the
house
of
forgetting

for Adrian & Laura

Con todo mi Cariño,

All blessing,

Other books by Benjamin Alire Sáenz

Fiction

Carry Me Like Water

Flowers for the Broken

Poetry

Dark and Perfect Angels

Calendar of Dust

the
house
of
forgetting

a novel

Benjamin Alire Sáenz

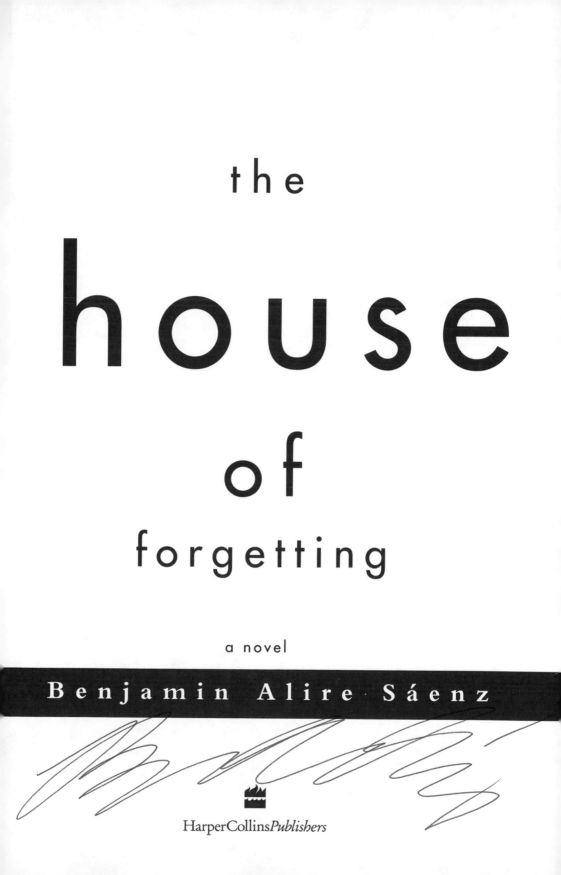

HarperCollins*Publishers*

HarperCollins books may be purchased for educational, business, or sales promotional use. For information please write: Special Markets Department, HarperCollins Publishers, Inc., 10 East 53rd Street, New York, NY 10022.

FIRST EDITION

Designed by Elina D. Nudelman

Library of Congress Cataloging-in-Publication Data

Sáenz, Benjamin Alire.
    The house of forgetting : a novel / by Benjamin Alire Sáenz. — 1st ed.
      p.   cm.
    ISBN 0-06-018738-7
    I. Title.
    PS3569.A27H6   1997
    813'.54—dc21   96-45019

---

97 98 99 00 01 ❖/RRD 10 9 8 7 6 5 4 3 2 1

This book is for two women who have graced my life with their patient and stubborn love
Erlinda Paredes and Gloria Woods
from a grateful brother

y siempre para Patricia (siempre, siempre, siempre)

part

1

The October wind moved through the afternoon air like a pair of sharp scissors cutting through paper. Thomas wondered what the leaves were carrying that made them fall from the trees with such a heavy weight. He motioned Claudia to come to the window. "Look," he said, pointing at leaves that fell like drops of lead. She stared out into his garden, could not see what he saw, saw only that the trees were fighting the wind as if they'd had enough of bending. The leaves made good their escape like pages fleeing from books they had been forced to be a part of. To learn to fall like that, she thought, to die like that. She looked at Thomas, noticed that the blue in his eyes was fading as if he was beginning to disappear. As she watched the wind and its work, she tried to think of something calm. Her mother's face. But she no longer remembered—only remembered her mother had been dark and smelled like the pine soap she mopped the floors with. The color of her skin, the soap, the mop. Her hands. Not her touch—that was no longer a part of her memory. Her touch was now in the place of forgetting, a forgetting she hated, a forgetting that made her feel as if she was not a part of what Thomas liked to refer to as "the army of the living." The living knew how to fight, but the fight was easier for Thomas than for her. He squeezed her hand.

"We'll look for flowers," he said. "A table without flowers is like a man without a woman." He chuckled at himself. Claudia liked that about him. He offered her his arm. She reached for his aging hand, which did not feel like a hand—more like a spider's web covering a fly, clinging to her skin.

They said nothing as they stepped through his garden. The wind seemed to calm as they walked. October's wind was unpredictable. He picked some white daisies that had miraculously reflowered in autumn. "Look," he said, "survivors." There was an expression of awe on his face, as if he were witnessing a miracle.

She nodded and wondered how anything lived through a season it was not meant to survive. He handed her the freshly picked daisies. She smelled them, held them tight as if they might fly away. "Here," he said, "rest." He pointed to the stump of the old willow tree. She stared at the stump, then sat quietly, as if posing for a picture. He looked at her approvingly. "I want to remember you just like this." She thought it was a strange thing to say—as if she were going away somewhere. The stump was an uncomfortable place to sit, but she pretended it was a chair. "Just rest," he said. She nodded and watched him as he admired the last of his miniature roses. He could make them bloom throughout the growing season. He knew how to do such things. "You like these?"

"Yes," she said. She smiled, grateful for the moment. She breathed in the smell of the roses. She wanted to hold it, to keep it—something that would be hers.

"I'll get my scissors," he said. He did not seem anxious about leaving her alone in the garden. Not today. She watched him disappear into the house. She looked out at the dying garden, the rusts, the golds, the fading yellows. The erratic October breeze picked up, then subsided again. Today it existed as a threat. Any minute the breeze would become a wind. The wind would become a storm. Everything would be gone. But the daisies. Somehow, they had survived.

She remembered how he had brought her here on summer evenings when she was a girl, how he had read to her, how his voice had been clear and steady, how she had felt he was a god who could still the world. She had touched the lithe limbs of the weeping willow as he read, the branches brushing the grass around it—softly—like a breath upon the waters. She remembered a poem he'd read to her when she was twelve, remembered the sound of his steady voice:

> *I loved a tree in my boyhood, a tree*
> *in my grandfather's garden, a weeping*
> *willow whose ancient limbs longed*
> *upwards, then arched downward, perfect*
>
> *bows which reached. . . . I played alone among*
> *the arches of leaves, pulling the green*

limbs around myself as if they were the great arms of God. . . .
I was so loved in that embrace of leaves . . .

She had wept when he finished. "Little girl, why are you crying?"
"Because it's sad."
"Not so sad," he'd said. "You must memorize it."
"I don't want to," she'd cried. "It's too sad. I don't want—"
But she had written it out in his presence and taken it to her room.
She could never resist giving him what he wanted. When she had mem-
orized it, she recited it to him as they both sat under the willow.

And then sickness came

to the garden one spring, the old willow
wrapped in a shroud of bugs. I could only
watch, could not touch it. I shouted
at the tree, and told it to live, and

She pulled herself away from that time. She hated him for making her
memorize that poem, had learned to hate *all* poetry. *He wants to remind*
me—won't let me forget, not even for a day. She looked up and saw him
carefully cutting the last of his red miniature roses. She stared at the
falling leaves and pictured herself floating away beyond the wall. She
picked up a leaf, stared into it as if she were reading a page in a book.
But she found nothing there.
"These will do nicely," he said as he put the roses in a small basket he
had brought with him from inside the house. He walked toward her
slowly.
"What were you thinking, my Claudia?"
"Nothing," she said. "Enjoying the calm."
"Strange how it's calm, then not. It's as if the wind were deciding."
"Deciding what?"
"I don't know." He smiled. "You weren't thinking about the willow?"
"Not at all. I'd forgotten all about it." She smiled. "It's been so long,"
she said, "more than twenty years, I think."

5

"You loved that tree."

"I was a child," she said.

He watched for a trace of anger. "You forgive me for chopping it down?"

"It was diseased, Thomas. You said so yourself."

"Yes, nothing to be done. The whole garden would have been infested."

She nodded. "And the garden's done so well. You can make things grow."

"Even you?"

She smiled, not a big smile. She nodded.

"Next summer I'll teach you how to garden."

She lifted herself off the stump and reached for his hand. "I'd like that," she whispered.

"We'll plant another willow," he said as they walked toward the house. "We'll start over—a new tree."

"Sounds lovely."

"Yes, it does." He stared at her. "Say my name."

"Thomas."

He nodded. "I like to hear you say it."

"You want me to say it again?"

"No," he said, laughing. He looked at her.

She hated to see so much affection on his face. "Do you remember the poem about the willow?"

"No."

"You wept the first time I read it to you."

"I don't remember."

"Strange that you should forget."

She caught a note of suspicion in his words. "Not so strange, Thomas. Girls have a way of forgetting."

"Or perhaps it's that you don't want to remember."

She shrugged. "There's not enough room to remember everything, Thomas."

"There's plenty of room." He laughed. She was relieved that he was taking the conversation lightly. Tonight he didn't have the energy to pursue his suspicions. Tonight he would not interview her at the dinner table as though she were withholding important and necessary information—information he craved though he had no reason to crave it, except that he was addicted to her thoughts. Tonight he wanted to believe she loved him.

She thought of the ground beneath her feet as they walked toward the house. Falling asleep for the winter, she thought; can't feel a thing. Peaceful, really. Resting until the spring. Better to be going to sleep for a long, long time. When they reached the house, they turned around and looked out at the garden. The soft breeze was beginning to turn colder, stronger, making the calmness of the last few minutes seem like an illusion.

"I think it's decided," he said. "A storm. It's decided on a storm." He locked the door as they reentered the house.

Still Air at Eventide

She turned from her task of setting the table, stared at the half-open door that led down to the cellar. The wind was growing stronger, rearranging everything in this large and fragile house that was her world. The leaves hit the windowpanes, banging to be let in like ghosts determined to reclaim what had once belonged to them. She wanted to give them what they clamored for.

She looked at the watch Thomas had given her. "To keep the time," he'd said. Measuring the hours was like measuring the desert with a cup. And yet she'd learned to do it. She stared at the time. Thomas had been in his wine cellar for over half an hour, *such a hard thing to choose the right wine, my dear.* She stared at the dead bolt on the door. *What if I closed the door? Slammed it shut?* Her heart skipped a beat, quickened, beat like a drum. It's hollow, she thought, my heart. She felt her skin tighten, pulling at her as if she were a snake about to shed its skin. She took a step toward the door. She could see it, the whole graceful and lyrical scene, and she in the center of it, could see it all, could see herself slamming the door, bolting it, and her, alone, dancing in the room, a ballet, dancing until she danced her way out of his house, her arms stretched toward the sky or a new lover like the limbs of a tree leaning toward the sun. She heard his footsteps coming up the stairs. *Now, before it's too*—he walked into the kitchen. She smiled at him, her heart returning to its normal rhythm. My heart, she thought. Hollow like the space between the ceiling and the roof. She rearranged the knives on the table. "You were gone a long time, Thomas."

He smiled back at her. "You missed me?"

She nodded, wondered if he could guess what she had been thinking.

"Claudia, you look a little flush," he said. "It's very becoming."

"You always say that." She fussed over the table.

He circled the room cradling a bottle of red wine in his thinning arms. He held it close to his breast as if it were a newborn child. She tried to ignore his movements, tried to pretend she didn't feel like prey. He gently wiped the dust from the bottle and repeated the year out loud: "1964." He whispered it several times, and it began to sound like the chant of a monk at prayer. He smiled at her, and again she smiled back. It was a cautious smile. Too cautious, she thought. He didn't seem to notice. "The year of your birth, my dear." She looked up at him—not at him, really, but at the air, as if she were following his words as they floated around in the room. She did not wish to be reminded of her birth, did not feel it to be anything worth celebrating. She continued ironing the white linen tablecloth with her restless hands. Always too many wrinkles. The fabric was rough against her fingers.

"A very good year. A lucky year. A lucky year for everyone." He smiled.

A lucky year for everyone? She offered him a broad smile. This time her smile was free of caution. He liked it, she could tell he liked it, exactly what he wanted, what he expected. She watched as he uncorked the bottle. So careful with his rare and fragile treasure. He was a careful man, she thought, careful with his shoes, his clothes, his books. "Such care is grace," he always said. She felt a chill run through her, as if someone had injected ice into her veins. "You can bruise it," he said, "if you're not gentle." She smiled at the sound of the cork being set free. Thirty years in one place, she thought. She stared at the cork lying on the table.

"We'll just let it breathe," he whispered, as if to speak too loudly would wake his sleeping child. She nodded, then continued setting the table.

He smiled approvingly at her labor, the forks, the gold-leafed china, the crystal wineglasses, everything neatly, properly arranged.

He placed the last of the fall flowers from his garden in a crystal vase at the center of the table. "Pretty," she said.

He had insisted she wear something elegant for dinner. "You look so lovely in dresses." She'd gone downstairs, to her room, the room next to his wine cellar, and changed. "Something white," he'd said. She'd decided on black instead. Tonight she felt there was a possibility that he would allow her this insignificant act of rebellion. "An excellent choice of dresses," he said as she reentered the dining room. "Not quite what I expected." She remained expressionless under his stare. "But it's charming nonetheless."

"You're not angry?"

"Not at all, my dear. You look stunning in black."

"I'm glad you like it."

"Black is fine," he said, "fine. Still, white suits you. A woman your age in black? It's really too sad, my dear. But black? Black is fine."

She didn't like the tone in his voice. She touched his arm. "I think I'd like to change," she said.

"Please don't go to all that—"

"I want to, Thomas. It won't take but a minute."

She disappeared down the stairs into the cellar. He walked into the kitchen, brought in the food and arranged it carefully on the table. He poured them both some wine and fussed with the placement of the wineglasses. "Perfect," he said. Claudia returned, wearing a long white dress. He stared at her for a moment. "Much better," he whispered.

She smiled. It was a weak smile, but he didn't notice. All he noticed was the dress. He pulled out her chair as if he were the maitre d' of a fine restaurant. He surveyed the scene: the white tablecloth, the white napkins, the white and red flowers, the crystal, the sparkling china, the silver tray of steaming lamb. The lovely woman in white. She watched him as his eyes moved across every object in the room. She wondered how anyone could look so comfortable wearing such stiffly starched shirts. She stared at his cuff links as he reached for his glass of wine. She noticed they were little mirrors reflecting everything in the room. She was there, too, in the cuff links.

"Well," he said, raising his glass, "a toast." He thought a moment. "What shall we toast?"

"Your garden," she said.

"It's the wrong time of year to toast my garden."

"Oh, but didn't we find daisies?"

"So we did. Still, it's bad luck to toast a garden this time of year. Bad luck, I'd say."

"To the coming winter, then," she said tentatively.

"Yes." He nodded approvingly, raising his glass. "There will be snow. Snow," he repeated. "I *do* love the snow. To a new season."

She tapped her glass against his. "A new season."

They both sipped the wine. She waited for him to comment on the taste. "Very nice," he said. "You like it?"

"I'm such a philistine when it comes to wine."

He nodded. "Not such a philistine, my dear." He took another small sip from his wineglass, swallowed it slowly, then placed his glass on the table. "Tell me," he said as he cleared his throat, "what did you do this week? I've been neglecting you lately. It's this damn book I've been writing. I must find more time for you." She was less sure of his mood now than she had been earlier in the evening. The weather in the house could change so quickly. His voice told her he had placed his darkness in some other part of the house, leaving the room where they dined warm and full of light. But his darkness was never far away, each room in the house connected. She would stay on guard. She would make sure the evening would remain calm.

"Let's see," she said as she leaned into the table. "I tried to read Proust, but it isn't working."

He smiled. "These things take time. I don't think you have the sensibility for Proust."

She detested his tone of condescension. "And I listened to Handel's *Messiah.*"

"Did you like it?"

"Yes."

"Yes doesn't sound like a glowing review."

"I don't know very much about music."

"But did it please you?"

She wanted to tell him music helped pass the day. That and nothing more. "I think I'd prefer something more cacophonous. It's so predictable. Perhaps it's the story line."

"You're not very religious, are you, my dear?" She could not tell if he was annoyed or not.

"I wouldn't say that."

"How *would* you characterize your feelings toward God?"

She would much rather be talking about Proust. He was temperamental and unpredictable about religion. "I pray," she said.

"And what do you pray for?"

She sipped her wine and weighed her thoughts carefully.

"Is it a difficult question?"

"Yes," she said.

"Why, my dear? It's simple enough."

She did not want to tell him what she prayed for, though the answer seemed obvious enough to her. And perhaps to him. "Prayer is such a private matter."

"You're not being evasive, are you?"

"Oh, Thomas," she said, a teasing quality in her voice. "Don't be silly." She touched his elbow and laughed. "When I pray," she said staring directly into his suspicious blue eyes, "I recite the rosary. It's old-fashioned, I know, but that's how I pray."

"I would have thought your prayer would be more original than that."

She smiled and shrugged.

He took a sip of wine. "Still, it's an old tradition." He did not say what she knew he was thinking. *It was bred into you.*

"Yes," she said, "very old."

"I, of course, abandoned that tradition long ago."

Always, he had outgrown anything she did or was doing. "Perhaps you didn't need it any longer."

"Quite right." He nodded. "I ceased to need it." He paused, placed his hand on her cheek. "Still, it's a start." He pulled his hand away. "And do you know where the tradition came from?"

She knew the answer, had read it in one of his books. She pretended not to know. "No," she said.

"Saint Dominic," he said, the teacher's voice pronouncing it as a kind of victory. "You must read more, my dear. Next time, you can tell me what century he lived." He took another sip from his wine. "His philosophy was work and pray. Work and pray. Excellent—and not nearly as simple as it sounds."

Thomas was wrong. It had been Saint Benedict's philosophy. She smiled to herself. "That's what you do," she said. "Work and pray."

He laughed. "So you've noticed."

"Yes," she said, "I've noticed."

"Tell me, what does praying the rosary do for you?"

"It centers me," she said. It was an answer he would understand.

"Yes, that's precisely the point." He looked around the table. "Oh, damn," he interrupted himself. "I've forgotten the potatoes—and the mint jelly." He rose from the chair and disappeared into the kitchen. She listened to the wind. If anything, the storm had grown stronger and she could still hear the leaves pounding against the windows as if they were being punished for a crime. The pounding and the leaves and the storm brought back the memories. So many memories. She would have preferred to keep them away, but she was too weak to fight them. She let them come.

He had left the back door open, had fallen asleep as he read. She took a chance, stepped out into the garden—a perfect day, the sun, a warm breeze, spring, and she was sick of being indoors. Just for a moment. He won't know.

She had lost track of time, had overstayed. He had found her—there, in his garden. His eyes angry and accusing.

"I was only admir—"

"Did I give my permission?"

She looked down at the ground, noticed a small weed making its way into his immaculate garden. She loved the weed but knew, too, it would be pulled from the ground.

"Didn't I tell—how many times have I told you?"

She continued looking down at the ground. She imagined the weed growing and growing until it overtook the garden.

"Look at me."

She refused to take her eyes off the small weed. A dandelion, she thought to herself. Her older brother used to pull them from the ground and give them to her.

"I said look at me." He grabbed her hair in his fist and pulled it until she looked into his eyes.

She dug her nails into his arm to make him let go. He pulled harder.

"Tear it out," she yelled. "Tear out my hair, Thomas, all of it. All of it!" She had worked so hard to show him nothing, and now he knew everything. She quieted herself, then stood motionless as he let go of her hair. She looked down at the ground again.

He softly lifted her chin. He looked straight into her eyes, then suddenly she felt the slap of his hand against her cheek. The power of his open palm made her fall to the ground. She lay there, not wanting to feel anything. She willed the sting of his hand to disappear, willed her cheek to stop burning. She felt the small weed near her hand and touched it.

"Get up," he said quietly, almost whispering. She walked inside the house. He punished her with his silence for a week. The next Saturday he took her up to his room and showed her a view of the garden. It was spring, and his irises were in full bloom. He pointed to the willow tree at the corner of the garden. "See your tree," he said.

She nodded.

"You love that tree?"

She nodded.

"It's a shame really," he said. "Diseased. I'm afraid . . ." His voice trailed off dramatically.

When the men came to saw the tree down, he made her sit and watch from the window in his room. "It's a shame really," he said again as they both stared at the stump. "Diseased."

Thomas walked back into the room, placed the potatoes on the table, then returned to the kitchen and back again, this time carrying a silver bowl with mint jelly. "There," he said, then sat back down. He looked a little tired. "Sorry," he said, "I'm getting forgetful—like you, my dear."

She smiled.

"What were we talking about?"

"Prayer."

"Ahh, yes." He looked at her. "You seem preoccupied."

"I was thinking about the storm. It's warm in here—safe."

"A home should be a refuge." He smiled, took his wineglass from the table and held it but did not drink. "Is that all you were thinking about?"

"Yes."

"I don't believe you."

He was getting angry. She would have to work hard to keep him calm. "Actually, I was thinking of something else—though it's rather silly. It had nothing whatever to do with what we were discussing."

"What's that, my dear?" He raised his eyebrows.

"I was thinking of Ezra Pound." She hoped her tactic would work. Talk of literature often distracted him.

"Why on earth would you be thinking of him?"

"I was thumbing through a book, and I ran across some pictures of him."

He smiled. The evening might go fine. "He had a brilliant mind."

"It's awfully hard to love a mind," she said, "especially when it comes in such a harsh and difficult body."

"Oh, my dear, but he was such a handsome young man."

"He looks dangerous."

"Other people thought so, too. You see, people just didn't understand Mr. Pound's—" Just as he was about to argue his point, the telephone rang. He lost his train of thought. He looked toward the phone. "The machine will answer," he said, and waited to hear the voice on the other end. He was in the habit of listening in on the people who left him messages, enjoyed listening to their awkward speeches as they spoke into a machine. Like him, she gave her attention to the telephone. She had learned to copy many of his habits. The phone rang four times, both of them sipping their wine quietly and expectantly. "Oh, damn," he said, "I've forgotten to turn on the machine." He hated missing phone calls more than he hated having his dinner interrupted.

"Well, I'm sure they'll call back," she said.

He shook his head. "You'll excuse me for a moment, won't you?"

She nodded. Her eyes followed his movements into the kitchen. *His walk is tired now. Are your limbs diseased, Thomas?* Through the open door to the kitchen, she could see the telephone on the counter. She watched his face as he answered the phone, heard his animated voice, noticed how he smiled into the receiver as if the person on the other end were studying him, admiring him, his voice warm and alive as he greeted his callers. "Robert, yes, how are you, my man?" That's how he spoke, she thought, my dear, my man, lovely, lovely . . .

He turned his back to her as he spoke into the phone. He never liked her to listen, always reminded her that she belonged to only a certain part of his world. She stared at the well-set table, trying to observe the scene as he had done a few moments earlier. She stared at the roasted leg of lamb, the mint jelly, the potatoes, the fresh spinach salad that sat waiting. To be consumed. She chastised herself: *Inanimate things don't wait. It's we who . . .* She had no appetite. She did not recall ever having been hungry since she had come to live with the man who was speaking into the telephone. She wanted his voice to go away, to disappear. Her eyes fell on the knife Thomas had brought in from the kitchen to carve the lamb. The knife, animate now, more full of life than the last of the flowers from his garden arranged on the table. The knife, staring. At her. Eyes as cold as Thomas's. The knife, like the crystal against the light, bright, luminous, full of possibility.

She did not even know she had picked up that shiny object until she realized she had cut her index finger on its well-sharpened edge. She rubbed her bleeding finger. She rose from the table slowly, moving toward the man with the voice she hated. All she could think of was the word *now.* Now, because already the moment was passing and would soon be gone—and she with it. Now, because the leaves were cutting themselves loose, freeing themselves from the trees. Now, because tomorrow the storm would be over. Now, because she had to seize this gift that was hers alone, this gift that was the first thing in twenty-three years that resembled hope—and she could taste the words in her mouth, sweeter than any wine Thomas had ever let her taste.

She was standing at his side. "Thomas," she said.

He kept his back to her and waved her off. He covered the phone with his hand. "I've told you never to—" But before he could say another word, she grabbed his arm and spun him around. He faced her angrily, did not even notice the blade, the sharp, shiny, clean blade. Everything happened in an instant, and yet it seemed to her that the entire world had slowed down just for her, everything moving in slow motion so she could watch herself, so she could keep this memory. She saw her own arm as she swung the knife in the air to better come down on him, hard, hard enough to make sure he would be cut, hard enough to stop forever his incessant talking. She saw her own raised fist, felt the weight of her whole body in her arm. She watched herself, her movements graceful, like a choreographed dance she had practiced and practiced, everything so controlled and yet so spontaneous. The knife came down slowly, full of the force of a body whose strength had remained bound for too long. She became a branch in a violent wind that was all the stronger for the force it was resisting.

She saw the stunned look on Thomas's face. He had not counted on this, she could see that, and that knowledge made her brave, made her feel strong. *I kept you safe, I gave you*—that is what she saw in his eyes as the knife entered his chest. She winced at the sound, such a strange sound—not at all like a blade cutting down a tree. And the blood, something so natural in the way it flowed out of the place where the knife had entered. She pulled out the knife and stared at it. His eyes opened wide as he dropped the receiver. She looked into his eyes, so full of rage and disbelief. He hated her, she could see that. She had always seen that look of hate lurking behind his kind words, behind his smile. He had tried to keep it hidden from her, but she had seen it. He kept that look on his face, *kept it like he had kept her,* and then she turned away. She had lost interest in that look, that face. She turned her attention to the place where he was bleeding. He has a heart, she thought. He bleeds.

He held on to the counter. She looked back into his face to see if that look had disappeared. His pleading eyes were as large as the windows in his house.

"I lied, Thomas," she said softly. "The poem. I told you I didn't remember. Do *you* remember, Thomas? I want to show you I remember:

> *though it fought to breathe without*
> *leaves, neither my voice nor the rain*
> *could heal . . .*

"You're crazy," he said softly, his voice cracking.

"No," she said. "Don't you like the poem, Thomas?"

"Help me," he said weakly as he clutched the place near his heart where the knife she was clutching had cut into him.

"No," she said as she stared at the blood that was redder than the sunsets she suddenly remembered seeing as a girl. That sunset was more real for her in that instant than the bleeding man who faced her. Not blood. It was a sunset. It was not Thomas. She could hear a voice coming from the telephone, a voice that kept repeating Thomas's name.

"Ingrate," he said, his hands full of his own blood as he clutched himself.

> *stripped limb by limb until there was*
> *only a stump. And the stump, too*
> *was pulled from the ground . . .*

"Ingrate," he repeated as he closed his eyes and moaned.

"I thought you'd like the poem."

"Lunatic," he whispered.

"Not at all, Thomas. I just turned out to be a weed in your garden. You should have killed me, you know? Instead, you killed the willow. Wrong choice, Thomas." There was blood on the white dress. She stared at the deep red against the white. She wiped the knife on the dress as if it were a cleaning rag. "Do you still like this dress?"

"You were safe," he said softly, using all of his energy to utter those few words.

"It was never safe."

"Why?"

She moved closer to him. And suddenly, unexpectedly, as if he had received a final gift of movement, his hand reached out toward her—not a hand that was pleading, not a hand that was begging, but a claw. She jumped away from his reach.

He became still again. "Why?" he repeated.

How could he not know? How could he not? She watched him struggle to speak again, then stared at the still body on the floor. She felt nothing, as if her whole body had gone to sleep. And yet she felt so awake. She picked up the receiver, stared at it, then spoke: "Robert, are you there?"

"What the hell's going on?" the voice yelled.

"I've just stabbed Thomas," she said calmly.

"What?"

"I've just stabbed Thomas," she said again. "Do you understand?" Her voice was firm, controlled, distant—it belonged to someone else.

"Who are you?" the voice demanded. It was such a long story. She did not want to talk. She stared blankly at the receiver. "Who is this?" the voice yelled.

She steadied herself against the wall. "Your friend is dead," she whispered. She hung up the phone, then walked slowly toward the table. She sat down, her stomach churning. She felt as if pieces of glass from somewhere inside her were spinning around—sharp—cutting, would not stop, would cut her just as she had cut Thomas. Perhaps his gods were taking their revenge on her body. She steadied her hand and reached for her glass of wine. She put it to her lips and drank the wine down. She stared at the blood on the dress.

She walked downstairs to her room, counting each step as she went. Sixteen steps. *I used to count them.* Inside her room, she stared at the door. *He won't lock this, not tonight.* She walked into the bathroom, washed her hands, her face, watched the pink water go down the drain until it was clear and pure again. She dried herself, looked into the mirror but did not see herself. She slipped off the white dress, changed back into the black dress she'd left on the bed. She looked around the room, then stared at the white dress stained with blood. She wiped her hands on the dress, then walked back upstairs, again counting the steps as she climbed. She sat at the table. There was nothing wrong. She poured herself another glass of wine. She stared at the deep, rich liquid, thick and red as his blood. She listened to the wind. The leaves had become heavier, were filling the sky, were knocking on the windows, would break into the house, carry her over the wall. She reached for her glass of wine. She drank. And waited.

Breaking

She could not bring herself to think of the body lying in the next room, refused to think of his face or his touch, or the smell of his breath on her neck. Or the way he had pronounced her name. "Just went to the kitchen and never came back," she said to herself. "Disappeared." She thought she heard him moaning. It was like an echo of a weeping penitent in a dark and empty church. It was the wind. It was only the breaking storm. She could not rise from the table, could not walk back into the kitchen. She tried to imagine what it would be like to walk outside and stand in the wind. She wanted to feel the night, wrap herself up in it as if it were nothing more than a shawl, throw herself on the cold ground and plant herself in it, grow roots. *Feel.* She could hear the rain, it was raining now. The rain would feel good against her skin. "I'll break a window." *Let in the rain, let it in, let it fill the house, wash it, leave no sign of life or* *blood, leave no sign of Thomas and me. . . .*" She thought she heard him groan above the sounds of the storm. *I saw him bleed. I saw him fall.* She placed the knife on the table and stared at it. Again, she thought she heard a soft moaning. *Thomas, are you dead?* It was true, she had wanted Thomas to die, but not like this. Just to die. Life. And then death. Death. Then peace. No philosophizing, no time for whys, for confessions, for explanations. No time for final thoughts. Reflecting was for the living. Just death for Thomas. She had not wanted him to suffer.

She stared at the floor to see if her heart was lying there, but it was not. She coughed, and again she felt herself going into spasms. Again she looked to see what she had ejected from her body. There was nothing. *If I could toss something out of my body, if only I could—then I would exist. I could have proof.* She breathed in and out slowly. She was surprised when calmness returned. She was tired. *I have never slept. I have never rested.* She wiped her dry lips with the perfectly folded white napkin, then licked them. If only she could drink the rain. *Was he still moaning?* She remembered how he sounded when they made love, how he shook, how the sounds that came out of him frightened her, and how she had learned to pretend she was not frightened. She stared at her hands and saw they were shaking uncontrollably. She felt as if the wind was shaking her, trying to free her flesh from her bones. "Stop," she said, as if she could command her hands to stop trembling, but they did not listen to her. Even her eyes would not listen. Everything was blurry, the tears falling fast as the rain. "Stop," she said again, but her eyes refused to listen. Her voice had no power over her body. Her voice was as powerless now as it had always been. She placed her head on the table and moaned.

And then it seemed that the wind died down, disappeared, left as if her prayers had banished it. Her prayers had never had any efficacy in this house—but tonight perhaps their power had returned. The quiet was soothing. She rocked herself. *You made me kill you, Thomas, you did, you started to get sloppy, careless, you wanted me to—leaving the knife like that . . .* "Freedom's too big a word for you, my dear." She pictured the leaves of the weeping willow in the calmest of nights—that is how she felt. Storms passed so quickly in this house.

She wiped the sweat and the tears from her face. She tried to make herself sit perfectly still. If she had learned anything at all in twenty-three years, she had learned to be patient. The truest gift Thomas had given her was the terrible gift of time.

She grabbed one of the crystal candlesticks in her hand, blew out the candle. Now there was only one. She held it, fingered it like she would a rosary. She remembered the day Thomas had given her one of his books, remembered how he had handed it to her—carefully—as if it were an animate thing that had to be kept alive but could only be kept alive if handled in a particular way. "I wrote it," he said, then left her to read it. His book was strong and passionate, and she had envied his ability to say what he believed. But she had not admired his work. "It's lovely," she had told him when she'd finished. "Such a mind." He had made love to her, had allowed her to sleep in his room that night. "When I was a boy," he whispered in the darkness, "I was afraid. My father wanted me to work with my hands, never even saw that I had a mind. *I have a mind.*" She remembered his exact words as she sat there, remembered how she had held him, made him feel protected, remembered how he had cried, how his tears had left his smell on her skin. *So many words, Thomas.* She let the piece of crystal she was holding drop to the floor.

She took the empty plate in front of her, closed her eyes, and slammed it against the table. She did not know if she was breaking Thomas or herself.

A Door Opens

As she sat in the light of the lone candle, she began to convince herself that nothing had happened. No phone call, no knife, no Thomas lying in the next room. Where was he, then? And where was she? She had brushed aside the broken pieces of her plate. She had drunk too much wine. She felt a little dizzy, out of control, felt like dancing.

Thomas had never cared for dancing. She hoped someone would come soon. Robert would have called the police. *They'll come. I'll go to jail. It will be better there.* She preferred anything now, anything at all to this house where she had been kept as a kind of gargoyle to keep out all the evil spirits Thomas had been afraid of. Those spirits would flood his home now. She was glad. She was not afraid of what might come after this. Freedom was anywhere away from this house.

She heard a banging on the front door. *They're here. They've come. Robert called them. Thank God, he called them. What is it like out there? What is that land like? There is a land outside this door, and I have never seen it.* The banging grew louder and louder, and a voice was shouting. She was not afraid. She would confess, would tell them everything, give them every detail of the last twenty-three years, and if they judged that she should die, then she would die, and if they judged that she should go to prison, then she would go to prison, and if they judged that she should be allowed to go free, she would go free. Thomas had wanted her to be like the women in the books he loved. Now she was no longer trapped there. Now she could see what was outside the door. Here there was nothing. She was not sorry and she was not afraid, though she did not feel brave. Odd that she felt herself trembling. Everything was so odd. She could not keep her body from shaking. What was wrong with it? She felt as though a wind was blowing through the empty house, blowing through her empty body, and everything that belonged to her was being carried away. She walked to the door and tried to make herself speak. "Yes," she heard herself say.

"It's the police."

"Yes," she repeated.

"Open the door."

She yanked at the knob.

"Open the door." The voice was loud and hard.

"I can't." Why didn't they know?

"Open the goddamned door! We'll break it down!"

Break it down, break the damn thing down. She said nothing. They did not know anything. She stepped out of the way and waited. She pushed her hair out of her face. She was sweating, and she felt her head throbbing, and her heart, racing like a pair of legs, running without knowing where it was going, lost and going just because it did not know how to stop. My heart is going to break. I'll die. With him—*not now when the door is*—She did not even hear the door being torn down, did not hear the voices of the men all around her, the gun pointed at her. All she saw was the face of a man she did not know, and his badge reflecting the light. It was like seeing the sun.

Some People Just Won't Die

When Lieutenant Murphy got the call on his cellular phone, he was in the middle of eating dinner at his favorite restaurant. The lighting was quiet, his pasta dish was even better than the last time he'd eaten it, and he felt shielded from the cold rain that was pelting the city like an angry father beating his useless sons. He had hoped the evening would pass without incident and he would go back home and get a good night's rest. His insomnia was catching up with him.

He cursed the weather, the city, his job, his wife, and himself as he drove toward the address he'd been given. He arrived at the scene a few moments after the ambulance. He walked into the house, then followed the action into the kitchen. He shook his wet hair as he walked. He stared at Thomas Blacker's body as the paramedics carried him away on a stretcher. He took out his pad, pushed his hair out of his face, then looked around the busy room. "Got a name?"

"Blacker. Thomas Blacker."

Detective George Johnson looked at him and grinned. "You look a little wet. Don't they pay you enough to buy a raincoat, Murph?"

He smiled. "Nah. I like looking like a wet lizard. Don't you ever call me Lieutenant?"

"Didn't know you were so big on titles." George smiled at him, his black skin glistening in the light of the room.

"What've we got?"

"Some broad cut him up pretty bad."

"And they say crime is down when the weather's bad."

"If that were true, we'd have an awful lot of slow days in this god-damned city."

"Yeah, well, least we're not getting laid off."

George laughed. "Didn't know you were on duty."

"Not supposed to be. Krociczk called in sick."

"Got here pretty fast."

"I was grabbing a bite on the North Side. Know a good restaurant."

"Still got a weakness for good food, huh?"

"Wouldn't eat out so much if my wife could cook."

"Why don't *you* cook?"

"She doesn't like that. Having a penis disqualifies me from setting foot in her kitchen." He winced, then smiled. He put a cigarette in his mouth but did not light it. "They take the suspect in?"

"Yup. Fell into the arms of the first officer on the scene. Fainted dead away. She's in a state. Won't talk. Doesn't seem like there was much of a struggle. Knew each other, I'd say."

"Guess he didn't know her as well as he thought. Poor bastard."

"Lucky bastard, I'd say. Guy should be dead."

"Yeah, well, some people just won't die."

I Am Only Sand

She did not blink when they photographed her, did not smile, did not frown, did not pose. She was tired of posing. She heard directions and she followed them. They asked her questions and she said nothing. When she was waiting for them to open the door, she had thought of telling them everything: how she had come to be in that house, what he had made her do, everything. But she did not remember everything, and what she remembered, she wanted to keep for herself. She did not know these people, did not want to let them hear her voice.

They looked at her as if she were a foreign and strange thing—like Thomas looked at the art he kept in his house. But Thomas had admired the art, and the people here did not admire her. "She won't say a god-damned thing," she heard a man say as if she weren't in the room. She looked at him. It was he who was foreign.

They took her to a room, and she waited. Two men walked into the room. One man was dark, so dark he was almost black. She had never seen a man with such dark skin. She did not know what to make of his smile. She wondered if it was a sign of happiness. The other man had white skin—like Thomas's—though he did not look like Thomas. He was younger, stronger, his thin lips sure and arrogant, and he seemed very serious. She liked the black man better. The white man told her his name. Lieutenant Murphy. He said something else, but it was difficult to remember. He asked her firm questions, firm as his face. "Were you lovers?" His fine hair kept falling into his face. He pushed it back, and again it would fall in his eyes. She sat in her chair as if it belonged to her. She pretended they did not exist. "Were you lovers?" he asked again. She did not bother to nod. The more questions he asked, the stiller she sat. "I'm gonna keep digging," he said sternly, "until I get some answers." *Dig all you want, Lieutenant. I am a soil that holds no ore. I am a desert. I hold only sand that slips through your fingers.*

I Don't Feel Like Talking

As Lieutenant Murphy pulled up into his driveway, he sat in his car and lit a cigarette. He thought of the dark woman who refused to speak, how she sat as if sitting was a way of life, as if she knew nothing but sitting. She had looked at him as if she knew what parts of him were missing, as if he was less important than the chair she was sitting on. His voice had meant as much to her as the fucking walls. *Goddamnit, I walked away with nothing.*

As he stared at the red ashes of his cigarette in the darkness, he felt numb and removed from himself. He wanted to sit there, not move, just smoke. "I should've been a priest," he said, then winced, unable even to laugh at his own ridiculous and miserable thought. He knew why he'd said it. He *was* a priest—that's what being a cop had meant to him. When it all started, he had wanted to be a pure being—flawed and yet still good—a being who would aid in dragging the helpless city along in some kind of salvific journey. He was not exactly searching for God, but searching for an image of harmony that was vague even in his own mind. Something had gone wrong along the way, and now he half thought the city was cursed—and he along with it. All of them edging closer to hell or whatever place was farthest away from God. Over twenty years in the department, twenty years of watching cops slowly become filthier than the alleys of the city—he could smell the stench on his skin. A part of him, now. Twenty years of blood—fathers killing sons, brothers beating brothers, husbands mutilating wives, strangers, lovers, rapes, knifings on streets and in homes, the confessions, the pathetic begging for mercy, the empty and insincere gestures of forgiveness—these were the litanies of his days. He was mesmerized and distanced from all of it, as repetitive as the Hail Marys in a rosary that lulled him to sleep as a boy, as distant as the voices that whispered the familiar prayers. Tonight the whole fucking thing made him sick. He had once found a baby in a trash can, both of its arms missing. The thought occurred to him that the whole of his career in Chicago's finest was about missing parts. So many things missing that it seemed to him nothing could ever be made whole. Least of all him. It was the woman, that woman who so stubbornly refused to give her name—the way she looked at him, as if she knew him, as if she was accusing him of something, as if she knew all about his sins of omission. *In what I have done and in what I have failed to do . . .* the words of the Act of Contrition came to his mind. He had never been able to control his Catholic imagination—always it had controlled him. *I should have been a priest. I should have been a goddamned priest.* He put out his cigarette and moved reluctantly toward his house, his feet dragging as he walked. When he opened the door, he smiled at his wife as she sat on the couch watching television. "Hi," he said.

"You're late again," she said flatly.

"It couldn't be helped, Becky."

"Fuck it."

"Let's not fight. You want a beer?"

"I'm going to bed."

"Stay up with—"

"You sit out there in the car for twenty minutes—just sit, don't even come inside, and you want me to stay up with you? Go to hell, Murph."

"I was just thinking, that's all. A man has to think. There was a stabbing, Beck—it couldn't be helped." He smiled at her. "C'mon, have a beer with me."

"I'm too tired. I don't feel like talking."

"Must be going around."

"What?"

"Never mind."

She glared at him. "I'm going to bed." She clicked off the television and tossed the remote onto the coffee table.

He walked into the kitchen and stared into the refrigerator. He was thinking not of his wife, but of the baby he had found, of the missing parts, of the woman who would not speak.

In the Country of Silence

She paced the small cell, back and forth, her footsteps almost as steady as the ticking of a metronome. There was no room to breathe, and yet she found herself breathing. She kept her eyes on the floor. She did not know if she liked being in this small cell that smelled of stale human urine, vomit, soap, and years of smoke. Her slow back-and-forth steps betrayed no exasperation, no anxiety. She could have been a nun in a convent, lost in fervent prayer. As if coming out of a trance, she suddenly became acutely aware of her surroundings, the dingy floor; and the odors became so sharp and pungent she wanted to lose her sense of smell. Strangely, she became convinced that someone had died in this place of her keeping. *I will die here, too.*

She made herself sit on the bed. She pulled her hair back and began to braid it. She had nothing to tie it with. It would come undone. It did not matter.

She hummed a song to herself, a song she remembered from childhood, a song her mother used to sing as she cleaned the house: *Ay, que laureles tan verdes* . . . When she finished braiding her hair, she unbraided it. She laughed softly, then covered her face with her hands as if by placing them there she could make herself disappear. She could hear a woman screaming: "Fuck all of you. Hear me? Fuck you all."

"Be quiet," she whispered. "Never let them see how much you hate them."

She tried to shove Lieutenant Murphy out of her thoughts. He seemed to be hovering over her. What was he doing there—in her cell? "Did he try to rape you?" His question had a kind of logic she understood. *Rape, Lieutenant? Do you mean did I cooperate? I have looked that word up in the dictionary a thousand times, and I cannot answer.* She almost liked his voice, strange and casual and new, and if it had been something solid she would have turned it over and over in her palms, felt it, touched it, held it up to her face—maybe even tasted it. She had looked at him, his thin lips that moved confidently, his almost kind and noticeably tired face. She wanted to tell him to go home and shave and get some sleep. *And let me sleep, too, Lieutenant.*

After a few hours, she grew tired of his relentless questions, grew tired of his voice. She wondered if he saw her. *I am something to be solved. I have read about men like him.* Maybe he was like Thomas—

Thomas never let her go until he got what he wanted. She wanted to shout at him. *If I answer your questions, you think you will know, but you will never know.* But she had not shouted, had said nothing at all. She had said nothing to the policewoman who had asked her question after question and fingerprinted her and made her change her clothes. *What is your name? Have you understood the rights you are entitled to? Would you like to have an attorney? Would you like to make a phone call? Why won't you tell us your name? We know you stabbed . . . your fingerprints all over the knife, the room. . . . What is your name? How long have you known Thomas Blacker? How is it that you came to be in his house . . . came to be in his house, came to be in his . . .* Her speech had left her, her tongue had become an immutable stone, as heavy as the harsh and gray winter sky she hated so much. *The talk will change nothing. It will not return what was taken. Ask Thomas. Thomas will tell you. He will answer your questions. He will not speak the truth, but you will understand him.*

She felt as though she had been asleep for a long time, and having been woken, she wanted nothing else but to return to her long slumber. The waking itself was exhausting. Suddenly, she felt a surge of panic. What if she *had* lost her ability to utter words? She had looked at the lieutenant and tried to say something, but her vocal chords had locked themselves into dumbness. And then she knew she would never be able to speak again because the man who had given her words was gone, and he had taken all words with him. He was gone. She wanted to summon him back. *Dead, dead, Gloria, not gone, use the right word, it's what he taught you, wasn't it? Always use the right word. Why did I think a knife could make me free? Gloria, that was stupid, that was a stupid thing to do. Your name? We can help. . . . How did you come to be in his . . .*

She had said nothing to the woman doctor who had asked her more questions. She had never seen so many women, all of them so different, all of them with their own voices, not at all like her. And so many men who did not look like Thomas. So many people, and all of them moving so fast, talking so fast, as if they were trying desperately to catch something that was just ahead of them—something valuable.

The doctor had asked if she could examine her. She had shrugged, but when the woman had tried to touch her, she heard herself scream.

She did not even know why she had screamed except that she did not want to be touched. She did not want anything—except to sleep.

She would tell them nothing, would not speak to them even if she *could,* even if Thomas sent them to her from the land of the dead. She could not tell them what had happened. She had been safer with Thomas. The safe place had been taken. He had exiled her from her former life, but he had also protected her—and her exile had not been torture. Not torture—that word, it wasn't *that* word. *It wasn't so bad, Thomas.* She wanted her bed at Thomas's house. *There,* she had at least learned to rest.

She thought the lieutenant would ask and ask and ask for an eternity—ask and ask until she fell to her knees and begged him to stop. Finally, he had given up and left her alone, though she knew he would be back. He would not leave her alone until she spoke. *Lieutenant, I don't know how to speak to anyone except to Thomas. You are not Thomas. You want me to remember—but I have tried to forget where I was born, where I used to live. Memory is a curse, Lieutenant. I don't know anything, Lieutenant, except a strange story about a willow. You don't know that story.*

A Thousand Ways to Hurt

The uncomfortable bed did not matter. Sleep took her body away as soon as she laid it down on the lumpy mattress. All night she dreamed she was reading a book in Thomas's living room, his omnipotent eyes watching her. When she woke, she felt as if his face were imprinted on her body. She wanted to rub away her skin until she was sure his image was no longer there.

She tried to stop thinking of Thomas, tried not to talk to him. But there was only him—him and the lieutenant. *Do you love him?* She hated the lieutenant for asking. I cut him like a loaf of bread, Lieutenant.

Thomas. His blue eyes, soft as water. Hard as ice. So cold, they burned like embers. They could melt her, those eyes, turn her from a solid to a liquid. The way his brow wrinkled, the way he nodded when he agreed with what he read, the way he got angry when something disgusted him. The passion in his voice when he spoke of things he loved. The way he laughed when he was pleased, the way his hand felt when he reached over and combed her hair with his fingers. His palm, callous from the work of his garden. The lines on his weathered face. The kindness in his voice when she sat next to him. The smell of the kitchen when she cooked for him. The scent of his coat. His books. The scar on his chest—from boyhood. The slap of his hand. *Do you love him?*

◆ ◆ ◆

The second day was better than the first. She was hungry, and though the food was bad, she ate. Thomas would not have liked the food, Thomas who loved good food. But good food did not matter. She was hungry.

I am getting used to Lieutenant Murphy's voice—but he would not believe me if I told him the whole truth. He wants simple answers. What is your name? My name, Lieutenant? Perhaps my name is Claudia? Perhaps my name is Gloria? Which of those names do you like? I have nothing simple to say. Thomas liked simple answers, too. And to think, Thomas, you thought yourself a philosopher. Perhaps you should have been a policeman.

On the third day, she still refused to speak. Lieutenant Murphy was losing his patience. She could see it in his eyes, could hear it in his speech. Once, he raised his voice. She wondered if he was going to hit her. Her body had jerked, a reflex. "I won't hurt you," he said. *There are a hundred ways to hurt, Lieutenant. Thomas told me we would plant a new willow. I wanted to tell him it was too late for resurrections. There are a thousand ways to hurt.* She wished she could have told the lieutenant—just that, and nothing more.

31

Benjamin Alire Sáenz

Lieutenant Murphy's Obsession

Lieutenant Murphy sat at the bar and sipped his bourbon. He ran
his hand over his unshaven face. He took out the newspaper he'd been carrying around with him as if it were a private document. He reread the article he'd already read a dozen times as if he were reading it for the first time:

WELL-KNOWN SCHOLAR STABBED IN HOME

Thomas Blacker, a well-known scholar, writer, and professor at the
University of Chicago, was found stabbed in his home early Sunday
evening. Police were called to the scene at about 7:05 P.M. when a col-
league reported to police that Professor Blacker was apparently assaulted
with a knife as he spoke to him on the phone.

The assailant, an unidentified woman, is being held by police for
questioning. A police spokesman said there were no signs of forced
entry, but police are not ruling out burglary as a motive in the stabbing.

Professor Blacker became a well-known advocate for a more rigorous
academic training based on a classical model of education with his book
Educating America. He provoked a national controversy when he attacked
"misguided progressives and reactionary conservatives" alike for "using
universities to further political ideologies rather than for producing students who are not only literate but who can think." In a noted address,
he proclaimed that universities "ought to be in the business of producing scholars—not professionals who merely go to college to find a job. A
fine mind is always marketable." He blamed the dismantling of the
Greco-Anglo tradition of education on progressives who "have forgotten the very idea of standards" and business interests "whose very idea of
education is completely corrupt." In a famed and influential essay that
has been widely discussed in the academic community, Blacker urged
universities to provide all students with a rigorous liberal-arts education
regardless of their chosen disciplines. "Having doctors, lawyers, and
M.B.A.'s who have read and thought about Western philosophy and art

can only be to the good." He attacked faculties for allowing universities to become nothing more than vocational schools. "It is one thing to be a specialist," he wrote, "but who can truly become a specialist, when one has not first been a competent generalist? If civilization is to survive, then we must ensure a civilized population."

Blacker's students and colleagues, who were shocked by the news of his stabbing, are organizing a candlelight vigil to call attention to growing crime in the city. Blacker lives in Hyde Park, and one of Blacker's colleagues stated that his stabbing was "just another example of how unsafe the city is becoming. Thomas Blacker has become just another victim."

Blacker is reported to be in serious condition at Mercy Hospital. . . .

He stared at the picture of Thomas Blacker's thin face, his studied smile as the university president handed him an award. Strange world, he thought. Strange people. Something about Thomas Blacker he didn't like. Maybe it was just that look of entitlement—no sense of surprise as the award was being handed to him, as if he expected it, deserved it. He laughed to himself. It was just a picture of a man. A man he didn't know. There was no reason not to like him. He tossed the newspaper onto the bar and ran his hand over his unshaven face again. Maybe I'll grow a beard, he thought. He shook his head. He hated beards. He put his fingers in his drink, fished out a piece of ice, and chewed on it. "Sexual frustration," he said, talking to himself, "that's what she says every time I put ice in my mouth."

"What's that? Talkin' to yourself again, Lieutenant?"

He laughed, then nodded at the bartender.

"The wife, huh?"

"You guys have to learn to read minds before you can land a job pouring drinks?"

"You're not that hard to read, Lieutenant."

"That's why I don't play poker." He looked at his glass. "Pour me another, will you, Danny?" He finished off his drink, lit a cigarette, rubbed his hands together. "Cold today," he said as the bartender placed a fresh drink in front of him. "Don't you guys ever turn on the heat?"

"The heat's in the glass."

Lieutenant Murphy laughed. He watched as Danny turned to serve another customer. "Nothing but regulars in here," he said to himself. He recognized every face even if he didn't know their names. He took a small sip of his drink, then pressed the glass against his lips and kept it there. He kept going back to her eyes. He pictured himself shooting questions at her. He placed his hands around his neck and rubbed it. His wife never rubbed his neck anymore. He let go of his wife and picked up the image of the stubborn woman who refused to recognize his questions. For the last three days she had taken up permanent residence in his mind. Nothing he or any of his colleagues did or said could force her to speak.

"Bet she's rich," he said. "Has to be rich." The rich, they carried themselves in a certain way—like they were used to owning, like they knew where you came from, how much money you got paid, just by looking at you. "Yup, bet she's rich." Someone had taught her to carry herself like she was the only thing in the world that mattered. She had a way of making him feel inferior without uttering a word. "Gotta be rich. Bet I'd hate her, bet I'd hate her voice." He laughed at himself, knew he was talking bullshit. He wanted to hear her voice, was convinced it would be haunting and sad and lovely. "Lovely," he said. It was not a word he used. He did not hate her, did not want to hate her. Something about her. He looked at his watch. George was late again. He thought of leaving. His wife would be waiting. They'd have dinner, they'd argue. Maybe he would wait for George. He played with his cigarette, stared at the ashes, wondered when he was going to give it up—this habit of his.

"Couldn't be that bad?" He recognized George's voice. He looked up and smiled at the ageless black man who was taking a seat beside him.

"It's bad," he said, "bad as the weather."

"Lighten up, Murph."

He nodded. He pointed at the bartender, then pointed at George. "Same drink," he said. "Got any news for me, George?"

"The professor, you mean?"

"And the woman."

"Got nothing on her—she doesn't exist—at least not to any of the professor's acquaintances. She's got no record, nothing. Never been arrested. She's got no sheet."

"Maybe she's not from Illinois."

"Maybe not. Doesn't matter. We only have prints—got no name. We don't have anywhere to go. Strange, huh?"

"Strange is what we do, George." Lieutenant Murphy winced as if he were in pain. "You know, maybe she doesn't speak English."

"There's a thought. Where do you figure she's from?"

"Mexico, I'd say. Maybe Italy. Maybe Greece. Latin America—who the hell knows."

"She's a real looker. This one put the *b* in *beautiful*." The bartender placed a drink beside him. George took a sip and smiled. "You know how to treat a guy right, Murph."

"Just don't tell my wife."

George slapped him on the back. "Still a funny guy, huh?" He took another drink. "You know that professor, everybody loves his ass. Everybody. It's incredible. Knows everyone."

"Think it's all professional niceties?"

"Maybe. I'll tell you one thing, though. Nobody has a clue who that woman is. No one even knew he had anyone on the side. I mean, she was really on the side. Everyone thought—thinks—that this guy's been mourning his dead wife for twenty-five years. One of his colleagues even gives me this sob story about how the guy visits his dead wife's grave once a year. All the way to England. She's a side of him no one ever heard about. You think this girl's a prostitute?"

"Don't know. If she is, she doesn't work the streets. Too classy. No signs of makeup. Ever hear of a hooker who didn't wear makeup? No perfume. Nothing. This one doesn't have to try to look good. Didn't even have a purse. No money, no credit cards, nothing. Nothing, nothing, nothing. That's what we got. Maybe she's just careful. Maybe an escort service—"

"From what I've heard, the professor doesn't seem the type."

"Who the hell talks about their sex lives?"

"My wife."

"There much to talk about?" They both broke out laughing. Lieutenant Murphy rubbed his hands together again, then combed his hair with his fingers. "I don't know. Something's not right here. She doesn't strike me as a call girl—not even a pricey one. There's gotta be something else. Sure wish she'd talk. I'm getting the public defender's office to send over one of their people—someone's gotta get her to say something." His voice lowered almost to a whisper. "Just hope they don't send over Jenny Richard."

"What are you muttering about?"

"Jenny Richard."

"Now, why do you wanna mess with her? She's a royal pain in the ass."

"I don't. I was just saying I was hoping they wouldn't send her over."

"You've gone and jinxed it." George laughed. "She's good, though, Murph. If her boss has any sense, he'll send her."

"You're right—she's real good. This case is weird enough without her in the soup, though. I'm just not in the mood to deal with another ball buster. She's a bigger pain in the ass than both my wives put together."

"Well, at least she's smarter."

The lieutenant glared at him. "Don't start."

"You brought it up." He smiled at his friend. "Lighten up, Murph." He laughed out loud.

"What's so funny?"

"Nothing. I was just remembering the last time you and Jenny Richard faced each other. Your case was thrown out of court." George laughed again. "What is it that you said?"

"I said I'd rather have prostate cancer than ever run into her again."

"Yup, that's what you said."

Lieutenant Murphy lit another cigarette. "Got anything on the professor?"

"Squeaky clean. Ph.D. Yale University. Classics professor, University of Chicago. He's the greatest. Students love the guy. Colleagues love the guy. I can't get anyone to say a bad word against him. Sounds like a bit of a dandy to me. Guy's kinda famous, wrote a couple of books that stirred things up about American culture. Big player. Gets his name in print all the time. Even the guys who disagree with him think he's a good Joe. Anyway, from what I can tell, the guy's kinda private—never has anyone over at his house. No crime against that. Nice house—"

"Yeah. Didn't think professors made that much money."

"Bought the house with his dead wife's money. Came from some big bucks in England. Oh—and one other small thing."

"What's that?"

"The professor changed his name. Used to be Thomas Neelon."

"Nice Irish name."

"Yeah—changed it to Blacker when he turned twenty-one. Had all his records changed."

"That it?

"That's it."

"That leaves us nowhere." He polished off his drink. "Well, if the professor doesn't kick over, we'll have a nice chat. Something tells me I won't like him."

"Hey, he's the victim, Lieutenant, remember?" George smiled.

"Right."

A Summer Dream

AUGUST 1990. TWENTY–SIX YEARS OLD.

The little girl walked up the aisle dressed in white, all the pews of the church filled with parents whose eyes were fixed on her. She could not make out any of the faces, all of them out of focus, grotesque, ominous. As she walked toward the altar she became more frantic. "Mama?" she whispered to herself. "Mama?" She could not find her mother's face in the crowd. She kept walking up the aisle. A priest stood large and still at the altar. His was the only face that looked vaguely familiar. As she moved closer to him, she began to make out his features, his blue eyes the color of the Immaculate Conception's robe. It was him, his face, his body. Thomas. He smiled and called her by name. When she turned to run, he appeared in front of her. "No!" she yelled. "I want my mama. I want my mama!"

She jerked herself out of her dream, then hugged herself. She wiped the sweat from her face, then stared at her wet palm. She sat up, then held herself perfectly still, breathing in and out until her heart returned to its regular, steady rhythm. *Maybe today,* she thought, maybe this was the day. She rose from the bed and wrapped her bathrobe tight against her body. *How often have I thought: Maybe today? Claudia, when will you stop thinking? Claudia? I'm not winning this war.*

Ingrate

Thomas lay in the hospital room unaware of where he was. Something in him knew he was near waking, but he wanted to keep himself in limbo, in that intoxicating liminal state despite the dull pain. He wanted to keep himself between worlds for as long as he could; no one could bother him there. His mind wandered as if looking in a book for a passage that might lead him home. Books. He had always turned to them like a penitent in front of an altar. Books had always saved him. He refused to open his eyes, kept them shut, his mind traveling . . .

"Reading? Reading again?"

He looked up and stared into his father's angry eyes. He felt the book being torn from his hands.

"A book? By a bloody Englishman? The English would step on you like you was a bloody cockroach—to them the likes of you ain't nothing. And you sittin' there reading their blasted, goddamn books." He opened the window and tossed the book into the street below. "Where'd you get the money for that bloody book, boy? Answer me," he said, raising his hand.

"I carried some groceries for Mrs. O'Conner. She gave me the book."

"Mrs. O'Conner? Reading bloody books by bastard Englishmen?"

He slapped his son across the face. "Next time, tell her to pay you with something useful. Now, go fetch that book and sell it."

He stood perfectly still.

"Go on," his father said softly. He touched the boy on the shoulder. "Don't mean to be so rough with you, boy. I'll let no son of mine read them that kept us down, understand?"

Thomas nodded.

"A far better thing to work than to read," he said. "Go fetch the book. The bookshop's bound to give you something for it."

The boy nodded and walked slowly out of the room.

I'm dead and gone to hell—have to live with him now, he thought. He kept his eyes shut. The dull pain in his chest growing sharper. The knife, the look on Claudia's face. *Ingrate—*

"Professor Blacker?"

He heard a voice in the distance. He opened his eyes.

"Professor Blacker?" The woman's voice was kind.

"Claudia?" he whispered.

The woman squeezed his hand. "It's a lovely name, Claudia—I'm afraid my name is Alice."

He moaned, the pain in his chest.

"Take this," she said. "It'll help you feel better soon."

He felt a pill in his mouth, then a tube in his mouth. He worked hard to swallow the water through the straw. His mouth was dry, and he wanted Alice to go away. "I want to die," he said.

She patted him on the arm. "There. Just like new before you know it."

"Ingrate," he whispered.

Mama

1971. SEVEN YEARS OLD.

In the beginning, she cried every morning. Cried every evening. In the day, she hid her tears. Crying made him angry. He was good to her when she was calm. It wasn't long before she taught herself to smile for him. Day by day, she learned. But she kept her mother's face locked away in a place where she could reach for it when she needed. Sometimes she pictured her mother praying in front of the statue of Saint Jude at Sacred Heart Church, her lips busy and lost in her prayers, the dance of the burning candles shining in her bright, black eyes. Sometimes her mother held her in her lap as she played with the thin and worn ring on her finger.

She willed her mother to come and see her. She tossed her voice to the night—Mama—as if it were a ball her mother would catch and carry back to her. A ball that resembled a large and glowing moon. One night, her mother heard. She came. Her mother would speak to her, tell her stories that made her happy. She would stand over her as she lay in bed, sing to her until she fell asleep. For a long while, nights were nothing but peace. Her mother's soft, protecting voice was everywhere, covered her like a soft rebozo, eased her to sleep. Every night she would come and make her visit.

The bad dreams ceased, and the days did not seem so long. Slowly, the visits became less and less frequent. Then she stopped coming. Stopped. And she began to forget.

What Every Girl Should Know

THIRTEEN YEARS OLD.

She searched for the source between her legs. At first she thought she was just urinating, but there was something different. She reached down and touched the slow trickle of blood. No pain. Blood. It was warm. There was something wrong, a hurt. She took a towel and placed it where the blood was coming from. Oh God. God. Don't cry. Thomas didn't like it when she cried. But he's not here—Oh God, he's not here, and when he comes back it will be too late. Mama, I'm scared. Mama, I want to go home. She sat on the floor of the bathroom and wept. She had not cried since the first few weeks she had arrived at Thomas's house. Crying would not get her back home. She sobbed quietly, sobbed until she felt all the water inside her had drained. She felt dry and old and tired. She fell asleep, the towel between her legs. Sleep would take her away. She dreamed she was swimming, and the water was not water. Blood. When she woke, Thomas was standing over her.

"Claudia, is there something wrong?"

"I'm sick," she said. She pointed at the towel between her legs.

He nodded. "Yes, I see."

"Am I going to die?"

He smiled. "Of course not, my dear."

"Then why am I bleeding?"

41

"Claudia," he said softly, patiently, "you're menstruating. I didn't think it would come this soon. You're growing up so fast, my dear. You'll be a woman in no time."

She stared at the bloody towel. Her lips were dry. She felt empty and numb. She wanted the bleeding to stop. *"Menstru—"* she stumbled over the word.

"Menstruating," he repeated slowly. *"Men-stru-a-ting."*

"Does that mean it will stop? I don't like it. It makes me feel—makes me feel scared."

"Does it hurt anywhere?"

"No," she said. *"Last night, I hurt a little, not much. And then, this morning, when I was going to take a shower, I felt something. And then—"*

"It's quite normal," he said. His voice was calm and sure.

"Did you bleed, too?"

"No. Only girls."

She took a deep breath. He did not seem worried or afraid. If she was sick, he would be worried. When she had caught a bad flu, he had looked concerned, but right now his eyes were absent of worry. She might be all right. *"Only girls?"* she said finally. *"Why only girls?"*

"Only girls have babies. This blood—it's like food."

"For the baby?"

"Exactly."

"Am I going to have a baby?"

He laughed softly. *"No, my dear. Every month, starting today, you'll start to bleed. More commonly, it's known as 'a period.' When a woman says, 'I'm having my period,' she means that it's time for her monthly letting of blood."* His voice was gentle, caring, confident. He knew so much about so many things. He felt her forehead. *"Sometimes, women get cramps—like the pain you felt last night. Sometimes, it gets very bad. Some women get no cramps at all. Everyone's different."*

"And it doesn't mean I'm sick?"

"Not at all. Quite the opposite, it means you're very healthy."

She looked into his eyes. She felt better now. She felt stupid for having spent the day crying.

"I'll tell you what," he said. "I'm going to the store to buy you something. Something that will help you catch the blood. You can't very well walk around the house holding a towel between your legs, now, can you?"

She nodded. She wondered what he was talking about.

"Now, you just clean yourself up. Take your shower, dear Claudia. And when I come back from the store, I'll show you what to do. You must pay close attention. You'll be doing this every month for a long time."

"I don't like it," she said. "It scares me."

"There's nothing to be frightened of, I promise. And tomorrow, tomorrow I'll buy you a book, and it will help you understand everything. And what you don't understand, you can ask me."

She nodded. He took the key out of his pocket. "Now, just this once, I'm going to take the shackles off your feet—because you've been so brave. Take yourself a nice hot shower, and I promise I'll be right back."

"I'll be fine?"

He placed his hand on her cheek, then kissed her. "You'll be just fine."

She smiled and wiped away the last of the tears on her face. Sometimes she liked him so much, so very much.

Visits of a Hungry God

SEPTEMBER 1987. TWENTY-THREE YEARS OLD.

Tonight he had the look of a hungry god who had found just the thing that would appease him. He would come to her, make his usual visit. But soon enough, he would leave. Sometimes she would count, lose herself in numbers. Sometimes he ran his tongue over her entire body until she broke down and groaned. She did not like his saliva on her ear, the awful tingling like cockroaches crawling all over her. Sometimes he just pushed himself in—and it was over. It would hurt, but it was quick. Tonight he'd had too much wine. It would take longer. The hungry god would stay a long time. She put down her book, changed into a nightgown he'd given her. It would go faster if she was ready. She hated it when he undressed her—hated it even more when he wanted her to strip him, make her run her hands over all his body. She always wondered what her face looked like when she did that. Calm? On fire? Her hands. On him. It wasn't his body she hated, not his age. It was him.

She heard the key in the lock, saw the door open. He smiled at her. She stood motionless. "Am I disturbing you?"

She shook her head. "I was waiting for you."

He placed his lips on her neck. "Come. I need you."

The whole night. He breathed her name softly. "Claudia." It sounded like a leaf falling from a tree.

Maybe She Wanted to Be Punished

Jenny Richard laughed quietly to herself as she sat at a win-dow table of her favorite coffee bar. She liked coming here, liked the loud conversations, the laughter, the whispers, the arguments. Better this than the silence of her apartment. Better all this. Her coffee was strong and hot. Black. No sugar, no cream, nothing to mask the taste of the drink she loved, of the drink that reminded her that bitterness could be sweet. She felt protected from the storm that had come in fits and starts, a storm that was as awful as Chicago had ever known.

She smiled as she saw the people rushing up and down the street, armed with their raincoats and umbrellas like warriors going into battle. Neither the weather nor their own fears of the night nor the knowledge that the streets could be as threatening as the sky, nothing, nothing could keep these people off the streets. They did not live their lives cowering in fear. When had she fallen in love with these people—these people and their city? When she had come here, she had been running from a place that was incapable of returning her affections. She had never belonged. But when she had arrived in Chicago, she had not belonged here, either. She remembered entering law school, the victory of having been accepted, and how that small victory had vanished as quickly as it had arrived. She remembered how her professors and colleagues had treated her—like some southern hick. "Cajun, what's that?" At the top of her class, and yet everyone had treated her as if her accomplishments had been meaningless. Meaningless because it was she who had emerged as the beneficiary. But she had refused to profit from her success. She had not taken a job with any firm, had refused to become a member of a club she had little desire to belong to. Or was it that she felt rejected—and so, in turn, rejected? She did not know the answer, and wondered why she was sitting there, remembering things as if the remembering would bring a clear answer. Perhaps her job was getting to her. Over fifteen years as a public defender. Too long, she thought.

She loved this city. She was sure of this—but her love did not allow her to have any illusions about what it was, what it could do to people. Chicago, like anyplace, was good to you *if you were successful*. But her clients were hardly portraits of success. Most of them had been born poor, and those who had been born to better circumstances had fallen from the graces of the middle class. She lost a good many of her cases, but she had, at least, learned how to live with losses. And she had also learned how to win. Mostly, she had learned not to measure herself by the cases she'd won. Or lost.

She remembered her most celebrated win. Cop killer. Of all her clients, she had been most certain of his innocence. Of all her clients, he'd had the least chance of getting a fair trial. And she had won. *Her client had won.* She reminded herself always that it had been *his* victory. That case had won her few admirers. She had been treated as an example of how the law protected criminals, and she had been vilified by cops with whom she was forced to have contact. But the man had been innocent. And the prosecutors had known it. And many cops had known it. She shook her head. She did not want to be thinking about this. Perhaps it was the storm that was reminding her of her own tempests. "Oh, Jenny Richard," she whispered to herself. "Stop remembering." She finished her coffee and walked out into the storm that seemed intent on punishing the city for its prodigal ways.

She stepped outside into the pelting rain. As she walked along the sidewalk, she sensed footsteps behind her. She did not hesitate, kept her steady stride, straightened her back. She wished she had brought her umbrella. Her raincoat kept her dry, but an umbrella could serve as a weapon. She felt at a disadvantage in the rain, so much harder to decipher her surroundings. She picked up her pace and listened, the footsteps still behind her. They seemed to grow closer. She noticed a familiar bar just ahead; she would go into it. It wasn't far, the footsteps so close. She walked faster, almost breaking into a run. Then she felt it—a hand on her shoulder. A hand, digging into her—*No.* Her heart beat as fast as the rain fell on the street. *No,* she thought, but her fear had made her mute. No, all this time refusing to be one of the city's victims, and now—"Jenny!"

She took a deep breath as she recognized the voice. She felt her heart almost stop, then return to its usual rhythm. "Charlie, you idiot, you scared the shit outta me!" She hit him on the chest. "You scared me on purpose."

"I did not—I just wasn't sure it was you, but then I noticed that tear in your raincoat. You should get a new one." He smiled. "I'll walk you home—and you can invite me in for a drink."

She felt her heart returning to its normal rhythm. "I shouldn't," she said. "Not after what you just did." She took his arm. "But I can be forgiving." Suddenly, the rain started to come down in sheets. Charlie held his umbrella over both of them, and she felt safe again. "Our sins, Charlie," she laughed nervously. "The gods of the city are pissed as hell."

◆ ◆ ◆

She turned the dead bolt on the front door after she saw Charlie to the door. It was late, and she was tired. She walked straight to her kitchen and checked her answering machine. She stared at the blinking light, pushed the button, and slipped off her shoes as the tape rewound. She listened to Dave's voice, decided she liked it. He didn't make himself sound like her boss; friendly without being full of bullshit: "Jenny, I know you're up to your ass in crocodiles, but you're on this new case. I've a feeling it's just up your alley. Yeah, yeah, so you have to work a little bit with your old friend Lieutenant Murphy. It's too much work to hate that guy. Just bury the goddamn hatchet. Come by tomorrow, we'll talk. You can yell at me, and I'll yell back—and we'll be in business. Oh, and Jenny, stop giving my new assistant such a hard time. He's good, Jenny, *and he's honest*, and that should count for a helluva lot. So what if he has the personality of a non-alcoholic, decaffeinated beverage that lost its fizz from being on the shelf too long?" She couldn't help but laugh. "I'll bet I made you laugh." She made a face. "Relax, Jen—and give my love to the lieutenant."

She sat down at the kitchen table and rubbed her feet. She shook her head. Dave's right, she thought, I gotta cut Peter some slack. Lieutenant Murphy was another story. From the minute they'd met, it was as if they were in a ring with gloves on. As the bell rang, the referee ran for cover, and they went at it. She was disgusted with her own behavior when she was around him—the way she became compulsively insulting. Was it her? Or him?

She opened the refrigerator and stared into it. "Oh, I get this feeling," she said, "I just get this awful feeling." She kept staring into the refrigerator. "And tomorrow I get to see Lieutenant Murphy. Try and be nice, Jenny. Shit, shit, shit." She took out a piece of cheese and popped it into her mouth.

◆ ◆ ◆

"I can't get her to say two words."

Jenny tried to smile at Lieutenant Murphy. "Serves you right for not having her lawyer present." I'm doing it again, she thought.

The lieutenant grinned at the public defender. He tried to pretend he didn't find something about her attractive. "Coffee?"

"Black," she said.

"She just looks at me as if I don't exist—reminds me of the way my first wife looked at me."

"How many have you had?"

"On my second—not so many."

"You keep looking at me that way and you'll go through the one you have in record time."

"Look at you like what?"

She noticed his wedding band as he handed her a cup of coffee. She shook her head and smiled. "Little boys, little boys."

"What's wrong with little boys?"

"Oh," she said, "nothing. I don't mind sleeping with them on occasion. I don't even mind feeding them. Why, I've even changed a few." She shot a grin at him. "It's working with them that's a pain in the ass."

"Your southern accent is showing."

"Ahh wasn't hidin' it," she said self-mockingly. She took a drink of her coffee. "Terrible stuff. Makes me want to light up a cigarette just to get the taste out of my mouth." She looked into his eyes, wanting him to look back, wanting him to see how stubborn she was. She wanted to make sure he understood. "How long has she been in?"

"Oh, I'd say about seventy-two hours."

"Seventy-two hours?"

"In Cook County, that's a second or two."

"Yeah, well—" She shook her head.

"And besides, I told your boss to get you here yesterday. Where the hell have you been?"

She wanted to yell back at him. She nodded calmly. "I'm here now, Lieutenant. Shall we get to it?"

"She's all yours."

"She in the little room?"

He nodded. "I'll tell you one thing, though. Whoever the hell this woman is, she's decided she doesn't have anything to say to me. She doesn't have anything to say to anyone. You may have a hard time reaching her. We're the enemy, I guess."

"*You're* the enemy," she corrected. "You're prosecuting her, aren't you?"

"Just because we've booked her doesn't mean we're prosecuting. We haven't charged her with anything."

"Not yet, anyway. Why the hell should she give you a rope to hang her with?"

"She knows her rights."

"Yeah, I'll bet. Made sure, did you? You guys recite Miranda as if it were the Hail Mary. Those who don't know the prayer don't have a clue. Not everybody's a good Catholic, Lieutenant."

"No, but we are, aren't we?" He grinned at her.

"Good Catholics don't get divorced."

He shook his head. "Always got a retort."

"Yup."

"So you wanna have a go at her?"

She wanted to belt him. She wanted to wipe that cocky grin right off his face. "I think it's a good thing I'm here."

He placed his hand across his mouth.

He looks tired, she thought. She almost liked him. It didn't stop her from wanting to slap him.

"Something about this woman," he mumbled.

"Huh?"

"Something about this woman," he said. "Something's not right."

"Like what? Give me a for instance."

"I can't—I just get this feeling."

"Well, it's nice to know you have them."

He laughed, then rubbed his neck.

"You implying she's not playing with a whole team?"

"Crazy, you mean? Don't think so. Smart—sane as they come, I'd say." He opened the door to his office and led her down the hall. They walked toward the interrogation room.

"What's her name?"

"She didn't say."

"Not even her name? You're slipping, Lieutenant. In three days, she didn't even give you her name?"

"Did you want me to torture her?"

"You think it hasn't been done? My guess is she's not black—not from the South Side, either."

"Anybody ever tell you you're full of shit?"

"Happens all the time."

"Doesn't surprise me at all, Counselor."

"Anybody ever tell you to go swim in the lake till you get cramps and drown?"

"Happens all the time. And how come every time I see you, you act as if you're in a goddamn war?"

"I *am* in a goddamn war."

He raised his arms. "Truce."

She shrugged. "Sorry," she said. She grinned. "You can take it." She shook her head, her hair flying everywhere. She placed a hand on her forehead. "Shit!"

"What's that?"

She half-smiled at the lieutenant. "Nothing—I just remembered something I forgot to do." She looked at her watch and shook her head. "No IDs?"

"Nothing—not even a purse."

"Maybe she's deaf."

"I don't think so."

"What makes you so sure?"

"She spoke to the guy on the phone."

"What guy? What phone?"

"We sent your boss a report. Didn't he give it to you?"

"Came straight here—soon as I got out of court. All I know is some gal stabbed some old professor. I told Dave you wouldn't be exactly pleased to see me on the case."

"Well, he was right about that."

"It's not as if I volunteered."

"Do your job. I'll do mine," he said stiffly, then smiled. "My friends call me Murph."

She was annoyed at his invitation. "Let's not call it a friendship," she said. "Friendships can get messy."

He shook his head and grimaced, then handed her his clipboard. "And I want it back," he said. "You've got your own damn copy waiting for you in your office." She glanced at the report as she walked.

"How's the professor doing?"

"He's still breathing."

"Oh," she said. "I read about this guy in the paper. He's famous. I mean, I never heard of him, but everyone else seems to know who he is."

"Yeah, he wrote a book—actually several. One of them was some kind of bestseller. Can't remember the name—something with *America* in the title.

"Sounds swell."

He laughed. "Caused quite a stir. The *Tribune*'s making a big deal out of his stabbing. Calling for an end to crime and all that shit. An end to crime—that's a joke. That goddamn newspaper's a crime. Anyway, I've been asking around, and it seems like everybody loves this guy."

"Not everyone. Guess we know how my client feels about him."

"Well, actually, we don't know diddly."

"Well, she sure as hell didn't stab him because she loves him. The old geezer going to pull through?"

"Hard to say. So far so good. I'm checking in on him myself soon as you're done here. Wanna meet him?"

She didn't even notice he was joking. "Maybe—don't really—" she lost her train of thought as she looked over the report. "Got any theories?"

"Well, at first I thought the professor must be banging her. She wants more—or maybe he wants to end it—or maybe she wants money. It's gotta be money, I said to myself. Why the hell else would a woman with looks like that be hanging around an old bastard who's already more dead than alive?"

She stared at the report. "He's not that old. Sixty-three. Maybe she was one of his students."

"She's too old for that."

"Ever hear of graduate school?"

He tried not to look annoyed. "So maybe she was his student," he said reluctantly. "So how come the university doesn't have a record of anyone who matches her description?" He waited for her to answer.

"I really do hate you," she said.

"Yeah, sure. Anyway, one of them wants to end it, and the conversation gets nasty, the phone rings, she gets mad, grabs the knife, well, there we have it. Never even got around to eating dinner. That's what I was thinking. Only I don't think so."

"Why not?"

"She's not the type to be banging anybody. And it doesn't seem that she'd kill out of rage."

"Oh, you know, huh?"

He nodded. "Well, I guess I don't. But something else."

"What?"

"She didn't run. She just sat there and waited. She fainted on some policeman as soon as they broke down the door. Not real criminal behavior, I'd say."

Jenny looked at Lieutenant Murphy, then shook her head. "Maybe she wanted to be punished."

"You *are* a good Catholic girl, aren't you?"

She couldn't help but laugh. He liked that she laughed at his joke. He grinned. "Or maybe," he said slowly, "she was waiting for someone to let her out."

"What's that supposed to mean, Lieutenant?"

"All the doors in the house were locked. Dead bolts. You need a key to open them. She didn't have one."

"Didn't the professor have one on his person?"

"No. They found his keys hidden in one of his shoes—in his closet."

"What an odd place to put them."

"Maybe he didn't want them anywhere near her. Anyway, I don't know what the hell it means, but that's all I know. It's all there," he said, pointing to the report.

"Yes, I see," she said as she turned a page. "When are you guys going to learn how to write in English? Maybe the professor could give you guys a few lessons." She kept her eyes on the report. "So what's your new theory?"

"Don't got one. You tell me." He stopped in front of a door along a busy hallway. "Here we are," he said. He turned to look at the public defender. "All I know is that she stabbed him. We know that much." He opened the door. "I want to see you after your interview."

"I'm not going to breathe a word, Lieutenant."

"All I want's an ID. Fingerprints gave us nothing. This gal's got no record."

He turned and walked back down the hall. She looked into the room. An officer nodded at her and wordlessly stepped out. In the dull light, she saw a woman at the table. Jenny stared at the eyes that were examining her—the darkest things she'd ever seen, as black and as large as a clear winter night. At that moment, Jenny thought those eyes took up the entire room, making it even starker than it already was.

More Than a Name

"The lieutenant tells me you're not much for talking." The woman across from her smiled faintly, then looked away. Jenny was disturbed by her smile—a smile that lacked the self-confident cynicism, even the rage, of most of her other clients. She seemed perfectly composed, as if she was wrapped in an innocence that seemed at once natural and incongruent, eyes soft, giving—and yet impenetrable. She did not belong in the light of this room, would be more at home in the natural light of day. *I wonder how many hearts she's busted up.* She shook her head and chastised herself for her thought. "You want to tell me how this all started?"

The woman shook her head.

"Well, at least we're communicating. What's your name?" The woman sat as still as a statue, and for an instant Jenny felt invisible. She had the urge to ask her where she learned her posture but shoved the thought away. "You have a family?"

Again, the woman did not respond.

"My name's Jenny," she said, "Jenny Richard. Actually, my name's pronounced Re-*shard*, but most people call me Richard, like the man's first name." The woman sitting across from her seemed to be listening, but her interest seemed faint. *Jenny, just talk.* "Why the hell do we let other people change our names? I grew up speaking French, and now I don't know a word." The woman shrugged her shoulders. "You don't seem as if you're from Chicago. You from Chicago?"

The woman just sat, though now she appeared to be a little more interested.

"The South, now there's a place to be from. It's no place to live, but a great place to be *from*." She stopped herself and smiled at the silent woman. "Couldn't get away fast enough after my mama died. Just looked at a map, packed my bags, and came to Chicago. Been here for twenty years, and you know what? Sometimes I feel as if I've never left New Orleans. To be from the South is to be owned—it keeps you without asking if you want to be kept." She thought she saw something that resembled a smile, as if she were about to laugh.

"You're awful quiet. Okay by me. I haven't had a moment's peace all day. I had court this morning at eight. I woke up at five to the sound of my dog barking in my ear. To hear her, you'd have thought that dog was dying of something. She's a hound—sounds like a dying seal when she barks. Sorriest-looking dog I've ever seen. You ever had a dog?"

The woman shook her head.

"Can you at least say 'no'?"

"No," the woman said.

Jenny laughed. "I'll write that down," she said. "I can tell the lieutenant that you never had a dog—and that you told me so."

She smiled, then turned her head away.

Jenny waited for a minute, but it was clear to her that it would take a lot more time and talk to get her to feel more at ease. *I'll make you talk if*

I have to tell you my whole life story. "You'd love this dog," she said, then stopped. *Cut the shit about the dog.* She stretched, turning her head from side to side. "Me? What part of town do *I* live in? Thanks for asking."

The woman smiled, almost laughed.

"You really want to know?"

The woman nodded.

"I live in a neighborhood not too far away from Wrigley Field. Right near what some people call Boystown. Roscoe Street—pretty close to the lake. You know the place?"

The woman shook her head.

"Great place. As Chicago goes, it's pretty safe. Most of the guys in my building aren't into women. They take good care of me. When my brother came to visit, he was a little uncomfortable. He told me people were going to think I was a lesbian. 'What people?' I asked him. And besides, I told him, God cursed me with heterosexuality—I'm damned to like men for the rest of my life. It's nothing to be proud of." Jenny laughed. "My poor brother. He's afraid of everything—afraid of black people—in Louisiana, mind you. Afraid of men. Afraid of women. Poor guy—maybe that's why he joined the NRA." She crossed her arms and looked straight into the mute woman's face. She seemed as lonely as she was lovely, almost as if she were in mourning. *No wonder the lieutenant likes her. Long as she just sits there, she can be anything anybody wants her to be.* Jenny was quiet for a long time, searching for the right thing to say, the right gestures. She fought her impatience. The wordless woman did not seem to be uncomfortable sharing the silent room, but Jenny could not help but be annoyed. She was tired of maneuvering, tired of strategizing. She had spent the entire day talking and responding and thinking on her feet. She wasn't in any mood to sit there and listen to the sound of her own voice. She wasn't interested in a monologue. *Everything is not about you, Jenny.* "You want me to come back another time?"

The woman shrugged her shoulders.

"Are you ever going to talk to me?"

The woman almost spoke but stopped herself.

"Maybe I should leave." She started shifting her body out of the chair she was sitting on.

A wave of panic moved over the woman's face, and then it quickly disappeared as if she had caught herself falling and picked herself up and pretended nothing had happened—*I didn't fall. I didn't.*

Jenny stared at her for a second, then stood up.

"I'll come back some other—"

The woman nodded, a blankness in her expression. She seemed as vacant as an empty lot, no signs that a building had ever existed on the premises.

Jenny watched her for a moment. "I just want to help you. I can't if you won't let me."

The woman stared at her, then nodded.

"Do you want me to leave?"

She shook her head.

"You want me to stay?"

She shook her head again.

Jenny put her hands on her forehead and brushed her hair back. Was this a game? Too hard to tell. "You're not making this very easy for me."

"Sorry," she said. She shrugged.

Her second word. "No" and "sorry." It was something. The lieutenant said she hadn't spoken a word. Not that she'd learned much. She looked at her watch. She looked up at the woman. "Well, I don't suppose it's your job to make things easy for me, now, is it?"

The woman opened her mouth, then shut it. She waited a moment, looked into Jenny's eyes, then whispered, "Thomas said I could be difficult."

A sentence. Progress. "You want to tell me about Thomas?"

The woman looked into Jenny's face as if she were looking for something in Jenny's eyes, something familiar perhaps, some kind of sign. "I'm tired," she said finally. She closed her eyes.

Jenny waited, weighed her options. The right strategy meant everything. "If I come back tomorrow, will you talk to me?"

The woman looked around the room as if she were looking for an exit sign.

"You want out?" Jenny hoped her voice was friendly and firm.

"Yes," the woman said, her voice heavy as drops of rain in a storm.

"I'm your only key."

The woman seemed to acknowledge Jenny's remark.

Jenny rose from her chair. She reached for the woman's hand.

The woman pulled away.

"I won't hurt you," Jenny said. She smiled at her, then walked slowly out of the room.

◆ ◆ ◆

"Well, did you get anything?"

"I got a few words."

"A few words?"

"It's more than you got, Lieutenant."

"It isn't enough. You get a name?"

"Tomorrow. I'll be back."

"It doesn't seem to me you tried very hard."

"Look, Lieutenant, I got a few words. I decided not to push it. Easy does it—you ever hear that expression? You have to know when to push and when to leave well enough alone." Jenny looked at her watch. "Look, I gotta go."

"We're going nowhere, fast."

"I wouldn't say that."

"We haven't even got a goddamned name."

Jenny glared at the lieutenant. "I'll get you a name. I'll get you more than a name."

No One's Ever Called Me Honey

The dark woman looked better rested—and slightly nervous. Jenny thought the slight look of discomfort on her face was a good sign. Jenny took out a pad and a pen, then noticed that the faint look of nervousness had vanished. "Now," she said as she settled into her seat. *Now what?* "Now," she repeated, "why don't we start at the beginning?"

The woman nodded.

Jenny's mind fumbled around for a while, lost, wondering what she should say first. Chess. She hated chess. Maybe this *was* a game. She looked at her client again, looked into her eyes. The woman did not look away. She had the urge to tell this woman that she was a lawyer, not an entertainer. Bad strategy, she thought. She looked at the woman, studied her for a moment, then smiled. "You don't look like you grew up speaking English. Did you grow up speaking Spanish?" Something in the way the woman turned her head told her she was on the right track. "I took Spanish in college, though I don't remember much of it." She reached into herself and let out a nearly flawless Spanish: *"Yo soy una abogada. Estoy aquí para ayudarla."*

The woman across from her wiped a tear from her face, then another. Her lips trembled though she remained as quiet as a Sunday morning in Jenny's native Louisiana. She pushed her palms into the table as if she wanted to push everything she felt onto that surface—push what she knew, what she was, into that inanimate object, make that object speak for her. "I haven't heard Spanish in twenty-three years," she whispered.

Good girl. Today she would get more than a name.

The woman looked around the room, then directly at Jenny. "My mother, she always spoke Spanish. So did my father." She placed her head between her hands.

"What happened to them?"

"I don't know. It's been a long time since I've seen them."

"How long?"

"Since I was a little girl."

"Did you run away?"

She shook her head. "Talking makes me—" She stopped and looked around the room as if she was looking for something. Or some*one*. "Talking makes me nervous." Her words were soft, but they seemed careful—well chosen, as if she only allowed herself to speak after she assessed her surroundings.

"Sometimes talking can relax you. It's like getting a massage—it helps you get rid of tension." Jenny tried to make her voice sound relaxed, calm.

The woman stared at her, opened her mouth to say something, then simply shook her head.

"I'm your lawyer," Jenny said in that same tone of voice she'd heard herself use for the last fifteen years. It was a maternal tone, firm and protective and stubborn. "Whatever you decide to tell me stops right here. I'm the wall with ears and no mouth, honey—"

Suddenly and inexplicably, the woman laughed.

"I must have missed something."

"No one's ever called me honey."

Jenny grinned. *This woman hasn't known enough laughter.* "Maybe it was about time." She seemed oddly self-possessed, not at all like a woman in need of help. She felt the echo of her laughter still in the room. Jenny looked straight into her eyes and wondered if she should continue asking questions. No, she thought, it was better to make her feel at ease, to talk for a while, to let her say what she wanted about *what* she wanted. The lieutenant and his friends have been shooting questions at her for days. *Better just to talk.* "Lieutenant Murphy thinks you're very attractive," she said, half making fun of him.

This time the woman did not hesitate before she responded to Jenny's remark. "Maybe it's because I didn't say anything to him. Thomas used to say that the less a woman said, the more attractive she was."

Jenny laughed. "I feel the same way about men."

The woman with the dark eyes smiled. "Do all men like quiet women?" There was no hint of cynicism in her voice. She seemed to be curious, if cautious, and the tone in her voice was open and friendly—especially for a woman who sat on a chair as if it were a throne.

"I don't know anything about men," she said flatly. She was surprised at her own candor, but she had not slept well and she was tired, and she was in no mood to censor herself. She did not feel like behaving like the consummate professional. "I've been around men all my life, and sometimes I think we live in different worlds. But there's something to that, I think. Men probably like quiet women—that's why most of them run when they see me coming."

The woman laughed. When her smile went away she looked down at the ground. She raised her head slowly. "Do you like them?"

"I'd be a liar if I said I didn't. You?"

"I don't think so. I only know one." She coughed, then cleared her throat.

"You only know one man?"

"Yes, the lieutenant doesn't count."

"He'll be glad to hear it."

"Is he nice—the lieutenant?"

"Sometimes I think I hate him. He doesn't like to lose, I can tell you that much. Maybe that's why he bothers me so much—I don't like to lose, either."

The woman coughed again.

"You look tired," Jenny said. "Maybe you'd like to rest."

"Yes, I'd like to rest."

"Can't you sleep?"

The woman said nothing.

"Is it the cell?"

The woman shook her head, then seemed as if she was about to speak. She shivered as though she were cold.

"Would you like a blanket?"

"Why," the woman whispered, "why are you being so kind?" She trembled, then hugged herself. "I'll never . . . I'll never—" the whole room was suddenly full of her voice, full of her quiet sobs. She clamped her teeth together as if by performing that action she could control the pain, could stop the tears from flowing out of her like a dam could stop a river. But there was still no controlling it. There was nothing but loss on her face, and knowing that the loss was so visible, she could do nothing but place her hands on her face, as if that simple gesture would keep Jenny from seeing anything about her. "Don't look at me," she said.

"You don't have to hide," Jenny said quietly. "You can't control everything, honey. It's not a bad thing to cry."

"You don't know." Something in her voice—not anger. It was more an unbearable, inconsolable grief that was as deep as the bayous of the

Louisiana Jenny remembered from her childhood—as deep as that—and just as stark and lovely and despairing.

Jenny reached for her hand.

The woman squeezed it as if to let go of her hand meant letting go of something crucial and necessary.

"It's okay." Jenny listened to the woman and, for no reason at all, she wanted to cry with her, tell her *I know I know*—but she did *not* know. She knew nothing of this woman. And she wondered why this woman reminded her so much of her own past, since their pasts had nothing in common. Sitting with her and her dark eyes and her haunting voice in this sparse and quiet room was no time to be recalling that graceless place she had run from. Jenny shook her head as if to shake off her own thoughts. She reached into her purse and handed the woman a tissue. "No one will cry for you. That's what my mama used to say. 'Cry,' she'd say, 'cry with everything you've got.' Good advice, I'd say."

The woman nodded and wept quietly, still holding most of what she felt inside like a treasure that would lose its value if she allowed it to hit the open air. Then she laughed. She blew her nose. "You have a nice voice," she said. "I haven't heard a woman's voice for a long time. A long, long time."

That Quiet Will Kill You

"How long is a long, long time?"

Gloria stared at the woman across from her, who sat patiently waiting for an answer.

"Take your time," she said. "I'm not in a hurry." She smiled and leaned back on her chair.

"I was just a girl." Gloria stopped, did not know what to say after she said the word *girl*. The beginning of the story was the hardest. The first word was the most difficult to pronounce. She remembered the beginning as clearly as she remembered sticking a knife in Thomas's chest, but she found she could speak of neither of these events. If she told someone, nothing would be left of her. She looked at the woman lawyer across from her—she seemed like such a miracle. But she was just a woman. She shrugged.

"Relax," the woman said, "or scream if you want."

"I've never screamed."

"It's not so difficult."

"I have had to learn the simplest things last—which made for difficulties."

Jenny laughed. "What?"

"It's a line from a poem that Thomas used to quote. He liked poetry."

"You want to talk about Thomas?"

Gloria shook her head. She shrugged again.

"Do you mind if I smoke?" the woman asked.

Gloria remembered her father. Her father had smoked. "I've forgotten what smoke looks like."

"You say it like it's a lost love."

"Maybe it is."

"It's awful stuff—only an addict could love it. Did you used to smoke?"

"No."

Jenny took a cigarette from her purse and lit it.

Gloria stared at her as she blew the smoke out of her nose. She didn't care for the smell, and yet she loved the way the smoke looked in the air, like a net catching light. She looked at the woman's face, her wavy hair, her deep brown eyes, the thin gold chain she wore around her neck. She wanted to know what hung at the end of the chain that was hidden behind the red sweater she was wearing. "Is there something at the end of your gold chain?"

Jenny took out the chain, the gold cross sparkling in the light of the room. "My mother gave it to me for my first Communion."

She stared at Jenny's cross, the working hands that held the tiny crucifix as if it were in danger of being lost, as if it might turn to dust if she didn't hold it just right. She said nothing for a long time. She watched as Jenny placed the chain back inside her sweater.

◆ ◆ ◆

"Where do we go from here?" Jenny tried to keep her voice soft.

"I can't go back?"

"Home? Why not?"

"I meant Thomas's house."

Jenny was troubled by Gloria's answer. "Was Thomas's house home?"

She considered Jenny's question. "No," she said finally.

"You want to go back there?" Jenny tried to hide her amazement. There was something here she didn't understand.

"Where, then?"

"We can figure this out. We're two intelligent women."

"I don't feel very intelligent."

"Well, I don't feel intelligent, either—but we are." Jenny tapped her finger against her temple. "Why don't you start by telling me your name."

"My name?"

"It's not a difficult question." Jenny winced at her own sarcasm, but the words had just come out of her. Sometimes her job was too much a part of her. "I was just being sarcastic."

"I know," she said, a hint of a smile on her face. Just a hint, and then she returned to her stoic composure.

"I'm sorry."

"It's okay."

Jenny watched her and thought how hard she was fighting herself. *God, don't blow it, Jenny.*

There was another awkward pause between them until Gloria continued. "Thomas called me Claudia." She clenched her fist. "I think sometimes he thought I was one of his flowers—just another thing that grew in his garden. Claudia. I looked it up in a dictionary—it means *lame*. A part of him must have always known what it meant. Thomas never told me why he gave me that name, just that he thought it was lovely—sophisticated. He liked things to be sophisticated—especially women. Lame. Do I look like a cripple?" She tilted her head slightly. "He had a garden with all kinds of plants and flowers and trees, and he knew their Latin names, but sometimes he renamed them. What was wrong with—*I had a name.*"

Jenny watched her face. She sounded angry, but there was no sign of rage on her face.

Gloria inhaled deeply and looked down at the table. She looked back up and stared at the gold chain. She tried to remember what her mother had given her for her first Communion. A rosary—it looked like it was made of pearls.

Jenny reached over and lifted her chin. "Are you okay?"

"I was just thinking." She hesitated, then spoke softly, as if to speak above a whisper would somehow break her. "My first Communion."

Jenny waited for her to continue.

"I was trying to remember what my mother had given me."

"Did you remember?"

"A rosary. I thought the beads were pearls. But they weren't. They couldn't have been. She was too poor. I was so happy, that's what I remember—or maybe I'm just making that up." She placed a finger in her mouth and bit it. "I had a friend—her name was Rosie. I remember holding her hand when we stood in line to make our first conf—" She looked up at Jenny and smiled weakly. "Sometimes I dream Rosie's hand." For an instant Jenny felt she could read what was on her face as easily as if she were a book—a children's book in which everything is simple and obvious and repetitive. *You won't hurt me, if I tell you everything, you won't hurt me?* Those words were as solid as the walls in the room. "My name is Gloria," she said, no longer whispering. "Gloria Erlinda Santos." She pressed her finger against her lip, then pulled it away. "Holy. Santos means holy—" She stopped talking and clasped her hands together as if she were praying—or begging. "But holy people don't go around—" She stopped and looked into Jenny's eyes. They were kinder, easier to read than Thomas's.

"I'm not going to hurt you."

"I know."

"I like your name."

She nodded. "Will you say it?"

Jenny smiled at her. "Gloria," she said, then repeated it. She wanted to reach out and brush her face as softly as a branch might sweep across a lawn. She kept her hands to herself. *She's just a little girl. My God, she's just an innocent.*

"My name isn't Claudia," she said. "It was never Claudia. Do you understand?"

Jenny nodded. They sat in the quiet for a moment until Jenny spoke again. "What did he do to you, Gloria?"

Gloria looked at her, trembled, opened her mouth, then shut it. She tried to push words out of herself, but nothing came out. She shook her head. She tried to speak again. "It hurts."

"It will hurt more if you don't say it."

"He stole me," she stammered. "He stole me. I was just a——" Her voice disappeared as if there were someone in the room who was stealing her words from the air as she spoke. She fell quiet.

"That quiet will kill you," Jenny said softly.

Gloria stuttered, held herself still. "There's no light in this room. I want to go outside. Please. Take me outside." She wasn't whispering anymore, was almost yelling. She began to sob, her body jerking as if she were having a seizure. Jenny reached for her, but she pulled away. "Outside," she yelled, "outside."

An officer quietly poked his head in the door. Jenny motioned him away. There was nothing for her to do but let Gloria cry. Jenny watched as she placed her head on the table and banged on it. Jenny wanted to look away, could not stand to watch this woman. That cry was the kind that possessed the body and the heart, the kind of cry that made you mindless. Awful and desolate like a large, swallowing desert. Inconsolable and despairing. Nothing could stop it. No hand was skilled enough to touch her, to take away that hurt. Jenny stared at her own hands. She would have to reach. Touch. It had been such a long time since she had comforted a client, such a long time since she had reached over and touched someone she did not know. She walked over and took Gloria in her arms—Shhhh, shhhh—she rocked her in her arms until she stopped. "We'll be outside, soon. I promise." *What has he done to you? What has that animal done?*

La Llorrona

"It was so long ago. It feels like it never happened, like the story of *La Llorrona* I heard as a child—" Her voice was steady, a monotone that did not distinguish emotion. And it did not seem to Jenny that the words were coming out of Gloria's mouth at all because the words did not seem human. "*La Llorrona* murdered her children— drowned them in a river. I don't remember why she drowned them except that I always felt sorry for her, because I knew she loved them. And she was condemned to wander the river for eternity searching for her children, and she would scream into the night shouting the names of her babies. That's all I remember of that story. It wasn't real. It could- n't be real. It was just a tale you could tell any way you wanted as long as you kept the ending. My story's like that—none of this ever hap- pened. Or if it happened, I pretend it happened to somebody else. That little girl wasn't me.

"She is walking down the street, going to school. She likes school, likes her teacher, likes her friends. And everyone likes her because she's always talking, always laughing, and she doesn't like other kids to be mean. She even loves the hot sun, the way it shines through the window in her room. El Paso—that's where she lives. El Paso, Texas. And the sun always shines in Texas. And I see that man who is not from El Paso. He is kind to the little girl, and he seems good. He has a gentle voice—soft— and when he smiles, the whole world looks just like that sun entering through the window in her room. He asks the little girl her name. And the little girl smiles and says, 'My name is Gloria.' And the man says, 'You ran away from me yesterday, Gloria. Why did you run? I just wanted to talk to you. I was lost, and I wanted to know where I was going.' And the little girl feels bad for running away from the nice man, and so she says, 'I'm sorry.' And finally, somehow, for some inexplicable reason, the little girl gets into the car with the man. Maybe the man has promised to take her to school. I don't remember. I don't want to remember.

"And then when the little girl realizes the man is taking her away from her home because he is driving down a freeway, the little girl tells him she wants to go back home. 'Please,' she says, 'I want to go to school. I've done my homework.' She takes out her homework and shows it to him, 'See. I did it all.' But the man keeps driving. The girl begins to cry. The man tells her to be quiet. He gives her something—it's a pill. And the little girl gets very sleepy, then falls asleep. They drive and drive, and every time the little girl wakes, the man makes her take another pill. Finally, when she wakes, she finds herself in the man's home. The little girl tells him she wants to go back home. 'I want my mom and dad. I want to go to school.' And the man tells her *he* is her mom and dad now. 'I am your new teacher.'" Her voice was dry, and though Jenny had never been to the desert, she was certain that the desert could not possibly be as dry as Gloria's voice.

Jenny sat perfectly still, a chill going through her as she heard the hollow voice. "Would you like some water, Gloria?"

"Yes." She seemed to take herself out of her trance. "I don't know the ending to this story." Her voice was more human.

"We'll have to write it," Jenny said.

Gloria nodded. "Are they going to make me stay in jail?"

"Not if I can help it. I'll get you out of here—soon as I can."

"I want a window."

"A window would be good."

"I want to live in a place without winter."

"What? You don't like Chicago winters?" Jenny smiled.

Gloria smiled back. "But where will I go?" Her voice betrayed her panic.

"You had a family, didn't you? We'll find them. We'll take you home, honey, back where you belong."

"Where I belong," she said distantly. "Did I belong with Thomas?"

"No. He's never going to hurt you again. I promise," she said, her voice cracking, tears rolling down her face.

"Why are you crying?"

"I don't know." Jenny rose from her chair. "I'm going to get some water," she said. "I'll be right back." As she headed for the door, a thought entered her head. She turned around and faced Gloria, who sat composed, calm, immutable. "How can you be so calm?" she asked her.

"I'm not calm. I'm not."

Jenny shook her head, unsure of what to say next. She smiled as she took a step toward the door and placed her hand on the knob. "Would you mind if Lieutenant Murphy listened to the rest of this story?"

"Will he ask more questions?"

"Yes."

"I don't trust him."

"If he asks you something you don't want to answer, then tell him to kiss off. And if he asks you something that I think he'll use against you, then *I'll* tell him to kiss off. He won't hurt you. I promise. He should hear this. It can only help you. He'll listen. All he has to do is listen."

"You think he'll believe me?" Her voice sounded concerned even if that concern was nowhere present on her face.

How does she do that? "Yes, I think so."

Gloria looked at Jenny and shook her head slowly. Her head suddenly looked like it had become too heavy for her shoulders. "I'm sorry I killed him," she said.

"You didn't."

"What? I saw him. He stopped breathing."

"Like hell he did. Didn't anybody tell you?"

"No," she said.

Jenny found it impossible to read what she was feeling in that momentary silence.

"I didn't want him to—I didn't even plan—but it seemed like the only way, and the knife was there and suddenly—I didn't even know what I was—" She paused, then took a deep breath. "Oh, thank God. Thank God. I didn't kill, I didn't—what do you think they'll—Will they let me—"

"Honey, I'd say he's in a helluva lot more trouble than you are. By the time we're through with him, he's going to wish he never set foot in El Paso, Texas."

"You won't hurt him."

"What?"

"I don't know. He's—"

Jenny stared at Gloria and shook her head. "He's what?"

"He's the whole world."

Next to His Bottles of Wine

Without bothering to knock, Jenny swung open the door to the lieutenant's office and slammed it shut behind her. He had his feet on the chair and was scowling into the telephone ". . . be helped—I told you that already. Goddamnit, you knew that about me before you married me." He shot Jenny a dirty look as he spoke into the receiver. "Look, I gotta go—Yeah—yeah—Okay, we'll finish this tonight—What do you mean, if you're home?—Look, never—" He shook his head and plunked down the phone in the middle of his sentence. He looked up at Jenny. "You often barge in on people as they're having private conversations?"

"Sorry, Lieutenant." She shot him a grin. "And things like this wouldn't happen if you didn't conduct personal business on taxpayers' time."

"Yeah, yeah, I'm responsible for the City of Chicago's deficit spending." He grinned at his own remark, pleased with himself. "And I'll just bet you never call home from the office."

"I'm not married."

"It's no—never mind." He took his feet off his desk. "Ahhhh, the whole of Cook County knows my business. You should have experienced the little scene at the policeman's ball last month."

"I guess you had to have been there."

"You missed it. Lucky you." He opened his drawer, took out a pack of cigarettes, and put one in his mouth. He lit it. "You mind?"

"You could at least offer."

"Didn't know you smoked." He pointed the pack at her.

"No, thanks."

He slammed the pack back on his desk. "You're annoying sometimes." He took a deep drag from his cigarette. "Well, you didn't come here to watch me smoke." He exhaled the smoke through his nose. "Did you get anything out of her?"

"Her name's Gloria Erlinda Santos." She stared at the lieutenant's lips. "And twenty-three years ago, Professor *Educating*-whatever-that-book's-called Blacker kidnapped her."

"What?"

She didn't know what to make of the look on his face. She stared at him, then almost smiled. "I think I *will* have that cigarette."

He tossed her one, then tossed her his lighter.

"If I were you," she said, her face as firm as her voice, "I'd get on the phone and call one of your colleagues in El Paso. It seems our Professor Blacker is in more trouble than you were at the policeman's ball. That sonofabitch kidnapped her when she was seven."

Lieutenant Murphy ran his hands over his face as if he were trying to push in his five o'clock shadow. He was quiet for a moment. "I don't know about this. Sounds a little—"

"Look, Murph, or whatever it is you like to be called, I know the goods when I see them. Just call El Paso, will you?"

"All right," he said, jutting his chin out. "But I'm going to tell you something—your client belongs in the loony bin."

"You said she was as sane as they come. You were right."

"So now I was right."

"It was you who said something wasn't right. The doors were locked, the keys were in Blacker's shoes. In his shoes—why the hell was he hiding them? I'd say he was keeping them in a place where she wouldn't get at them. Why couldn't she open a door? Why was she just sitting there— waiting? You said so yourself."

He shook his head. "I hate it when people remember what I say."

"It doesn't seem to keep you from talking."

The lieutenant laughed. He picked up the receiver and stared at the buttons.

"Not now," Jenny said. "Later."

"Now, later, now. Make up your—"

"You wanna hear her story or not?" She looked at him. "She's waited long enough."

He straightened himself up, ran his hand through his hair, and put out his cigarette. "How'd you get her to talk?"

"It's an old trick," she said as they walked out the door. "First off, you don't make them feel as if you're going to eat them for dinner." She offered him a smug smile. "Then you talk. And be nice."

"Is this a lesson?" He returned a version of the same smile.

"Take notes. If you talk, then they talk. You follow? It's not so difficult. It's an exchange."

"Kind of like, I'll show you mine if you show me yours."

"Put a lid on it, Lieutenant."

◆ ◆ ◆

"We'll try to make this as easy as we can." The lieutenant's voice was steady—not harsh, but not quite friendly. "You told Ms. Richard that Professor Blacker stole you. When was that?"

Gloria looked into the air as if she were staring at his words, rereading them, pondering their meaning.

The lieutenant poured her a glass of water. "Would you like something else instead?"

"No. Water's fine. I like water."

"Sometimes," Jenny said softly, "questions sound harsh. Just take your time. And you can tell us to go to hell when you want."

Gloria took a sip of water, then another.

"It's hard to believe you've been, well"—the lieutenant stumbled over his own words—"it's hard to believe you've been in his home for over twenty years."

Gloria nodded. "That didn't sound like a question."

"Why should we believe you?"

"Because it's true."

"No one ever saw you together?"

"No."

"How is that possible?"

"I was a secret." There was a hint of a child in the way she answered the lieutenant's question.

The lieutenant nodded. Jenny wondered what was going through his stubborn head.

"I never left his house," Gloria said watching the lieutenant's face.

"Never?"

"Well, sometimes he'd take me out to his garden. He has a huge backyard, and he turned it into a garden. Sometimes he took me there."

"Did he ever take you anywhere else?"

"No."

"Nowhere?"

"Nowhere."

Jenny looked at Gloria, tried to keep the tone of disbelief out of her voice. "You mean to tell me you've never even been anywhere—not even to a store?"

"The last time I was in a store, I was seven years old. A grocery store; I was with my mother."

"You've never even been anywhere else since then? Never?" The lieutenant couldn't help but sound suspicious.

"I never went outside his house. I told you that." Her words were strong and deliberate.

Good girl, Jenny thought.

"For twenty-three years you never went out? What have you been doing for all those years?" The lieutenant combed his limp hair out of his face with his fingers.

"Reading books and learning from Thomas. Sometimes he let me watch television, but not very often. He thought it was a waste of time. Sometimes he'd rent videos of his favorite movies, and we'd watch them—but not very often. He said he didn't want me to lose my hunger for books." She looked into the lieutenant's face, then looked at Jenny. "Once we saw a video about the Holocaust. Thomas kept shaking his head. 'Horrible,' he kept saying, 'just horrible.' "

"Such a civilized man."

Gloria watched Jenny's lips, the bitter tone in her voice. Their eyes met for an instant, each trying to read what was there. Such a civilized man, Gloria thought. What did she mean by that?

"Why didn't you just run?"

Gloria stared at the lieutenant's thin lips. "I couldn't."

"Why not?" His voice was hard, challenging.

"He kept me in chains." She wanted to smile at him, though she thought it an odd thing to want to do. "Well, not chains, really. Shackles, he used to keep me in shackles. He said I'd earn the right not to be kept in them. He said I was difficult—so he kept me in them. He kept them around—to remind me. He liked to remind me of things. When I was eighteen, he took them off. He said I wasn't wild anymore."

"You wore shackles from the time you were seven until the time you were eighteen?" Jenny could tell the lieutenant was trying to believe her, but the cop in him wasn't letting him.

"Only around my ankles—and not all the time. When he'd take me out to the garden, I didn't have to wear them. When I slept, he took them off. Sometimes he'd go away, and I'd have to wear them the whole time he was gone. But he was never gone for more than two weeks at a time."

"When he was gone, what did you do?"

"He left me books to read. And he left food in the refrigerator. He kept a refrigerator down where I lived."

"So you were his prisoner?"

"Yes." She looked at Jenny and waited.

"You said he stole you," the lieutenant broke in.

"Only I think the word is *kidnapped*." Her voice cracked.

Jenny reached for her hand. This time she didn't pull her hand away.

"And where did he keep you?" Jenny detected a note of sarcasm in the lieutenant's voice.

"I lived," she said, staring deeply into the lieutenant's eyes, "in the basement. That's where he kept me—in the basement—next to his bottles of wine."

"The basement?" the lieutenant asked. His pale face turned red as a wave of panic moved over it.

Jenny glared at the lieutenant. "Did you check the basement, Lieutenant? I didn't see anything in the report about a basement. What kind of half-assed investigation are you running?"

The lieutenant slammed his fist on the table. "Damnit!"

Gloria jumped back, almost falling off her chair. The look of terror on her face disappeared as suddenly as it had appeared.

Jenny squeezed her hand. "It's okay," she said. "He's not going to hurt you."

"I'm sorry," he said. "Look, why don't we finish this in the morning? Would you mind that, Gloria?" He smiled, as if he was making an effort to be gracious. He only succeeded in sounding awkward.

Gloria looked at his lips but said nothing.

"Can we let her go?"

"Let me go where?" Gloria asked. "Where?"

Jenny reached for her hand and squeezed it.

"We'll sleep on it," the lieutenant said.

"I don't want her here another day," Jenny said firmly. She looked at Gloria. "I'll come up with something," she said. "Don't worry. I'm getting you out of here." She looked at the lieutenant. "Make sure she doesn't have to room with anyone."

"We're pretty overcrowded. We've gotten some new—"

"You telling me you can't arrange it?"

"I can arrange it," he said. "I'll take care of it."

◆ ◆ ◆

"What kind of monkey show are you running, anyway, Lieutenant?" Jenny didn't bother hiding her irritation. She'd learned a long time ago to scratch where it itched. People didn't like you for it, but she could never be accused of beating around the bush.

"Look, I'm on it. I'm on my way right now."

"You're on it? You searched the house and you didn't even check the goddamned basement?"

"It didn't seem relevant."

"It didn't seem relevant? How do you know what's relevant until you case a joint?"

He just stared at her. "Look, we screwed up."

"Yeah, well, you're never going to make captain, Lieutenant."

"Who the hell says I want to be captain. And stop being such a b—"

"You can use the word *bitch*—I've heard it before—even in reference to my person. Didn't kill me."

"Yes, I can see that." He couldn't help but smile.

She laughed.

"Always deflect everything with that cackle of yours, do you?"

"I'll worry about my cackle, and you worry about what's in that goddamned basement."

"I'm on it. I'm in the fucking car. I'm driving toward that goddamned basement."

"The hell you are. You get a judge to get you in that place before you do anything. I'm not going to have that evidence dismissed just because you fucked up—*again*—and got in a hurry."

"Calm down, will you? Take it easy." He ran his hands through his hair. "And you don't need a judge's permission to return to a crime scene."

"I'm a lawyer, not a cop."

"Exactly what I was thinking. Have a cigarette."

"I will," she said as she took out a cigarette and lit it. "How the shit am I supposed to quit smoking when I got screw-ups like you messing up my clients' lives?"

"Don't blame me for your pack-a-day habit."

"I don't smoke a pack a day."

"Yeah, well, look, I'm not the guy who kidnapped her."

"Then I suggest you book the man who did."

"We gotta check out her story first, and you know it. You just can't go around arresting people just because somebody says—"

"You do it all the time."

He waved his hand at her. "And besides, he's still in the hospital. It'll be a while before he recovers. I just talked to the hospital not half an hour ago."

"Well, wheel the son of a bitch into jail."

"You have the instincts of a prosecutor, Counselor." He was pleased with himself. He was beginning to enjoy fighting with her.

"Don't insult me." She took a puff from her cigarette, then stared at it. She looked at him. "Pretty weird, huh?"

"She's lucky," he said quietly.

"Lucky. Twenty some-odd years in a basement is not my idea of lucky."

"Maybe not. But she lived to tell the story. After some of the bodies I've found, I'd say she was real lucky."

"Yeah, great." She took another puff from her cigarette, then another. Trying to calm herself. "Lieutenant—" She paused and looked into his eyes. "You believe her?"

"I'll believe her when I see the basement."

"Right." She put out her cigarette on the ashtray sitting on the lieutenant's desk. "Lieutenant, I'll see you tomorrow." She enunciated her words deliberately, as if biting down on a piece of meat. "And I want to see a report." She walked toward the door. She turned around and smiled at him. "And don't forget to call your wife." She walked out the door and shut it softly behind her.

Painkillers

"I wish I'd died."

"You mustn't say that, Mr. Blacker." The nurse handed him a glass of water and a pill. She looked at his breakfast, untouched. "You must eat. The sooner you get your strength back, the sooner we can let you go back home."

He imagined his house, empty now; everything was gone, the flowers he had planted, the shrubs, the fertile soil. What good was the soil without a man to harvest it? His garden had seen its last season. He knew that now, felt it, knew he could never return there. He pictured Claudia dressed in black. *She had it all planned. She was waiting. All this time. As I grew kinder and kinder, she grew colder and crueler. Was I so cruel to you, my dear?*

The nurse waited for him to take his pills. "Just swallow, Mr. Blacker."

He took his painkiller, then looked at the nurse. "Take this food away."

"But Mr. Blacker—"

"Professor Blacker," he said sternly. "Just take this, this food, or whatever it is, just take it away. I'm going to die anyway—don't you know that? Just go away."

"Shhh. You're just a little tir—"

"Go away."

She looked like his mother, the nurse, big peasant bones. Even talked like her. *As Irish as they come. Go away.*

The Necessary Graces

His first wife had been from a wealthy English family. He wasn't sure what had attracted him more—her perfect upper-class accent or her old money. He never lied to himself—she was everything he had always wanted to be. If his parents had been alive when he'd married her, he would not have invited them to the wedding. He had broken with them long before they died, broken with their Irish name, their Irish God, their peasant immigrant ways, broken with all their broken-ness. His father had been so in love with poverty and work, had spoken endlessly about the rich he referred to as pigs. The romance of poverty—that is what his father had loved. And he had hated everything about the way he had grown up, punished for reading, punished for learning, punished for being clumsy with his hands.

On the eve of his wedding, he had taken a walk, banished the memory of his family, remembered the day he had changed his name to Blacker. He loved the memory of that day because he had felt the freedom of divorce. His father had felt that the rich were evil, but his father had been wrong. His father had held educated people with suspicion, but his father had only been in love with his own ignorance. Leaving his name had freed him to become whatever he chose to become. And now that he was marrying Denise, his change was complete. He was a new man. Nothing of the peasant left in him, nothing of the worker. He had become everything his father hated. On the night before his wedding he caught himself wondering if his father could see him from his burning seat in hell.

He and his wife were wealthy enough to afford solid stone walls and privacy and a library that was the envy of his colleagues. "I don't like neighborhoods," she had told him before they married. He had wanted to live in England, but she had decided that she needed a change. Like her, he had not liked neighborhoods, either, and so the wall they built around their property became a monument to their flight from an America that existed mostly as a threat. The America they lived in was a country in decline, a country of violence, a country that understood the cheap making of new money more than it valued the honing of the mind. He had been content with her. And she with him. If their marriage lacked passion, then at least it gave them both a sense of discipline.

Ten years into their marriage, she had been killed in a car accident. He had returned her body to England, visited her grave yearly. He was free to enjoy what she'd left him. It was as if she was a companion who'd served her purpose. She had taught him the necessary graces, taught him about gardening and cooking and collecting rare books. She had left him to live a quiet, civilized life, the kind of life he had always dreamed of leading, the kind of life he believed everyone envied. Everyone wanted to be like him.

But in the ten years they had lived together, he had grown more and more uneasy with life in Chicago. The city remained the object of his disdain—it was large and ugly and crass in the way it behaved. The city was loud and careless. And he—he was a quiet, private, and careful man. After Denise died, he had lived a quiet and lonely life. His mind had been passionately alive, but his body had felt numb and dead. He did not even know why he had taken his trip to the desert. Mexico. For some reason, he felt his body might find something in Mexico. He had been warned about the poverty there, but there was art and culture there, too. He had never arrived. When he saw Claudia, he had felt he had a body again. She was just a child, a child like himself, poor and hungry for knowledge, hungry for another world far away from the animals who had bred and given her life. He could sense that yearning in her as she walked past him. She was like him. It had taken him so long to free himself. So few had helped him along the way. Why should that hungry creature wait as long as he had waited? Taking her was difficult. But leaving her, after hearing her voice, would have been more difficult. To take. To steal. As if she were a thing. But if he had left her, she would've become just that—a thing—just as he had been a thing to his father—just another thing to bring in money. She was meant for something better. He would teach her to be hungry for the better things of the world.

So he was alive again. She consumed his heart, his mind, his body. He was making her new. But he also discovered a side of himself he never knew existed. He was irrationally jealous. She saw no one but him, so there was no reason for his behavior. He rarely allowed Claudia to wander in his garden unaccompanied. Inside, he would often let her roam where she wanted—but not in the garden. In the summer, he would often take her into his room before sunset and let her sit at the window with a glass of sherry so she could enjoy the view of the garden he had spent years shaping with his own hands, his own imagination, his own labor. He loved her even more when she was appreciative. He did not know that every time she was allowed to look out into the garden, she searched for some sign—however small, however insignificant—some sign of imperfection.

They Cannot Be Saved

She had to be watched. You let yourself believe she could be trusted. You let yourself believe she could be taught to be something more than another resident of a barrio. You should have let her rot in that place where she was born—in that family that could teach her only to be like them. So many years of tending to her, of feeding her, of teaching her, of giving her the best of what I had. I should have left you in that place where I found you—left you there to become nothing, to live and die there surrounded by men who breed like rabbits and women who throw themselves at the feet of statues made of cheap plaster. Thomas, you should have known. They cannot be saved. God damn me to hell. Stupid man, stupid, stupid man.

Gloria, Claudia, Gloria, Claudia

Winter 1980. Sixteen years old.

Snow fell for days. Winter disturbed her sleep. She wondered what it would be like to walk into the snow—and just keep walking. Sleep would not come. Almost ten years, but the years did not seem to matter, the years did not seem to measure anything, not even the time. There seemed to be nothing but whiteness and snow and cold. She fell asleep trying to picture her mother's face, but she knew she had forgotten.

When sleep finally came, an angel came to her in a dream. The angel hovered over her as she walked through an endless desert of snow, everything dead except a breaking wind. Miles and miles of blinding snow. The angel, whiter even than the snow, spoke her name: "Gloria." Hearing her name, she knew she was safe. Then she saw a man in the distance. He called her Claudia. "Claudia," he yelled as he opened his waiting arms for her to come to him. She wanted to walk in another direction but could only move toward him, the wind pushing her, carrying her into his arms. She looked for the angel, but she had disappeared. When she was close enough to the man to feel his breath, he grabbed her by the arm and pulled her toward a light in the distance. The angel reappeared. "Gloria," she whispered. She looked at the angel. "Mama," she yelled. "Mama!" The angel reached for her hand and pulled her toward an even brighter light. The man tightened his grip on her other arm. Each pulled until her arms began to ache. "Stop," she yelled. "You're hurting me." The angel who'd whis-

pered Gloria and the man who called her Claudia pulled even harder, as if they were incapable of letting her go—she was nothing more than their battleground. They pulled and pulled until she felt her arms being ripped away from her body. She saw herself turn pale as the snow. She felt her arms tear away from their sockets. She managed to whimper as she saw both her arms fall into the perfect snow. She could not find a way to pick up her arms and put them back on her body. The two figures gone, no one to help her now, she watched as the snow fell harder and harder until her arms were buried in the snow. There was nothing to do now except keep walking into the cold, cold, white.

Dresses

"Goddamnit, George, I can't believe we missed this. What the fuck did we think we were doing?"

"No harm done, Murph."

"You know what your problem is, George? You forgive yourself too easily."

"Excuse the hell out of me for not being Catholic."

The lieutenant flashed George a smile, then laughed. He looked around the room: a shelf full of books, a desk, a double bed, a white, satin dress stained with blood lying on the floor.

"Well, that explains why there wasn't any blood on her dress," George said shaking his head.

"I thought—"

"You thought what?"

"I guess I'm a little kinky. I thought she'd taken off her clothes just before she did it."

"Almost like sex?"

"Yup. Goes to show you how warped I am."

"Ahh, I thought the same thing, Murph."

"I thought you said you weren't Catholic."

They both laughed. They looked around the room again, neither one of them speaking. George pointed at some shackles sitting on the shelf in the midst of all the books. The lieutenant walked up to them. "You'd think they were a trophy, the way they're sitting here. That sonofabitch. Wonder where he got a hold of these damned things?"

"Hey, Murph, look over here." He followed George's voice into the bathroom.

"Holy shit!" he said as he walked into the room. "I got a wife who dreams this room nightly. It's bigger than our bedroom." He stared at the expensive tile, the thick carpet—old but still in good shape. It reminded him of some of the carpets he'd seen in old movie theaters. And mirrors everywhere.

"You like?" George asked. "It looks like a fucking dressing room in a department store. He slid open a mirrored door, then whistled. "Uhhh, it gets better." He walked into what was another room. "It's kind of like a library for frickin' dresses, huh, Murph? How much you figure these dresses are worth?"

The lieutenant walked toward a row of hanging dresses, ran his fingers across each one. He stopped, rubbed one of the gowns between his thumb and index finger. "I'd say, this one right here would cost you more than you make in a month."

"Yeah, well, too bad they're all gonna wind up in the property room."

The lieutenant let go of the dress. "This is really strange, you know that?"

George nodded. "Weird guy. You don't think he built this room just for her, do you?"

"Nah. I'd say most of these fixtures have been around a long time. Expensive. You can't find most of this stuff anymore."

George laughed. "I forget you're into houses."

"Well, I'm not into houses like this one." He reached into his coat, took some notes, stared at the dresses, at least a hundred. No, more than a hundred, he thought. George was right, it *was* like a library. "My bet is that his first wife had this built. She was some kind of rich dame— English. Died about twenty-five years ago. Left him all her money." He shut his pad, stuffed it back in his coat. "This place gives me the creeps. Let's have another look upstairs."

◆ ◆ ◆

"What do you think these are, George?" The pills were in a plastic bottle, unlabeled, sitting among a row of pills.

"The guy has pills up the ass. Look at all these. Who the hell knows?"

"How much you know about women, George?"

"Enough."

"What kind of protection you and Lisa use?"

"Protection?"

"You know, sex?"

"What the hell kind of question is that?"

"I mean, is she on the pill?"

"Yeah. So what?"

"Don't like rubbers, huh?" He laughed. "You ever watched her take them?"

"No."

"Never?"

"Nope."

"Well, they look just like these. My bet is that he has her taking them. He didn't like rubbers, either." He placed the pills back on the counter, then took off his plastic gloves. "I hate these things. We'll get these to a lab. Get ID and Records over here, pronto. Tell 'em to videotape the whole damn house. No telling what else we missed. Bet I'm right about the pills." He lit a cigarette.

"You think the professor would appreciate you smoking in his bathroom?"

"Nope. That's exactly why I lit it, Sergeant." He grinned.

"I'm not a sergeant, yet, Murph."

"Looks good on you, though, doesn't it?"

Two Nice Irish Boys

The room was filled with flower arrangements, tributes from students, colleagues, readers, nameless admirers. Lieutenant Murphy looked down at the near-broken man lying on the bed who looked back at him like a hungry dog in an alleyway. He almost pitied him. He handed the professor a newspaper. "You've made the papers," he said. "I thought you might be interested."

The professor placed the paper on the bedside table but did not glance at it. "Newspapers don't interest me. And I'm not taking visitors, didn't they tell you? Especially visitors I don't know."

The lieutenant was surprised at the strength in the old man's voice. "Lieutenant Murphy," he said, taking out his badge.

Thomas glanced at the badge disinterestedly. "I should have known." He pointed at the newspaper. "Didn't you read all about it? I can't talk."

"You're doing just fine, Professor."

"I suppose you want a statement—that's what you people want. Asking people questions—it's no way to live one's life."

Lieutenant Murphy ignored his remark and took out his pad. "Just a few questions, then I'll let you get your rest."

"I was on the phone, my back to her—and she stabbed me."

"Why would she want to do that?"

"I have no idea."

The lieutenant nodded. "How long have you known Ms. Santos?"

"A long time."

"Were you lovers?"

He looked at the lieutenant but did not answer.

"It's not a difficult question."

"Personal questions are always difficult." He looked away from the lieutenant. "Yes, yes, we were lovers."

"Did you always lock her into your house when she came to visit?"

"I have no idea what you're talking about, Lieutenant."

He nodded. "Where does she live?"

"You mean her place of residence? I have no idea."

"You were lovers—and yet you had no idea where she lived?"

"We always met at my house."

"And you never visited her? Never asked her address?"

"She was very secretive. Her place of residence was no concern of mine."

"How long have you been lovers?"

"A long time."

"She's only thirty. How long is a long time?"

"Ten years perhaps."

"That would have made her only twenty at the time."

"Our affair had little to do with age."

"Ten years, huh? That *is* a long time," Lieutenant Murphy said smiling. "My first marriage only lasted two years. What's your secret?"

"I have no wish to discuss my private affairs with a stranger."

He pointed to the newspaper. "It's not so private, anymore, Professor." He looked down at his pad. "Where did you meet?"

"I don't remember."

"A man of your intelligence doesn't remember?"

"One should not confuse memory with intelligence."

"There is no intelligence without memory—didn't you write that in one of your books?"

The professor almost smiled at him. "So you've read my books?"

Lieutenant Murphy shook his head. "Call me a dilettante."

"Precisely what I was thinking."

The lieutenant ignored the insult. "And you have no idea why Ms. Santos would want to kill you?"

"I don't read minds, Lieutenant."

"Then you don't know what I'm thinking, do you?"

"Don't be ridiculous—I have no idea."

"Then let me tell you."

"I'm not the least bit interested."

"Humor me."

"I don't suppose I have a choice, do I? I'm your captive audience."

"Captive, there's a word."

The old man glared at the lieutenant. "Just say what you want to say, and leave me in peace."

The lieutenant could not help but grin. "Well, Professor, I was thinking that twenty-three years ago—give or take a few months—a little girl was kidnapped as she was walking to school. She lived in El Paso. You ever been to El Paso? Of course you have, haven't you, Professor? And I was thinking that this little girl might have been drugged and brought to Chicago, and—"

"It's a strange thing to be thinking, Lieutenant. But as I said, I have no interest in—"

"I'm not finished yet, Professor."

"I am not even remotely interested in what you think, Lieutenant. If you must ask me questions, then ask me. And though I am in no condition to be interrogated, I will answer them to the best of my ability."

"To the best of your ability? Really? I asked you how long you'd known Ms. Santos. You said 'a long time.' And yet you know precisely how long you've known her. I asked you why she might want to stab you, and you answered that you had no idea. No idea, Professor? I asked you where she lived, and again, you insisted you had idea. No idea, at all? For a man who's built a career on ideas, you have an amazing lack of them." He stared into Blacker's eyes. "I've been to your basement, Professor. I've seen Ms. Santos's place of residence. I even saw the shackles she used to wear. I've taken them as a souvenir."

"You have no right to enter my house. No right whatsoever."

"Oh, there's a judge who says I *do* have a right. And you know what else, Professor? One of my assistants has done a little homework. You have an old car in the garage—and it matches the description of a car that a little girl in El Paso once stepped into, a car that took her away from her mother and father—and never took her back home."

"I never use that car."

"Oh, I imagine you wouldn't."

"I'm the one who's been stabbed."

"Yes, I see that. But you know what I think, Professor? I think a real killer would have cut you to pieces."

"Why aren't you questioning the woman who put me here?"

"I have. I don't think there's a jury in this country that would find her guilty of anything."

"That only goes to show you what this country's come to. And I have no wish to continue this discussion. If you'll excuse me—"

"Sure thing, Professor." The lieutenant shut his pad. "Oh, Professor, I have one more question: Why'd you change your name?"

"My name is Blacker."

"Legally, it's Blacker, but it used to be Neelon. Nice Irish name—like Murphy." He grinned. "Why'd you change it?"

"It's none of your concern."

"Maybe."

"It has nothing whatever to do with Claudia."

"Her name's Gloria, Professor. Gloria Erlinda Santos."

"I know what her—"

"Then call her that." He looked at the man lying in the bed. He felt a surge of adrenaline run through his blood. He felt his pulse quicken. He knew this familiar feeling, recognized his hate instantly.

"I can see everything about you, Lieutenant. A man like you could never understand."

Lieutenant Murphy clamped his jaw shut, then opened his mouth slowly as if he had to chew his own words before he could spit them out because they were too large to be let out whole. "A man like me doesn't understand virtue, Professor. You're right about that. A man like me is like a bloodhound. And believe me, Professor, I know what I smell. Thank your Greek gods I'm not hungry." He moved toward the door. "Oh, and if I were you, Professor, I'd take my time getting out of this joint, because as soon as you're able, I'm throwing the book at you—and it's not the kind of book you're used to."

Deformities

When she was ten, Lieutenant, she caught the flu. She was so sick, you should have seen her. I thought I'd lose her. I stayed with her for a week, hovered over her, was a perfect angel—for her, Lieutenant. Would you have done that? Do you know about caring? Ask her, Lieutenant. Ask her if I cared. Ask her if I loved. Day and night I watched over her. I missed my classes, made up excuses, said I was the one who was sick. I lived for her, Lieutenant. She was my life. Have you ever loved a woman so much that she became your life? A man like you would never—what do you know? What do you know of love, of women? Irish. What do the Irish know except the streets? Do you know why Joyce left Ireland, Lieutenant? Do you even know who he was? Joyce knew. But you know nothing, Lieutenant. You are a hunter who smells its prey. All you know is the hunt. You see only a young girl who was taken from her family. But do you ask: What would that family have given her? What did those people have to give her, Lieutenant? I see the woman she has become, the woman I knew was inside her when I first saw her. What would you have seen, Lieutenant? You would have seen a dirty Mexican girl. You would not have noticed her. She would have been nothing to you. You would have watched her like you watched an animal in a zoo. It is you who put her in a jail—not me, Lieutenant. And now you imagine yourself her savior. You see someone who is frightened, don't you? You think she is lost and afraid. It was she who frightened me, Lieutenant. Do you see how she sits, Lieutenant? She learned to carry herself like that in my house. In her house, they would have taught her how to work. Does this creature look like she was meant for working? If you see a woman, Lieutenant, then thank me for it. But you want only to punish me. You think I have deprived her of something? Tell me, Lieutenant, what have I deprived her of? Of the wretched city? Of the city that makes endless and futile noises? Of the city that takes women like her and destroys them? Is that what I have deprived her of? We should all be deprived of that, Lieutenant. It is useless to talk to you. You see Gloria Santos. I see Claudia—Claudia who has no need of a last name. Not even my name, Lieutenant. You cannot see, cannot see anything. This city has deformed you.

What Would They Do If They Knew?

The Tragedy of America is, and always has been, that she has no memory. Great civilizations became great precisely because the history of their tribe was revered, its citizens standing in awe of the accomplishments of their ancestors whose actions enabled them to come into being. In late-twentieth-century America, we have come to a crisis regarding our sense of history. (It is ironic that one of the youngest countries in Western civilization has abandoned its commitment to history just as she is beginning to acquire one.) And having lost our place in time, is it any wonder we have lost our sense of purpose?

The wind turned the page as Herald Burns read one of his favorite passages from one of Thomas's books, the words disappearing from his view. The sudden gust continued turning the pages of the book like a newsreel in a movie theater that was running too fast, the images utterly indecipherable. He did not fight the wind, was content to watch the pages of Thomas Blacker's book as if the wind—like him—was hungry to absorb his words.

He remembered the first time he'd ever heard Thomas Blacker lecture. He had been passionate and articulate and brilliant. *This land will disappear*—his words had been a warning, and Herald had been more mesmerized by Blacker's prophetic voice than he had ever been by any woman's whispers. He remembered finally gathering the courage to seek him out. He had considered how he should dress, had spent an hour getting ready. Look like a student, he had told himself, like a real student. Even as a youth he had instinctively understood the power of projecting an image. Thomas Blacker, he, too, had understood that. He recalled what Blacker had been wearing the day he had seen him as he sat in his office: a perfectly pressed white shirt with silver cuff links and a thin tie with a matching tie clasp. His tweed coat had been hanging on an empty chair as if it were a prop. He had thought Thomas's office was a kind of haven, everything calm and perfectly arranged. It was a place of meditation, a place to collect thoughts and organize them. He remembered how Thomas Blacker's eyes had examined him. He had smiled as if he had decided he approved of what he saw. The older man had reached out and taken Herald's paper from his hands and read the first few paragraphs aloud. "You have some promise," he said, "a way with words. But do you have the discipline?" He had looked straight into him. "People without discipline are rarely happy—and almost never successful." Herald Burns smiled at the memory.

It had been twenty years since their first encounter. His professor had grown old, but he had hardly declined. His mind had grown sharper, his passions deeper, and he had become one of the most influential public intellectuals in America. His books sold millions despite the fact that he wrote about serious matters. And he, *he*, Herald Christian Burns, had become his friend—and he had also become one of the most successful attorneys in Chicago. He had gotten by on his looks, on his uncanny gift of sensing people's strengths, sensing their weaknesses. A great seducer, that is all he had been before Thomas Blacker. Good looks and no money—and a talent for pleasing. Where would that have gotten him?

They had so little in common, the two of them—except that they had both lost themselves in their work, been consumed by it. Both of them were revered. But revered by different people. For different reasons. Thomas had chosen the nobler profession. It was he who had managed to stay the course, he who had remained true to the things he believed in. America was a nation full of bad listeners, but many had listened to Thomas. He had stayed the course, his heart a moral compass that could guide him through any storm. He wondered why some men

were born with hearts and others were not. He did not lie to himself—
he was not the kind who was born with a heart.

After he had won his first big case, Thomas had attended the party
Herald's first wife had thrown for him. Two hundred people had
attended. And only Thomas's presence had mattered to him. Thomas had
whispered in his ear, "Just remember, Herald, after this, you'll never get a
bad meal. And you'll never again hear the truth." He laughed at the
thought. He had been right, of course. He wondered how Thomas had
remained so aloof from the fame that had come with the success of his
books. It was a strange thing, not to care about success. Not me, Thomas,
he whispered, I love what I have earned. And I would do anything to
keep it. He whispered it like he was whispering a confession to a priest.
And he knew Thomas would keep the confession to himself.

He stared at Thomas's open book whose pages obeyed the wind. He
picked it up and held it. He looked out into his yard, then turned and
looked at his house. He owned all this—and could own more. He loved
the owning—that's what living was. He noticed the wind was no longer
just playfully sparring. Now it was fighting. He would go inside, pour
himself a brandy, and spend the evening rereading Thomas's masterpiece
in a warm room where it was not necessary to think of the wind or the
city whose name was synonymous with it. If he listened. *If he listened* to
what Thomas had written, maybe he could find something that resembled a heart. Beating, beating in his chest.

♦ ♦ ♦

The next morning Herald Burns awoke, his head spinning and aching as
if he had spent the evening drinking in a bar. He looked at his watch,
jumped into the shower, dressed, then decided to have coffee over the
morning newspaper in his office. Lately, his office seemed more like a
home than the place where he lived.

When he walked into his office, his coffee was waiting for him. His
secretary was as good at making coffee as she was with screening his
phone calls. He took a sip, opened the newspaper, and stared at the headlines in disbelief. He shook his head as he squinted into Thomas Blacker's
face. He read, then reread the article. He said nothing to anyone about it,

kept his appointments, bailed out a client accused of raping his mistress. "How do you rape a mistress?" his client had asked. For the first time in many years, he had wanted to spit in the man's face. It was this man who should've been stabbed—not Thomas. Not Thomas Blacker.

That evening he drove home, had several drinks, then called one of his lovers and asked her to come over. He made angry love to her, made her afraid. When he finished, he asked her to leave. "You called me just to fuck me like that? Like that?" she yelled.

"Get out," he said. He had thought sex would help, but it did nothing but make him feel worse. "You sonofabitch," she said. "I never want to see you again."

He didn't care.

◆ ◆ ◆

Thomas looked up from his hospital bed and smiled in the direction of the familiar voice. "Herald. Wonderful to see you." He pressed the button to the hospital bed and raised himself higher. "That's better," he said.

"You're looking well for a man who's been through such a shock."

"The doctor says I'll be fully recovered in no time—at least from the stabbing."

"You look a little thin, a little pale. But that's to be expected." Herald looked around the room. "You seem to have a lot of fans."

He nodded as he stared out at all the flowers. "Thanks so much for the plant you sent—it was very thoughtful. I know you're a busy man."

"Never too busy for you, Thomas."

"You're very kind."

"It's the least I could do for the man who's taught me everything I know."

"Not everything, Herald. I certainly don't know anything about the law."

"The law is only a tool. It's the mind that counts—you taught me that."

Thomas smiled at the man who once sat in the front of his classroom taking furious notes as he lectured. "You stopped being my student a long time ago, Herald."

"I've never stopped being your student, Thomas. And I have all your books to prove it—all of them dog-eared at my favorite passages."

Thomas smiled. "You're medicine for an old man's heart."

Herald Burns shook his head and loosened his tie. "Everything I have, Thomas, I have because of you."

"That's not entirely true."

"I was going to drop out of school. You wouldn't hear of it."

Thomas nodded, accepted Herald's compliment as graciously as he could manage. "I'm very grateful." He looked away from him, looked instead at the flowers that flooded the room. He thought of his garden. "All those people—" his voice trailed off.

"They believe in you, Thomas. They believe in what you've—"

Thomas interrupted him, did not want to hear the end of that sentence. "Do they?"

"Of course, they do. You've touched people you don't even know—changed people's lives."

"Have I?"

"I've never known you to doubt yourself, Thomas."

"Herald—"

Thomas spoke his name with such feeling, affection, and yet Herald sensed there was something wrong. "Thomas, what is it?"

"What would they do if they—"

"If they what, Thomas?"

"What would they do if they knew?"

"I don't like the expression you're wearing."

"I'm afraid it's a very long story." Thomas looked away from him.

"I have time. What's a little time?"

"I haven't got time, Herald."

"Thomas, what's wrong?"

The old man waited before he answered. He might as well tell him everything. From the cancer to Claudia. Everything. It would be a relief to tell someone, someone he could trust, someone who would not hurt him with the information, who would not judge him. "I have cancer," he said softly.

Herald said nothing, reached for his arm. "Henry's the best," he started to say.

"Henry says there's nothing to be done."

"I see." Not this man, he thought, God, not this man. He fought back the tears, hoped Thomas would not notice. He swallowed hard, then composed himself. "It's all right if people know, Thomas."

"That's not what I meant."

"What *did* you mean?"

"I did something—"

"You can trust me, Thomas. You can trust me with anything."

"Friend to friend, Herald, or client to lawyer?"

"Whatever you think best."

"I think I may be in a bit of trouble."

"Client to lawyer—that would be best."

Thomas was quiet for a long time. "Are you as good as they say?"

"You've seen me in action, haven't you?"

"Not really, Herald. You did a wonderful job with our estate even though that's not your specialty, but I've never seen you in action—not really in action."

"Thomas, I'm the best criminal attorney in the city, in the county—in the state. And that's the damn truth."

Thomas nodded.

"Is Thomas Blacker in need of the services of the best criminal attorney in the state?"

Thomas nodded. "He is. I'm afraid he is."

◆ ◆ ◆

This is not the time to give up the fight, Thomas. As he sat in his office and held one of Thomas's books, he repeated his own advice. He had pretended not to be surprised when Thomas had told him the entire sordid story. *What have you done, Thomas? What in the hell have you gone and done?* In the end, he had comforted him. He was unable to resist the fragile and shaken man in front of him. He did not want to see him die so broken—not this man. "Maybe no one has to know, Thomas." That's what he'd said. He had promised to do everything in his power. *Your work, Thomas—everything you've worked for.* "I know," he had kept repeating. "I know."

He had returned home and had been surprised by his own compassion for Thomas, and surprised, too, that his hands were trembling. So the great Thomas Blacker had a dirty little secret. Part of him mourned the loss of a hero. The perfect statue had fallen from its pedestal. Would he put him back up? Would he let him lie there? Part of him was glad. Even men with more than their share of virtues had Achilles' heels. The thought occurred to him that he enjoyed his new position, liked having this power over the man who had had so much power over him. He half grimaced to himself, half smiled.

Certainly, he could keep Thomas out of jail. That would be the easy part. Henry had told him no more than six months. Perhaps a little longer. Even if he lived another year, he could prevent a trial. Was that enough? He knew the lines. He tried not to think about the times he had crossed them. He had gone to great lengths to defend worse men, men who had committed crimes that had even disgusted *him*, men who had contributed nothing to the world, men who were interested in nothing more than their crass power, their need for wealth. His other clients were nothing compared to Thomas. Thomas had made his mark. Could he do less for Thomas than he had for men he did not even know? Thomas had made him possible, had formed him, had made him hungry, had given him ambition, had taught him how to discipline his mind. He could not abandon this man—not now. It was too late. Too late for both of them. He would do better than keep Thomas out of court. No one knew this woman. What had she given to the world? She was just a woman. She had no money. She had no friends. Thomas had been wrong to take her, to keep her. It could not be undone. But he knew. He knew he could not allow her to destroy Thomas Blacker. What he had stood for—what he had written—maybe it could be saved. To save a man's reputation—wasn't that an honorable thing? He laughed. He was disgusted by his own cynicism, but he also knew it had become his great addiction. *This is not the time to give up a fight.* He picked up the phone. When the familiar voice answered, he enunciated his words as firmly and deliberately as he knew how. "I need you to get me some information. I need it fast . . . "

You Know Anything About This
Thomas Blacker?

Jenny picked up the phone on the second ring. "Jenny Richard." Her Louisiana accent always rose to the surface when she pronounced her name.

"So how's our Lieutenant Murphy?"

"Are you calling to gloat, Dave?" She shut the report she'd been reading and rereading for the past hour.

"Just calling to see how it was going. Interesting case, huh? How's it looking?"

"Strange, if you want to know the truth. Not your average attempted murder."

"I take it you can handle it."

"You still have to ask?"

He laughed. "Just checking."

She nodded into the telephone. "You know anything about this Thomas Blacker?"

Dave was quiet for a moment. "I hear he's well connected."

"He's just a professor."

"Not *just* a professor, Jenny."

"What's that supposed to mean?"

Dave paused as if he was thinking about something. "Well," he said finally, "for one thing, he's famous. Very famous, Jenny. Don't you read?"

"Not that shit, I don't. And so what?"

"I was getting to that. He's not only famous, but he's rich. Very rich. Rich and famous people attract power."

"You know something I don't?"

He paused again. "No. I read the report. I read the newspapers. There's something a little off. Can't put my finger on it. That's why I wanted you to handle it."

"I think that was a compliment."

"Damn right it's a compliment."

She smiled into the receiver. "I'll let you know if I need anything."

"Just ask, and you got it. Anything, Jenny."

She nodded, looked at her watch. "Thanks for the call, Dave."

"Is that your polite way of saying this little chat is over?"

"Gotta go," she said. "Miles to go before I sleep."

"Me too," he said, then laughed. "Look, I just wanted to let you know I was behind you on this one."

She nodded as she heard him hang up the phone.

She stared at the file but did not open it again. That was strange, she thought. Dave never called her if he didn't have anything pressing to say, and certainly he never called her to assure her of his support. Not his way, she thought, not a hand-holder. He had seemed hesitant about something. She shrugged, then rubbed her shoulders. She lit a cigarette.

She turned the file over in her hands and thought of Lieutenant Murphy, the way he looked at her. He didn't hate her, exactly—not exactly hate. Sometimes it almost seemed as if he admired her. But he also admired her legs. In their last encounter, he had been less than gracious. So, he had lost. She'd thought she'd seen that look in his eyes, that look she sometimes saw when she met other cops: *You're the bitch who let off that cop killer. You're the one.* That case still haunted her, followed her around like an orphaned, smelly dog that had claimed her as its owner. She still felt the accusing stares. It was the jury who'd let him off. And the prosecution had had no case. He was just a small-time junkie, an easy patsy from the South Side with a long sheet of petty crimes. The cop had been as crooked a cop as Chicago had ever produced. Murphy had known the score on that one. He had never said a word. Not that there had been any reason to speak up—he was not involved. Still, she resented him. He was one of them, after all. But hadn't she wanted to make them all angry? She enjoyed fighting them almost as much as they enjoyed referring to her as someone in need of a good lay. She knew what they said. She knew the rules. She played by them as much as they did. But she couldn't help but feel she was expected to pay a higher price. At least they knew better than to screw with her. It was not the same as respect. She had learned to control the anger. She had not yet learned to make it go away.

"File your rage, girl," she whispered. She stared at the phone. Something about Dave's call bothered her. She knew him, had worked under him for six years. He had seemed so hesitant—and Dave was only hesitant when he was hiding something. She picked up the phone, pressed the button that automatically dialed his office, and waited to hear his secretary's voice. "It's Jenny," she said. "Can you put Dave on?"

Again she waited. She fumbled with her cigarette as she held the phone between her neck and her shoulder. She heard his voice. "Dave?"

"What's up, Jenny?"

She paused a moment. "I have a question for you."

"Shoot."

"What was that phone call about a few minutes ago?"

"I don't know what you're talking about."

"The hell you don't, Dave. I know when you're bullshitting me. You want me to take a stroll into your office?"

"No," he muttered, "don't bother."

She waited for him to speak.

"I got a phone call."

"From who?"

"Doesn't matter from who, Jenny. Let's just say someone doesn't want you on this case—and that someone isn't Lieutenant Murphy."

"Higher up, huh?"

"Look, Jenny, I told 'em to go to hell."

"In just those words?"

"Well, not in those words—not exactly those words."

"What *exactly* did they ask?"

"They asked me to put someone else on the case."

"What was their excuse?" She put out her cigarette.

"That you're a pain in the ass. That no one can work with you. That Ms. Santos would be better served by someone else. I told 'em I couldn't spare anyone else right now."

"Did they push?"

"Yes. Not to worry. I didn't budge."

"Anything else?"

"I feel like you've put me on the witness stand."

"You're behaving like a hostile witness."

"Look, I just didn't want to worry you."

"I'm already worried." She paused, reached for another cigarette. "And your analysis?"

"Someone thinks you're good. Too good. And too honest. They want you off."

"Who is that someone, Dave?"

"Don't know."

"What do you mean, you don't know?" She lit her cigarette.

"Someone told someone to tell me. And where it began, nobody knows."

"And where it will end, nobody knows." Jenny sneered into the telephone. "Was it a threat?"

"I don't know, Jenny. And it doesn't matter. What the hell can they do? It's not the first time someone wants to tell me how to do my job—and I'm sure as shit it won't be the last. I don't run my office by committee."

Jenny laughed. They were both silent for a moment. "Listen, Jenny," he said finally, "I got you on this case because I thought you were just the right woman for the job. I know you didn't want it. I'll give you an out."

"You're saying you want me off?"

"No. I'm saying it's your call."

She took a deep drag from her cigarette. "I think I like this case, Dave. I think I'll stick with it."

"That's the Jenny I know and love." He laughed as he hung up the phone.

Portrait of a Lady

JULY 5, 1982. EIGHTEEN YEARS OLD.

She heard him unlock the door to her apartment, what he liked to call it. She pretended to keep reading. She was tired of him, angry. "I love you."

He loved to say that, but he wouldn't love her so much if she were free.

"*Reading so early?*"

She looked up at him and nodded.

"*A new book?*"

"*Yes,*" *she said, showing him the cover.*

"*Ahh,* Portrait of a Lady. *Mr. James is the finest of writers.*"

"*Yes,*" *she said without emotion,* "*but it will end badly for her.*"

"*You know the story, then?*"

"*It's a very old one.*"

"*Ahh, but the story's in the telling.*"

"*Yes, I suppose you're right.*" *She smiled at him. It was useless to be angry with him. She tried not to appear interested in the box he held.*

"*Eighteen years old now, my Claudia.*" *He took the book out of her hands.* "*Happy birthday.*" *He handed her a gift wrapped in silver foil and white ribbon.*

She stared at the box, smiled, and looked up at him. "*May I open it?*"

He paused, took a key out of his pocket, and undid the shackles around her ankles. His hands were warm against her skin. "*I don't believe these will be of any further use. You're a woman, now. Time to put away childish things.*" *He pulled out a delicate gold chain from the inside of his coat pocket and placed it around her neck.* "*This is much more becoming, don't you agree?*"

She nodded. She kept her tears far away from her face.

He placed the shackles she'd worn off and on for eleven years on the bookshelf next to Claudia's books. "*We'll keep them right there—in case we should ever need them again. But we won't need them, will we?*"

"*No,*" *she said,* "*never.*"

"*Good girl.*"

"*Why don't you open your gift?*"

She gently fingered the box, careful not to wrinkle or rip the pure satin ribbon. Slowly, carefully, she unwrapped the box and opened it. She folded back the tissue paper and felt the soft fabric.

"*Take it out and look at it,*" *he said quietly.*

She extended the long silk negligee in front of her.

100

"It's so soft," she said. "It's very beautiful." She looked up at him. "Thank you for remembering my birthday."

"Not at all." He rubbed the negligee she was holding between his fingers. "It's to sleep in."

"I know," she said.

The look in his eyes frightened her, but there was no reason to be any more afraid of him than she had ever been. He had put away the chains, had remembered her birthday, had given her these gifts. She did not understand the curious look on his face. This is new, she thought. She wanted to rub her ankles, rub away the feel of the chains. Is he setting me free? Is he letting me go? "Thank you," she said. She touched the gold chain around her neck. "Everything's so beautiful."

"Are you happy?"

"Yes, Thomas."

He leaned down and kissed her on the cheek. She didn't like the feel of his face against hers, the smell of his cologne.

"Oh, I almost forgot. He took out a pill from a small plastic bottle. "I want you to take one of these." She remembered the pills he had given her in the car, when he'd taken her, pills that made her sleepy.

"What are they for?" she asked.

"It's just a vitamin." He walked into the bathroom, filled a glass with water, and walked back over to where she was sitting. He handed her the pill. She took it quietly and placed it in her mouth. He handed her the glass. She drank it down.

"That wasn't so bad, was it?"

She smiled. "Will I get sleepy?"

"No," he said gently, "of course not. I told you—it's a vitamin. We don't want you to get sick, do we?"

She rubbed her hand over the negligee on her lap.

"You'll take one every day. That way you'll never get sick. You'll stay nice and healthy."

She rose from her chair. "I'll hang this up." It was good to walk across the room without any shackles.

As she hung up her new garment, she felt his breath beside her. She felt his lips on her back. He kissed her skin softly. She did not turn around until he had left the room.

Jenny Richard, Jenny Richard

"I'm telling you, that woman's a lot of trouble—"
Herald Burns didn't like what he was hearing on the other end of the phone.

"—and the public defender's not budging an inch."

"Push him a little harder," he said.

"He won't be pushed—not when it comes to her."

"Do they have something on the side?"

"Don't think so. DA's a straight arrow."

"Find out everything you can—her friends, where she goes. Everything."

"Done that."

"What d'ya got?"

"Likes to hang out with fags."

"She one, too?"

"She's had her flings—all of them with men. This woman doesn't like messes. She cleans up after herself—and nobody likes to fuck with her. Clean as your ass after you've washed and shaved it."

Herald shook his head. He leaned back on his chair and stretched his neck, moved it from side to side. "What about Murphy?"

"He's straighter than she is."

"You're telling me that in a town full of cops and lawyers that sell out for a dime, we're dealing with the milk-and-cookies crowd? Is that what you're telling me?"

"That's exactly what I'm telling you."

"What about her family?"

"I'm working on it."

"Well, stay on it. If they're as poor as Thomas says—" He stopped. "Just stay on it. And stay on Jenny Richard. Don't let up for a god-damned second, or a goddamned sandwich, you got that?" He slammed down the phone, then loosened his tie. Jenny Richard and Lieutenant Alexander Murphy. He had never heard of them. If Lieutenant Murphy started causing trouble, it would be easy enough to get him removed from the case. One phone call. Jenny Richard would prove to be a bigger problem. "Milk and cookies," he said. "Goddamnit!"

This Is How the World Begins to Die

Jenny looked around her apartment, the shelves filled with secondhand books she'd bought in shops that smelled of dust, run by old men who smelled like the objects they sold. She stared at her mother's antique furniture that wore its varnish like an old woman wore a gown— dignified and yet grotesque. Each piece too scratched and chipped to be valuable, but still of use. She eyed her painting of the bay-ous, the trees choked in Spanish moss, the dark waters surrounding them. She asked herself about the woman who lived in this apartment. There was something so unfamiliar about her. She told herself it was normal not to recognize herself. On certain days, it happened. Nothing to be alarmed about. "Strange day," she whispered as if addressing the trees in the painting.

She was cold. She had taken the bus from her office to the garage where they were fixing her car. As she waited at the bus stop she had lost herself in the conversations of the people who waited with her. *Shit, girl, get rid of that no-good man—he ain't good for nothing but sleepin' and waggin' his tail. Get yourself a dog. . . . I bought this dress and it's like, it's like soooo great. . . . I bought her flowers—fifteen years tomorrow. Best years of my life. Don't know what I'd do without her. . . . I swear my boss is part chicken, part pit bull—I never know which one is going to show up at the office. . . .* All those lives. All those words. She wondered how the pieces fit together—or if they fit. On the bus, she had stopped listening, had wrapped herself in her own thoughts, had shut out the voices. Sometimes too many voices. She was tired of them. And yet she did not feel like resting. Her dog nudged at her ankles. She reached down to pet her. "How's my girl? How's my good Bessie? Did you go for your walk with Charlie?" The dog barked and lay over on her back. She laughed. "Silly dog." She walked into the kitchen and put on a pot of coffee. "Who is this neatnik who lives here? The woman I know couldn't organize a backyard picnic." She laughed.

She felt uneasy, nervous, waiting for something to happen. Her back was stiff. She paced around the living room waiting for the coffee to brew. She stared at the painting on her wall. "It swallows the whole damned apartment." She thought for a moment that Gloria would like the painting. It was dark enough for her to appreciate. She could not get that arresting and lonely woman out of her mind. It was as if Gloria Santos had decided to claim a piece of her—a piece of her she had no wish to relinquish. Something about the whole damn mess made her feel uneasy. *Over twenty years in a goddamned basement. I would have killed him long before now.* She was not surprised by her own violent reaction, but she thought less of herself for having thought it. *How unimaginative, Jenny. Solve everything with a gun, with a knife, with a bomb.* From the minute she laid eyes on Gloria, she had not stopped thinking about her childhood, about her mother and brother, about New Orleans. She wondered why. She thought of Gloria's sobs, how her body had become limp as if her bones had suddenly ceased to function, no longer able to hold up the weight of her grief. She remembered how she herself had sobbed that way on the morning she had stood over her mother's grave. She shivered, walked into her bedroom and undressed. She suddenly felt trapped in her work clothes. She hated the way they made her feel. Her clothes owned her, told her how to act, what to say, told her how to walk, when to cross her legs. She ripped off her clothes and left them in a pile on her neatly made bed. She threw on a pair of jeans and a sweater. She looked at herself in the mirror. She tied her hair back. "Forty-five," she whispered to herself. Fifty in five years. Then what, old girl?" She remembered her first lover when she came to this city. She had sent him away. "What will become of all that beauty then?" he had asked. She had been right to send him away. He loved words and ideas. That's all she had been to him—an idea. They did not speak each other's language. All that beauty. She sneered. Fifty in five years.

She remembered watching her mother change every day when she came home from work. She would walk in the door, give her a kiss, then change into the same cotton dress. She would cook dinner for Jenny and her brothers and try to pretend nothing had happened. She hugged herself. *I refuse to think about this, refuse*—She thought of Gloria, who wore the same kind of look her mother had worn—only there was more hope for Gloria because Gloria was stronger and had discipline. Her mother had had no discipline, had lived a life completely ruled by her emotions. She had been incapable of thinking, of reflecting. All she could do was feel. But Gloria had something her mother had never had—she had power over herself. *And she's only thirty. Damaged goods, but maybe the lieutenant's right—maybe she is lucky. She managed to survive, escaped—and she's gonna be fine. But not before*—she smiled—*not before we put that bastard away.* Somehow she just knew. *I have an extra bedroom. My clothes should fit her. She'd look good in them—better than me.*

She had been in the public defender's office for more than fifteen years, and in all those years she had never let her clients near her—not personally—not ever. *Not part of my job.* She wondered why Gloria was the exception. She was just another client. Didn't they all have stories that could make you want to scream until your lungs collapsed? Didn't they all have a tale to tell? And hadn't they all been victims in one way or another? She used to think of her clients as Job's messengers who came to her bringing news of the destruction of the world: *And I alone have escaped to tell you.* It occurred to her that it had been a long time since she thought about the world she lived in. She had ceased thinking about that difficult subject. It was better to concentrate on defending her clients as best she could, and then forget about them. They were too heavy—all of them too goddamned unmanageable for her to carry around. And she had no place to take them. Jail was a better place for them than her home. It was better to think about the condition of her wood floors, her new cappuccino machine, which she never used. But Gloria, Gloria belonged to a different category of clients, a category she rarely encountered. "Gloria Erlinda Santos, who the hell are you?" She knew she would let this woman into her house, this stranger who had stabbed a man. But there was nothing frightening about her. Haunting was not the same thing as frightening. She would give her a home for as long as she needed one. She wondered about her own generosity. Perhaps it was as simple as doing a good deed—nothing profound—maybe just that.

She found herself staring into the mirror. She kept looking at herself as if she were seeing her own face for the first time: "Am I Gloria?" she whispered softly, though she did not hear herself ask the question.

◆ ◆ ◆

She looked at her watch in the dim light of the living room. Eleven o'clock. Shit. She put down the magazine she was reading, then pulled herself up from the couch. She rubbed her eyes. She wasn't tired. She stretched her arms out, walked into the kitchen, and stared into the refrigerator. She reached for the bottle of wine. As her hand touched the cold glass bottle, the front doorbell rang. After a pause, it rang again. She walked back into the living room. "Who is it?" she asked through the closed door.

"It's Harriet Nelson."

She laughed and unchained the door. "Charlie," she said, giving him a kiss on the cheek. "Come on in."

The dog ran up to him, barked, wagged her tail, and flopped herself on her back.

"I'm just returning your book."

"At eleven o'clock at night? What's with the glasses?"

He shrugged, then reached down and rubbed the basset hound's belly. "Good girl. Good Bessie." He looked up at Jenny.

"What happened?" she said as she slid off his sunglasses. She stared at his swollen eyes. "Charlie?"

"I got jumped," he said, then shrugged. "It happens."

"What do you mean, it happens?" She took him by the hand and sat him down on her couch.

"Your place has been so clean lately," he said smiling. "Getting domestic?"

"I've decided to turn this place into a real home," she said. "I'm working my way into the bedroom."

"That's where you should have started." He laughed.

She looked at his eyes. "Does it hurt?"

"It's better now. I was lucky—no broken teeth. See?" He smiled.

She put her hand on his cheek. "Oh, Charlie. Poor, sweet, Charlie."

"I'm not so sweet," he said.

"Yes, you are. Don't argue with me—I'm a lawyer."

"Yes, ma'am."

She saw his lip was swollen and noticed the stitch tape above his forehead. "Would you like some wine?"

"Sure," he said.

She walked into the kitchen shaking her head. Gloria looks like that, she thought as she poured them both a glass of wine, only Gloria wears her bruises where no one can see them. She walked back into the living room and handed Charlie his wine.

He sipped it. "Not bad. Your taste in wine is a little more refined than mine."

"I never skimp on the wine," she said looking into his eyes. "Who hurt you, Charlie?"

"It happens."

"What the hell's that supposed to mean?"

"Queer-bashing."

She nodded, then shook her head. "When did this happen, Charlie?"

"A few hours ago."

"Did you call the cops?"

He nodded.

"And?"

"And—nothing. They're not going to do anything. Cop says they'll never find them."

"Right," she said. "Did you get the cop's name?"

"Yeah."

"Good."

He put his glass of wine down on the coffee table. "Funny thing is, though, this time was different than the other time."

"How do you mean?"

"The last time"—he threw out a plastic smile—"the last time, the guys just kept calling me faggot! 'You like that, huh, faggot? You like it like this?'"

Jenny winced, wondered how he could tell this story so casually. She wanted him to stop, but she let him keep talking.

"But this time they didn't say much, for one thing. Two guys—they just jumped me. I could have sworn one of them said, 'That's him,' right before I felt the first blow. One of the guys kept saying, 'You like hanging out with lawyers, huh, faggot?' And the other one, I could have sworn he said my name."

"What?"

He shrugged. "Strange, huh?"

"How many lawyers do you know?"

"Just you. Most of my friends are low-lifers."

"Just me, huh?"

"I don't like that look on your face, Jen."

"It's nothing. You're sure I'm the only lawyer you know?"

"I'm positive."

"What about any of—" she stopped.

"One of my one-night stands?"

"I wouldn't have put it like that."

"Yeah, well, I haven't lived like that for a long time. I don't sleep with anybody I don't know. Not safe. Haven't you heard?"

"Had to ask," she said. "I ask questions for a living." She played with her glass of wine. "It's odd, though, isn't it?"

"And another thing"—he touched his swollen lip—"they just stopped. The first time this happened, if someone hadn't come along, I'd have been dead. These guys just stopped, and then one of them said something to me—as if he was warning me."

"What did he say?"

"I don't remember. I was just lying there. And all I could think was *thank God, thank God they've stopped*. I was still breathing. That's all that mattered."

"Can you remember anything else, Charlie?"

"I'm just not sure, Jenny. I was pretty drunk. If I wasn't all beat up, I'd swear it was a dream. I wouldn't make a very good witness under oath. Wish I hadn't been so drunk."

"You have to trust yourself, Charlie."

"I was getting hit all the over the place, you know, Jen? I think I heard them say those things—*I think,* but I'm not sure. 'That's him'—maybe they said it, maybe they didn't. It all happened so fast. Maybe they said my name, maybe I was saying it, maybe I was talking to myself. All I know is that these people are lunatics. Sane people don't go around beating up other people—especially people they don't know. Why try to make any sense out of it? It's all fucking crazy. You go around asking why, you'll go stark raving mad."

"Sometimes we have to ask why, Charlie."

He nodded, took a sip of wine. "Yeah, we can ask why, and we can ask who. But we don't know, do we, Jenny?"

"Do you remember anything else? Did you see their faces?"

"I didn't get a look. Only—" He paused. "Maybe it's—"

"What?"

"One of the men—one of his hands—his left hand, it had scars. Not scars really. Discolored patches—I remember. I could see it under the streetlight."

"What kind of patches, Charlie?"

"Like it had been burned in a fire or something. Maybe it was just the shadows." He shrugged. "Doesn't matter, Jenny."

"It does matter, Charlie. A scarred left hand. It's a lead. A good lead. It's something. We gotta follow up on—"

"What's the point?" He placed his hands over his face.

"The last time this happened, was anything ever done?"

He shook his head.

"Charlie," she whispered, "we've got to do something."

"Like what? Scour the streets for a guy with patches on his hand? I don't think so." He clenched his teeth, then laughed. "Anyway, you kinda get used to being hated."

"You can't let them do this to you. You can't. That's how we begin to die, Charlie. That's how *the fucking world* begins to die."

"That cop didn't give a shit, Jenny. He just looked at me. I know that look, Jenny. It says, 'You had it coming, faggot.'"

She nodded and took a big swallow from her glass of wine. "But Charlie, you and I know you didn't have it coming, goddamnit." She began waving her hands in the air as she spoke. "They'll break you. They'll treat you as if you deserve to be hated. They'll do that, Charlie."

"So I'm given the job of changing their minds? Forg—"

"No. You're never going to change their minds about anything. They've already decided."

"That's my point."

"But you can fight them. You can't teach them to love you, Charlie, but you can teach them not to fuck with you."

He smiled at her. "You can't fight the world, Jenny."

"I don't want to fight the world—I just want to fight bastards like the men who did this to you."

"How come you're so angry?"

"It's not anger, Charlie." She laughed. "It's love."

He smiled. "Love, huh? So how come you don't have any lovers?"

"You don't want to know, Charlie." She took his hand. "You know, I'm talking to a lieutenant in the morning."

"Friend of yours?"

"Well, let's say he is. Yes. Anyway, this isn't his beat, but maybe I can get him to—" She stopped. "Just trust me, Charlie." She looked straight into his swollen eyes: There was something broken in them—like Gloria's. She wondered why she was seeing that woman in every face she looked at. *This is how the world begins to die.*

part
2

Lieutenant Murphy's Obsession

Lieutenant Murphy stared at the picture of the little girl as he held it carefully in his right hand. He placed it on his desk, then stared at it again, as if he were trying to memorize the face. He fought the urge to smoke a cigarette, then decided to stop fighting. He stuck a cigarette in his mouth but did not light it. He reread the newspaper articles, the fuzzy printing on the glossy fax paper making the stories appear even farther away than the twenty-three years since they had appeared in print:

GIRL MISSING FROM SOUTH EL PASO

A seven-year-old girl has been reported missing since early yesterday morning. Gloria Erlinda Santos was last seen walking to school early Thursday morning, but school officials reported that she never arrived. The girl's father, Ramiro Santos, told police that his daughter had mentioned that a man had stopped her on her way back from school the previous day and had asked her questions. Mr. Santos also reported that the stranger had told her he was lost and asked for directions. "But my daughter," Santos said, "did not believe him because he did not look lost to her."

Witnesses say they saw the young girl walking to school and saw a man speaking to her on the corner of Fourth and Stanton. The man, they said, was white, and he did not appear to be bothering the girl in any way "I thought he was just asking for directions," one witness said. "He wasn't from the neighborhood." The man, a suspect in the girl's disappearance, was reported to be driving a new, black Buick, and is decribed as a white male in his forties, about six feet tall with a medium build. . . .

He spotted a misspelled word, the *s* missing in *described*. He fought the urge to circle it with a pen. He looked at the note Jenny Richard had left for him. Her handwriting was firm, almost careless—no nonsense, nothing to hide, nothing decorative in the way she formed her letters:

113

She remembers her address. 507 Fifth Street near the corner of Fifth and Ochoa—an apartment building, not a house. She says it was right around the corner from Sacred Heart Church. Says she made her first Communion there, and was probably baptized there. She can't remember having lived anywhere else. Her mother's name was Eloisa, but she can't remember her father's name at all. She went to Father Rahm Elementary School, and her second-grade teacher's name was (get this) Mrs. Murphy. I'm sure there are records. No fingerprints on her, as you've already discovered. I don't know if her parents are still alive—there's a good chance they might be, but who knows? But she has a brother who can ID her. He should be about thirty-three years old, and hopefully he still lives in El Paso. His name's Ricardo, and I'm sure you'll find him without too much trouble. I'll come by tomorrow. I don't know how you want to handle this, but I want you to get the DA's office to sit on this for a while. I'll have someone on my end lean on them. I think we should hold off on prosecuting—perfectly understandable in view of the circumstances. She's been through enough, don't you think? I want her out tomorrow. I'm sure we can come to an agreement. Sorry I've been a little rough on you—very unprofessional of me.

JENNY

Don't forget to call your wife. "You're a pain in the ass, Ms. Jenny Re-shard." He elongated her last name as he spoke it aloud. He remembered meeting her. Six years ago—seven? What did time mean in this job? His cases—that's how he kept track of the years. *A helluva way to live.* He smiled at the first thing she'd ever said to him. "The last name is pronounced Re-*shard.* Repeat it until you get it right." He wondered why he fought with women like Jenny and married women like Becky. He had always found himself attracted to smart-ass women, but he always managed to run from them. He'd found himself getting involved with unambitious, nice-legged women who wanted him to protect them. *I'm not even good at protecting myself.* "Leave your personal life at home,

Lieutenant." He lit his cigarette and set aside the dialogue he was having with himself.

He picked up the picture of the little girl. No doubt about it, the same dark eyes, the same face, the same lips. Sometimes people changed; they grew into utterly different adults as if they were tadpoles who had turned into frogs—complete strangers to what they had been as children. But not this woman. Even at seven she was an arresting, beautiful child with the poise of an adult. But something *was* different, and it was not just the passing of time that made the little girl in the picture different from the woman who was sitting in the Cook County Jail. The little girl in the picture was happy. There was nothing happy about the woman who had filled his thoughts from the minute he first saw her. For some inexplicable reason, this woman's sadness disturbed him. There was a complete lack of joy in her face—as if she had never heard that word, did not even know the idea of it existed. He wondered about Blacker, what he had done to her, wondered what had made him do it. Taking a child. He was some kind of devil. Had to be a devil. The city bred devils as fast as tenements bred cockroaches and rats. He wondered how a man like Blacker managed to live with himself. To kill someone in a rage—that was not so difficult for him to understand. But to keep someone like a prized animal in a zoo—that he did not comprehend. To live each day with the reminder of what you had done. He could not imagine such a life. He had tried to talk about it with his wife, but she had gotten angry.

"I don't want to hear about any woman or any man that stole her."

"Honey, it's not—"

"I don't want to hear it, Murph."

"What do you want to hear? Just tell me so I can say it."

"Why can't you talk about normal things?"

"Like what?"

"I don't know—just don't talk about some woman who sits in jail and looks sad. I don't care about that, Murph. She probably asked for it, now plays innocent—"

"Shut up. Just shut up . . . "

"Oh, screw it."

"Screw what?"

He stared up from his desk and saw Jenny Richard standing at his door. He pushed his argument with his wife to the side of his mind that did not talk. "Don't you knock?"

"The door was open. Talking to someone?"

"I like to mutter. Something I picked up in college."

"You went to college? I thought you just went to one of those police-academy places."

He glared at her. "You're relentless." He spoke firmly as if to push his words into her thick, impenetrable skull.

"Can't help myself."

"Yeah," he said, "I know." He shoved the faxed newspaper articles toward her. "Have a look."

She picked them up from his desk and read them. He watched her face, calm and sure.

She looked up at him. "How the hell did he get to Chicago in a car without being stopped? And what the hell was he doing in El Paso?"

"Good question. Only the professor can answer that one."

"You have your chat with him?"

"This morning. I had a look at the basement last night."

"You believe her now?"

"Always did."

"That's not what you said yesterday."

"There's something you should know about me: I don't always tell the truth." He looked at his watch, then looked at her for a moment. "Wanna have lunch?"

"I didn't come here to—"

"A business lunch, Counselor. I'm a married man."

"You buying?"

"Dutch. I don't have your kind of money."

Jenny laughed. "Oh yeah, being a public defender has really put me in the bucks."

How, If You Wake in the Night

It was impossible to sleep in a hospital. Thomas wondered how they expected anyone to recover when they pinched you and poked you and took your temperature all night. They told you to rest and then did not let you do the very thing they asked of you. All he wanted was sleep—and sleep was what would not come. He shut his eyes. He tried to think of good things. Claudia was all that came to him. Wasn't she a good thing? He remembered how she looked when she baked bread, the sweat on her brow, the dough on her hands. When he would watch her, he remembered thinking how he wanted to be that dough. Her image faded away, and the darkness of the room returned. Nothing but that smell. What was that smell that hospitals had? He would rather be smelling Claudia's sweat.

He wondered where they were keeping her. Were they treating her well? Did they know she liked the color yellow because it reminded her of the sun? Would they let her come back to him? "No," he whispered, "she put me here. I should have let her starve in that basement. I should have kept her in chains—" But the clean smell of her skin after she'd bathed. The way her lips moved when she spoke. The rare sound of her voice, soft as the petals of the finest flowers in his garden. Her body in those dresses. His name in the air when she called him.

Keep Telling Yourself That He's the Enemy

"I'll have a burger, no fries." Jenny placed her menu back on the table.

"The same, only I'll have the fries." The lieutenant shut his menu, reached for the one Jenny had put down, and handed them to the waitress.

Jenny tried not to look at him too closely. *Nice-looking man. Bet he likes brainless broads.* "Well, what do you think?"

"Well, I'll tell you," he said, playing with his glass of water. "If it were up to me, I'd send this woman back home."

"Think everyone else will see it your way?"

"Judgment call, really. I mean, the professor's not going to die—not from the stab wound, anyway."

"What's that supposed to mean?"

"It seems as though our professor has cancer."

"Mind if I ask how you come by this information?"

"Ran into his doctor—an old friend of his. Supposed to be a pretty famous oncologist. I asked a few questions, and you know—"

"In other words, you tricked the guy into telling you."

"Why don't you call me Murph?

She shook her head and wrinkled her nose. "Murph sounds like something you'd call a dog. Why don't they just call you Alexander?"

"Hate my first name."

"Not very Irish. I like it."

"Just stick with Lieutenant. And I didn't trick this guy. He wanted me to know."

"How come?"

"Not sure. Sympathy, maybe. This doctor knows something—and certainly he knows his friend's in trouble. George did some checking—these two guys have been friends for a long time. Much longer than you and I have been fighting."

She smiled, then nodded. "Makes sense. What kind of cancer does our professor have?"

"Prostate."

"Right where it hurts." She winced, then smiled. "Serves him right."

"Well, we're full of compassion today, aren't we?"

"Don't tell me you liked the guy."

"Hated the sonofabitch, but that's got nothing to do with it. He's just the kind to insist the DA prosecute."

"Sounds like you've taken my client's side, Lieutenant."

"I don't have a side. It's my job to gather evidence, to build a case, to decide when I have one and when I don't, and to pass on a recommendation. In Gloria's case, I'd recommend we not prosecute."

Jenny nodded, was interested to know how he thought about things. It wasn't often she had the opportunity to have lunch with a cop. "And your recommendation would be based on what?"

"The evidence. For one, she's been through enough—she doesn't need to go through a trial. And—" He paused. "For another thing, who'd convict her? Prosecuting would be a waste of everybody's time. We can't count on compassion—bad way to play the game. Money, time, the odds of conviction. Be pragmatic—that's the angle. I'll tell you one thing, though, that bastard's up to something. I figure right now, they're playing the compassion game. Soon enough, they'll find out that it's a strategy they can't win. Gloria Santos holds all the cards. Poor girl from the barrio gets kidnapped. They'll get pragmatic. They'll do what they have to do. He knows a lot of important people—"

"That's what Dave said."

"Yeah? Does he know something?"

"No." She hesitated. She didn't trust him enough to tell him someone had wanted her off the case. "He just said a man like Thomas Blacker was bound to have attracted people in power. Powerful people like to collect artists and intellectuals."

Lieutenant Murphy laughed. "Well, sounds right to me. They all stick together, these guys. And his lawyer was walking in the door."

"Anybody I know?"

"Burns."

"Herald Burns?"

"The one and only. Blacker only hangs with designer types. He's got his designer doctor, and he's got his designer lawyer. These folks give lots of money to politicians."

"How do you know that?"

"I make it my job to know. Information comes in handy, sometimes. Major-leaguers, all of them. Those guys don't play to lose. He kidnapped that girl sure as you smoke cigarettes. But I'll bet my goddamned badge that Blacker and his lawyer aren't finished with Ms. Santos. Not by a long shot."

"Wouldn't it be better on Blacker if he just let the whole thing go?"

"Seems like it would be—but talking to Blacker—I don't know. You could be right. Still, I have a hunch he's not going to make anything easy for her. This bastard really believes he's the victim here. He wants her to pay. And besides that, he's got a reputation to salvage."

"He's dying. What's a reputation?"

"To these people? You really have to ask?"

"Maybe he figures he lost—that it's over."

"The man spends a lifetime building a reputation. His books have sold millions. Essays everywhere from academic journals to the *New York Times*. Think of it as a legacy. Ever read his work?"

"Can't say I have." She was impressed by the lieutenant's homework but did not feel moved to tell him.

"Checked out some of his books. Nothing new, really. Articulate. Smart. He's a sort of academic evangelist. A true believer. I don't trust people like him. Never have. Think they're clean. Real clean. I think he'd do a lot to leave behind what he built. It's like a church. It's what he lived for. And besides that, he's a sick puppy. Anybody who'd keep a girl for twenty-three years has to be sick. Sick people are hard to second-guess."

He's thought more about this than I have. She smiled. "So what's your plan?"

"Don't have one. I'm going to turn over everything I have to the DA's office. It's up to them to worry about it."

Jenny parked her elbows on the table and placed her face between her hands. "And in the meantime?"

"Oh, I don't know that we're in any hurry. Maybe they can be persuaded not to rush into anything."

Jenny smiled. "It's pretty high-profile."

"We'll see." He rubbed his hand over his mouth as if he were trying to erase something on his face. "I can release her."

"She doesn't have anyplace to go."

He couldn't help but grin. "I'd only release her to your custody. She'd be *your* problem."

"And what am I supposed to do with her?"

"Not my place to say. All I can say is she can't leave the city. I got someone working on finding her brother—shouldn't take long. If we find him, we'll fly him here. Who knows, maybe she can go home."

"What made you change your mind?"

He smiled, though his smile closely resembled a wince, as if the sun was in his eyes. "The basement was the clincher. The shackles. That place was like a cross between a bank vault and a department-store dressing room. Gave me the creeps."

"What?"

"The professor liked to buy her dresses. Expensive ones, the designer type—like I said. As a matter of fact, his ex-wife didn't trust banks, so she kept her valuables there. Had it built special. I talked to some old geezer who did the job for them. He's still around—he remembers it like yesterday, or so he says. Says it was his first big job. Some of these guys, I tell you, they stay around forever. Anyway, he says he still remembers putting in the soundproofing. State-of-the-art—back then, anyway."

"Why would they want to soundproof it?"

"Rich people do strange things—and they have the money to do it. There's a bathroom down there, and a huge closet—I mean huge. Mirrors in there and a vanity—like a room in an expensive department store. Seems like Blacker's wife used to go down there and try her things on. Who knows? Anyway, it was the perfect place to keep her. No doubt in my mind—she's telling the whole damn truth. You gonna take her?"

"I have a choice?"

"Sure you do." He took a drink of water. The waitress placed their hamburgers in front of them.

"I don't normally take in clients."

"Think of it as an adventure."

"Yeah, just what I need—an adventure." She reached over and took a french fry from his plate. "I should have had the fries."

"Help yourself," he said.

"Thank you, I will."

He laughed. He seemed preoccupied, as if part of him wanted to be somewhere else—though Jenny was trying not to notice anything about him.

"Oh," she said, "before I forget." She had decided to risk asking him. What could it hurt? The lunch had gone well—he was nicer than she thought he'd be. And she had promised Charlie. "Can you do me a favor?" She threw out her question casually. She didn't wait for an answer. "I got this friend—he got beat up last night, pretty bad." She searched his face for an expression, but there was no reaction. "He talked to some cop, but the cop said it was a waste of time to go looking for someone they'd never find. Frankly, I think they blew him off because he's gay."

"Gay? Probably a typical case of queer-bashing."

"You say that so casually."

"Sad fact of life."

"So we should just accept it?" She bit her lip and stared at the lieutenant. "And besides that, I don't think it's that simple. He said they seemed to know who he was—said his name. They told him they didn't like lawyers. Doesn't sound like a typical case of fag-bashing to me."

"I take it he's not a lawyer."

"No."

"Does he hang out with lawyers?"

"Just me."

"Hmmm." He shook his head. "Strange. Is he sure?"

Jenny shrugged. "Well, he was getting beaten up."

"So he's not sure?"

"No, I guess he's not."

"Doesn't sound like a good witness. What did the cop tell him?"

"Basically told him what you just told me—that they'd never find them."

"Did he get the cop's name?"

"Yup."

"I'm sure they won't do shit about it," he said. "They figure another fag got beat up."

"Just like you did."

"I'm not saying it's right."

"And he said something else. He said the guy had scars on his left hand."

"Scars?"

"Yeah. Like he'd been in a fire—discolored patches. That's what he said."

The lieutenant nodded. She thought she saw something in his face.

"Scars on his left hand, huh? Is he sure?"

"Well, it could have been the shadows. It was night."

"How could he see?"

"Under a streetlight." She took another one of his french fries.

He slapped her wrist. "What part of town did they jump your friend?"

"Somewhere in Boystown."

The lieutenant nodded again. "And you want me to go looking for this guy, that what you want?"

"It's your job, isn't it?"

"Not my beat."

"In other words, no."

"Look, Jenny, it's a wild-goose chase."

"If it had happened to you—"

"If it had happened to me, I'd have to let it go."

"Yeah, I'll bet. So you won't do anything?"

He sat perfectly still for a moment. "Okay. I'll look into it."

"You don't sound very enthusiastic."

"Can't say that I am."

"Look, just forget—"

"*I said I'd look into it.* But you know the score in this town."

"So we can just let creeps like that beat up on anybody they please—because it doesn't matter."

"I didn't say that."

"Yes, you did, Lieutenant."

"I'll look into it, goddamnit. What do you want from me?"

She glared at him. "You guys are all alike."

"You don't—"

"Not once in my career have I ever asked a cop for a favor. And all I'm asking is that you do your job."

"Look, I said I'd try. That's all I can do. If I'm less than enthusiastic, it's because—"

"Look, Lieutenant, just release Ms. Santos to me, will you?" She took a deep breath. She lit a cigarette. "You know what I'd like to do. I'd like to take this hamburger and shove it down your throat." She laughed. "Of course it would be a waste of a perfectly good meal."

"You have a temper."

"And now you're going to tell me you like that in a woman."

"As a matter of fact I don't."

Jenny played with her cigarette. "I don't think we understand each other, Lieutenant. And I don't think we ever will." She took out a pen and wrote down her home number on her business card. "If there are any hitches about Gloria Santos, you can reach me at home. And it's not an invitation to get friendly."

"Getting friendly with you is like trying to kiss an alligator."

She smiled at him. "I see you have a temper, too."

"Just defending myself, Counselor." He took the card and put it in his coat pocket.

She saw the pleading in his face, knew it was there, knew that he wanted to say something to her, tell her that he was not a bad man. But what was he doing to change the way things were done? To do nothing—that was not acceptable. "I'm sorry, Lieutenant." She looked at him, searched his face. "I'm just a little angry. He's my friend, Lieutenant. He's not just a faggot to me. He's a real friend. You have a friend like that?"

He nodded.

"Well, if we can't fight for the people we love, then who the fuck are we gonna fight for?" She shook her head. "I'm sorry." She rose slowly from her chair. She looked at him, and for a fleeting second his face was as silent and impenetrable as Gloria's.

"Can't we just sit down and finish a meal like decent human beings?"

"Are we decent, Lieutenant?" She turned her back on him and walked away, his voice echoing in her head: *You know the score in this town . . . Goddamnit, Lieutenant, I want to change the score.*

I Love This Town

"You're off the case, Murph."

Lieutenant Murphy made a face, then pressed his lips together. He nodded at the captain. "I was about to hand it all over to the DA's office, anyway."

"It's not that you haven't done a good job—"

"Yeah, sure. I love this town."

"C'mon, Murph."

The captain offered him a sympathetic stare. The lieutenant hated his new boss for the look of unconvincing compassion he had pasted to his face. It was as though he were wearing makeup. It was embarrassing. He looked at the captain blankly and bit the side of his mouth. "What do you want me to say?"

"Look, Murph, you did your job."

"And that's why you're taking the case away."

"There's plenty of other cases, Murph. You've done what you could—and thorough as hell. I'm serious. Very thorough. Well, there was that screwup about the basement. It happens. No harm done. You more than made up for it. And you've held off the press. You play 'em close to your chest, Lieutenant. Nobody ever knows—"

"I'm a lousy poker player, Captain. Never play the game."

"Oh, so it's Captain today."

"I'm feeling a little formal."

The captain nodded. "You and George, well, hell, you did a nice job here—always thorough," he repeated. "You guys are a good team. You like working with George, don't you?" Murph understood his veiled threat. Nothing subtle about it. The captain continued looking through the file. "Nice writing, too."

"So maybe I'll become an English teacher."

The captain laughed. "Don't see you in a classroom, Murph." He shut the file and placed it on his desk.

"I'm really sorry about—"

"Yeah, yeah—I know. High-profile case. I've heard this story."

"It's out of my hands, Murph. No hard feelings?"

"Hard feelings? Nah, it's not the first time. Won't be the last."

"Tough case. We want to have a good hard look at it before we turn it over to the DA's office. This comes all the way from the top."

"Professor has friends, huh?"

"Yeah, well, sometimes it goes like this—"

"Only one thing."

"What's that?"

"I'm letting her go—the woman—she's all set to be released."

"Can't let you do that, Murph. Not until—"

"Save it, Captain."

"It's out of your hands, Lieutenant."

"You feeling formal, too, Captain?"

"Look, I'm telling you that—"

"I said save it." He put a cigarette in his mouth but did not light it. He spoke through the unlit cigarette. "You don't let that girl out of the can, there's gonna be press wiggling in and out of your ass."

"You're not gonna do that, Murph."

"Who said anything about me? Did you have a look at who her lawyer is?"

The captain remained quiet, then looked at Lieutenant Murphy blankly.

"Jenny Richard."

"Name means nothing to me."

"I forget you're new around here." The lieutenant smiled. "I bet you've heard of her, though. Ever hear of the Franklin case?"

"Everybody's heard of the Franklin case."

"She got him off."

"So she's the bitch that—"

"Convinced a whole jury that her client was innocent." The lieutenant smiled again.

"That bitch let off a cop killer."

"It's a free country," the lieutenant said matter-of-factly. "Well, it's sort of a free country, anyway. You can call her a bitch if you want to. Won't change a thing."

"We'll just get the public defender's office to get her off the case."

"Not going to happen."

"We can make it happen."

"I'll buy tickets when you get in the ring with her. Jenny's not letting go of—"

"Oh, it's Jenny now, is it? Sounds cozy."

"That's her name. And if you want to know the truth, she treats me like dogshit. But I've worked with her before, and I know how she operates. Ever seen a pit bull? They don't let go of anything they get a hold of. She's not gonna let go of this client—I'd stake your job on it. Public defender's not gonna yank her—not her. She's the best he has, and he knows it. And I'll tell you what else. If you don't let Ms. Santos go, Jenny's gonna have the press all over the goddamn place. Is that what they want upstairs? If that's what they want, that's just what they'll get. All this bullshit at the university about crime and victimhood—they're gonna look like patsies. They're gonna look like patsies anyway." He smiled through the unlit cigarette in his mouth. "You wanna keep it nice and quiet, you'll let her go. Later, the chief wants her prosecuted, the DA wants her prosecuted, they'll know where to find her. She's not going anywhere."

"Awful cocky, aren't you?"

"Like you said, I'm thorough. I saw that basement." He pointed at the file. "It's all there. Pretty clear, I'd say. I don't give a shit how many friends the professor has. This thing goes to court, it's gonna last a day, and the professor's career is going to be in the toilet. I may be a lowly lieutenant, but I know one thing: Kidnapping a seven-year-old kid isn't gonna play well in the press. Hell, it's all gonna come out in the wash, anyway. And we're gonna look like horses' asses for having kept her in jail. You want some good PR, Captain, let her go. She's been kept long enough, wouldn't you say?"

"Oh, so now we're playing the hero with a heart?"

"Nah. Nobody who knows me would ever call me a hero. And a heart, Captain? Not even my wife thinks I got one." He took the unlit cigarette out of his mouth and smiled at the captain.

"If you let her go—"

"If I let her go, what?"

The captain glared at him, as if his glare would be enough.

"I'm gonna let her go, Captain. And you're not gonna to try to stop me." He walked toward the door.

"You'll never be anything but a grunt lieutenant."

"That's an old song, Captain. I hum a few bars every morning."

"You ever think of transferring, Lieutenant?"

"What? And ruin what we've got?" He slammed the door on his way out.

A Door Opens

"I want to have a baby, Thomas."

"Out of the question."

"I'm begging you. I've never begged you for anything."

"That's only because you're entirely too proud, my dear."

"Thomas—"

"Claudia, I won't hear another word. You know very well we're quite incapable of caring for a child."

"I'm not incapable."

"You think because you can breed, you can raise a child. I raised you, my dear. That was quite enough. You'll never know what you put me through."

"I'll stop taking the pill," she said stubbornly. "I swear I'll stop taking it." She felt his hand grip her arm, his finger digging into her skin.

"I don't think so." He grabbed her chin and squeezed it between his fingers.

"Perhaps you're right," she said.

He let her go but remained silent. He waited for her to apologize.

"I'm sorry for being so childish . . . "

She felt her belly. She sat on the edge of her bed and rocked herself. She wanted to stop thinking about Thomas, willed herself to stop hearing his voice. Since the night she stabbed him, it was as if he had entered her body and possessed it.

She had fooled him, had stopped taking the pill—but her body had not cooperated. Her own body had betrayed her, had sided with Thomas, had not given her what she wanted most—a baby. Her body had decided that Thomas had been right, that babies were not possible.

She felt shivers down her spine, felt cold, felt tired and heavy and wanted to scream and never stop screaming. No matter what she did, she could not keep herself from returning to his house. He was everywhere in the world, ubiquitous as God. That was what he was—God. She remembered her first Communion classes—the questions she'd had to memorize: *Who made the world? God made the world. And why did God make you? God made me to love, honor, and obey him . . . love, honor, and . . .* She was Eve running from the voice of God. But the garden was his. There was no escape.

"Are you okay?"

She recognized the lieutenant's voice. She did not want to speak to him. She would speak to him only in Jenny's presence. "What do you want?" she heard herself say. She did not know why she was speaking. She did not want to—"Did you come to put chains on me?"

"What?" he asked. He had a puzzled look on his face.

"Chains," she said.

"No," he said.

She thought he looked softer today, the part of him that was a boy showing through. She stared at him.

"You okay?" he asked. "You look a little sick."

I'm sterile, she wanted to say. She said nothing.

"You want me to get a doctor?"

"No," she said.

"Are you sure?"

She nodded.

"Well, I just—" He stopped. "I just came to let you know that we'll be releasing you."

She said nothing. She heard her heart as if it wanted to speak. But her heart felt brittle as a bone. If she spoke, that chamber might shatter. She showed the lieutenant nothing of what she felt. She did not know him. And *he* should not know *her*.

"We're releasing you to the custody of Ms. Richard. She'll be here first thing in the morning."

She smiled. She wondered what was making her smile. She wanted to laugh.

"Nice smile," he said. "You should do it more often."

She stopped smiling. "And what about Thomas?"

"Oh, the professor's going to be fine."

She placed her hand over her mouth. "Will you send me back to him?"

"No," he said, that same puzzled look returning to his face.

"I'm glad he didn't die," she said.

He nodded.

"I don't know what happened to me." She suddenly felt the need to explain. Thomas, she thought, has me addicted to pleasing.

"Look, you don't have to explain—not to me anyway. It's better that you talk to Ms. Richard."

"Am I free?"

"For now," he said.

She remembered how Thomas had told her freedom was a big word. Thomas was right: She knew nothing about that word. Suddenly she had a thousand questions for the lieutenant, but he did not seem to be as talkative as she had been in the past few days. For a man who had pushed her so hard to speak, he now seemed not to want to talk at all. "But what—"

"I'm sure Ms. Richard will answer all your questions." He smiled and turned to walk away.

"Thank you," she said.

"I didn't do anything," he said.

She wondered why she had been afraid of him. He looked tired and sad and far away. He was kinder than Thomas, was not as interested in power as she had first thought. She wondered why she had thought they were alike.

He smiled again, but it did not seem to her that he was smiling at all. "You'll be getting your clothes back before you go—and your personal effects."

"Personal effects?"

"You were wearing a gold chain and a watch."

"Keep them," she said. "I don't want them."

"I'm afraid," he said firmly, "you'll have to get rid of them yourself."

In a Cold Chicago Bar

Alexander Murphy decided to walk to his favorite bar. It wasn't far, and he felt like getting some air, felt like feeling the cold wind against his face. As he walked, he chastised himself for having treated Gloria Santos so distantly. She deserved to be treated with more kindness. Lunch with Jenny Richard and his meeting with the captain had rattled him, and he had spent the rest of the day trying to recover his sense of balance. *Are we decent, Lieutenant?*

As he walked, he wondered about Gloria Santos. Tomorrow she would walk down the street, would do something he did every day without even being conscious of it. What would she see? He thought he would like to see everything around him with her eyes. His own sight was beginning to fail him, and it had been a long time since he had been awed by the sight or the thought of the city. He thought of what Jenny Richard had said. Maybe she was right about him. When she'd mentioned the scarred left hand, he had immediately thought of Tim Cain. But Tim Cain was a cop. A cop maybe, but a real sonofabitch. He wouldn't put it past him to go queer-bashing, and maybe he was—he shook his head. He had said nothing to her. Tim Cain. He gritted his teeth. Maybe he *was* as corrupt as Thomas Blacker, as corrupt as the captain. Maybe they were only separated by a few degrees.

◆ ◆ ◆

"It's gonna be one of those winters." He raised his glass at George and put it to his lips. "Hey, Danny," he said, looking toward the bartender, "give us some heat."

"I thought I told you—"

"Don't give me that crap about the heat being in the drinks—it's fucking cold in here."

"It's early yet, Lieutenant—give it a few hours. By ten tonight, this place'll be downright hot."

"Yeah, yeah," he muttered. "By ten tonight I'll be home in bed. But you know, at least I have a coat."

"What are you muttering about, Murph?"

"Nothing, George. My grandfather used to say that. He'd come in from the cold and say: Ahh, at least I have a coat."

"Sounds like your grandpa had a good attitude. And speaking of attitudes, how was your meeting with the captain?"

"Not good. It's never good." He took a drink, then played with his pack of cigarettes on the bar. "Tell me something—you think it's likely that the captain didn't know Jenny Richard was working on this case?"

George shook his head. "He's known she's been on the case from the get-go."

"Yeah?"

George looked at Murph oddly. "Sure. Heard Tim Cain tell him. Heard it with my own ears."

"When?"

"The first day Jenny interviewed Ms. Santos. Like I said—from the get-go."

Murph smiled. "You eavesdrop often?"

George laughed. "Every chance I get." He looked at Murph. "What are you getting at?"

"The captain made like he didn't know who the public defender's office had sent over. He pretended not to recognize Jenny Richard's name. It just got me to thinking." He winced, lit a cigarette. "Tim Cain, huh? I hate that guy." He looked at his drink, then looked at George. "What kind of game do you figure the captain's playing?"

"Don't know. I'll keep my ears open." George stared at his drink.

"George?" He paused. "What do you know about Tim Cain?"

"Captain's lick-ass."

"Yeah? And what else?"

"Crooked, I'd say. Can't prove it. A real motherfucker. Why do you ask?"

"No reason."

"I know you, Murph, there's a reason."

"I'll get back to you on that one—that okay?"

George laughed. "Heard that before, my man." He polished off his drink. "How's our Ms. Santos?"

"I let her out."

"Freed the caged bird, huh?"

"Yeah." Murphy nodded.

"It was the right thing to do, Murph."

"Yeah, I'm a real saint."

There Is a World

She woke exhausted, unable to place herself in the world. She felt like someone had blindfolded her and spun her around as if it were her turn to swing at a piñata—but there was no piñata and everyone had gone, leaving her alone, disoriented, not knowing which direction to take to search for the necessary things she'd left behind. It was a room. But whose? And where was the room? A peculiar taste sat on her tongue, bitter, as if she'd slept with half-chewed food on her tongue. She had tasted one of Thomas's roses once—that was the taste. *Maybe I've been dreaming.* She tried to comb her hair with her fingers, knots everywhere. *Thomas loved this hair, more his than mine.* She rubbed her eyes, then paced the cell. She felt dirty, in need of a bath. The smell of her body disgusted her—and then she remembered.

Today she would walk out into the world. Today, there would be no cells, no basements, no worry about what to say to Thomas, no fretting over the darkness that sometimes overcame him. Today there would be no boundaries, just open city streets. There was a world. There was a real world, and she could see it for herself, think good of it or bad of it—be a part of it. She remembered the maps that Thomas had made her memorize when she was a little girl: *The capital of Italy is Rome, the capital of England is London, the capital of Holland is Den Haag, the capital of the United States is Washington, D.C.* She remembered the pictures, the art that each country produced, the lines on maps that showed you roads and streets and highways. *If you have a map, know how to read one, then you'll never get lost.* Thomas had been wrong. She knew how to read a map—and yet she was lost.

She stretched out her arms toward the sky as she paced the small cell faster and faster. She was making herself dizzy—and then she laughed. She felt like a girl. She tossed her long hair around and around and around. Today she would walk on a city street. Chicago, the city in which she lived. The city she had never seen. Today she could go where she wanted—but where was that? Where was there to go? She had no money—did not even know how to go about getting a job. The word *job* was as strange and meaningless and foreign to her as *money* and *love* and *happiness*—they were words in a dictionary, and though she knew how those words were defined, they were not real—just as the city and the world she lived in were not real. Real was a room in a basement. Real was Thomas's voice, his aging face. She sat back down on what passed for a bed. What did city streets look like? But today there were endless possibilities, though she knew nothing was endless. Thomas said there was only a mind. The world did not matter—only the mind. Maybe the world had no possibilities, maybe he was right, maybe the possibilities were only in her mind.

"Chicago," she whispered, "Chicago." The thought of it made her heart beat faster. The city would be peopled. The city would be full, though what it would be full of she did not know. She only knew that *it would be full,* as full as her life had been empty—it would be *that full.* She let her mind wander: The city would be beautiful; the people in it would be happy. Thomas said the people in the city were miserable and mean and small-minded, that they were ignorant and greedy, and that they cared for nothing but superficial things, spent their lives in silly stores, and did not think—did not ever bother to think. *The life of the mind.* She could hear his voice. But what of the life of the body? And if he had not needed the body, why had he needed her? She stopped herself. Today she did not want to argue with him. He was gone now, anyway. He was gone. She thought of Jenny, and wondered how she lived—Jenny, she could think. She wondered what Jenny thought of the life of the mind, and wondered, too, what her house looked like, wondered if she had books, wondered what kind of clothes she wore, clothes she bought with her own money, wondered if her house would be anything like the house where she had lived for most of her life. Perhaps it was more like the house she grew up in. She remembered her room in her apartment in El Paso. Not like Thomas's house. Where she was from, no one lived in a house like Thomas's. Her apartment had been connected to other apartments, had not been separate, had had no yard—only a street in front and an alley in back. There was always noise, always talk, always children playing in the streets, and always someone was singing. In Thomas's house, there had been no singing.

She wondered if her parents were still living, wondered how they had changed. And her brother, her brother who had always been so kind to her—was he alive, too? Yes, he had to be alive, alive and part of a city. He was not much older—only three years. She tried to remember them as they had been, but their faces would not enter her mind; it was as if a wall had been constructed to prevent their images from entering. But she would know them when she saw them. She would know them anywhere. She would never let them go again. She would take care of them. She was strong, and she would learn about the world and learn how to make her way in it.

Perhaps Chicago was like El Paso. There would be people here who lived like she had lived in El Paso. She wondered, now, whether she could go back. That strange place had once been her home, but it now seemed as far a thing as her own body, as far a thing as the Spanish she had grown up with, as far a thing as the bright sun that never seemed to stop shining. But she was here—in Chicago. It wasn't warm. Winter was coming. But today she did not care about the cold. She wanted to walk the streets—alone, free—in any weather. Today, she was free. *I don't even own a coat.*

And then she was suddenly terrified at the thought of the city. What did she know of this thing called Chicago that was full of people and voices and buildings? Thomas had told her she was lucky because she was safe. She always felt he was lying, but the possibility existed that he had told her the truth. She thought of Jenny and the lieutenant. They seemed tough to her—hard. Nicer than Thomas but in some ways harder, as if they had learned to take care of themselves, and having learned to take care of themselves, they had also learned what to do, what to say—what *not* to do, what *not* to say. She knew none of these things. She knew she did not have the necessary skills.

She felt heavy—felt as if she were carrying around all the books in Thomas's library in her belly. That heaviness was hers alone. *What would Thomas have done if he would have found out she had stopped taking the pill? What could he have*—she hugged herself. She knew what he was capable of. *Maybe I stabbed him before he stabbed me.* No, she thought, he loved me. I was everything. She felt herself getting dizzier and dizzier. *Yes, he would have. He would have done something. He would not have let me have a baby.* She eased herself toward the sink, leaned over it. She felt spasms in her stomach, in her throat. She looked at what had come out of her and half expected to see pieces of Thomas. Little pieces of Thomas.

Say Your Prayers, Catholic Girl

"It's not so bad." Jenny stared at the extra bedroom she used as a giant closet. She had stayed up late cleaning. Everything was neat and in its place. The furniture was nothing special—except the vanity, which had belonged to her grandmother. "It's clean, anyway—and it isn't a basement." She moved to the window and looked out into the dawn. The view faced the street, unlike the view from her own room, which faced the alley. She gazed out the window. Not a bad view, she thought. Pleasant, really. The dog, who had followed her into the room, barked at her. "Hungry, girl? Let's get you some food." She looked out the window again. *It was pleasant.* She loved the morning, loved the quiet of her apartment. *She'll like this. Now, if only the sun will come out.* Three days of rain and cold and gray had dampened more than the city. She gave the room another careful look. It would do. It was nice. She walked into the kitchen, poured some dry food into Bessie's bowl, and watched her tail wag as she ate. *Wish I had it so good.* "We're going to have company for a while, so be good. Be a good dog. No chewing on shoes." The dog, intent on eating, ignored her commands. Jenny poured herself a cup of coffee and looked up at the clock on the stove: 5:50. Plenty of time. She didn't have to be at the jail until 8:30. She'd taken the day off to get Gloria settled. She was apprehensive about bringing her home, but she saw no other options. "Can't turn out a woman in need, can we, Bessie?" *What the hell are we going to do with her? The room will be fine. We'll all be fine. And maybe her family*—she heard steps outside the door, Charlie dropping off the morning newspaper. She smiled at her delivery man. Such a nice guy—*he's got to find himself someone nice. And maybe I do, too.* She opened the door to the hallway and picked up the newspaper. She sat down at the kitchen table, retied her bathrobe, and opened up the newspaper. She shook her head at the photograph of students gathered in a circle, all of them holding candles beneath the headline that read: U CHICAGO STUDENTS HOLD VIGIL AGAINST CRIME. "Poor bastards," she whispered. "Who's going to tell them the truth about their squeaky clean leader?" Just as she started to read the story, the phone rang. Who would call her before six in the morning? She let the phone ring three times before she rose from the table and answered it. "Hello."

"Sorry to call so early. I wanted to make sure and catch you." She recognized Lieutenant Murphy's voice immediately. "This is Lieuten—"

"I know," she said. "I know who this is."

"Sorry," he said again. He paused. "Listen, I know you're not too happy with me. Truth is, I'm not too happy with you, either. You're too hard, you know that?"

"This a lecture, Lieutenant?"

"No, no, let's not get into all this. I just wanted to let you know you may be up against some tough odds here—I mean with the Santos case."

"I'm always up against tough odds, Lieutenant."

"Yeah, yeah," he said. "Well, listen, he's got a lot of friends, the professor. They've taken me off the case."

She was suddenly more interested. "How come?"

"Higher-ups—they want it. I'm off—that's all I know."

"Was it the basement fiasco?" she asked.

"No, that's not it. Someone wants him protected, I'd say."

"So what are you suggesting?"

"Just be careful. And don't back down from anything."

"I never do."

"Then keep it that way. I don't get a good feeling here. You may be right about me, but—well, hell, just use the press if you have to."

"What?"

"You heard me. If they try anything, just use the press. That's exactly what they don't want."

"You hate the press."

"Of course I hate the press. Nothing but entertainment. But this time, our friend the professor is gonna be the show. Use the goddamn press, if you have to. They don't want that—boy oh boy, they don't want that at all."

"What makes you so sure?"

"I used it on him."

"What? On who?"

"The captain. We got this new captain, and he's a little—well, never mind. He smells to high heaven. Anyway, when the captain pulled me from the case yesterday evening, I told them I'd arranged to have Gloria Santos released under your supervision. And just remember it's your ass if she makes her way out of this town."

"Don't you think I know that? Jesus Christ, Lieutenant."

"Yeah, well, anyway, he said I couldn't let her go. No way in hell."

"He said what? If that sonofabitch doesn't—"

"Take it easy. Just come and get her. It's all arranged—everything legit, aboveboard."

"How'd you get your captain to let her go?"

"I was getting to that."

"Get to it, then."

"Can't you be nice?"

"I'm not good in the morning."

"You're not good during lunch, either." He laughed. "So I told them you were on the case. He pretended he didn't know. He knew, all right. And my guess is he wants you off. Make sure your boss stays behind you on this one." Jenny listened intently and reached for her cigarettes in her robe pocket. "And I told them that if they didn't let her go, you were gonna make a big stink to the press. I've mailed copies of the file to your home address. Everything's in there—including police reports from El Paso when she was kidnapped."

"How'd you get my address?"

"I'm a cop."

"Pretty smart guy, huh, Lieutenant? How'd you get the file if they've taken you off the case? I'm sure they're not letting you anywhere near that damned file."

"You got that right. But this time I saw it coming. Kept my own copies. Just wanted to make sure it didn't get lost. Sometimes they get lost—know what I'm saying? Anyway, the captain bought it—you going to the press. He wants everything nice and quiet. All they want are pictures of Norman Rockwell students holding candles in the night. Seen this morning's paper?"

"Yeah, I've seen it. Up pretty early, Lieutenant."

"Always. Can't sleep. Oh, and George tells me that one of the captain's cronies called El Paso and told them the lead they had on the missing girl didn't pan out."

"What? Jesus Christ."

"Say your prayers, Catholic girl—and use all your trump cards. George is trying to locate her family. Hope they're still around. He'll be in touch. Oh, and—you got a pencil?"

She reached for a pad and pen next to the phone.

"Write this number down." As he gave her the number to the *El Paso Times*, she nodded. "You may need that number. I think they'd be very interested. Story was real big down there when she got kidnapped."

She lit her cigarette. "So how come you're letting me in on this?"

He cleared his throat. "Maybe you've misjudged me."

"I'm not willing to concede that."

"I'm sure you're not. That's what makes you a good lawyer."

"Trying to win me over with flattery."

"Not a chance. Listen, sometimes you see things. I saw those ankle things he made her wear—" He paused. "I'll be in touch. And you owe me a meal, Counselor. You stiffed me—I wound up paying for two meals."

Before she could say anything else, the phone went dead. She stared into the receiver, then hung it up. She looked over at her dog, who was watching her. "Well, Bessie, it's getting *verrry* interesting." She sat down, stared at the faces of the students, and set the newspaper on the table. "I can't read this shit." She put out her cigarette, then finished her morning coffee. *Say your prayers, Catholic girl—and use all your trump cards.* This would be a fight she was going to enjoy, a fight she was going to win. She smiled to herself. *Lieutenant, you may turn out to be the biggest trump card of all.*

A Door Opens

Jenny and Gloria walked down the heavily peopled hallway, neither of them speaking. Gloria imagined she was at some kind of circus as she turned her head right, then left, then turned herself completely around and started walking backward. "May I ask what you're doing?" Jenny finally asked her.

"I'm looking," she said. She searched Jenny's face for a look of disapproval. "I'm sorry," she said softly, then stopped walking backward. "I shouldn't have—"

"I wasn't asking for an apology, honey. I just wanted to know why you were walking backward."

"It was a silly thing to do."

"Not necessarily."

"I just did it—it was very—" she paused, "it was very—"

"Spontaneous," Jenny said.

"Yes." She nodded. "I've never been in one place with so many people."

"Better touch them to make sure they're real." She laughed.

"I don't think I'd like to do that."

"Don't blame you. Most of them aren't really people, you know—they're cops."

Gloria laughed. "Where did you learn how to do that?"

"What?"

"Make people laugh."

"It's a small thing."

"No, it's a very big thing."

They continued walking down the crowded hall. Jenny could not keep herself from thinking, could not stop the thoughts that ran through her mind like Sunday joggers running through Lincoln Park. She wondered what is was like, for her, wondered what she was feeling now that she was able to walk out the door with no one to stop her. What would it be like to come out of exile? There was a thought—to see the world for the first time, with eyes that were not clouded with the filth she had seen here. Maybe she would hate this goddamned city because it was ugly and unfair and violent and overcrowded and would make her feel as invisible as Thomas Blacker's stare. But after having been deprived of it, maybe she would see something that was good and pure, something none of the rest of them could see. Maybe she would see that the city had a heart. To walk on the sidewalks for the first time, to see the lake for the first time, the park, the buildings, the people rushing about. Maybe I would feel as if I were being born. Maybe I would feel as if I were dying.

As they reached the door, Gloria stopped, stopped as if something were preventing her from walking out into the street. *A world. I have spent my life far from the noises of the city. What was it like? Maybe the city was another name for freedom. Maybe it was another name for prison.* She looked at Jenny. "I don't want to go out there."

"All you have to do is push open the door."

"What's it like?"

"If you want me to tell you that it's not a frightening place, then I can't. It's ugly and it's beautiful—and it's cruel—" She paused a moment, then looked directly into Gloria's dark eyes. She gently grabbed her arm. "You asked where I learned how to make people laugh." She pointed toward the door. "Out there," she said. Then she smiled.

Gloria nodded, reached for the door, and walked through.

She felt the cold wind against her face. She had no coat, but today she did not hate the cold, was not bothered by the fact that there was no sun to greet her as she walked out into the streets for the first time since she was seven years old. She stared at the people on the busy street. She did not know where they were going, but they were all going somewhere. *Somewhere.* She looked up at the tall buildings, and she wanted to go to the top of each one of them, wanted to look down at the whole scene to see what it looked like, to see it, all of it. To really see and understand this thing called a city. *Oh my God. Oh my God. Look what we can build. Thomas never said a word about the buildings.* As she stared in awe of the towers reaching out toward the sky like fingers, she felt a jolt. Dazed, she looked up, and a man grabbed her shoulder. "I'm sorry, I wasn't looking where I was going. Are you all right?" He had a nice face and a nice voice, and she liked the way he said, "I'm sorry."

She nodded. "A pleasure," she said.

The man smiled, laughed, then kept walking down the sidewalk.

"Gloria, are you okay?"

Gloria had almost forgotten Jenny was with her. "I'm fine."

"Lesson number one in the big city: Never tell a strange man that he's 'a pleasure.'"

"It's not what I meant."

"What did you mean?"

"I don't know. I've never run into a man on the street."

"You'll get used to it. It won't be such a pleasure when it happens every day."

"Maybe. But I made him laugh, didn't I? Isn't that a good thing?"

"Yes, you did. You want to see your new home?"

Home, she liked the way the word sounded. "Can we walk around for a while?"

"Sure."

"And can you take me to the top of the highest building?"

Jenny stared at the black dress Gloria was wearing. She must have been wearing that dress when she was arrested. There was no blood on it that she could see. There must have been no blood—otherwise it would have stayed in the property room. She made a mental note to ask the lieutenant about it. The dress was sleeveless, and looking at her made Jenny feel cold. "Here, put this on. At least I'm wearing a sweater. And be careful as you walk."

"I'll be careful. I'm good at doing what I'm told." She laughed softly. It was nice not to have to hide her own laughter.

"I'm sorry," Jenny said softly. "I didn't—"

"It's okay." She stood in the middle of the sidewalk putting on Jenny's coat. She stretched her arms out toward the sky—like the buildings. *So this is the world. This is what the world is really like. I'm free, Thomas Blacker. Not lame. Come and watch me walk.* She did not even notice she had dropped her gold chain on the sidewalk. She had worn it since her eighteenth birthday.

An Ordinary Courtship

She resisted—but only in the beginning. It was the newness of sex. Women always found it more difficult to enjoy their bodies, and I overpro-

tected her, trained her to think of herself as pure. She was so inexperienced, so unprepared for me. But it was better that way—better to teach her. I could feel her resistance, could feel the tenseness in her when I reached out to touch her. But she liked the flowers and the dresses and the perfumes. She liked the dinners and the wine. She liked my eyes on her. And yet she pretended to be indifferent to the attention, but I could sense the quickening in her pulse. She learned to kiss like a fire raging across a dry savanna. And I could make her moan.

On many occasions, she almost begged me to let her spend the entire weekend in my room. I never denied her request. So many years together, each of us knowing what the other thought. And all of it gone in an evening. A moment of insanity, and all those years of wooing and loving were gone. How the world could change . . .

He read over what he'd written. He wondered why he could write nothing unless it was about her. Why was he writing about the memory of that body? He was writing about a time with a woman, a time that was gone. So hard to accept the loss. And yet, it seemed to him, it was *the only* time he wanted to remember. She had been so sweet, her struggles so naive, he had never loved her more than the time he had taught her to respond to his body. How had *that* time escaped him? Perhaps it was not her failure, but his. He had failed to teach her something essential. He stared at his own handwriting, wanted desperately to re-create his past with Claudia, go back, retrace their whole time together and discover where he had failed. He had felt they had been so successful together. Watching her learn was like watching himself. She had learned as quickly and easily as he had, but he had given her what he had lacked—a mentor. *You never even knew what you had, did you, my Claudia?* He shook his head, looked around the hospital room, wondered if he would ever see her again. He wondered how he would feel if he saw her again. *I will see her,* he whispered. *I will teach her.* He would teach her something she still needed to learn. He would—

"I see you're writing again."

He looked up at the unwelcome voice. He hated the sound of the nurse's voice—overly friendly, unrefined, nothing subtle in its cadence.

He tried to smile. "Yes," he said. "And I write much better when I'm left alone."

"I see." The nurse tried to smile. "I just need to take your vitals."

"I can tell you they're fine."

"Well, we'll just—" She placed her hand on his arm.

He shoved her away. "Get out!"

She looked into his angry face. "I'll call the doctor," she whispered, then walked out of the room.

Thomas returned his attention to his journal. He was tired of writing. He was tired of thinking of her. Wasn't it time to let her go? He clenched his jaw. "Never," he whispered, "not after all this. I've earned her."

Cars

Gloria hesitated as she stood on the passenger side of Jenny's car. "Are you okay?" Jenny asked as she opened the door for her. Gloria stood motionless, stared at the car, then looked away. She became a statue or a model who was posing for an artist who demanded she become not something human but something still and inanimate and unfeeling like a painting that created the fiction of realness but was in fact only dry paint. Dry paint that looked wet. "Are you okay?" She placed her hand on Gloria's back.

"I'm cold."

"Let's get you inside. Once we get you home, I'll make you the best cup of coffee you ever tasted."

Gloria refused to move. "I'll never be warm again."

"What is it?"

"I'm cold."

"We'll get you warm."

Gloria stared out into the city, not seeing any of it, as if it had disappeared. "It's a nice car—smooth as a magic carpet."

"What?" Jenny shook her gently.

"It's what he told me."

"What?"

Gloria shut the door to the car. "Thomas. It's what he told me. He said his car was as smooth as a magic carpet. 'Do you want to see?' That's what he asked." She looked directly into Jenny's eyes. "And his voice, it was as soft as the light of the candles my mother lit to her patron saint, the softest voice I'd ever heard. And later it turned to ice. And I was always cold. Do you think it's possible to be warm in this world?"

"Yes," Jenny whispered.

Gloria placed her hand on the hood of the car. "Red," she said. "I like it. Thomas wouldn't like a red car. It was the first time."

"I don't understand."

"It was the first time I'd ever been in a car. My parents didn't own one. I'd always wanted to ride in a car. 'Would you like a ride?' And I did—I wanted a ride. That's all I wanted—a little ride. If I hadn't wanted—" She bit her lip. "Be careful what you wish for."

"It's not your fault."

"I wish I was so sure."

Jenny grabbed her by both shoulders and shook her softly. "I'm sure enough for both of us." She smiled at her.

"Were you a happy child?"

"Sometimes." The wind blew Jenny's hair across her face. She pushed it away from her eyes, then hugged herself. "Let's get out of this weather."

"Your girlhood—was it warm?"

"Sometimes. And sometimes it wasn't. C'mon, let's go someplace where it's warm."

"Yes, let's go someplace warm. Is it warm where you live?"

"Absolutely—and I have the heating bills to prove it."

But still Gloria refused to move.

"We don't have to take the car. We can take a cab—or a bus."

"No, it's okay. You don't have a basement, do you?"

"No basements. Just an old basset hound who likes to have her stomach rubbed."

Gloria took a deep breath, almost put a finger in her mouth, then pulled it away. She went back to a day in El Paso—and then the day disappeared. She stepped inside the car.

The Geography of Blue

The two women slowly made their way to the entrance of the John Hancock Building. Gloria said nothing as they walked, just stared at the people rushing through the cold streets. Their hurry seemed so intense, so urgent. She had never known that kind of hurry. She wanted to feel it. Inside the building, Jenny took some money out of her purse and handed it to a woman behind a counter.

"Is seven-fifty a lot of money?"

"No, not really."

They walked around the corner and waited for an elevator. Gloria looked at Jenny. "Are we supposed to do anything?"

"No. We just step inside, and the elevator takes us up." Just then they heard the sound of the elevator coming to a stop. A group of old women slowly made their way out of the elevator, their excited laughter filling up the space around them. When the elevator was empty, a man waved them inside. They stepped in, and Gloria grabbed Jenny's arm as the elevator doors shut. She said nothing. She squeezed Jenny's arm as the elevator began rising. Her stomach felt as if it had been left behind, as if it had to run to catch up with the rest of her body. She took a deep breath.

"You okay?"

"Sure," Gloria said softly. "It feels like I'm stepping on clouds."

"Just wait till you see this view."

Gloria noticed the man watching them. He smiled at them. Jenny smiled back.

"Cold out there, huh? Clear though. At least it's clear." His voice was friendly.

"Won't stay that way for long," Jenny said, her voice as friendly as his.

"That's for sure. I think we're really in for it this year."

"Well," Jenny said, "we gotta pay for our sins one way or another."

The man laughed. "Guess you got that right."

Gloria was amazed at the easy way these two people spoke to each other. Strangers, and yet they were not at all shy or hesitant, not at all distrustful or suspicious. They were not afraid to say things, their banter something calm and casual as if this was part of what made a day. She would have to ask Jenny about the etiquette of speaking to strangers, ask her if there were rules to be followed. She suddenly felt the elevator coming to a halt. She let go of Jenny's arm and held on to her stomach. Her legs suddenly felt like rubber, as if they were incapable of holding her up. She tasted the familiar salt in her mouth. She took a deep breath, then another.

"You sure you're okay?"

"Yes," Gloria said. "I'm just not used to elevators."

Jenny noticed the slight edge in her voice. Once she saw the view, she would calm down—she was certain of it.

The door opened. The man smiled at them as they stepped out of the elevator.

◆ ◆ ◆

When Gloria entered the floor—not a room really—she felt as if she were stepping into an ocean of blue. Everything blue. She became completely unaware of Jenny's presence, as if she had disappeared. There was only this blue. There was only the brightness of the day, the sky, the lake attacking her eyes through the huge glass windows, not windows exactly, but walls, walls of glass. *Oh, I didn't know.* She stared out at the blueness of the lake that had a beginning but had no end. As large as an ocean, though she had never seen an ocean, only on maps and globes and photographs. She could see the buildings, the tops of many of them. It was a kind of forest. She walked around the building looking out at the city from every direction, could see cars and yellow taxis, and little dots she knew were people—and the sky was as blue as Thomas's eyes—only vast and free. Thomas's eyes were blue and lovely—but they were enclosed and seemed more like a cage, but this—*this* was not a cage. This was the world, and it was open, and from here she could see where the things of men met the things of earth, and she felt like she was in a church, like the church where she had made her first Communion—only that church had been dark—and this church, this church was full of light and air and buildings that eternally reached out to touch the perfect blueness. *Oh, I didn't know. I didn't know.* She was happy to see, to know, to be here, to be lost in this geography of blue. She felt something beginning in her—something for which she did not yet have a name.

What You Have Inside You

Bessie rolled over, wagged her tail, and waited for Gloria to rub her belly. Gloria laughed, then sat on the floor and rubbed the hound's stomach. "Funny dog."

Jenny walked into the living room with two steaming cups of coffee. "That damn dog thinks it's everybody's job to love her."

"Looks to me like she gets what she wants." Gloria stopped playing with the dog and moved over to the coffee table, where Jenny had placed her cup of coffee. The basset hound followed her and lay down at her feet.

"Looks like you have a new friend."

"I could use a few new friends." She looked up at Jenny and smiled. "I never had a dog." She took a sip and nodded. "Good coffee. Nice and hot."

Jenny nodded. "You hungry?"

"Not really." Gloria stared at her.

"What?"

"You changed."

"Yeah, I always change when I get home."

"Thomas never changed. Sometimes he'd take off his tie, put on slippers. But he never changed. Are they comfortable?"

"What—the pants?"

"Yeah."

"Nothing like a pair of jeans."

"Thomas only bought me dresses."

"Maybe we should swing by his place, pick up all those dresses, and go pay him a visit at the hospital. We could make *him* put them on—see how *he* likes it." Jenny laughed.

"How come you're always laughing?"

"Just remember men don't like funny women." She looked at Gloria's dress. "You know, I have an extra pair—I'm sure they'll fit you."

Gloria nodded, "I'd like that. I hate this dress. When he came back from a trip, he'd bring me a dress. I'd model them for him as he took notes in his journal. Like he was painting me."

"What?"

"Like he was painting me."

"He keeps journals?"

Gloria nodded as she sipped her coffee. "Is that important?"

"What did he write in them?"

"I don't know—he never let me read them—but he wrote in them faithfully. Every day—well, maybe not every day."

"Anything in there about you?"

"He said there was." She tapped her teeth with her index finger. "He was in love—I mean I was every—do we have to talk about this?"

"Course not. You know, I think I'll give the lieutenant a call." She put down her cup of coffee.

"Are you going to tell him about the journals?"

"Yes."

"What are you going to do with them?"

"Use them as evidence."

"But they're his."

"So what?"

"They're private."

"Private isn't sacred—not always."

"And you'd use his own words against him?"

"Absolutely."

"What about his rights?"

"My personal opinion is that I don't give a damn about his rights. My professional opinion is that his journals don't apply to his First Amendment rights of self-incrimination." She lifted herself off the couch but did not move toward the telephone in the kitchen.

"It just doesn't seem right, Jenny."

"Just because it doesn't *seem* right doesn't mean it isn't right."

"I'm not so sure." Gloria saw a look on Jenny's face she didn't like. "Jenny, I'm not a child."

Jenny nodded. "No, you're not."

"Then don't treat me like one. You don't know him."

"Goddamnit, he kidnapped you—" She stopped herself. She realized she was raising her voice. She cleared her throat. She couldn't help but feel frustrated with Gloria's defense of Thomas Blacker. "I'm sorry. I didn't mean to yell."

Gloria nodded. "He didn't invent me, you know?"

"I know," Jenny whispered. "I'm sorry." She sat back down on the couch. "You love him?"

"I don't know."

Jenny nodded. "Well, that's an answer, too. But you sure as hell want to protect him."

"Isn't that what he did for me?"

Jenny shook her head. There was a long silence between them. Jenny wondered if she wasn't pushing her too hard. It was too soon. Gloria was no longer Thomas Blacker's possession, but that in itself did not make this woman free. *Free*—what kind of a word was that? *Free*—that's what she had wanted to become when she had moved to Chicago, but she had come to understand that the business of freedom was no easy thing. Not for her. Not for Gloria. Not for anyone. *Be patient, Jenny.* "It's a new life, Gloria."

"Thomas used to say that every time he started working on a new book. I never understood what he meant by that—the new life looked a lot like the old one—for me *and* for him."

"This isn't a new book that someone's writing, Gloria. This is a life."

Gloria said nothing, looked away from Jenny. Suddenly, she couldn't stand looking at her, at her self-confidence, at the sureness of the way she talked and carried herself. She wondered how long a new life lasted. She forced herself to look at the woman who was sitting across from her. She had a good and decent name. She had been kind enough to open her doors to her. She didn't know what to say, what to do. She knew how to act around Thomas. Nothing in her life had prepared her for this woman named Jenny. She looked at her, nodded, then almost smiled. "I'd like to try on your jeans," she heard herself say.

◆ ◆ ◆

Gloria reluctantly stepped out of the dress she was wearing. She had wanted to take it off, get rid of it, but now, as her body felt the dress's absence, she felt as if she had shed a necessary layer of skin, a layer she still needed to survive the coming winter.

She placed it gently on a hanger. She was as careful with dresses as Thomas was careful with his wines. He had taught her to take good care of her things. She hung it in the closet of her new bedroom—but noticed the closet was empty. Nothing like the closet she had had in Thomas's house. She stared at the lonely and singular dress for a long time. She looked at the bed where Jenny had placed a pair of jeans, a T-shirt, and a bathrobe. She would take a shower, change into her new clothes. She knew they would feel strange. She looked back at the dress, touched the fabric with her fingers. She let it drop reluctantly, then shut the door to the closet.

◆ ◆ ◆

"Yes, I'd like to speak to Lieutenant Murphy." Jenny lit a cigarette as she leaned against the refrigerator. "Yes, I'll wait." He's probably not in, she thought, as she inhaled her cigarette. Gone for the day, gone home to fight with his wife. Her mind wandered around the room. *Dinner, maybe I'll make dinner. She's got to eat something, must be starved. She hasn't had a good meal in days. Hell, I haven't had a good meal in days, either. And tomorrow, a counselor—that girl could use a good counselor. She needs to get that guy out of—*"Yes. Oh, he just stepped out?" She placed her cigarette in the ashtray on the counter. "Well, could you please have him call me first thing in the morning? The name's Jenny. Jenny Richard." She pronounced her last name like the man's first name—she didn't have the patience to explain yet one more time the fine points of Cajun pronunciation to a receptionist who didn't care, who didn't get paid enough to care. She hung up the phone and searched the refrigerator for something edible. Chicken—baked chicken and baked potatoes. "Perfect." She sensed Gloria's presence in the room, turned around and faced her as she leaned against the doorway.

"Thanks for letting me take a shower," she said. "I feel better."

"It's the water," Jenny said. "Nothing like water on the body. Did you know that the body is ninety percent water? The other ten percent is just junk."

Gloria nodded. She was a funny woman. Logical and illogical. Thomas would not have known what to do with her. She combed her wet hair back with her fingers. She looked down at herself. "How do I look in your jeans?"

"Stunning, Miss Gloria, absolutely stunning." She placed the chicken on the counter and took out a baking pan from one of the cabinets. "Have you ever worn any makeup?"

"Thomas wouldn't allow it—he said he liked women who looked natural."

"Natural, my ass. That's why he had you on birth control pills. That's why he took you from your *natural* family." She shook her head. "Would you like me to teach you how?"

"To wear makeup?"

"Not that you need much—just enough to make you feel like you spend a little time on yourself."

"I'd like that. Would you like some help with dinner?"

"Can you cook?"

"That's one of the few things—besides reading—that I can actually claim some expertise in. That and cleaning."

"He made you clean his house?"

"Don't say it like that. It helped pass the time."

Jenny nodded. She would have to let a lot of things pass. She smiled. "My mama used to say every girl should know how to cook. I *hate* to cook. And if I ever succumb to that moment of insanity we call marriage—then my husband's going to do the cooking—and I *do mean all the cooking.* Tell you what—you do the cooking, and I'll make the coffee." She laughed.

Gloria stared at her.

"What?" Jenny asked.

"Nothing. It's just that you carry yourself in a certain way." Gloria moved toward the counter. "Like you're not ashamed of having a body. Where are the spices?"

Jenny opened a cabinet. "Here."

Gloria placed the chicken in the pan, turned on the oven, and began spicing the chicken. She reached for an onion and began dicing it.

"Well, of course," Jenny said as she watched her, "I'm not ashamed of having a body—but I don't have your perfect posture."

"I'm tired of standing up straight. I want my body to change."

"It will," Jenny said. "And you won't like it one damn bit. Our bodies are always changing. Makes us crazy."

"Yes, there's that." There was something distant in Gloria's voice—as if there was something bothering her, something she did not want to speak about. Maybe she was just tired, Jenny thought. She watched Gloria as she scraped the diced onions into the pan with the chicken, poured a little olive oil on top, and then added some wine.

"Looks good," Jenny said. "That didn't seem very hard."

"It isn't. Whoever told you cooking was hard? You have rice?"

Jenny nodded, opened one of the cabinets, and took down a clear canister filled with white rice.

"Is this all you have?"

Jenny nodded, then smiled. "You don't approve."

"I didn't say that."

"You didn't have to."

"I don't like being that transparent."

"It's not such a bad thing," Jenny said. "Hiding everything is hard work."

"Yes," Gloria said, "and it's also an addiction."

"Like cigarettes?"

"I suppose so. Have you ever tried to quit?"

"I don't have it in me."

"How do you know?" She thought of herself making love to Thomas. Then saw herself standing over Thomas's body with a knife. "You never know what you have inside you—not until the time comes."

A Door Opens

"I don't understand what you want from me."

"I thought you were supposed to be the smart one in your family."

"A smart Murphy? That'll be the day."

"Well, you got that right, buddy."

He stared at his wife, turned off the television set that was always on too loud.

"Turn it back on," she said. "I was watching it."

He sat down next to her, put his hand on her lap, his hand pleading, searching for hers. "What's wrong with us? What happened to us, Becky?"

"I married a crybaby, that's what's wrong. I thought I married a cop, but you're no cop. You can't even give me a kid."

"It's that again. I told you," he said, his face turning red as his voice grew louder, "I fucking told you I didn't know I was sterile when I married you."

"Yeah, well, that doesn't do me any good, does it?"

"Why don't we adopt? We can adopt, damnit."

"I want my own."

"Well, there's nothing I can do about it."

"I can."

"What the hell's that supposed to mean, Becky?"

"It means I'm pregnant."

"What?" He moved away from her, jumped off the couch, and stood up, keeping his eyes on her as if he were pointing a gun—about to place her under arrest. "What?"

She looked down at the coffee table. "I said I'm pregnant."

"Anybody I know?"

She nodded her head softly. "I love him," she whispered.

He walked into the kitchen, opened the utility drawer, and took out a hammer. He walked back into the living room, pointed the hammer at his wife, then walked over to the television and pointed the hammer at it. "See this hammer," he said.

"Don't!" she yelled.

"See this television," he said.

"You're crazy, Murphy."

"No," he said. "No, I'm not crazy." He leaned down and pulled the plug on the television. "We wouldn't want anyone to get hurt, would we?"

"I'll call the cops, Murph—I swear I will."

"What are you gonna tell 'em, Beck, huh? Are you gonna tell 'em that I clobbered my own television with a goddamned hammer?" He swung the hammer at the screen. Becky screamed and shut her eyes as it shattered. Murph dropped the hammer on the floor. "Tell him to buy you a new one."

"You're fucking crazy, Murphy. I don't know why I married you."

"I don't want to talk about it, Becky. Go take a ride in your car. I'm packing my bags, and I'm leaving. I want to do it in peace, god-damnit—" He shook his fists in front of his chest. "I want to do it in peace."

Becky slowly got up off the couch, grabbed her coat from the closet, and walked toward the front door. She turned around and looked at him as he stood motionless in the center of the room. "You know what?" she said numbly. "I'm not even sad. I won't even miss you. This has been the most miserable three years of my life."

He nodded. "And don't think you get the house, either—I'm just loaning it to you. You got six months to get your shit together and get out."

"If I want the house, Murph, then maybe I'll take it."

"Let me get this straight—you would take the house my grandfather gave me? You would do that? You would bring another man whose baby you're carrying and live with him in the house my grandfather left me—my grandfather who worked thirty-five years in the police department, and built it himself—you would claim his house as yours? You would do that, Becky?"

She said nothing. She turned her back on him and opened the door.

"Answer me, Becky! You would take my house?"

She slammed the door on her way out.

◆ ◆ ◆

As he walked through the empty house, he found himself looking through an old shoe box where he kept things from his childhood he could never bring himself to throw away. He took out a letter his grandfather had written to him just before his death. He had willed his house to him in that letter, had given him advice—advice he had failed to take. *You don't have to be a cop, son. Too many cops gone bad in this family.* He stared at his grandfather's handwriting, then folded it, put it back in the envelope. He carelessly thumbed through the letters his grandparents had written to him when he had gone away to college in southern Illinois. He retied the shoe box with an old shoelace. He hugged the box, then placed it in the suitcase he was packing. Besides his clothes and these letters, he could think of nothing else he wanted. He walked around the house in a daze, from the kitchen to the basement to the back bedrooms to the dining room. This was the only place in the world that had ever given him a sense of belonging. This house was his heart, and he felt lost and numb and exiled. There should have been tears, he thought, but he had been taught to banish them. So he could only feel blank like a clean chalkboard. Nothing to say. Nothing to teach. He sat down at the kitchen table. *Where should I go? After a week, I'd go crazy in my father's house. Cheap hotel? George, maybe George will put me up—at least for a while.* "I will miss you," he said to the empty room. He packed an old picture of his grandparents as they held him in their arms.

You're a fine man with a fine heart. Don't lose it—that's what his grandfather had written. "I have lost it, Grandpa. *I have.*" He closed the suitcase and opened the door. He was afraid to walk through it. He turned around, found a pad in the kitchen, and wrote out a note to Becky: "You think I'm not strong? I'll tell you one thing—you got two months to get out of my house. Two months. I'll burn it before I let you have it." He didn't bother signing his name. He walked through the front door and looked out into the cold, clear night.

Roommates

A robed and exhausted Jenny stood in the doorway to Gloria's room holding a glass of wine. "Would you like something to read?"

Gloria was staring out the window watching people walk by on their way to places she could only imagine. A part of her wanted to tag along, go someplace where someone was expecting her, where someone would open the door, smile at her, embrace her. Thomas? Would Thomas embrace her? If she went back, would he take her in? She turned around and shook her head. "I'm too tired to read." She looked out the window again.

"Would you like some tea before going to sleep?"

"Thomas loved tea—"

"Would you like some wine?"

"Thomas loved wine. He kept it in a cellar. Right next to where he kept me." She continued staring out the window. "I love wine," she whispered.

"What?"

Gloria kept her face toward the window. "Where do people go so late at night? Don't they sleep?"

"Oh, they go to bars, they go to friends' homes, they go out to eat, some of them are up to no good. Most people don't stay home and read books."

Gloria laughed. "Yes, I can see that. It sounds like fun."

"Oh, sometimes—depends who you go out with."

Gloria walked over to the bed and sat on it. She placed her hand on the mattress and pressed down. "Firm," she said. "I'll sleep." As she was speaking, the basset hound slinked into the room and attempted to climb onto the bed.

"No, Bessie, stop that." Jenny laughed. "Don't let her onto the bed—otherwise you'll never be able to get rid of her. That dog loves to sleep with people." The dog rolled over on her back at Gloria's feet.

Gloria reached for Bessie's belly and rubbed it. "Such a sweet dog. Why aren't people more like dogs?"

"I know lots of men who act just like them."

Gloria grinned at Jenny. She patted the bed. "Will you sit here for a while?"

Jenny moved slowly toward the bed and sat at the edge of it.

Gloria crossed her arms as if she were cold. "Jenny, can I ask you a question?" She had a little-girl tone in her voice again.

"Sure, shoot."

"What's a lesbian?"

"What?" Jenny was surprised by the question. "Why do you ask?"

"You said a lot of men who didn't like women lived around you, and you also said your brother thought that living here, people might think you were a lesbian."

Jenny paused, then opened her mouth to speak, then shut her mouth again. She shook her head. "Do you know what a gay man is?"

"I don't think so."

"The word means homosexual—a male homosexual."

"Oh," she said, then laughed, though her laughter seemed to lack conviction—as if she were hiding her embarrassment. "I know what that is—Thomas and I talked about it once. But he didn't have much to say on the topic. He just explained it in a hurry and told me I shouldn't concern myself about it. He said it wasn't important." She nodded. "Then a lesbian is a woman homosexual?"

"Yes."

"I know what you're thinking. You're thinking, how is it that a thirty-year-old woman didn't know what a lesbian was."

"I know the answer to that one."

Gloria uncrossed her arms. "There are so many things I don't know. *I am crippled.*" She looked at Jenny, her eyes bright in the light of the room. "Have you ever known anybody like Thomas?"

"No, not like Thomas. I've never dated intellectuals. I've only dated morons."

Gloria only half smiled at her remark. "You're lucky. Morons don't kidnap people." She paused. She shrugged her shoulders and whispered into the room as if she did not wish to hear her own words. "Jenny, I know this doesn't make sense, but he could be a very kind and generous man."

Jenny nodded. "Try not to think about him too much. Just remember, it's over, honey."

"That isn't true."

"Look around this room—it's got windows and curtains. The doors are locked to keep bad people out—*but not to keep good people in.*"

"Good people. Bad people. Thomas thought he knew the difference between the two. But I've never known. Do you?"

"I know whose side I'm on, and I think I might even know why."

Jenny's voice was as soft as the light in the room. Gloria was soothed by the sound of it, like soft hands across the tight muscles of her back.

"Then you know a lot," Gloria said firmly. "It's so cold." She rubbed her hands together. "It's so strange to be here. This is like something out of a novel—curtains, a comfortable bed, a window to peer out of—a dog at your feet. Is this a dream?"

"Tomorrow when you wake, this room will still be here—and so will you. And so will I."

"You're very generous."

Jenny laughed. "Go to sleep. You're so tired that you're beginning to talk nonsense." She rose from the edge of the bed and walked toward the door. "Come on, Bessie, it's time to get some shut-eye." The basset hound reluctantly waddled out of the room.

"Please don't shut the door," Gloria whispered.

◆ ◆ ◆

"Well, look what the cat dragged in." George eyed the suitcase Murph was holding at his side. "And what have we here? Come bearing gifts?"

Murph sneered at his friend, then chuckled. "You gonna let me in or are you gonna make me stand out in this hallway till I do a dance?"

"No dancing. Too painful to watch a white boy dance." George swung open the door and stepped out of the way. *"Mi casa es su casa."*

"Your Spanish really sucks, George."

George laughed, then grabbed Murph's suitcase. "Trouble at home?"

"Yeah, sure."

"How long you want to stay?"

"I gave her two months to get out of the house—but I just need a place to land for a while. Maybe I'll find a room—"

"Hey, no problem, Murph—two months is fine. You pay half the rent for two months, and I can put some money away for a rainy day."

"What about Lisa?"

"We mostly stay at her place. She's also a better cook. Wanna beer?"

"Beer sounds good." George walked toward the kitchen, then appeared back in the room holding two beers. Murph took one and opened it, then sat down on the couch. "You two ever gonna get married?"

"And ruin a good thing? What's wrong with you, anyway, Murph? You're always getting married. Someday, some woman's gonna try and take that house your grandpa left you."

"Yeah, well, this one's already threatening. It's a good thing she's an airhead. The house was all mine before I met her. She hasn't got a legal leg to stand on. Not only that, she's pregnant." He lit a cigarette.

"I thought you told me you were shooting blanks."

"Yup."

"Well, then it ain't your kid."

"You're brilliant, George. No wonder you're a detective with Chicago's finest."

"Fuck you, Murph—" He stopped himself and laughed. "Good old Becky. She's always been a pain in the ass, anyway."

"No loss to you—you never liked her."

"Not much to like, if you don't mind my sayin' so. She didn't like black people—in case you didn't notice. And she treated you like shit. You're a good guy, Murph, but there's something definitely wrong with you."

"Why is everything all my fault?"

"It's your fault you pick women who are bad for you. Why don't you pick someone nice and smart and decent?"

"Like who, for instance?"

"Someone like Lisa."

"Lisa's taken."

"Yeah, but I'm sure as hell you could find someone who doesn't enjoy shitting all over you. Becky was to you what a pigeon is to a fucking sidewalk. And your first marriage was the same way. Buddy, it's morning in America—it's time you smelled the coffee."

Murph smiled and took a deep drag from his cigarette. "Goddamnit, I've got Ann Landers for a roommate." He downed some beer. "What d'you suggest? You want me to hook up with someone like Jenny Richard?"

"Now, there's a thought—why the hell not?"

"You think Becky was a pain—old Jenny Richard would kill me."

"No, she wouldn't. I bet that woman knows something about lovin'."

"Since when are you a big fan of hers?"

"She's smart, Murph—you gotta give her that. And she has morals. I mean, let's face it, Murph, most of the women you hang out with have the morals of yellow dogs in heat. And I'll bet ole Jenny Richard knows how to love a man. Good-lookin', too."

"She's not that good-looking."

"Neither are you, Murph."

"Thanks. She's not my type."

"I know. That's your problem."

Murph held his can of beer out in front of him. "A toast. A quick end to ninety-four. A bad year, if there ever was one." He took a drink. "And how much is half the rent?"

"Four hundred and fifty bucks."

"Four hundred and fifty bucks! Shit!"

"It's the market, baby. Not everybody's grandpa leaves them a house—most people gotta pay rent. Besides, it's a nice place."

"Nice my ass. The walls are made of cardboard. Wall-to-wall carpeting—I hate that shit. Wood floors, that's the way to go. You're going to charge me four hundred and fifty bucks to live in this joint? You're gonna break me."

"You should be grateful. You got a place to stay, and the company's good." George smiled, "Reaaaaal good. A bargain at any price. And look at it this way: You got off cheap—at least you don't have to pay child support."

Murph blew out a perfect smoke ring. "Don't you ever give it a rest?"

"Not me, not ever." George looked straight at his friend. "You gonna be okay?"

"Yeah. I'm a little beat up right now. I'll be okay. I suppose I should hit the sack—work's waiting for me in the morning."

"Yeah, well, work's always there." George played with his can of beer. "You know, sometimes I really hate—" He stopped and looked at Murph. "Oh, shit! I forgot to tell you. I got some news before I left work today. You know that girl, Gloria Santos?"

Murph nodded. "What about her?"

"Well, more bad news—no lucky stars for that baby. Looks like all her family's dead. Parents both died of cancer—one year apart. Brother died in high school—too much cocaine. Found him in a hotel room after he'd been dead a couple of days. Haven't been able to trace down a single relative. Mother was an only child, and her dad—well, seems like he left his family in Mexico. Looks like she's pretty much on her own."

"Not quite. She's got Jenny Richard."

"That where she staying?"

"Didn't I tell you?"

"Well, she could do a lot worse. I'd say having Jenny Richard as an advocate is pretty good going. Maybe she can do something for you?"

"Forget about it, George."

"You want to break the news to her?"

"I'll call her in the morning, then we'll be done with it. We're off the case."

"Did you send her a copy of all the files?"

"Yup."

"Captain wouldn't like that."

"We hate the captain."

"Yup."

"But we're off the case, anyway."

"We're as off as we want to be."

"What's that supposed to mean?"

"It means we can put our two cents in if we want."

"Do we want?"

"We might want."

"Captain wouldn't like that."

"We hate the captain."

"Yes, we do."

Cars

The little girl is walking down the streets of the barrio, everything around her dark and bleak. But the light. The light shines where she walks. He sees her as he sits waiting in his car. It is her, the one he has been waiting for. The one who has been promised. He steps out of the car and waves at her. She waves back. He asks her why she ran away from him. She shrugs.

"Do you like my car?"

She smiles and nods. "My papa doesn't have one."

"Do you like cars?"

"Yes."

"You like this one? It's a nice car—smooth as a magic carpet."

"A magic carpet?" She laughs.

"I'll show you."

As she stepped into the car, Thomas Blacker woke from his dream. "The car," he whispered. The room was lit with sunlight. A nurse smiled at him and gave him a pill. He took it wordlessly. He asked her the time. She told him it was eight-thirty. "You slept well," she said. When she left the room, he picked up the phone and asked for Herald Burns. When he heard his voice on the other end, he took a deep breath. "The car, Herald . . ."

How, If You Wake in the Night

She woke, startled, in the middle of the night. A speechless dream lingered, swam around in her like a lost fish in search of scraps to eat. Her fingers moved through the air, spelled her name, then looked for a place to rest. She wanted to be held like a cup held warm coffee. She felt tears on her face as her fingers moved in the dark. She wiped the tears, then rubbed her wet palms over her neck as if the salt were a potion that could make her seven again. To be seven, to be that young and wake to a room full of sunlight and watch the trees of spring sprouting leaves.

Then she remembered.

There was no Thomas, there was no basement, there was no library full of books that always threatened to fall in on her, crush her. There were no lessons, no mental tests. There was no garden. There was no wall. She was suddenly awake, felt as if she had been sleeping for years, and now, well rested, she was ready to run, to jump, to play. *She was seven.* And wherever she was, it was a playground, it was a church. It had been such a joyless life, and now this. It was a kind of death, she thought, what she was feeling. Still and quiet and timeless, as if she had ceased to exist. It was her pain, that dull pain that she had lived with and embraced— that indelible and immutable sorrow that had become a part of her because she had always been mourning the life that had been taken from her—that awful pain. It was missing. And even if it was missing for just this moment, it was enough. She laughed, then hugged herself. *"Me llamo Gloria Erlinda Santos,"* she said. She had not heard herself speak Spanish since the day she left the barrio, but she had not forgotten how to speak it despite the fact that Thomas had insisted that *that* language was not worthy of her. It was the only language she spoke before she started school. And though she mastered English easily, Spanish had remained the language of her dreams. Thomas could not banish *that* language.

She rose from the bed, turned on the light, looked around the room. It's like Christmas, she thought, and I have received this room as a gift. All that was missing was a tree with lights that twinkled as if they were beating to the tune of a song. She could almost smell her mother's tamales in the room. She had loved the taste of them, something of the taste of her mother's hands in them. Tamales. The memory of the cornmeal in her mouth made her feel warm and hungry. In Thomas's house she had never felt hungry. She ate, she cooked, baked bread—but she had no appetite. Thomas sometimes told her she overseasoned the food when she cooked. All she wanted to do was to taste something.

She stared at the open door. *An open door.*

She touched the oversized cotton T-shirt Jenny had given her to sleep in, soft with wear. She stared at the words written on the shirt in black and pink: SILENCE = DEATH. She was puzzled by the words, and yet she felt she could have written them. She smiled, walked into the kitchen almost expecting to find tamales. She laughed, walked back into the bedroom. She didn't want to go back to sleep. If she went back to sleep, she might find Thomas there, the basement, his garden, the dead leaves of a willow lying at her feet. She wanted to feel this thing, this freedom, if that's what it was. Maybe it was not such a big word.

She picked up a magazine that sat on the desk. She stared at the nearly unclothed young men on the cover, and then smiled at the big stylized letters: ROLLING STONE. She read it slowly—cover to cover, the article on the politics of the environment, the reviews of music and musicians she'd never heard of, the interview with a woman who made sex films for a living—"Queen of Porn"—the advertisements for perfume and clothes with beautiful men and beautiful women who were all so young and confident and dressed in costumes she thought were appealing in a foreign kind of way. They lived in America, she knew, just as she did. But they lived in separate countries, and she wanted to be part of *their* America—it seemed infinitely more interesting than the country Thomas had taught her about. She wondered about these people who posed for this magazine, wondered about the photographers, the publishers. The world in those glossy pages was a world of which she knew nothing. She wanted to know it, wanted to be just like them, feel like them, dress like them, talk like them, understand the world as they understood it. She understood so little. Then she knew: She had never lived—not here—not in this country.

She remembered reading a magazine with glossy pages like this one—just once. She did not remember the name of the magazine, but Thomas had told her it was a magazine best left unread. But *he* read it. She had liked the magazine, but she liked this one better. Everyone seemed so relaxed, so casual, so free in these pages. She saw a dress she liked and decided the first thing she would do when she had her own money would be to buy a dress—soft and comfortable and made of cotton. And she wouldn't wear a bra—just like the woman in the picture. Thomas had always made her wear a bra. "Only prostitutes go braless," he'd said. He'd said it with such disgust. As she thumbed through the magazine, she wondered why Thomas had disliked prostitutes. It was because he knew, she thought, knew that he had turned her into one. A prostitute. That's what she had always felt like when she touched him. And not a dime to show for it. Why did it matter? She and Thomas, what they had been for each other, why didn't it just go away?

She noticed that it was no longer dark outside, the light slowly erasing the night. It was morning. The sun. It seemed as if she'd never seen it. She walked to the window and stared out at the street. She touched the pane of glass, then opened the window. It was cool, almost cold. She shivered, but it didn't matter. Nothing mattered except the morning air, the coming of the day. Light, such a plain and simple thing. And such a simple thing, to open a window—and yet she had never done it. She saw a man running down the street, a dog running beside him. He seemed peaceful, the rhythm of his movements steady and graceful and strong. She could see his breath in the air. She wanted to shout at him, wave at him. "Run!" she wanted to yell. "Run!" She smiled and urged him on in her silence until he disappeared down the street. She stared at the trees that lined the street, lovely and strong and quiet in the silence of the morning, unbothered by the shedding of their leaves. They were not afraid of the coming winter.

She was suddenly tired. And happy. It had been such a long time since she had been happy. She shut the door but did not shut the window. She crawled back into bed, covered herself with a blanket that had no trace of his smell. And slept.

We're Not Even Dating Yet

Jenny looked at her watch as she finished taking notes on her notepad. "Christ," she sighed, a kind of bitter and cynical disgust in her tone, "the whole world's gone to hell." Sometimes her clients disgusted her. She stared at the neat stack of files she had just looked over, then smiled. She ran her fingers through her hair and thought she'd take a shower before Gloria woke up. They'd go to the market, buy some groceries. She'd let Gloria spend the afternoon doing whatever she'd like. She'd give her a map to the city—maybe she'd venture out. Why not? She had to learn. She remembered Gloria's face as she stared down at the world from the top of the John Hancock, the vastness of the entire city in her eyes as if she were looking down at Eden. The view from her office was another matter. All she saw were files of people who inflicted their rage on others—mostly on people they knew. *Be afraid of the people you know,* her mother had warned. As she sat there, she wondered about Gloria, wondered if she would ever find a place in the world. A place that was hers. She had been transplanted by force—but hadn't most of them? By force or otherwise. "You got to grow somewhere, girl. We're like trees." She remembered when she'd been to California. Her cousin who'd moved there told her that the eucalyptus trees had all been brought there from somewhere else. "And look at the way they've taken over. Fragile as hell and no good for lumber—but look at them—everywhere you step they're growing." Maybe Chicago was a place where Gloria could grow. But grow into what?

She got up from where she was sitting, poured herself another cup of coffee, and was startled as she heard someone place a key in the front door. She reached for the phone, then laughed when she heard Charlie call for Bessie. She walked into the living room and found Bessie on her back as Charlie rubbed her belly and repeated, "Such a good girl."

"Actually, she's a very bad girl," Jenny said. "Snored all night—worse than a man."

"Jenny! How's my favorite drama queen? What are you doing at home?"

"You just scared the hell out of me. It's becoming your favorite pastime."

"You're never home during the week."

"Well, today I'm home."

"What's the occasion?"

"I have a guest. I'm taking the morning off."

"A man? In the bedroom?"

"Actually, it's a woman."

"You experimenting?"

Jenny laughed. "Nothing like that, Charlie. She's a client."

"Didn't know you brought your clients home."

"Not generally. It's a long story."

"I'm sure it is. When are you going to bring home a man?"

"Men are evil."

"That's why we're so good."

"You really are a piece of work, Charlie."

"Yup, we both are—that's why we're both still single—though I met someone."

"I hope he's not like the last one."

"Go ahead, rain on my parade." He winked at her, got up from the floor where he knelt next to Bessie, opened the closet door, and took out a collar. The basset jumped all over him and barked. He laughed. "I have that effect on women." He kissed Jenny on the cheek. "We'll be out all morning," he said.

"Going anywhere special?"

"Nah. I have the day off—thought I'd take a walk and take Bessie with me. I get more attention when I'm with her." Just as he was speaking, the phone rang.

"Have a good time," Jenny said as she walked back toward the kitchen. "Be a good girl, Bessie." She picked up the telephone and recognized the voice immediately: "Why the hell aren't you in your office?"

"Good morning to you, too, Lieutenant."

"I've been leaving messages at your office all morning. Ahh, tell him to go to hell," he shouted.

"What?"

"Not you—I was talking to Geor—Detective Johnson."

"How does he put up with you?"

"We get on so well that we've become roommates."

"What happened to the wife?"

"We're not even dating yet, and already you're asking me about the other woman?"

"Very funny," she said. She kept herself from laughing. She reached for her pack of cigarettes on the counter.

"Are you about to light a cigarette?"

"No," she said, pulling her hand away. "Did you just call to annoy me?"

"Actually I called to give you some information—though, if you're annoyed, it somehow makes my day." He waited for her to respond, but she said nothing as she lit her cigarette. He heard the familiar sound of a match over the phone and heard her inhale. He smiled. "Listen," he said softly, "I've got some bad news for our friend, Ms. Santos. Just don't shoot the messenger. Her family. George tells me her folks are dead.

Died a few years back, a year apart. Cancer—both of them."

Jenny bit her lip and placed her cigarette on the ashtray next to the phone book. "What about her brother?"

"He died before the parents. Cocaine. Was still in high school when it happened." He waited for Jenny to say something. "She there with you right now?"

"No, thank God. She's still asleep. Must be exhausted."

They were both quiet for a moment. "Listen," he said, "more bad news. The car—the car that matched the description when Gloria was taken."

"The car in the garage?"

"Yeah, well, it's missing."

"How does a goddamn car disappear?"

"Car thief, the captain said. Just a simple case of car theft."

"You buy that pile of buffalo shit?"

"Hell, no, I don't buy it. Car sits for over twenty years, then all of a sudden, just when it's going to be picked up as evidence—bingo!—it disappears."

"Oh, shit!" Jenny said.

"Oh, shit is right."

"No, I mean, Oh, shit."

"What?"

"Gloria told me something last night—his journals. She said he kept journals, wrote in them all the time."

"Well, he must have quite a collection."

"You think we can get our hands on them before they wind up in the same place as the car?"

"I'm on it."

"Just don't steal them."

"I don't do stuff like that."

"Yeah? And I'm a virgin."

"Me, too. I regain it every time I lose a wife." He laughed. "I'm an honest cop, Jennifer."

"It's not Jennifer, it's Genevieve, Alexander."

"Alexander? Are you flirting with me?"

"I'd rather kiss a flea. Just get those journals."

"We're on it."

"I'm counting on you."

"Really?"

"Don't get too flattered, Lieutenant, I don't have too many choices."

"Are you smiling?" he asked.

"I don't smile in the morning," she said, then hung up the phone.

Orphaned in Eden

"Sleep well?"

Gloria stood in the doorway between the kitchen and the hallway and stretched out her arms as far as she could. "I could almost fly," she said.

"Coffee?"

"Sounds wonderful." She walked to the coffeepot and poured herself a cup, then looked around the room. "Where's Bessie?"

"She's out for the morning. Charlie, my neighbor—he's crazy about her. Takes her out for a walk every day."

"That's nice of him."

"Well, he's a very nice man."

"Friends," she said as if the word was something she had just discovered. She sat down at the table and stared at the files.

"Let me move those for you," Jenny said, reaching for the pile of manila folders.

"You work a lot, don't you?"

"I don't mind."

"I'd love to have a job. Any job. I've never had one."

Jenny nodded. "You'll find something." Jenny tried to sound enthusiastic, though she wasn't at all sure it was a good idea. There would be plenty of time to worry about money and a career.

Gloria placed her hands around her coffee mug. "I don't have a degree."

"Degrees don't mean shit."

"*You* have a degree. So does Thomas. I never even went to high school."

"High school was a bore. And the boys were lousy lays."

"I would have liked to have been bored in any high school. I don't know what a lay is, but I'm sure I would have loved that, too."

"A lay is when you sleep with someone."

"Of course," she said, then smiled. "I would have loved a lousy lay."

"You wouldn't have. You would have stayed a virgin—I can tell. You would've been a nice girl—and all the other girls would have hated you."

"It would have been nice to be hated by silly, jealous girls." Gloria laughed, then looked at her. "Jenny, how old are you?"

"Forty-five."

"You seem younger."

"I don't feel younger. I'm going through menopause."

"Menopause?"

"Thomas didn't tell you?"

"Is it painful?"

Jenny laughed. "It only hurts my vanity. I don't miss having a period. I always hated it, anyway. It was so—well, messy." She made a face.

Gloria shrugged. "It's just a little blood."

"Well, good riddance to that little blood." Jenny looked at her hands. "I'm getting older, that's all. I'm a little young, the doctor said, but it happens. Anyway, I'm not worried about it."

Gloria stared into Jenny's face. "You don't even seem to have many regrets."

"Oh, honey, I have a long list of regrets. But what's done is done. You know, the first time I was with a man—well, he was a boy, really—the first time, I felt bad. I'd lost my virginity. It was supposed to be such a sacred thing. But you know something, it didn't matter. I let go of feeling bad, just let it go. I'm not going to live my life feeling bad because I made mistakes." She fought the urge to lecture her. Gloria's regrets were nothing like her own. She had nothing to teach her. They were quiet for a while, both of them staring into their coffee mugs as if they could fish out the word *regret* from them.

Gloria looked up and took a deep breath. "I owed him everything. Not that he put it that way—he had more finesse than that. He paid a lot of money for those dresses he liked to buy for me. Sometimes he left the price tags on them—by mistake."

"You know something? If I were you, I'd take Thomas Blacker to the cleaners—milk that bastard for all he's worth. He's loaded. You've got a great civil suit on your hands."

"What I have is blood on my hands." She shook her head. "You really think there's such a thing as compensation for being someone's possession for twenty-three years?"

"You should have *something*."

"I *do* have something," she said. "I just don't know what it is."

"Think about it, honey—just think about it."

"You sound like my mother. Don't mother me, Jenny—I already have a—" Gloria noticed the look on Jenny's face at the mention of her mother. She understood what that look meant, what her silent eyes were saying. They stared at each other for a few moments, searching each other's faces.

"I'm sorry," Jenny said. She looked into Gloria's dark, expectant eyes—so dark they were almost blue. "The lieutenant called this morning—" She got up from her chair and poured herself another cup of coffee. "I didn't offer you another—"

"How long have they been dead?" Gloria's voice was hollow and numb.

"Your brother died when he was in high school. And your parents—" She made herself stare into Gloria's eyes. "Your parents died a few years ago. Cancer—both of them."

Gloria's lips were firm, her face absent of pain—as hard as the trunk of an oak. "It doesn't matter."

"That isn't true." Jenny reached for her hand. Gloria moved away from the table and walked out of the kitchen. Jenny followed her but stopped.

She heard the door to Gloria's room shut, heard the click of the lock.

"Shit," Jenny whispered, "shit, shit, shit. Damnit, this won't help."

So it was gone now. Everything she'd dreamed about. A mother, a father, a brother. El Paso. A sun that rose. All of it. Even Thomas was gone. *He wasn't even man enough to give me a child.* She grabbed the bedspread with a fist and yanked it off the bed. She sat on the floor and pulled at her hair. *Tear it out, Thomas. Tear it all out.* She put herself away like an unwanted dress in the deepest part of the closet. She refused to unlock the door. She was used to locked doors, something about their refusal to open made her feel secure. No one could get at her when the door was locked. Not even Thomas. She had learned to be a room that not even *he* could enter.

She could hear Jenny's voice through the door. "Please, you don't have to go through this alone. Not anymore." Her voice was muffled, had no power, spoke no truths. It was as far and distant as the leaves. Just something the wind would blow away.

◆ ◆ ◆

After so many years of being alone, Jenny sensed Gloria had learned how to find a private comfort. And anyway, she thought, Gloria was entitled to be alone; to push others away, *to push her away,* to win this small battle, though Jenny was not convinced the battle was worth fighting. *I am not the enemy.* But it was not up to her to measure or judge the battles Gloria needed to wage. She left her alone.

A little while after lunch, she left Gloria a note on the table:

GLORIA,

> *Had to go into work. I'll probably be back around 7:00 or so (though it could be later). I'm leaving you some keys to the house—in case you'd like to go out. (The big one is for the dead bolt—sometimes it sticks.) If you go out the door and take a right, you'll literally run into the lake. If you take a left, then you'll hit*

Broadway—lots of stuff to see. If you walk down a bit, there's a movie house—a movie would do you good. Here's some money in case you need anything. Look, honey, things can't get much worse. You'll get through this—you'll get through this just fine.

JENNY

P.S. Eat something. And if it's any consolation, I know what it's like to lose a set of parents. The day I buried my mother—that was the day I understood the word orphan. If only I didn't have a heart—that's what I thought.

She left two twenty-dollar bills and the keys on the kitchen table next to the note. As she walked out the door, it occurred to Jenny that she felt guilty for leaving Gloria at home, felt guilty for not being able to offer her comfort—though she knew there was no comfort. *Maybe she'll need me.* She shook her head. *I can't feel bad about this. She's not a child.* She would try not to act like a parent. She hated worrying.

◆ ◆ ◆

Gloria heard Jenny as she left the apartment. She felt paralyzed, unable to move, as if the parts of her that could move had turned to solid granite. She was a headstone announcing the names of the dead. She remembered she felt exactly like this when Thomas had taken her to her new bedroom in his house. She remembered that day more clearly than she remembered her own room, her own mother's face, her own brother's voice. A part of her had refused to forget, had kept them locked in herself, had refused to accept that she would never see them again. Her father, her mother, her brother. They had ceased to exist. The word *family* had disappeared, and yet there had been shards of them left in her that cut her like broken glass. Their memory was a hurt, but that hurt had been the only thing in her days that resembled hope. That hope had been a gift that had held her together, that had kept her from falling apart. That hope had given her a form.

She remembered that awful day when she entered her new room in a strange and lonely place, a place devoid of her father's cigarette smoke, devoid of her brother's voice as he read a book aloud because he had not yet mastered the art of reading to himself, devoid of the smell of her mother's sweat as she rolled out flour tortillas with a rolling pin as worn as her hands. She had once lived in a familiar house, a house full of smells and voices, a house where every room had a window you could open and listen to the sounds of the day, the sounds of the living, the sounds of the night. She had never been afraid in that house. But then she had just been a little girl—and now she was a woman. Now, after the passing of so many years, she found herself in another strange and lonely room that she could not locate on a map. This was not the house that had been in her dreams. The house in her dreams was small, and everyone was accustomed to each other's smell, addicted to each other's touch. She was lost. Again. She had grown numb. A piece of ice. Unmeltable. "What does it matter?" she whispered. "It does not even matter."

◆ ◆ ◆

But didn't she still have Thomas? He had not died. He had not abandoned her. Maybe he had gone back home. Maybe she would go back to him. He would forgive her. There was a place for her there. She reached to finger her gold chain. It was gone. Where had she lost it? She tried to remember. How could she have lost it? How could she have been so careless? *No, my chain. I've lost it.* She jerked herself out of bed, walked to the closet, stared at the black dress, touched it. She could smell him. She took off her robe, let it drop to the floor. She took the dress from the hanger and stepped into it. She looked at herself in the mirror and tried to see herself through Thomas's eyes.

The house was quiet. She walked into the kitchen and read the note Jenny had left. She looked at the keys, the money she had left. She could take the money. She would go back. But Jenny had been so kind. It would be wrong to take her money. She was lost, did not know what to do. She closed her eyes, then opened them. She walked away from the money and the keys and returned to her room. She threw herself on the bed and traced Thomas's address in the air with her finger. She had seen it on his mail a thousand times. She traced it and traced it and traced it.

Then traced his phone number. She had not forgotten. She smiled. She had lost the gold chain, but she had not lost her memory.

◆ ◆ ◆

Jenny found the note exactly as she had left it, the two twenty-dollar bills and the keys, untouched. She thought she would drag Gloria out of her room, but then decided to leave her alone—what could it hurt? The next morning she banged on the door. She heard nothing. She decided she would break the door down, afraid that Gloria had hurt herself.

"If you don't open this door, I'll break it down, goddamnit!" Finally, a muffled voice came from the other side of the door. "I'm tired. I need to rest." Jenny was relieved to hear Gloria's voice. She was fine. She had not hurt herself. Good, she's breathing. "I want you to eat," she said.

"I'm not hungry."

"Don't make me act like a crazed woman," she said. "I'm going through menopause, and I can get downright scary."

"I'm not hungry," Gloria said again.

"Do you know what menopause is?"

"Yes. You told me."

Well, she's talking anyway. She did not see Gloria for three days (though she spoke to her through the door, the conversations consisting of pleadings and two- or three-word answers). When she left for work, Jenny would leave a pitcher of water and some bread and cheese, and every evening, when Jenny returned home, the empty plate would be sitting on the kitchen counter along with the pitcher—empty of water.

The Smell of Coffee

When Gloria at last emerged from her bedroom, she looked tired and tormented, not at all like the controlled, poised woman Jenny had first met in the interview room at the Cook County Jail. "You're home," she said, her voice dry as sand.

"It's Saturday," Jenny said. "You look awful."

"Do I?"

"Take a shower. And then I'm going to feed you."

Gloria nodded. "I feel like going back to bed."

"The hell you are," Jenny said. "We're going out this afternoon."

"I don't want to go anywhere."

"You can't do this. You're not dead."

"I want to die." Her voice cracked.

"Don't say that."

"I don't feel alive."

"Pretend."

"That's all I know how to do."

Jenny placed her hand over her mouth. "I'm sorry. I'm sorry I said that. I don't know what to say."

"It's better not to talk."

"That's not true, Gloria. It's time to wake up, honey. No more sleeping. Sleep won't take away the pain."

◆ ◆ ◆

After twenty minutes, Jenny walked into the bathroom. "Are you drowning yourself?" she yelled.

"I'm trying to wake myself up. I'm just taking your advice."

"Soup's ready." She walked back to the kitchen and stirred the canned tomato soup she'd warmed in a pan. She put some cheese and crackers on a plate. She stared at her arrangement and laughed. "Who the shit cares, anyway?" She placed a bowl on the table and a soup spoon beside it. She turned around and smiled at Gloria, who stood in the doorway to the kitchen. Her long hair was still wet, and she was wearing the robe Jenny had given her. "Hungry?"

"A little."

"Sit." Jenny served her a bowl of soup as she sat at the table. "It's not exactly homemade."

"It's okay." Gloria put a spoonful in her mouth. If the soup was too hot, there was no sign of it on her face. "It's good." She finished her soup quickly, then reached for a cracker, then another, then another.

"More?" Jenny asked.

"You're watching me."

"Well, I'd rather talk than watch, but you don't seem very talkative."

"What would you like to talk about?"

"How about a therapist?"

Gloria smiled. "Did you have that line rehearsed?"

"No, not exactly—"

"When Thomas was angry, he told me I was insane. You think so, too?"

"No. You're in a bad space, that's all. You're a—" she paused looking for the right word. "You're a survivor, honey—"

"That kind of talk is a little inappropriate, don't you think?" There was a hard stubbornness in the tone of her voice. "I wasn't in a concentration camp."

"How many people have to be in a room before it's called a concentration camp?"

"It wasn't like that."

"Maybe not. Just because you were well fed didn't make you any less of a prisoner. What could it hurt to talk to someone?"

"I can't talk to a stranger."

"You know how to read people."

"As if they were books." There was something bitter in her voice.

"Don't beat up on yourself."

"I'll go." Gloria's voice was stiff as a dead branch. "But I don't want to talk about this anymore."

"What *do* you want, Gloria?"

"I want to be a little girl. I want to be in El Paso and be seven and have a brother and a mother and a father. I want to taste my mother's cooking, and sit on my father's lap and he can call me *angelita*. That's what I want. But I can't have that, can I?" She bent the soup spoon she was holding in her hand. She bit her lip.

Jenny took the bent spoon out of her clenched fist, then placed a hand on her cheek. "See, you can talk just fine."

◆ ◆ ◆

The air was crisp, the last leaves floating to the ground like feathers as the two women walked toward Broadway. They spoke of small things, no hurry in their pace, no worry in their movements. They walked as if they were afraid of losing each other on the street. The darker woman constantly pointed at things as a child would point at something curious and rare. Her companion was happy to explain, to answer questions, her hands moving in the air almost as if she were trying to catch the leaves. They smiled and laughed. They could have been girls in the sunlight wearing sweaters their mothers had bought for them. They could have been girls—except something in their eyes made them both look much older—much older even than their faces.

◆ ◆ ◆

"Treasure Island?" Gloria said pointing at the sign. "It's the name of a book Thomas once gave me to read."

"Well, in this neighborhood, it's where we get our food."

Gloria took a deep breath as they walked into the store. "God, it smells good in here."

"It smells like rotting vegetables, if you ask me." Jenny reached for a cart. "Didn't make a list. We'll just go aisle by aisle."

As they reached the produce section, Gloria began touching all the tomatoes—not feeling them to see which were too ripe or which were too firm—just feeling them. "They're beautiful, Jenny."

Jenny handed her a plastic bag. "Pick a few?"

Gloria nodded as she searched for the best tomatoes. Jenny smiled. She was used to being all business when she zoomed through the grocery store—shopping for food was not one of her favorite things to do. She fought her impatience and decided to let Gloria enjoy herself as she examined the fruits and vegetables. She seemed to know exactly what everything was—and yet she touched everything as if it were something exotic. "Jicama!" she yelled as she picked up what looked like an oversized potato.

"What the hell is that?"

"It's a root. It's great with lime and paprika."

"You sure know a lot for someone who hasn't been out much."

"I know my foods." She searched the store and stared at everything as if she were in a church full of masterpieces. "I smell coffee."

"The coffee's way the hell the other side of the store."

"I can smell it. Where is it?" Her voice sounded like it belonged to a little girl asking if she could open a present. But even as her eyes pleaded, her face remained calm and distant.

How does she do that? Jenny shrugged. "Just follow me."

As they reached the coffee aisle, Gloria walked up to one of the canisters, pulled one of the drawers, and let a handful of coffee beans fall into her cupped hands. She brought them toward her face and stuck her nose into the beans. She breathed them in like Jenny inhaled her cigarettes.

Jenny watched her in awe. Who was this woman? This strange and lovely woman.

Sanctuary

Charlie looked at himself carefully as he finished shaving. The swelling had gone down, his face almost normal, his boyishness beginning to reappear. He thought of Jenny, what she had said to him: *You can teach them not to fuck with you.* "How do you do that, Jenny?" He loved her for her fight, something so innocent and decent about the way she lived her life. What she had was hard to come by in this town, he thought. She was tough enough to hold on to her integrity. He was not as tough as she was—and not as innocent, either.

He put on his shirt, tried not to think of the feel of the fist on his face. *Not the first time it had happened.* When he was a senior in high school—that was the first time. That small town in southern Illinois had known him all his life, had known what he was—its sons had no use for him. Walking home from school, the boys had taunted him, beat him, taped pictures of naked women to his clothes to remind him of the correct objects of desire. They had followed him, made sure his parents would see what they had done. He had finished high school in silence, never speaking to anyone. No one speaking to him. The night of his graduation, he packed his bags and moved to Chicago. His mother sent him away with a blessing: "It will be safer there," she said, "for you." He had understood perfectly what she had meant.

He never looked back, never visited. Chicago became his haven, provided him a place where he could live without the tauntings, without the voices that whispered his name. Chicago was too big to whisper—that is what he loved about the city. It was too big to care who he slept with, who he loved, where he went. Too big to care. At least that's what he'd thought. He laughed as he looked at himself in the mirror. He looked every inch the country boy. He had toyed with the idea of starting his own farm. His grandfather had been a farmer—and the happiest days of his boyhood had been spent working at his side. But the country and its people had not loved him, and they had banished him from their piece of earth. The city had taken him in, had become the closest thing to paradise he would ever know. He felt the cut above his eye. There would be a scar.

He had never understood why he was so hated. At first he had hated in return, but that hate slowly went away—though fragments of that hate remained. When he had come to Chicago, he had met others who were hated. Over time, he and his friends had formed themselves into something that resembled a secret society of soldiers. The only real goal of their ragged army was to help one another survive the wars of the city. The endless wars of the city. "Some paradise, huh, Charlie?"

Something about his attacker bothered him, but the whole matter was unclear to him. He had had too much to drink, and he had been exhausted from lack of sleep. It was impossible to tell what had really happened. But he had a feeling that one of the men had been trying to convey a message to him. If only he could remember. All he remembered was the sound of the voice, that strange thing he said about lawyers—and did he ask him to tell someone something? He shook his head. It was no use to think about it. Just another hate crime that would go unpunished. He had lived. He was fine. He promised himself he would be more careful. He would warn his brothers yet again to be careful, to watch where they walked. They would all stay on guard. Ever-vigilant sentries. Survival did not come easy.

◆ ◆ ◆

He walked to the coffee shop, opened the book Jenny had lent him. She was always lending him books, telling him to read this or that. They would talk about them, talk about everything. In a way, they had become each other's teachers, each of them filling in the blank spaces of the other. They had become like brother and sister. They had both been transplanted, migratory birds in search of a sanctuary.

They had argued once, had not spoken for weeks. Then one day she had shown up at his door. "Forgive me," she said. It had been difficult for her to say the words. In the end, perhaps they had not found their sanctuary. Or perhaps they had abandoned their futile search for a perfect place. What they had found, instead, was each other. What they had found was a fierce loyalty, a sense that, between them, there would never be any betrayals. She was home, he thought. A good place.

As he drank his coffee, he tried to relax. He had the feeling that there was something unfinished—it was nothing. He shrugged, shut the book. Today, it was hard to concentrate. As he sat there, a waiter walked over to his table. "Your name Charlie?" he asked.

"Yes," he said as he looked up at him. Nice-looking, he thought.

"A man asked me to give you this." He handed him a note.

"What man?"

The waiter looked toward the other end of the coffee shop. "That man over—" He shrugged. "He must've left. He was sitting over there. Anyway, he said to give this to Charlie—and he pointed at you."

Charlie held on to the note. "What did he look like?"

"Old man," he said. "Too old for you, anyway." He smiled at Charlie and walked away.

Charlie stared at the note, then opened it. He stared at the letters:

Did you give her the message?

That was all it said. He shook his head. Sick joke, he thought. He had no idea what it meant, though he had an uneasy feeling at the pit of his stomach. He placed the note in the book and walked out of the coffee shop.

In a Room at the Contagious Hospital

"Well, Thomas, you're doing just fine. I'd say you can go back home in a few days."

"A few days, Henry?"

The doctor made a few notes on the chart attached to the clipboard he was holding. His freckled hands had turned to leather. His bedside manner was distant, though he was friendlier with Thomas than he was with his other patients. He'd known him for nearly thirty years, had attended his wedding, had watched him grow old, had taken care of his health, had told him he was dying. Both of them had been young and ambitious and had superb careers—the best in their fields. Both of them had lost their wives. "Soon, maybe by the middle of the week—if nothing changes."

"What day is today?"

"Saturday."

"I've lost track of time."

"Time, Thomas?" The doctor sneered. "What's time?"

"It's what I have so little of."

"There's enough," he said as if the matter of his cancer were a small detail. "But the wound is healing nicely. Amazing really."

"It will never heal."

"Oh, but it will."

"There'll be a scar. I'll feel it."

"What's a scar to men of our age? What's a little scar?"

185

"And the cancer, Henry?"

Henry looked at Thomas, almost severely. He hated the subject of the cancer. Cancer had made his career. He had made a great deal of money on it. As he watched his friend lying on those beds he hated, the irony was not lost on him. "I wish there was something I could do."

"But there isn't," Thomas said, almost as if he had lost interest in their conversation.

"Well, at least they have her in custody."

"Who?"

"The woman who put you here."

"I don't want to talk about it."

Henry nodded. "Well, we'll have you back home in no time."

An empty house, Thomas thought. Claudia would not be there. "Home," he muttered.

"You know, Thomas, you can stay with me. Kids are gone. It's a big house. Don't know why I kept it, really. And I have a good housekeeper. We'll get a good nurse. I insist."

Thomas shook his head. He was grateful for the offer, but his house, no matter how empty, was better than dying in a strange place. To die in a place like that would be no better than dying homeless, no better than dying in the Philadelphia slum where his father had taken his last breath. His house, even without Claudia, was home. He reached for his plastic cup of water and took a sip. "I'm so dry," he said. "If we're nothing but water, why is my mouth so dry? It can't mean anything good. My wife died here—at Mercy. Denise had a thing for Catholic hospitals. I was raised Catholic, did you know? But the Episcopal church had so much more dignity." He drank. "Can you help me up?" he asked. "I'd like to walk around. I've been told I have a view of the lake."

Henry helped his old friend up from the bed. Tired as Thomas looked, he was awed by his strength. He was recovering remarkably—at least physically. He wasn't sure about his mental state. It was hard to tell. Thomas had always been such an enigma. "Take it easy, Thomas. Just go easy."

"I'll be fine." Thomas stood up, then slowly shuffled his way to the

window. "It's a lovely day," he said. "But already the trees are almost bare."
He looked out at the lake. It might have been an ocean. To drown in.

The Water Is Cold

Gloria sat on the quiet beach and watched her toes as they
wiggled in the sand. It was too cold to go barefoot, but she had never
been on a beach and the sand was soft. Her feet were getting cold. She
reached for her socks, put them back on, then rubbed her feet. She
looked up at the sky, at the birds. She didn't know anything about birds,
didn't know any of their names. She watched Jenny as she walked near
the water. She looked so graceful and natural as she walked along, the
basset hound trailing her and barking. Even from this distance, she could
hear Jenny's laugh. She was born to laugh. She understood something
about living. *A survivor. Is that what I am? So is she.*

Two men jogged by, and as they passed, they said something to her.
Jenny laughed and said something back. She knew the world, knew how
to talk to it, knew how to talk to its people. Gloria was too far away to
hear what they said to her, but it seemed that everyone in the world was
compelled to say something to Jenny Richard, to be a part of her in the
same way that she was a part of everything around her. She was a part of
the neighborhood, she was a part of the grocery store, she was a part of
the lake, a part of the sky. Everywhere she went, she belonged. Gloria
waved at her, and wanted to yell her name: *Jenny, Jenny, Jenny!* She waited
for her to wave back. She saw her hand go up in the distance. "Come
on!" she yelled. "Stick your feet in the water."

She took off her socks again, placed them in the tennis shoes Jenny
had lent her, and walked toward the place where the lake met the shore,
the place where Jenny was standing. When her feet touched the water,
she backed away from it. "It's cold."

"Of course it's cold. It's cold even in the summer."

"I didn't know it would be this cold."

"It's in novels, you know, the coldness of water in lakes."

"I'm sure it is, but my feet didn't know that until now."

"Just walk a little while. You'll get used to it. You can get nice and chilled."

Gloria edged toward the water again. After a while, the icy water felt good, almost painful. It wasn't such a bad thing to feel, not a bad thing at all. She wanted to dive in the water. She wanted her whole body to feel what her feet felt. She smiled to herself.

"What are you thinking?" Jenny asked.

"Nothing, really. The water feels good."

"You look like you're feeling better."

"It was the homemade soup."

Jenny laughed.

Gloria hugged herself. "It's getting chilly." She looked up at the sky. "I've been feeling so—I don't know. I don't feel alone—not right now. The sky. The water. The sand." She reached for Jenny's hand and squeezed it. "Thank you."

"I should be thanking you."

"Me?"

"Yes. I've been lost in my work for a long time. It took us less than ten minutes to walk here. And I haven't been here in over a year. You haven't had a life for twenty-three years. But that's not your fault. What's my excuse?"

"At least you've been helping people."

"Not as many as you think."

"Me," she said. "You've helped me."

Jenny smiled. "I have two bedrooms. I gave you the one I don't use—that's not so generous."

Gloria said nothing, then squeezed her hand again.

Jenny looked around for Bessie, then laughed as she saw her dog in the distance jumping in and out of the water. "I better go get her," she said.

Gloria watched her as she moved calmly away, no hurry in her walk. *I have two bedrooms. I gave you the one I don't use.* It struck her that Thomas Blacker did not have any of Jenny Richard's virtues—was incapable of even acquiring them. He, with his big and empty house. Jenny with only an apartment. Houses—spaces for the living—they were such strange things. In the place where she had lived before Thomas, every room had been small. Each room big enough for a bed, a chest of drawers, and a small space at the foot of the bed to pace—or place a chair. Two bedrooms, a bathroom, a kitchen, and a living room where her brother slept and studied. She did not remember feeling crowded, needing space. Only that everything felt close and intimate, every inch of the house and everything in it as familiar as her own fingers. There had been no secrets in that house. No use for them. And Thomas—Thomas had a painting of the sea, blue and restless as his eyes. It was in a living room he rarely used. It was as if the room existed as a space for the painting. He walked through it every evening to reach the library. He read in the den, cooked in a large kitchen. A dining room, an entryway, stairs, four bedrooms, each one large and sunny, three of them fully furnished with antiques— and never used. Always clean—she had seen to that. He used to watch her as she cleaned. She always left everything as immaculate as his garden. His room overlooked the backyard so he could step out on his veranda and view what he had grown. But the house had never been warm enough. So much art, paintings on walls framed in heavy woods. No frames in the house where she was raised. No paintings on canvas. No stairways.

And his wine cellar. Row after dusty row of bottles. Her room. Far away from the light of the rest of his large and hollow house. He was a stingy man, she thought. Jenny was not stingy. She did not have the same sense of space that Thomas treasured. Houses, she thought. But at that moment, she preferred this place to any house. The cold air, the blue of the water, the soft sand on her feet. They seemed such simple and clear things. Not at all complicated—not at all like people's houses. She looked out at the lake and noticed the leaves floating on the water. Hundreds of leaves on the water. They did not care where the currents of the lake would take them. They would go. They understood the cycles, their purpose. She thought it would be a great thing to be a leaf.

House Call

Jenny watched Gloria as she stood over the stove and added some red pepper flakes to the sauce she was making. "Well, all I can say is this apartment never smelled this good. Maybe you should open a restaurant. All we need's the capital. I still think you should sue the pants off Thomas Blacker. I really do."

Gloria nodded good-naturedly but ignored Jenny's remark. "I'd rather go to school than sue. You think they'll let me into college?"

"Why not? All you have to do is take a high school equivalency exam."

"Will that get me into a good school?"

"That's Thomas talking. He was a snob—don't you understand that?"

Gloria looked as if she were about to say something, then smiled. "Let's eat. I'm starving." She stared at the table: bread, pasta, chicken, tomato sauce, salad.

"Gloria, we have enough food for four."

"Guess I went crazy. I'm a little hungry."

"Very hungry, I'd say." Jenny rolled her eyes. She fought the urge to argue with Gloria about the man who'd kept her under lock and key. The doorbell rang, disturbing her train of thought. Bessie ran to the door and barked at it. "Maybe that's Charlie," she said. "He comes by a lot." She walked toward the front door. "Bessie, be quiet—it's embarrassing." Her words had a magical effect, and the dog immediately stopped barking—though her tail kept wagging and she kept leaping. Jenny looked through the peephole. "What in the hell is *he* doing here?" She unbolted the door and stared at Alexander Murphy as he stood in the hallway holding a cardboard box. "Are you lost, Lieutenant?"

"No," he said smiling, "I think I know exactly where I am."

She looked at the box he was carrying. "Come bearing gifts?"

"You bet. My mother taught me never to visit anyone empty-handed. She was third-generation Irish—could never refrain from immigrant behavior."

Jenny laughed. "I suppose I'm forced to let you into my home." She stepped aside and let him in. He immediately saw Bessie, plunked down the box, and began petting her. Predictably, the dog rolled over on her back. "Good girl," he said. He looked up at Jenny. "I used to have a basset hound. Got her when I was six—she died when I was a senior in high school. Saddest day of my life." He rubbed the dog's belly, then forced himself to stand up again as he moaned. He placed his hand on his back. "I'm not as young as I used to be."

Jenny rolled her eyes and laughed. "You sure can put on a show, Lieutenant. To what do we owe the unexpected pleasure of your company?"

"Just came by to drop off the professor's journals. Drop them back off to me on Monday. And I made a notarized copy of them—in the box, too. The copies you can keep. You just might need them." He noticed Gloria as she entered the room. He stopped talking and smiled at her. "Looks like Ms. Richard is taking good care of you," he said. If he'd have been wearing a hat, he'd have tipped it. He felt awkward and stupid, and waited for her to say something, but she just stood there looking at him. He could feel himself turning red. He wished Jenny would say something, but she seemed to be enjoying watching him as he stood there looking like a guy who had shown up for a date a day early. Women always made him feel so uncomfortable. George had told him it was because deep inside he just didn't like women very much. If anything, it was the opposite—he cared too much what they thought about him. He cared too much what everyone thought about him. Maybe that's why he liked playing cop—when he played cop, he didn't have to care what anyone thought.

Finally, Gloria smiled slightly. She moved toward the box and its contents, walked toward it as if Lieutenant Murphy had disappeared. She opened the untaped flaps and looked at the journals. She recognized them immediately. It was almost a relief to see them. She picked one up, felt it in her hands as if it had once belonged to her, and was glad it had returned. They still smell like him, she thought. She remembered the last time she had seen him writing in his journal. "What do you write in them?" she had asked him. "They're all about you, my dear." He had smiled at her. She kept rubbing the leather cover as if it were a magic lamp. "Beautiful," she said, then dropped the journal back into the box.

Jenny and Murph couldn't help but follow her movements with their eyes. They said nothing.

Gloria looked at them. "Did you have to bring them here, Lieutenant?"

"I'm sorry," he said.

"They don't belong to us," Gloria said almost inaudibly.

"I'm sorry," Murph repeated, "I shouldn't have come." He took the photocopies from the box. He looked at Jenny. "Where do you want me to put these?" He looked at Gloria. "No one has to read these—" Then he looked at Jenny. "But someone should have an extra copy. In case the originals get lost."

Jenny pointed at the coffee table. "Put them there, for now. I'll put them away later."

He placed three stacks of copy paper on the table. "The professor wrote a lot," he said. "Look, I'm sorry. Just wanted to—I think I should go."

"We're about to have dinner," Jenny said. She was moved by his awkwardness, felt sorry for him. There was something raw and vulnerable about him this evening, and she found his lack of grace appealing.

He shook his head.

"We've got plenty of food."

"No, thanks," he said as he opened the door to leave. He bent down a little and scratched Bessie behind her ears. "Good girl," he said. He grinned at Gloria and Jenny, then shut the door behind him.

◆ ◆ ◆

"I'm sorry," Gloria said, "I didn't behave very well, did I?"

"It doesn't matter."

"And then I—I don't know. When I was with Thomas, I learned to measure everything I said. How do I measure what I say with people like you—and *him*?"

"You measured because you were measured."

"I don't know how to stop." She shrugged. "I have a confession to make. I wanted to hit the lieutenant when he brought in those journals."

"I absolve you of your sin."

"Was it a sin?"

"Yes. You wanted to hit the wrong guy. For your penance I'm going to make you read Thomas's journals." Jenny smiled. "You'll hate him if you do. Gloria, you just don't hate him enough."

"Why do I need to hate him?"

◆ ◆ ◆

Jenny rinsed the last of the dishes as Gloria dried them. They spoke of small things, the way their mothers laughed. "Mine laughed like a chimpanzee in heat," Jenny said.

"Mine laughed like the rain falling on the desert," Gloria said. Jenny could see a hint of nostalgia in her eyes, as if she was beginning to teach herself to relax the muscles in her face. They spoke of dreams they remembered when they were children, the trees they loved.

"I loved the tulip tree," Jenny said. "The flowers smelled like the armpits of angels."

Gloria laughed. "I loved the cottonwood," she said. "In the summer, the light cotton floated to the ground and my brother and I would chase them." It was odd that they felt so close, these two women who were as different as the trees they loved, as different as their mothers' laughs. "I would go insane without you right now," Gloria thought, but she did not say it. She did not know how to say it. It's nice not to live alone, Jenny thought. I have lived alone for too long.

Crime in the City

As Charlie walked out of the bar, he looked around the street. Since his attack, he'd felt a little uneasy, suspicious, only felt safe when he walked on major streets. He thought of the note the waiter had handed him. He was beginning to think the note and his beating were somehow connected. He had forgotten to tell Jenny. He wondered where he'd put the note, was always losing things. In the book, he thought, he'd left it in the book he had been reading. Tomorrow he would show the note to Jenny, ask her what she thought. He pulled himself out of the world of his thoughts. Pay attention, he said to himself. He turned the corner. No one on the street but him. He had this feeling, thought he heard footsteps, was too afraid to look back. He kept walking, had the urge to run. He calmed himself. He didn't have far to walk—still, he felt something. Something wasn't right. He walked faster. Too many dark patches on this street, he thought. He felt calmer as he reached a streetlight. But the street was so empty. Then he heard the footsteps behind him. He stopped, then began to turn his head—"Freeze, faggot!" The voice was in his head—it was all in his—"Keep your eyes in front of you, faggot! You know the meaning of the word *freeze*? Huh, faggot?" He felt the man's arm around his throat—from behind, the hot breath at his neck. "If I squeeze, you'll be dead. One less of your kind in the world." Charlie stood perfectly still, his heart thumping, the sound of it like an open palm pounding a hollow drum. "Just listen," the voice said, the arm tightening around his neck. He noticed the hand. The left hand. The scars, the patches of discolored skin. Just like the first time. Only this time he wasn't drunk. He was sure of what he was seeing. He tried not to panic as he heard the man's voice. "I've been watching you, faggot. You got friends—they're not good for you. Tell 'em they've been bad." The man laughed, spun him around, then kneed him between his legs. As Charlie fell over, he heard the man laughing, the sound of his voice mixing with the pain shooting through his body. He heard the voice near his ear, spit falling on his face. "That one was for the bitch lawyer." He felt the man pull him up by his hair, then felt a fist across his face. "That one was for Gloria Santos." As he lay on the ground, he felt numb, wondered if he wasn't dreaming. The man's voice did not seem real, like something from one of his boyhood nightmares. But the pain—that was real. He felt a kick against his ribs. "That one was for you, faggot. That one was just for you." Where were the lights, he wondered. He could see nothing—the blackness of the night all around him.

Poor, Sweet Charlie

"I'll do the dishes," Jenny said.

"I'll help."

"Why don't you rest?" She looked at Jenny as she heard the doorbell ring. "You get a lot of visitors."

"I never get visitors."

Gloria followed Jenny to the door. As the doorbell rang again, Jenny heard a pounding at the door. "It's me, Jenny, it's Charlie." Bessie barked at the sound of his voice, then ran to the door.

"Charlie!" she said, a lilt in her voice, as she opened the door. She stared at her bloodied friend as he leaned on the door. "Oh, my God," she whispered. "Charlie, what have they done to you?" She reached to help him.

"Easy," he said.

"Where does it hurt?" She placed her arm around him gently and led him to the couch. The dog jumped onto the couch and snuggled up against him. "No, Bessie, bad dog."

"Let her stay," he said. "She's all right."

Jenny shook her head. "A boy and his dog." She looked up at Gloria. "Get me a wet towel."

"Have you done something, Jenny?" he whispered.

"What? Charlie, what happened?"

"I didn't see him. It was dark. He just grabbed me from behind. It was the same guy. The same voice. The man with the scarred hand. He said he'd been watching me. He said I had friends that weren't good for me. He said, 'Tell 'em they've been bad.'"

Gloria handed Jenny a towel. Jenny took the towel and cleaned the blood off Charlie's face.

"Ouch. Easy."

"There's a bottle of bourbon in the kitchen cabinet," Jenny said, "just above the glasses."

Gloria walked into the kitchen, grabbed the bottle and a glass, then poured. She wondered about what Charlie had said. *Tell 'em they've been bad.* It was her—all her fault, she thought. She walked back into the living room and handed Charlie the drink. She smiled weakly at him, wanted to tell him she was sorry. The room was completely silent.

Charlie's hand trembled as he brought the drink to his lips. He swallowed, licked his lips, then took another drink. "Better," he said. He smiled at Gloria. "Thanks." He shook his head. "What kind of trouble are you girls into?"

"Oh, Charlie," Jenny whispered. "Poor, sweet Charlie. I should have known. You tried to tell me the first time. I should have known."

Poor, Drunk Murphy

They sat in the living room, Jenny drinking a glass of bourbon, Gloria drinking a glass of wine. "You think Charlie's going to be okay?" Gloria said, a look of worry passing over her face.

"John will take care of him. He'll be fine."

"It was good advice—telling him he shouldn't be alone. But why didn't you want him to call the police?"

"We don't need the police. The doctor in the ER will have a record of Charlie's wounds. And besides, I think it would be better if we deal with Lieutenant Murphy."

"Do you trust him?"

"At least he's on our side."

"Will they hurt him again?" Jenny heard Gloria's voice crack. "It's all my fault."

"The hell it is. That's what they want. They want us to think it's us. It's not us, goddamnit. It's them. They want to scare us."

Gloria sipped her wine, then wiped the tears from her face. "But why Charlie?"

"Because they know he's my friend. And it's safer to get to me through him—that's why. And they're chickenshits."

"Was it Thomas, you think?"

"Maybe. Or maybe someone who wants to protect him."

"From what?"

"From you—from what you might say."

Gloria was silent for a long time, nothing written on her face. Finally, she opened her mouth to speak. "Can we make them stop?"

"We need to know what they want." But Jenny knew what they wanted. They wanted silence. She was not about to let them scare her into dumbness. "Lieutenant Murphy. He'll help us." *He damn well better help us.* She stirred her drink with her finger. She shook her head as she heard the doorbell ring. "Again? Who in the hell is ringing the doorbell at one-thirty in the morning?" She walked up to the door and yelled through it. "Who the hell is it?"

"It's just me."

It was a familiar voice. She looked through the peephole. She unlatched the door and stared at Lieutenant Murphy.

He stared at her. "Hi," he said.

Jenny looked at him and shook her head. "I can smell you from here. Is there something you need?"

"I need," he said, "I need—" He leaned against the door. "I don't know—I don't know why I'm here. I just—" As he spoke, Bessie came slouching into the room and rubbed her nose against Alexander Murphy's shin. "She likes me," he said.

"You're drunk."

"Yes." He squatted down, rubbed the basset's ears, then promptly fell over.

Jenny looked back at Gloria, who showed no emotion as she witnessed Lieutenant Murphy falling on the floor. "Have you ever seen a drunk man?"

"Not like this."

"What do you think?"

"We can't just leave him there like that."

"Help me get him to the couch."

They managed to get him to stand up, then pulled him toward the couch in an awkward three-way waltz. Jenny slipped his shoes off.

Gloria stared at him. "Why would he do that?" she asked.

Jenny couldn't help but laugh. "He's out cold." She couldn't help but be a little amused. "I can't believe he did this to me. He walks into my house *and passes out.* And this is the man we're counting on to help us?" She laughed. "Look at him—Chicago's finest. I can't believe this night." She stared at the man lying on her couch.

"Why would he do that?" Gloria looked a little confused, but after the incident with Charlie, she seemed comforted by his presence.

"Oh, the poor drunk sonofabitch is having problems with his wife. This is what men do when they're in pain."

"What would he have done if you hadn't opened the door?"

"Oh, he knew I'd open the door," Jenny said. "He knew."

Dear Jenny

Jenny woke up in the morning and remembered Alexander Murphy was sleeping in her living room. "I'm dying to hear his explanation," she said to herself as she changed into a pair of jeans and a T-shirt. She put her hair up and brushed her teeth, then walked into the living room. The couch was there, but the body she and Gloria had placed on it was gone. She was surprised at her disappointment. She found a note on the coffee table:

DEAR JENNY—

> *I don't exactly remember how I got here. I was sitting in a bar on Broadway, having a few drinks, just thinking. I've been doing a lot of thinking lately. Guess I was mostly feeling sorry for myself. I don't know what's wrong with me—well, yes I do, but it's a long story. You know, I'm forty-seven, and I'm trying to figure out what the hell I've done with my life. I don't remember. I guess I just wandered over here in a stupor. I haven't had that much to drink since I was in the police academy. I've gone home to take aspirin*

and drink plenty of water. I think I'll sleep all afternoon. And when I wake up I'll feel ashamed—it'll give me something to look forward to. Catholic boys are like that. It dawned on me when I woke up in your apartment this morning that I liked you. I must have been a sight last night. I apologize.

Sincerely,
Alexander Murphy

P.S. I hope Ms. Santos didn't see me in my delicate condition. If she did, tell her cops are strange people and that she should never become one.

Jenny smiled when she read the letter. He had not written it out in longhand, but had printed it. He wrote like a boy. She folded the note and put it in the book she was reading. She would take the journals to him on Monday. She would pretend to be angry with him. She walked into the kitchen and put the coffee on. She watched it as it dripped into the glass pot. "A watched pot never boils," she said. When the coffee was ready, she poured herself a cup, then walked into the living room, grabbed a journal, and began reading.

The World According to Thomas Blacker

16 September 1971

I thought I was lost, just wandering the West like Satan wandering to and fro upon the earth. Two years, I'd been without Denise. Two years, and I wanted the numbness to go away. The desert was desolate, and somehow I had thought I would find something there. I could hardly stand to drive through that wasteland, its people as flat as the land. But I was determined to drive to Mexico, a place Denise had always wanted to go. I had it all mapped out. Like all foolish men, I believed in my own schemes, my own plans. And instead, something else. Instead, a new life. A wrong turn. The wrong street. One street led to Mexico, and another led to that barrio. Instead of finding myself in Juarez, I was in that broken neighborhood. She was like an angel walking through hell, nothing around her capable of harming her. Perhaps I had not been lost at all. Perhaps I was supposed to be there right at that spot at that hour, as if something in me knew I had an appointment. Perhaps I was supposed to see her walking down the street. I spoke to her, but she ran away from me. I'd lost her. But the next day I went back. I had to find her, had to see her again—this child. I waited for her on the same street corner. She would come to me. I waited and waited, and prayed. And then I saw her—that happy child. Perhaps we carried each other's names in our bodies. Perhaps in a past life we were one. And now we would be one again. . . . She said her name was Gloria. But that is not the name she is supposed to have. I, too, changed my name. It was not my name—it was not my name.

23 SEPTEMBER 1971

. . . I've had to put her in shackles, though I find this sort of thing distasteful. Distasteful things are sometimes necessary. I had to pay Rusty a good deal for them, but he managed. I don't much care to associate with him. He doesn't bathe enough. The drugs—it must be the drugs he takes—they leave a certain smell on him. He's predictable, though. That makes him both boring and easy to work with. People like him will do anything for anyone for a price. There are some people in this world who cannot be tamed, cannot be taught. They care nothing for the world, for the life of the mind. But they can be bought. That, too, is a kind of taming. . . .

Claudia was so wild the first few days. At one point she almost clawed me. She was more like an animal than the poignant little girl I saw walking gracefully down the street. I had to protect us both. She is calmer now. In time, the shackles will come off. They're nothing more than a tool. . . .

16 AUGUST 1972

It has been a year now since Claudia has been with me. She seems to have adjusted quite well, all things considered. She's quite strong. Her will serves her, and I cannot help but admire her sense of self. She is less cold toward me, as I knew she would be. She is less suspicious and more trusting, though she tests limits. Eventually, she will know her boundaries. . . .

She lets me hold her hand, asks me questions. Last night, she kissed me on the cheek. I was quite moved though I did not allow her to see how pleased I was. She sees me as her father now, and does not seem as sad. It pained me a great deal to take her, and her sadness very nearly broke my heart. But I could not allow myself to give in to that kind of sentimentality. I had to think of her, of her future. Her past will mean nothing. Meant nothing. Where she came from, there was nothing for her. Nothing for her in that El Paso slum where I found her. Before I saw her in that neighborhood, I stopped to ask someone for directions. The man looked at me, could not understand a word I said. I could smell urine on him—so much like the smell of so many men I remembered as a boy. I hated having the memory, wondered why things still came back to me, things I had no use for. And when I saw her, I could not help but think of that slum in south Philadelphia where I had been born, nothing but immigrants and work— no one around me to notice if I had a mind or a will to be something more than just a body who drank and ate and worked. It was as if she were a gift to me. And I—I could be a gift to her. She had such a hungry look about her—a haunting kind of hunger on her face that made her appear to be much older and wiser. I think now she was never a child. She was always a woman waiting for someone to see what she had inside her. And there I was. And I saw. I saw. There was a reason why I was in that neighborhood. Fate, perhaps (though I am suspicious of that word). I was lost in that godforsaken city—and there she was, the most elegant creature I'd ever seen in my life. She was a miracle. At the age of seven, there was something of a woman in her walk. I believe she was sent to me. Yes, there was a reason why I was in that neighborhood. There was more grace in her than I'd ever seen in any one human being. She didn't belong there in that squalor with those people. She's much more at home here, now. I am strict, but I am also kind. . . .

27 SEPTEMBER 1972

I had the willow tree chopped down today. I had no choice, really. Claudia loved that tree more than she loved anything. Love to the point of idolatry. She used to hug it, perhaps even pray to it. I was jealous of that tree, though it seems a ludicrous thing to admit. I told her it was diseased, that if we didn't chop it down, the whole garden would get infected and die. She said nothing as the tree was chopped, but I know she was reciting the poem, the poem I made her memorize. She was poised and controlled, completely charming, really. Not a sign of sorrow or grief or rage anywhere on her face. She owes that poise to me. But if she ever shows signs of loving anything more than she loves me, I will destroy it. . . .

I wonder sometimes if I have done the right thing. I suffered over the decision to take her for a long time. It was as if I was punishing myself for having taken something that was not mine. So many sins we have committed on this earth. It's true, I took her, true I robbed her of her life with her family. But was her family such a loss? I cannot help but think that her family would have molded her in their own image—an image that needs no reproduction. I have forgiven myself my transgression. So many evil acts are committed—and committed every second. Does the world have anything to fear from men like Thomas Blacker? If the world is an ugly place, it is not because of men like me. I know this. I am certain of it. The streets are filled with violent and disgusting men who are brainless and heartless and soulless. What does anyone have to fear from me? Even Claudia, what does she have to fear? Someday, she will understand everything. There is such a thing, I think, as perfect understanding. Claudia is capable of such a thing—I can sense it in her. She will become perfection itself. She will know it was I who made her perfection possible. If there is anything to forgive, she will forgive me. . . .

2 JANUARY 1980

Claudia is turning into an amazing young woman—even more amazing than I had hoped. She is lovelier than the spring, lovely as the rain, the loveliest woman I have ever seen or met. I should have named her Grace instead of Claudia, though it's too late for renaming. I'm tempted to change it, but I think I've confused her enough as it is. Some days I want to touch her, hold her. But she is still too young. I am learning self-control. The time will come for us. But not now. I will teach her other things. It's not the right time, not yet.

I taught her how to make a pesto sauce yesterday, and she made homemade bread. She picks things up easily. She almost doesn't need a teacher. I only direct her and let her discover things for herself. She reads and understands and wants to rebel against what is written in the books she reads. She has a mind. She wants to use it. She could be in any one of my classes at the university and more than hold her own (though I think she would spend a great deal of energy disagreeing with me rather than reading the material). She seems patient, but I sense she is not. She is, among other things, a fine actress. . . .

She wanted to know why she could not listen to the radio (a typical teenager). I told her she was free to listen to any and all of my music col-

lection. Mozart and Haydn bore her, and though she hasn't said it, she finds Vivaldi too sweet. There is a dark side to her, dark as the alleys of the city at night. Perhaps it's her background. She broods though she does not wear that brooding on her face. She hides what she feels from me—but I can see it in some of her gestures. She'll learn to control those, too, in time. And then our game will become much more interesting. . . .

3 JUNE 1982

She is almost ready. I got the pills today. Rusty charged me a great price, but I'm afraid I'm going to have to pay it every month. Well, I can well afford what he asks. I do not care to deal with men like Rusty. But he is not difficult to work with. All I have to do is offer him money. Everything for him is money. It makes things very easy for both of us. I try to keep my personal contact with him to a minimum. He's inarticulate and crass, and when he takes the money I give him for his services he appears to me to be a dog slinking away with a bone in his mouth. I try not to give him much thought. I give him what he wants. And he will bring me the birth control pills. And then we will be together, Claudia and I. I want her desperately. Not even as a young man did I ever feel this way. Perhaps my growth has been delayed. It is difficult to control myself. I am grateful for my discipline. I know I must get her started on the pills as soon as possible. I cannot wait forever. There must be no complications. There must only be a mutual enjoyment of each other. We will know each other completely. This is all that matters. Soon, touch will be possible. We will both be new again.

16 SEPTEMBER 1986

Claudia has just finished reading Prescott's The Conquest of Mexico. *She was quite taken with it, I think. She's quite interested in history and*

204

philosophy and literature. I cannot help but feel she is drawn to these inter-
ests partly because of my influence. She asked me what kind of man I
thought Cortez had been. I told her he was probably an ambitious and
greedy man. But also told her he was an intelligent man. Certainly, he was
more intelligent than Montezuma. History has proven that. . . .

Of course, I have a certain admiration for Cortez (though I'm sure he
must have been a crude man—and cruel). When Cortez saw Doña Marina,
I know how he must have felt. He must have seen her, a slave, and known
she had been a princess by the way she carried herself. His heart must have
stopped beating for an instant. He must have asked her name. Malintzin.
The name did not suit her. Doña Marina because she was as calm and as
stormy as the sea. Cortez knew that she was the heart of the New World.
He knew he had to have her. That is how I felt when I saw Claudia, though
she was still a child, in that barrio. She has become my heart.

6 OCTOBER 1990

Claudia did not wish to make love to me last night. I could tell. I had to
raise my voice. But when she made love, she was very nearly perfect. She
knows what I like. She knows what I want. She knows how to please. She
is always able to please.

This morning, when I awoke, she was lying beside me. I realized I had
fallen desperately in love with her. She does everything I ask, and yet I
know she is not compliant. She behaves like a genteel woman because I
expect it of her, but she does not show me what she really feels. I want her
to love me. That is all I want now. It is not too much to ask. . . .

As Jenny read the entries in Thomas Blacker's journal, she skipped
over the sections that had no mention of "Claudia." She was in turn fas-
cinated, appalled, amused, and disgusted by what she read. That evening
she finished reading the last volume. But even she was not prepared for
what the last entry said.

The Geography of Leaves

Jenny sipped coffee as she drove toward downtown. Gloria stared out the window, neither of them interested in conversation. As they passed a park, Gloria noticed the trees. She had not been born to trees, she had been born to a vast and endless sky. The sky had been everything. And here there was nothing but buildings and trees and the blue of the lake that would be gray all winter. Here, in this season, there was nothing but dying leaves, and she was lost in their falling. She didn't know where she was, didn't know the name of the park, was afraid of getting back to Jenny's apartment by herself. She fingered the directions in the pocket of the coat that Jenny had given her—and the map of Chicago. She wanted to ask Jenny if she was sure the directions were correct. She looked over at her, then changed her mind. Jenny had already explained everything carefully—she had even circled her street—just in case. "Just give it to any cabdriver if you get lost," she'd said. "After I leave you off at the therapist, I don't want you wandering the streets. Not after what happened to Charlie. Take a cab—and come straight home. And don't open the door for anyone. A cab will get you home. You don't have to know where you are." She wanted to tell Jenny to stop the car so she could pick up a leaf. A leaf was a map, the veins on them were streets and rivers. She remembered. That's what her brother had told her. If she could only remember what his voice sounded like. That would help her know where she was. If only she could walk the streets without care, without seeing Thomas's face, which followed her like the great eyes of God. She was still lost. *I do have to know where I am, Jenny. I do.*

◆ ◆ ◆

Jenny pulled into a no-parking space and smiled at Gloria. She pointed at the building in front of them. "Her office is on the ninth floor," she said. "You're appointment's at nine o'clock." She looked at her watch. "You're right on time."

Gloria nodded. She wanted to tell Jenny she'd changed her mind about seeing a therapist. I'm only doing this for you, she wanted to say.

"You have the map?"

Gloria smiled. "Yes. And the money for the cab. And go straight home. We've gone over this."

"Sorry, you'll have to forgive me for being a little worried. I just want to be sure you'll be all right."

"I will be," Gloria said as she opened the car door.

"And you have my number?"

"Yes," Gloria smiled, "I have your number."

"Maybe I should go up with you."

"Jenny, will you just let me do this?" She shook her head and grinned as she stepped out of the car.

"Just be careful, Gloria. It's a big bad city."

Gloria smiled and waved at Jenny as she drove reluctantly away.

◆ ◆ ◆

The receptionist smiled at Gloria as she stepped into the waiting room of the therapist's office. "You have an appointment?"

"Yes," Gloria said, successfully hiding her nervousness. The woman behind the desk seemed nice, genuine; there was nothing forced in the way she smiled or spoke. People could be friendly; she thought Thomas wasn't right about people.

The woman looked into a book on her desk. "You must be Ms. Santos."

"Yes," she said. She thought she should say something. Jenny would have said something. "Yes" was all that came to her. She watched as the woman picked up the phone. A wave of panic moved over her, and she felt herself trembling. "Wait," she heard herself say.

The woman looked at her. "Yes?"

"I only came to—"

The woman smiled and waited for her to finish her sentence.

"I only came to cancel my appointment. You see, I have another matter that I must take care of, and it's quite impossible for me to keep this morning's appointment." It was not such a difficult thing to do—to lie.

"I see," the woman said, putting down the phone. "Would you like to reschedule?"

Gloria nodded, wondering what she should say. "Yes," she said.

The woman looked into the book again. "What about tomorrow—eleven-thirty? She's had a cancellation." She grinned. "See, you're not the only one."

"Yes, that's fine." Gloria smiled, then looked at her watch. She remembered the day that Thomas had given it to her. "Thank you so much—I really must go." She left the office in a hurry.

Call Me Sandy

He picked up the picture he kept on his desk, stared into his wife's smiling face, then dropped it into the trash can. "How many times can you fuck up a life?" He thought of his mother and father, of how they had spent a lifetime together. Raised children, made their own kind of peace with each other. After sleeping off his hangover, he had gone to their house for dinner. He had told them his marriage had dissolved. *Dissolved*—that was the word he had used. His father had looked at him, shaking his head in disgust. "Alex, marriages aren't like Alka-Seltzers—they don't just dissolve." He hated the small fact that his father called him Alex. Everyone else in the family called him Sandy—everyone except his father. Sandy sounded too feminine for his father's taste. "It's my fault," he had confessed. His father had glared at him. "How many times can you fuck up a life?" He had spoken in that tone of his, that tone that never approved, that only knew how to humiliate. But his mother had kissed him on his way out the door and told him, "I adore you, Sandy." He shook his head, then opened a file and began reading. "Goddamnit," he said, "people are always killing each other." The phone rang. "Another goddamn murder," he muttered. He let it ring a second time before he picked it up and put on his nonchalant cop voice as easily as he put on his shoes: "Lieutenant Murphy."

"Are you feeling better this morning?" He recognized Jenny's voice immediately. He smiled into the receiver.

"I'm feeling just fine," he said. "Look, I'm sorry about Saturday night."

"Oh, don't be sorry, you gave Gloria Santos her first look at a really drunk male. In your own way, you're helping to educate her in the ways of the evil city."

"I'm sorry she saw me like that."

"You even managed to pet the dog before you passed out."

"Did I say anything to embarrass myself?"

Jenny laughed. "Actually, you confessed undying love for Gloria Santos."

"I did not."

"You said you didn't remember anything."

"That's true. But I know myself well enough to know I wouldn't have confessed undying love to Ms. Santos."

"What makes you so sure?"

"Alcohol's a truth serum. I don't happen to be in love with her."

"Tell me something. What brought you to my apartment in a drunken stupor?"

"I was in the neighborhood, and I was too drunk to drive."

"Such a good citizen. You could've taken a cab."

"I didn't think of that."

"So you just dropped by my apartment?"

He was silent for a moment. He reached for a cigarette, put it in his mouth.

"Are you about to light a cigarette?" she asked.

"Yes. And the reason I went to your apartment was that I remembered I forgot the journals."

"In that state—that's what you were thinking? Nice try, Lieutenant."

"Look, I know it's in your nature to give people a hard time—especially if those people happen to be men—and most especially if those men happen to be cops—but won't you cut a guy some slack? Hell, I don't know why I went to your apartment. I was drunk."

"I don't like drunks," Jenny said.

"As a rule, I don't, either."

"I'm glad to hear it, Lieutenant."

He lit his cigarette.

She waited for him to say something.

"I'm sorry," he said. "I've been fucking things up lately. It won't happen again."

"You can make it up to me by taking me to lunch."

He smiled. "You won't storm out again and leave me with the bill?"

She laughed. "No promises."

"Well, I'm not—"

"If you come, I'll tell you about my friend Charlie."

"What about him?"

"He got beat up again."

"And?"

"The message was this: 'Tell your friends they're being bad.' The guy hit him three times. Once in the balls—that one was for the lawyer. Once across the face—that one was for Ms. Santos. And a kick in the ribs—that one was just for being a faggot. It was the same man—the man with the scarred hand."

The lieutenant said nothing, took a puff from his cigarette, then winced. "We should've made something out of his first attack. Clues were all there."

"Well, I'm as guilty as you are."

He nodded into the telephone. "Fuck. I don't like these people." He took a deep breath. "Frontera Grill on Clark? One-fifteen—it's less crowded if we take a late lunch."

"Good place," she said. "I'll bring the journals. I spent all day yesterday reading them."

"They're something, huh?"

"Yeah, you could say that. The sonofabitch." She paused a moment. "See you at the restaurant, Lieutenant." She quietly hung up the phone.

He held the receiver for a moment. "Call me Sandy," he said—as if Jenny were in the room with him.

Maybe Someone Borrowed Them for Sex

Alexander Murphy walked into his office, took out his notepad, rewrote his notes, then made more notes.

"Whatcha got?" He looked up and saw Tim Cain standing at his doorway.

"You know, they give me this small cubicle of an office—"

"Which you practically share with Detective Johnson—"

"What's that crack supposed to mean?" The lieutenant glared at him until he was satisfied that Sergeant Cain was sorry he'd raised the issue of his close collaboration with George. "As I was saying, I have this small cubicle of an office, and nobody ever bothers to knock. Granted, it's not a big place—in fact, it used to be a storeroom before I begged to get it. In fact, I groveled for a year—"

"And lucky you are that you have it. I mean, detectives don't have offices."

"No, but lieutenants do. And the only reason George comes in more freely than the rest of you dopes is that half the dicks in this pop stand still don't want to work with a black guy."

"That isn't true."

"Okay. It isn't true. I made it up. You're right, Sergeant. Just knock when you come to my office."

"The door's always open."

The lieutenant glared at his visitor again. "I don't like you much, you know that?"

"I do my job."

"And you do it well. Lick the captain's boots like a pro. I'd say you were great at it. I don't much care for the new captain, myself. And I sure as hell don't like anyone who licks his boots. You'd probably lick something else if he asked you."

"I just came in here to be friendly—that's all."

"I don't like friendly people."

"Actually, Murph, I came to deliver a message from the captain."

"Tell the captain to deliver his own goddamn messages."

Tim Cain had the same thin lips as Alexander Murphy. They could have passed for brothers. "The captain says you got a warrant for some journals in Thomas Blacker's house. He wants to know where the hell they are. And he wants to know why you and George went to a judge to get a warrant for them when you're off the case. And he wants to know why you picked them up yourself when you know damn well that's not normal procedure."

"Tell him I don't know to the first question, and I don't know to the second. And to the third question, tell him I saved somebody a trip. Now get out before I make you shine my shoes." He turned his attention to his notepad.

"Just watch yourself, Murphy."

"Thanks for—" He looked up from his papers and noticed Cain was gone. He shook his head. "I don't think I know why I became a cop."

"I don't know. Why *did* you become a cop?"

He looked up and grinned at George. "Shut the door. Where you been all morning?"

"Been working. Could've used you—you were supposed to come out on a call."

"Aren't there any sergeants around?"

"No one's around.

"What's the deal?"

"Suicide—but maybe not. Looks fishy to me."

"Sorry. I was doing a favor for someone. Kind of a payback."

George looked up at Murphy and grinned. "Guess what?"

"A space alien abducted the captain."

"No. The captain *is* a space alien. Guess again."

Murph looked at him and shook his head, then leaned forward and placed his forehead on the desk. "If it's bad news, don't tell me."

"It's bad news."

He banged his head against the desk. "Don't tell me."

"The shackles are missing."

"The ones we found in the basement?" He banged his head on the desk one more time.

"Yup."

"I told you not to tell me." He banged his head a third time.

"Stop that, Murph, you're gonna do some damage."

He sat up straight and smiled from ear to ear. "Maybe someone borrowed them for sex."

"Not funny, Murph."

"Just a theory."

"You know what I think?"

"Do I have to listen?"

"I think the people who took the car took the shackles."

"Maybe they're having sex in the car."

George ignored him. "There's more bad news. The pills are missing."

"Keep going."

"And the videos of the basement." George shook his head. "But not the videos of the crime scene. Those are all still down there. And the dresses—they're all still there."

"Big deal. Dresses could have been his wife's. Keep looking for that stuff, will you?"

"Sure thing. Won't do any good, but I'll keep looking."

"Maybe somebody mislabeled them without actually lifting them."

"I'll look into it." George shook his head. "You know what I think? I think somebody somewhere likes Thomas Blacker."

"Well, me and you and Jenny Richard and Gloria Santos—we don't like him, do we, George? And we're gonna make a lot of trouble for him and all his friends. *I mean, we're gonna make a lot of trouble.*"

"We better not make too much trouble."

"I don't care, George. I'm pissed off as hell."

"Well, I kinda like it when you're mad."

"You know what happened Saturday night?"

"You stayed over with Jenny Richard."

"Drop it, will you? Not that. Charlie—he got beat up again."

"Charlie?"

"Jenny's friend. I told you about him."

"Yeah—and?"

"It's not him they want. They only want to get at Jenny. This time, the warning was loud and clear."

"And the message is," George smiled, "Keep your mouths shut about Thomas Blacker."

"You got it."

"What are we gonna do about it, Murph?"

"Oh, I think we ought to do some damage."

"Can we?"

"Yup." Murphy looked at his watch, then got up from his desk and put on his sports coat. He ran his fingers through his hair.

"Where you going?"

"Having lunch with Jenny Richard."

"First you spend the night at her place, and now you're having lunch with her. Usually, it's the other way around, but—"

"I told you *I didn't sleep with her.*"

"Tell me you don't like her."

"It's none of your business anyway."

"Well, since you're living in my house, it is my business. And next time you stay out all night I want you to call me." He laughed. "Tell me you don't like her, Murph."

"I still like you better," he said—then smiled, then walked out the door.

An Ordinary Courtship

Lieutenant Murphy pushed his plate away. "Well, we managed to get through a meal without an argument."

"This time, anyway," she said.

She tried to avoid his eyes. He tried to avoid hers.

"Well," he said finally, "at least we know how he managed to get her all the way across the country without getting caught. While the cops were looking for someone to cross the Mexican border, he got to

Canada. Then straight across. Then back down to Chicago. Smart man."

Jenny was glad to get back to business—their conversation during the meal had been awkward, both of them trying to talk about themselves without being self-conscious or defensive. He had spoken in fits and starts about his doomed marriage, and she had told him about the man she almost married. Both of them had suffered through the conversation.

"He could just as easily have been caught," she said. "He got lucky."

"Yeah. Lucky for him. *Un*lucky for her."

He noticed her hands as she held her cup of coffee. Worker's hands. He wanted to ask her about that. He smiled awkwardly. He decided to ignore her comment. "What did you think of the journals?"

"What did you think, Lieutenant?"

"Well, they were compelling—in a way."

"Compelling? In a sick way, I suppose. He's paranoid."

"And an egomaniac."

She thought a moment, kept turning her cup of coffee around and around. "He really has a thing about America."

He smiled. "It's an obsession, isn't it? It's almost as if he wanted to save her from what it's become."

"Maybe. But he also wanted to save her from her poverty—"

"Something like that. And he gets to be the hero."

"Except that he had enough of a conscience to suspect himself of having less-than-pure motives."

"But that's only when he came to the sex part." She laughed. "The sonofabitch waited until she was of age before he raped her."

"No, no, no. To him, it was an ordinary courtship. He was the perfect gentleman in his own novel. He certainly liked to buy her presents."

"And he lists them all as if he couldn't help but congratulate himself for his generosity."

"And she gets the role of the exotic virgin."

"She's beautiful, isn't she?"

The lieutenant looked at Jenny and smiled. "Yes, she is. That doesn't mean I'd want to own her. It's enough to make you spit."

Jenny found herself admiring his reactions. "History just keeps on repeating itself. It's a wonder we don't die of boredom."

"Except that what keeps repeating itself is so sick that it's killing us— even before we realize how fucking old the story is." He put a cigarette in his mouth but didn't light it.

"But there's more to it than that. There's a big leap between being an elitist snob and being a kidnapper."

"We're trying to understand something that we can't possibly understand. We only have pieces. And the puzzle is in Thomas Blacker's head."

"It's a fucking mess—that's all I know." She looked at Alexander Murphy, his gray eyes studying her, or perhaps just studying.

"What are you thinking?" he asked.

"Offer me a cigarette, and I'll tell you."

He took out his pack, tapped it until a couple of cigarettes stuck out, and pointed them at her. She took one, and he offered her a light. "Just like in the movies," he said, grinning.

"Yeah, sure." She thought it was a charming thing to say. She tried to ignore his grin. That was charming, too. "Gloria," she said. "I want them to leave her alone." She inhaled the smoke, then exhaled it. "Leave Charlie alone, too. Leave *me* alone. I don't like it one damn bit that an innocent man is used just because he happens to be my friend."

"They know your weaknesses. That's the name of the game. They know he's important to you."

"It's a shitty way to play the game."

"Someone's playing for keeps. Or maybe someone's getting desperate."

"Thomas Blacker?"

"Yup. But he has help."

"Herald Burns," she said.

"They've been friends for a long time."

"Think Blacker called in a marker?"

"I don't think Blacker had to ask. Anyway, five will get you ten that Mr. Burns will be in touch with you. Sooner or later, he'll get in touch."

"He already has, Lieutenant. I'd say Charlie's broken rib was getting in touch. The sonofabitch didn't even say what he wanted."

"He'll get to that."

She shook her head. "Those bastards. Can you imagine having Herald

Burns as your lawyer? And even worse, can you imagine having Thomas Blacker as a guardian for twenty-three damned years? Just the thought of it makes my skin crawl. You know, he taught her everything about the world—how to look at it, how to interpret it. And he gave her his oh-so-lovely vocabulary. It's disgusting."

Lieutenant Murphy winced. She wondered why he always did that—as if he were in pain.

"Well, she has to find a way out, damnit," Jenny continued. "At some point, we all have to unlearn the crap we've been handed."

He watched her as she spoke. He liked her even more than he had suspected. He wanted to say something smart, but he didn't feel very intelligent.

Jenny made a face. "I really would like to castrate that man."

"Nature's doing it for you."

"It would be a little more satisfying if I could do it myself."

"Hold grudges, do you?"

"Sometimes." She bit a nail, then removed it from her mouth as if her mother's voice played inside her like a tape. "And the creep really thinks he did her a favor."

"Jenny, that's how he lives with himself." He noticed she didn't object when he called her by her first name. He tried to hide his smile, but it was there.

She tapped her nose with her forefinger. "And what do you make of this Rusty person?"

"Well, he's black, probably hates the professor as much as the professor hates him—"

"It's a wonder Thomas Blacker would work with a black man."

"It was a mutually beneficial business proposition."

"His wife, Lucy, sounds like a piece of work."

"I don't remember her," he said. "Must have skimmed that section." He pointed his finger at her. "This Rusty guy, he probably lives somewhere on the South Side, near the university. That would be my guess, anyway. And either he knows people who can get him drugs illegally or he—"

"Or he knows a lot of women. Any woman can get a hold of birth control pills."

"Yes, but wouldn't she want them for herself?"

"Not if she couldn't have a baby."

"Good girl," he said.

"And if he ever needed anything for a woman, this guy Rusty could get his woman friend to get them for him. They passed on middleman prices to the professor."

The lieutenant nodded. "That'll work."

"You think we can find this guy, Sandy?

He smiled. "Sandy?"

Jenny laughed. "Can we find Rusty?"

"George is on it. I'm joining him this afternoon."

"I thought you were off the case."

"Well, he's supposed to be working on another case right now. But he reports to me. And me—well, a lieutenant has some leeway." He shrugged. "We'll find this guy. A Rusty Rayborn shouldn't be too hard to find. Bet he has a sheet on him."

"Where'd you dig up his last name?"

"The journals."

"I must have missed that one."

He leaned back on his chair. "I wonder what the world according to Thomas Blacker looks like."

Jenny almost spit out her coffee. "Alexander Murphy, thank your Catholic God you'll never know."

Little Girls

Gloria wondered if Jenny would be angry with her. She wanted to please her, though Jenny didn't seem the type to demand things of her—not like Thomas. *I didn't want to go, Jenny.* Maybe she wouldn't tell her. But wouldn't the therapist call her? *No, I've rescheduled.* I'll just tell her I have another appointment on Friday. She'd been so nice. *I just can't go, Jenny. I just can't.* What was a little lie? She needed her secret—though she did not know why she needed it.

She stared at the map of Chicago Jenny had given her. She reached in her coat pocket and made sure the money was still there. She felt her fingers rub against the new bills. Three twenty-dollar bills. New. *Just grab a cab. I don't want you wandering around the city after what happened to Charlie.* How did you grab a taxi? She watched a man in a suit come out of the building she had just been in. She watched him as he raised his arm. She noticed a taxicab headed in his direction. Miraculously, the taxi stopped in front of him. The man got in. "Easy," she said to herself. How did they know how much to pay? "It's not difficult, Gloria. I'm sure the man will tell you." She smelled coffee. She wondered why she was always smelling coffee. She noticed a coffee shop across the street. *Go straight home.* What could a cup of coffee hurt? She walked to the corner, waited for the light to turn green. She looked at the white letters that said WALK. She smiled. Easy.

The coffee shop was crowded, but she noticed an empty table. She made her way to it, looked around, then sat down. A man walked in the front door, took an empty chair at a table across from a woman who was sitting alone. He began reading the newspaper. He did not walk up to the counter like the other people. Perhaps you did not have to order coffee, perhaps you could just sit and read. She watched as people stood in line and ordered their coffee, watched as they sat down with friends. She supposed they were friends. Jenny was her only friend, she thought. One friend in the world. She wanted more. But what would she do with them? They would ask questions—what she did, where she worked, where she had gone to school. What would she say? *I went to Thomas Blacker University.* A joke. She smiled. She got in line behind a man who was ordering coffee: "A double latte," he said. She watched the girl behind the counter prepare the coffee he'd ordered. *I could do that. Maybe they need—* The woman behind the counter smiled at her. "What can I help you with?"

"A double latte," she said. What she was doing was normal, so she pretended to be that word. Normal. It would be nice to have a normal life.

Or maybe not. Jenny didn't seem to have a normal life. Neither did the lieutenant. But there was something normal about them—the way they behaved, the way they spoke.

Nobody noticed her. She was doing everything right. When the woman handed her a cup of coffee with foam at the top, Gloria handed her a twenty. The woman handed her some change. She stuck it in her coat pocket and made her way to the table. She studied her map. She saw all the streets that were between where she was and Jenny's apartment. Lots of streets. She would have liked in that instant to walk them all. Know them all. Explore. She wondered about the people who had made these maps. Cartographers. Amazing. To see the world and map it.

"Do you mind if I sit here?"

She looked up at a young man dressed in a gray suit. She didn't know whether she should let him sit there or not. Jenny had told her to be careful. But he seemed nice. How could he hurt her with all these people around? She remembered the car. But he was kind. Thomas had been kind the day that—"I'd rather you not," she said. Her voice was sure and forceful.

He seemed surprised. "But there aren't any more seats," he said.

So stand, she wanted to say. "Okay," she said. She went back to studying her map. The coffee was good. She liked the sweetness of the hot milk, the way it mingled with the bitterness of the coffee. She drank slowly and studied the map.

"Are you looking for something in particular?" the man asked.

She looked at him, then shook her head.

"Are you a tourist?"

She nodded.

"Where are you from?"

She did not want to talk to him. You could never tell by looking. You could never tell by their voices. Jenny would have spoken to him—but Jenny knew the city, knew men, knew things she had not yet learned. She sipped her coffee. "I'm from Texas," she said finally.

"You don't have an accent."

She shrugged.

"Don't talk much, do you?"

"Do you always talk to strangers?" she asked. The words just came out of her. She did not want to talk to this man. Maybe he would offer to show her his car. She was sorry she'd spoken.

"Not always." He smiled.

She didn't smile back.

"Maybe I can help you find something?" he said. "Born and raised in this city. Know it like I know the back of my hand."

She nodded. It was harmless to ask him a question. She would ask him a question and then leave. "Do you know all the buildings?"

He chuckled. "Well, not all of them."

"I want to go to the top of the John Hancock Building."

"Oh," he said, "it's a perfect place to see the city—"

He was going to say something else, but she interrupted him. "Show me on the map."

He stopped talking and looked at the map. "You're here," he said. "Go here," He ran his finger along one of the streets on the map. "Three blocks to the west and four blocks south—to right here." He tapped his index finger on the map. He seemed pleased with himself.

Gloria circled it. She drank from her coffee.

"I can take you there, if you want. I have some—"

"No, thank you," she said. And before he could say anything else, she rose from the table and headed for the door.

"You didn't even say thank you," he yelled as she reached the door.

She turned around. People were watching. "Thank you," she whispered. She walked out into the street.

◆ ◆ ◆

The day was sunny. Peaceful enough, but the air seemed as if it were a set of cold teeth wanting to bite down on the city. It was almost November, but already there was a great deal of January in the steady breeze. Was it November now, already? She had kept track of the days on a calendar Thomas had given her. She had not seen a calendar since the day she had left his house. She needed to know. She should've checked before she left the apartment. She should have asked Jenny. It was an important thing to know where she was, the day, the hour. *She had to know.* When she got back home, she would find out. She noticed a metal stand with newspapers in it. The newspaper would have the date, they always had the date. She walked up to the stand and stared at the newspaper. She looked for the date. November 2. She held on tight to the map. She walked toward the building. Three blocks, then four. She walked slowly, sometimes looking at her watch. It was almost noon. She suddenly had the funny sensation of being watched. She looked around. No one even noticed her. Still, she felt the eyes. Perhaps the eyes were somewhere inside of her.

She peered into windows of stores. Such lovely things. In one of the stores, she saw a dress. It seemed to beckon her into the store. She found herself inside, staring at the clothes. She touched a dress, backless, made of satin—so blue it was almost black.

"Would you like to try it on?"

She looked into the face of an older woman who smiled at her. The woman wore too much perfume and too much makeup. She wondered what she would look like without all that powder, what she would smell like without all that perfume. This woman would not hurt her. She was hiding something—just like her.

She shook her head. "I was just looking," she said softly.

"Well, if you need anything, you just let me know."

"Yes, of course." The woman went away. Gloria kept her eye on the dress, soft as the slip she wore on her first Communion. Maybe she would pretend. Nobody knew her. The older woman thought she was just another shopper, just another consumer. What was the harm in pretending? What was the harm in trying it on? She could pretend it wasn't quite right. She didn't have to buy—did she have to buy it if she tried it on? Of course not. That wouldn't make any sense at all. Yes, she could pretend. There would be no harm, no harm to the saleslady, no harm to herself, no harm, even, to the dress. That's what people did—they pretended. She could see that. It was easy to see, could see all the pretending that was going on in the street.

She touched the dress again. She wondered how and where Thomas had bought all those dresses. He'd had a good eye—they all had fit her perfectly. "Are you sure you wouldn't like to try that on? It would look lovely on you." Gloria thought the lady was kind—or pretending to be kind. She wanted to sell a dress.

"No, thank you," Gloria said. She looked at her watch. "I'm actually in a bit of a hurry." *Very good, Gloria, that wasn't so hard. Not difficult. It will be easy to pretend in the city.* That was what she would do. Thomas had told her once she was a fine actress.

On the way out of the boutique, she thought she saw a man walking slowly down the street. She thought she had seen him in the coffee shop. The man reading the newspaper. The man who did not order coffee. She was sure of it. How could it be the same man? It was a big city.

◆ ◆ ◆

She felt uneasy for spending $7.50 to get to the top of the John Hancock Building, felt she was doing something wrong. Jenny had told her to go home. And here she was spending Jenny's money. She was not used to spending money—hers or anybody else's. It was not like spending time. Seven dollars and fifty cents sounded like a lot of money. It wasn't even hers.

When she reached the lobby where the elevators were, she paced the building. There was no one in there but her. She felt those eyes on her again. When she looked up, she saw him—the man with the newspaper. He stared at her and smiled. He walked slowly toward her. She could not bring herself to look away from his blue eyes. Not unlike Thomas's eyes. She felt he would hurt her, but for some reason, she was incapable of moving. His smile grew bigger as he walked slowly toward her.

She heard a bell ring, and a group of people walked out of the elevator, coming between her and the smiling man. She walked into the elevator and stood close to the man in the elevator whose job it was to go up and down all day. She wanted to tell him that a man was frightening her. It sounded like such a stupid thing to say. And what had he done to her? All he'd done was smile. She wanted to hold on to the elevator man as she'd held on to Jenny the first time she'd walked into the elevator. The man would think she was crazy. Her heart skipped a beat when the big man who'd been following her stepped into the elevator. He smiled at her again. She looked away. He reached for her arm. The elevator doors began to close. She felt a scream rising in her head. And then she heard a scream: "Hold the door." The elevator man pressed a button and the door opened again. "So sorry," a woman said, as she got onto the elevator along with a group of little girls. "It's just that we didn't want to wait. It's hard to keep them still when they have to wait. Children don't like to wait." The elevator man nodded. "No trouble." Gloria was relieved to hear the undisciplined chatter. She wanted to look into all the small faces, get lost in them. She noticed a pair of eyes looking up at her, eyes almost as dark as her own. "You're pretty," the little voice said.

"You're pretty, too," Gloria said.

The little girl laughed. "Did you hear that, Mrs. Podolinski? Did you hear that?"

The woman laughed. "Yes, yes, we all heard." The ride up made her stomach feel like it wanted to break free of her body. Her legs felt like they might not hold her up as the elevator came to a stop. Why had she come here? Why hadn't she gone straight home? She walked out alongside the children. Again, she found herself in a geography of blue. Only now, the only blue she could really see was the man's eyes as they followed her around the glassed-in floor. She slowly made her way around the building, seeing nothing of the sky, nothing of the lake. When she had circled the building, she turned around and faced the man. Her heart was pounding, but Thomas had taught her never to act afraid—especially when she was. She looked straight into his eyes. He moved toward her. He smiled. "Are you afraid?" he asked.

"No," she said. She noticed the girls through the corner of her eye. She moved toward them. "There's that lovely little girl," she said. She felt his eyes. Watching.

The little girl clapped her hands. "I'm five," she said. "How old are you?"

"I'm ten," Gloria said.

The other girls laughed. The older woman smiled at her. She continued speaking to the girls until they headed for the elevator. She walked with them, laughed with them. She knew the man was still following her. When she and the group of girls got onto the elevator, the man with the smile and the cold blue eyes stepped in just before the doors closed. Gloria pretended not to notice him. She edged close to the doors as the elevator went down. When the doors opened, she ran out of the building, did not even look to see if the man was still following her. As she walked out into the cold, she looked up and down the street. She noticed a man and a woman getting out of the cab across the street. "Taxi!" she yelled. "Taxi!" The man looked up, nodded at her, then pointed at the corner. She turned around and saw the man coming out of the building. She ran to the corner, then crossed the street and got into the cab. "Eight thirty-one Roscoe," she said as her lungs gasped for air like a child's hand groping for its mother. She thought it a miracle that the address had come out of her mouth. As she caught her breath in the cab, she looked around, saw the buildings and the people. They could not touch her. She remembered a trip with Thomas in a car. She leaned over to make sure the driver was not Thomas. He turned his face sideways. "Need something?" he asked.

"No," she said. He was dark, had an accent she could not place. The man was not Thomas. She was safe. Little girls, she thought, saved by little girls.

◆ ◆ ◆

As she sat in the back of the taxi, she felt calmer. She thought of her room in Jenny's apartment—how empty her closet was, how unfamiliar and foreign it felt. She thought of her room at Thomas's house—how it had belonged to her, how she had learned to find comfort in that room. It had been hers. In Jenny's home, she was just a guest. Welcome perhaps—but a guest. She wondered about Thomas; was he doing better? He would need help. He would be alone. She had always taken care of him when he needed her. Who would help him now that she was gone?

When the taxi arrived in front of Jenny's apartment, she could not bear the thought of her room there. So little comfort in that room. The driver turned around and looked at her as she sat quietly in the backseat. "This the place?"

She nodded, then smiled. "I've changed my mind," she said, then gave him Thomas Blacker's address.

Hit and Run

Neither of them had bothered to look at their watches all through lunch. It was as if they had all the time in the world, the lawyer and the cop, their busy worlds not so busy to stop and have a long lunch. With each other. The waitress poured them both another cup of coffee. The lieutenant mulled over what Jenny had told him about her friend. "So while you were taking care of Charlie, I was in a bar getting shit-faced. Not a pretty picture." He nodded, then winced. It was the closest thing to a smile he could manage. "I think I might be able to make up for it."

"How's that?"

He kept nodding. "I think—"

"Stop bobbing your head. You're making me dizzy."

"Sorry. Bad habit. You know, we really should've known. We had all the clues."

"My best friend gets beat up—twice! Twice, because I don't know how to use my head."

He laughed. "Want to walk over to the nearest Catholic church? We can beat our breasts at the feet of the Sacred Heart of Jesus."

She grinned at him.

He grinned back.

"Are we going to sit here all afternoon grinning at each other?" There was a softness in her voice. He liked hearing it.

He shook his head.

"Ahh, your head has changed directions."

"How you guys doing?" The waitress handed them the check.

Murph looked up at her and smiled. "You just saved my life."

He was a goofy man, Jenny thought. Goofy but sincere. She wondered how she had missed his virtues.

"You know, I think I know who's been beating up on your friend."

"What?"

"Will you trust me on this one—just this once?"

"You can't just say something like that and—"

"Oh, I hear that thing in your voice. Relax, will you? Can you just trust me?"

"I have a choice?"

He smiled. "Let's get out of here."

◆ ◆ ◆

He lifted the box of journals out of Jenny's trunk.

"Don't hurt your back," Jenny said.

"Not heavy. Damn things. They'll save us, though."

"Us."

"Gloria, I mean."

They moved to the sidewalk, Jenny looking at her watch. An hour till her next hearing.

He stared at the box. "Can you believe he was going to—" He stopped and shook his head.

"He would have done it, all right." She made a face. "*He'd have done it.*"

"It didn't surprise you." He didn't wait for her to answer. "It did me."

"Why?"

"Because he loved her."

"It wasn't love."

"It was warped, Jenny. It was sick. But he *did* love her. Love her till he dies."

"People who love don't—"

"People who love are capable of doing anything. A person's love is only as virtuous as the person who's doing the loving. You don't know that by now?"

Jenny looked at Alexander Murphy. It suddenly occurred to her how hard it must be for him to stay honest, to stay clean, when everything around him was so dirty. She had the sudden urge to place her hand on his face to see what it felt like. He hadn't shaved— it would be rough, but maybe there was a softness underneath that shadow. She was suddenly aware that she had not responded to what he'd said. "I didn't know you thought so much about the philosophy of love."

He laughed. "Just a student of human nature. Like you."

"How's that?" She wanted to hear him talk. To hear his voice in the almost cold afternoon, there in the sun in the middle of a busy sidewalk.

"You and I, we deal with people who kill. I arrest them. You defend them."

"They need defending—"

"I'm not arguing that point. But we know what they're capable of. They love, don't they? Yet they kill. And often they kill the ones they love."

"Yes," she said, "that's true."

"He loved her."

"He would have done it."

They both nodded.

"Jenny, has she read them?"

"She won't."

"Tell her she has to."

"She's stubborn."

"Good, it will help her to survive."

Jenny looked at her watch. "I have to go."

"Me too. I have to turn these in as evidence. I'm in deep shit over this. And just you watch, these journals are going to go the way of the disappeared car and the missing shackles."

"You think so?"

"Just watch."

"How are you going to explain your continued interest in a case you've been dropped from?"

"I'll tell him I've gotten emotionally involved with the woman. I'll make myself look like an idiot—apologize for my unprofessional behavior, maybe get written up—and it will be over. Easy. Things are easy so long as you don't care about looking good."

She laughed. "Involved with the woman. I thought you said you weren't interested in Gloria Santos."

"I'm not. It's her lawyer I'm interested in." He walked down the street before she could respond, not even waiting to see the smile on her face as he said the words. Hit and run—sometimes that was the best policy.

Fire and Water

He was so thirsty. If he could reach water, bathe in it, drink it. If he could do that, then the flames could not touch him. Everything felt so far away, so strange, and he was not sure where he was. He walked toward the window—then remembered. Mercy Hospital. He had been in this hospital for such a long time, he thought. Years, perhaps. He looked out at the lake. It had moved, he thought, the lake now reaching the doors of the hospital. Strange, but so lovely—as if the lake had come to take him away. And the waters of the lake, they were as blue as a summer sky. The waters seemed to call him by name. He opened the window. Strange that the window opened, he thought. He had never been able to open it. He smelled the freshness of the air, as clean and pure as the waters below him. His mouth so dry. He wanted only to drink. If only he could drink. The waters had come for him, he knew that, they had come to save him. And then he saw her: Claudia. Claudia in the water. She swam as gracefully as a mermaid. He yelled her name. She looked up, smiled, waved at him, then dove into the water. She has come back, he thought. He waited for her to reappear. When she came back up from the depths of the water, he heard her call his name. She has come back. He smiled, looked down into the soft, warm, waiting water, then stared into the dark and distant eyes of Claudia. She, too, was waiting. She disappeared into the water again. "Wait!" he yelled. "Wait!" When he jumped out of the window, his body moved through the air with the grace of a young man diving into a lake on the first day of summer. He saw nothing as he moved through the air except the blueness of the perfect water. He whispered her name. Claudia. He felt her warm skin in the cool water . . .

When Thomas woke from his dream, he knew. She would come back to him. He felt strong again. He had been wallowing in self-pity. Now it was time to return to the army of the living.

◆ ◆ ◆

"And you've taken care of everything, Herald?" Thomas wore a severe look on his face as he sat up in his hospital room.

"Everything's under control, Thomas."

"You must understand. Do you understand, Herald?" He looked directly into the younger man's eyes.

"I'm trying, Thomas."

"And the lieutenant?"

"He won't be any more trouble."

"And that lawyer?"

"She'll come around."

"You're certain."

He was not so certain, but he nodded convincingly.

"And everything's been taken care of at the house?"

"Yes, yes, no sign of what happened. I made sure of that. The police have what they want. I've arranged everything. It's safe to go back. You're sure you wouldn't like to stay at my house instead? There's plenty of room."

"Henry made the same offer. I appreciate the gesture, but I want my house back." There was a firmness in his voice that made Herald Burns want to smile.

"The police have things that belong to me."

"It can't be helped, Thomas. I'm doing what I can." He smiled at his old friend. He had regained the fire in his eyes—though something about them almost made Herald feel ill at ease. Still, the fire—it was good to see it. "Everything will work out—you'll see."

"Yes," Thomas said.

"When will they let you go?"

"Tomorrow morning."

"You're looking great, Thomas."

"Not great, Herald. Not great—until all of this is done."

"Patience, Thomas."

He nodded. "Help me up. I need to walk around."

Herald Burns smiled. He wasn't beaten—not yet. The fire was return-ing to his eyes.

Fallen Angels

Getting Lieutenant Murphy out of the picture would be an easy move—or so he had thought. But he had moved too slowly. Everything would have been simpler if Gloria Santos had remained in jail. Now she was out. And Murphy was responsible. The luck of the draw. If Murphy had never been on the case to begin with, everything might have gone as smoothly as a ride in a limousine. No matter: He had been assured that Murphy would cause no more trouble. One less player to contend with.

But there was always the unexpected. The unexpected made things more complicated, more difficult, but it also made everything so much more interesting. Jenny Richard. Jenny Richard was still in the game. By now, she would have received his message. She would know they were serious. And Ms. Santos, she would be the easiest to—he nodded as he lost himself in his own thoughts. If he had any misgivings, he had buried them with his first phone call. The game was on now, and there was no repenting. There was only the winning and the losing. This was how life in the city was meant to be lived—and he was the heart of it. He had no doubts. He spent every evening rereading Thomas's book. He was almost finished. He was sleeping well.

He walked to the window and looked out at the city. He could see no darkness there—only the lights. The lights of the city—the sight of them. It was more than enough. He could see almost everything, the buildings, the lights, the power that lit them. No need for stars. He moved away from the window reluctantly, then sat back down on his chair. He leaned back, then stared at the painting of Saint Michael the archangel, his foot on Satan's face, his arm poised to ram his spear through the demon's neck. "Too good to actually do it," he thought. Even in the midst of battle, the archangel's face remained virtuous and pure, as if the battle could not touch him. The same was not true of his opponent. Satan's veins bulging, his face twisted with the rage of defeat. His first wife had bought it for him in Spain—a relic from the sixteenth century. She had been in search of the likeness of Saint Thomas More, the patron saint of lawyers. But she had remarked that his image would have been out of place in his office. She had decided to look for something more appropriate. She had happened on the painting, had been completely taken with the image of Saint Michael fighting a holy battle against heaven's usurpers. She had been a good Catholic, a believer in good and evil—categories he found charming but useless in the world to which he belonged.

As he stared at the picture, he thought of Thomas. The first time Thomas had seen it, he had fallen in love with it, had stared at it for a long time, saying nothing, just nodding in approval. He had, on many occasions, decided to give Thomas the icon. In the end, he had been unable to part with it. But he always thought of Thomas when he stopped to admire the dueling angels. Thomas, who had given himself to fighting the good fight. Thomas, the true believer. Thomas, the pure. *And all this time, Thomas, you've been nothing more than a disfigured, fallen angel.* He smiled, then laughed. Fallen angels—they'd had a taste of heaven. Those were the worst kind. Those were the kind to be careful of.

At the Gates of Hell

Gloria sat passively in her seat as the taxi pulled up in front of
the gates. "This your house?" the driver asked.

"It used to be," she said, then stepped out of the car. She walked up to
the gates and peered at Thomas's house. She did not remember the night
the police had taken her away, had never seen the front of the house. So
different from the house she had known.

"Have you lived here for a long time?"
"Oh, not so long."
"And did you plant all these flowers?"
"Yes, all of them."
"They're very beautiful, Mr. Thomas."
"Not as beautiful as you."
She laughed, then placed her hand over her mouth.
"Don't, Claudia, don't hide. It's so rare that you smile. Let me see it . . .

. . . I shouted
At the tree, and told it to live, and
though it fought to breathe without
leaves, neither my voice nor the rain
could heal it . . .

"We'll plant another willow. We'll start over—a new tree."
"Sounds lovely."
"Yes, it does."

All the words she had ever spoken seemed to be coming back to her.
Her life with Thomas had not been so bad. Why, then, had she taken a
knife and stabbed him? She laughed at herself. It was funny—the whole
thing. She felt she could laugh until she died, then laugh all the way to

hell. All she had wanted was to be free of him. She had hated him. Now she wasn't so sure. Maybe it was just the way it ended. It was no way to end—with a knife. She owed him more than the sharp blade of a knife. She whispered his name—such a natural thing to do.

She wondered about her room, wondered if the house had grown dusty—no one there to make sure it was clean. *Thomas, was it you who sent that man? Did you send for me? I never meant to hurt you. Goddamn you, Thomas. Did you love me? Did you?* She kept her eyes focused on the distant house. It seemed alone and deserted. Thomas wasn't home. He was still in the hospital, but she knew he would come back. She had taken him away from his house, taken him away from everything he loved. Somehow, she felt that if she stood here long enough, he would appear. He would open the gates. She placed her hands on the iron gates and shook them, but she was not strong enough to force open the gates.

"Lady, you forgot to pay me."

The cabdriver's voice startled her. She wiped the tears from her eyes. "I'm sorry," she said. "There's nobody home."

part
3

Gloria. In a Different House.

When she'd reluctantly left the closed gates protecting Thomas's house, she had not wanted to return. To this different house. Jenny's apartment was only a temporary place of keeping. What did it matter where she was being kept? And *who* kept her—that matter was up to her. She had returned only because she could think of no other place to go. And she felt a kind of loyalty to Jenny—to her kindness. Thinking of Jenny made her feel calmer. But the calmness was strange.

She made herself some coffee, thumbed through a magazine, then took a nap. She slept deeply, dreamed Thomas's hands. She felt them on her legs, her thighs, her breasts. She felt them on her neck, her face. Her hair.

She sat in that room. In Jenny's home. Jenny who did not treat her as if she were nothing more than a rare and luminous stone. In Jenny's house she was not expected to glisten in the sun like a blade of grass in a well-tended garden.

She should be happy. She *had* been happy the first day she walked out onto the street. But that feeling had gone away, gone away like her mother and father and brother. As she stared at herself in the mirror, she felt as sterile as the basement she had lived in for most of her life. She remembered the mirrors in the bathroom, how, when she looked into them, a hundred images appeared before her eyes—as if there were more than just one of her, as if all those reflected images of herself were there to keep her company, giving her the illusion that she was not alone. She had sometimes seen her family in those mirrors: a quiet father who lived in a calm place, a mother whose busy hands never rested from work, never rested from touching. And a brother who made it his job to make sure his younger sister felt protected, always safe. A part of her had always felt that her family had been destroyed on the day she was taken, their home decaying into a place of mourning, in ruins—the curtains closed—no sun—the residents shutting out the world. Another part of her hoped they had survived—had commended her memory to vigilant saints, then continued as if she had never existed. She had tried to do that, too, had tried to pretend she was born in the house where she lived, the house of flowers and wine; the house of many books; the house of gardens and knowledge; the house of mirrors—mirrors that were nothing more than extensions of Thomas's eyes. She had been born there, she told herself, had never lived anywhere else. Just there. But she could never bring herself to believe that lie. There was the memory of her family. And the hope of return—that hope had been more seductive than Thomas's voice. When she had walked out of jail that day, she felt for an instant that she had become light. The pure light of morning. She could go anywhere. She could be anything. When she had looked down at the city, its beauty, its miraculous and overwhelming largeness—she had felt at that moment that she was free, felt she was close—at last—to the land of the living. She remembered a look on Jenny's face, a certain look that told her that the door she had waited a lifetime to open would never open. Other doors would open, but never that one. Behind the other doors, no faces of her family. Other doors, and behind them—hope? More hope? Not that. She was tired of that. Maybe the only thing that was left behind the other doors was a man who followed her like a ghost, reminding her that she was not—would never be—free. He was a messenger from Thomas—and the message: She was bound to the man who had claimed her as his. Bound, never to be unloosed. Behind every door, the ghost of Thomas Blacker. She had seen him in the mirrors of the room where she was kept. She had escaped the room, but she had not escaped his voice or his face or his grasp. She had once thought she could elude his reach by tricking him. When she had stopped taking the pill, she had thought: I have escaped. He cannot reach me. She was certain she would have a baby, and she often pictured herself handing the baby to him. *You see. I have done this. You could not prevent it. You cannot own a body that is not yours.* But she had only managed to create one more false hope. Like the hundred images of herself in the mirrors, the power of her body had been an illusion.

In a different house now. With Jenny. But she missed his voice, missed the way he spoke to her. She wished she could hear that voice one more time. Just one more time.

Secrets

When Jenny came home that evening, she found Gloria lying on the couch. She seemed tired or disturbed or aloof. It was such a difficult thing to read her. "Are you okay?" she asked.

"I'm fine," Gloria said. She knew Jenny did not believe her.

"You don't look well, honey."

"I'm fine—really I am."

"Maybe you should go to a doctor?"

She did not want to go to a doctor. What would a doctor know about her sickness? She thought of what to say. "Just my period," she'd said finally. "Sometimes I get cramps." It was only a small lie.

Jenny walked away and returned with some tampons and a glass of bourbon. She handed them to Gloria and smiled. "This and a hot shower will make you a new woman." A new woman? She hated Jenny in that instant, hated her for her generosity. Go away. You're so addicted to talking. Talking is your god, your salvation. Jenny Richard, I was saved because *I did not talk.*

"How was the shrink?" she heard Jenny ask.

"The shrink?"

"The therapist."

"The therapist was fine."

"Did you like her?"

Gloria nodded. Jenny knew enough to leave her alone, knew enough to sense that she was in no mood for talking. That was all she wanted—to be left alone.

Gloria walked into her room, stared out the window. The sun was not out today. It was gray. A mirror for the city. There was only gray.

She would say nothing to Jenny about having gone to see Thomas. There was nothing to talk about. And she would not understand. She would say nothing about the man who had frightened her, who had followed her. Maybe he wasn't real. Maybe Thomas was right. Maybe she *was* insane.

◆ ◆ ◆

Jenny combed her hair with her fingers as she sipped a glass of wine. Gloria's visit to the therapist had probably upset her. But there was no way out for her. Each exit would be painful. But she had to find a way out. *In love with that sonofabitch.* Stockholm syndrome—that's what Dave had said. Yes, yes. So easy to diagnose—as if the diagnosis itself was a kind of cure. But the cure could not be worse than the disease. There could be no worse disease than being in love with a man like Thomas Blacker.

But she would be difficult to heal—if healing was possible. She was such an enigma, as elusive as a sunny day in winter. How she withdrew sometimes, how she went away, hid—and then came back as if nothing had happened, as if she had led a charmed and easy life. How she refused to speak of her grief over discovering that her family was dead. Of this she never spoke. Whatever she felt was hers alone. And yet, how she reached out, laughed like a girl, wanted to be alive, struggled to understand what had befallen her. How she did not deny anything, wanted to embrace, wanted to face the loneliness and the horror of what she had lived, the role she had been forced to play—struggling to let loose the shackles. Prisoner. Captive. And yet how she would not speak those words—refused to wear them. How she hated Thomas, was appalled by his cruelty. How she was so acutely aware of how he had damaged her. And yet, how she remained so loyal to his many acts of kindness—and felt like a traitor when she thought of her attempt to kill him. How she so quickly learned to respond to her new freedoms. How there had been joy on her face when she'd looked out and seen the city as if she were looking into the eyes of God. How she was so deeply afraid. And yet so unafraid. How she would always be scarred.

Good Morning, Chicago

Thomas sat at the edge of the bed, dressed himself. His clothes felt good. He was a little thinner, but he had always been thin. He felt strong again, did not feel as if he were dying. He thought of his house, wondered if it would look different without Claudia. The house had meant everything to him once. But so had Claudia—and she had betrayed him, betrayed him in *his house. In his own house.* He tried to push the bad things away. He was alive. He felt as if he had died, then risen from the dead. He was clean. He was new. He remembered his dream—how she had come to him, and they were together in the cool ocean. Together. She would come back. He would make sure she would never leave him. Never again.

"Are you ready, Thomas?" Henry gestured toward his friend.

"Ahh, Henry. How's the good doctor?"

"Just fine, Thomas. You're sure you want to go back there?"

"It's my house, Henry." He could feel his face tightening. He smiled.

"I spoke to Herald. He said he'd stop in tonight—to look in on you. I'll look in on you periodically as well. That is, if you don't mind."

"Not at all, Henry. Not at all." He slowly pulled himself off the bed and held his side. He forced himself not to groan. "I'm still a little sore."

"That's to be expected, Thomas."

He nodded, walked to the window, and stared out at the distant lake. He wondered what Claudia was doing, wondered if the city had seduced her. "Living in that lawyer's apartment," he muttered.

"What's that, Thomas?

"Nothing, Henry. Nothing at all." *Take me home. I'll wait until she comes.*

◆ ◆ ◆

"It's a lovely morning, *que no,* George?"

"What's with the Spanish, Murph?"

"I like Spanish when I'm happy."

"I see Jenny Richard written all over your face."

241

"You're full of shit, George."

"Yeah, well, maybe so—but I still smell that lady lawyer all over you."

"Impossible. I was home all night. Which you weren't."

"I was out. And you were supposed to meet me—I called on your cellular. Only got that damned message of yours." He tossed a file on his desk. "Got another one for you. Captain wants us on this one right away."

He reached for his coat. "Ahhh, life in the city. Another damned day, another damned death."

"Well, we *could* be on the drug beat."

"At least those motives are less messy."

"Bodies bleed, Murph—don't make any difference who shot 'em. Don't make any difference why."

"Let's vamoose."

They walked out the door, down the hall. As they walked toward the car, George smiled. "Captain's pissed. Says when we're off a case, we're off a case." He opened the door to the car. "And guess what?"

"Why do you always do that?"

"Do what?"

" 'Guess what?' Why do you always do that?"

"Blame it on my mother."

"I like your mother. Leave your mother out of this."

"So are you gonna guess—or what?"

Murph nodded. "The journals—they're missing."

George smiled. "You're getting good at this game. Was just in there, checking something out. And guess what else? They don't even have the paperwork on them. They were never there. No one ever saw them. Lots of traffic in that evidence room. Lots of traffic, Murph."

"We got a judge who says we got them."

"No, Murph, we ain't got shit. We got a judge who says we got permission. Far as anyone knows, *we* lost 'em. It's our ass, Murph."

"And the captain—"

"Captain won't say nothin', Murph. We don't say nothin', *he won't say nothin'*. Simple. Next time, he says we're off a case, he means we're off a case." George laughed. "I love that look on your face."

"That sonofabitch. That bastard. That dirty rat fucker."

Ahh, Love, Let Us Be True . . .

"I have to go back to the therapist today."

"So soon?"

"She wanted to see me again."

Jenny nodded. "Not a bad idea." Gloria put down the morning newspaper. "You like her?"

"Yes," Gloria said.

"It went well yesterday?" Jenny wanted to ask her more about her sessions, but it was clear Gloria had no desire to talk. It was difficult to respect her distance, but she had no choice.

Gloria nodded, then poured herself a cup of coffee, her back to Jenny.

"What time's your appointment?"

"Eleven-thirty."

"You think you can find your way there?"

Gloria turned around and faced her, coffee mug in her hand. "I'll take a cab, like I did yesterday. It was easy."

Jenny lit her first morning cigarette. "I don't know. Maybe——"

"Maybe what, Jenny?"

"I don't know—this thing with Charlie. I was thinking I shouldn't leave you alone."

"What could happen? I lock the door—I won't let anybody in. I'll go, then come right back." She looked at Jenny, tried to read what was in her head.

"I think you should spend the day in my office—you could organize my files—they could use——"

"You're acting just like Thomas." She paused, then continued, her voice firm, studied in its anger. "He controlled everything I did. He had to keep me close—always. Either that or lock me up. Is that what you want?"

There was something in Gloria's voice that almost made Jenny afraid. *This girl's about to explode.* It was good she was going to see the shrink again. Whatever it took. It was out of her hands—she refused to lock her up as if she were a rare animal in a zoo. "I'm sorry," Jenny said softly.

"You don't need to be kept anymore, do you?" She smiled. "You have enough cab fare?"

◆ ◆ ◆

Gloria shook her head, was disgusted with herself. She had used Jenny's reaction as a weapon. But Jenny would stop her from trying to see Thomas—she would not understand. She picked up the phone, her hand almost trembling. She dialed Thomas's number. She had heard him give it out to people over the phone; people he called, people he thought were important. She remembered it like she remembered the way he said her name, the way he touched her. The body remembered everything. She waited for the phone to ring. She would speak to him. She would beg him to tell that man to stop following her, tell him that the man was scaring her. She would tell him she needed him. No, not that she needed him, but that she needed him to listen. Just to listen. He owed her that. She would tell him she was sorry. He was intelligent. He understood so many things. The phone rang, then rang again. She knew the machine would answer after the fourth ring. *Please, Thomas, please be home.* When she heard the answering machine, she almost smiled at the sound of his voice. Familiar and friendly—easy and graceful. He was so good with words, as if he had invented them. She heard the beep, opened her mouth to speak—but it was so useless to leave a message. She hung up the phone and stared at it. Whatever she had to say, it would have to wait.

◆ ◆ ◆

Gloria picked up the phone again, then dialed the number on the card Jenny had given her. She listened to the receptionist's voice, explained again how she could not possibly make the appointment. Perhaps next week. She would call and reschedule when she was feeling better, couldn't talk, was feeling ill, yes, yes, she was sorry. She was very sorry. Couldn't be helped, she was feeling so tired, had not slept. But the woman was kind, told her she could come in the morning, had an opening. Yes, yes, she would go then. She promised. Why had she promised? She had no intention of keeping the appointment. She hung up the phone, put on a coat, then walked outside. She walked the streets aimlessly, felt eyes on her again. She didn't care, didn't feel like running. What could he do to her? There were people all around. They would protect her. She saw a cab, stuck out her arm. It stopped in front of her. A miracle. The ways of the city could be so civilized. She looked around, thought she saw the man from the day before. She wanted to wave at him, tell him she knew it was Thomas who had sent him, tell him she needed no messengers. *I will go to him myself.* She gave the young cab-driver Thomas's address.

◆ ◆ ◆

Henry held the door open for him, but Thomas shook his head: "I'd rather sit in the back." Thomas's voice was hard and stubborn, as unbending as a skyscraper against the Chicago wind. Henry nodded. "That's fine, Thomas." He watched as his friend eased himself into the back of the car. He got into the driver's seat, smiled at Thomas, then started the car. He'd assumed Thomas would want to sit in the front seat with him. He felt like a chauffeur. *Needs his space, I suppose.* He looked at the rearview mirror and noticed that Thomas appeared to be talking to himself, muttering. He saw him open the window to his right. "It's a little cold, Thomas, don't you think?"

"I need the air, Henry. I need to feel it. Do you mind?"

"Not at all."

They fell silent, no words coming to either of them. Henry wondered what Thomas could be thinking, wondered if he was doing the right thing by taking him home. Thomas wondered how long it would be before he would see Claudia. He willed her to come before he became too weak. He would keep himself strong until she came. Henry kept his eyes on the road—a deliberate and careful driver. Thomas stared out the window, sometimes nodding as if he were greeting someone familiar. Finally, he tired of the scenery. He wished Henry would drive faster. *Get on with it, man. Just get me home.*

◆ ◆ ◆

"Fancy neighborhood," he said, then laughed.

"Yes," Gloria repeated. "Very fancy. You know it?"

245

He laughed.

She laughed with him.

When they arrived at the address, she asked him to wait. If the gates were open, it would be a sign—and she would pay the driver, tell him to leave. If the gates were closed, she would wait. He would be coming. She knew. She stood at the gates for a long time. She wanted to yell his name: "Thomas! Thomas!" She uttered his name to herself over and over, screamed it to herself, until his name shook her, until she turned red with rage or love or exasperation. She felt her knees buckle. She kept hold of the gates, did not fall—they held her up. She wondered why she could not bring herself to shout out the name of the man. The man she loved. His name. It had become more than the name of a man.

The cabdriver had the urge to drive away, was certain something was not right with this woman. But something about her made him want to help. She seemed like a penitent wailing silent prayers to a god who had abandoned her. He walked toward her, watched her for what seemed an eternity. Finally, he spoke to her. "Maybe I should take you back home," he whispered.

She nodded, slowly made her way back to the cab. But she hesitated, did not get in. She smiled at the driver. He was good, she thought. He was good like Jenny. But she, she was not good. She would never be good. She stood next to the car, disgusted by the control she exerted over her own body. She was always so composed. *Composed.* That was a word Thomas often used. *You are so composed, my dear.* Jenny would never use that word. "I'm sorry," she said, then looked toward Thomas's house again.

He smiled back at her. "Oh, it's all right. Nothing to be sorry for. Long as you got the cab fare, it don't much matter to me."

She laughed. He was very funny. He was funny like Jenny.

◆ ◆ ◆

"That's odd."

"What, Henry?"

"There appears to be someone in your driveway. It's a taxicab. Were you expecting someone?"

Thomas lurched forward and saw a woman leaning against the bright yellow taxi. She was wearing a long, dark coat, and her hair—her hair was as dark as a winter night. He would've known her anywhere. He watched as she stepped into the cab, watched as the car took her away from his grasp. So close. He could almost touch her. "Stop them," he yelled. "Henry, stop them!"

"What are you yelling about, Thomas?"

"Stop them, I said. Are you deaf, man?"

Henry stopped the car in front of Thomas's gate. "What's all this nonsense about?"

Thomas fell back into his seat. *It was her. Can you see nothing?* He sat still, controlled himself. This man knew nothing, could not heal him, was incapable of understanding. "Never mind, Henry." *You idiot, if you'd have driven faster, she'd be mine again.* He smiled at his old friend. "Let's just get me inside the house. I need to rest."

◆ ◆ ◆

As they drove slowly away, she looked back and noticed a car pulling up into Thomas's driveway. It was him, she thought, though she saw no one. He was coming home. "Stop," she said. She could feel herself trembling. "Never mind. Just take me home." She wondered why she had used the word *home.* She gave the driver Jenny's address but kept looking back toward Thomas Blacker's house. *He's back. We'll plant a new willow, would you like that?*

A Man's Home Is His . . .

"Let me help you, Thomas."

"That's very kind of you, Henry. I can manage." He opened the car door, took a deep breath, then stepped out of the car. He held his chest as he looked at his house, the largeness of it. Such lovely architecture, he thought. He stood as motionless as a gargoyle guarding a cathedral. Henry watched his old friend who did not look weak, did not look like a man who had been stabbed, like a man who was dying. Such a miraculous recovery. He wondered how it was that this man refused to give up. Was it his mind? Or was it something in his genes? His look was so determined that it almost frightened him. He was such a stranger, this man he'd known for so many years—this man he'd known but never known. And what about that car? He'd known who was in it. *That woman.* It must have been her. He did not understand any of this. He watched as Thomas walked slowly, almost painfully toward the front door. His walk betrayed him. He was old. The spring in his step would not return. Even men like him grew old, he thought. He watched as Thomas reached in his pocket and searched for his keys.

"Oh, sorry." Henry laughed nervously. "I completely forgot. Herald dropped off the new keys."

"The new keys?"

"The police broke down the door. Herald had a new one put in."

"Broke down my door, did they?" He examined everything carefully. "Yes, I see. It's just like the old one. You can hardly tell."

"Herald's very careful.

"Yes, he is."

Henry handed him the keys. Thomas took them, turned the lock, opened the door. He walked into his house half expecting to see Claudia waiting for him.

But she had left again. In that cab. She had not noticed he was arriving at his house. If she had seen him, she would have returned. Maybe it was better this way. He would be more prepared the next time she paid him a visit.

◆ ◆ ◆

He wandered the house, walking into each room. The same house, his favorite paintings untouched, the kitchen clean and spotless, the dining room as immaculate as the day his wife had furnished it. No signs of that night. Everything in its place. Herald had made sure there were no reminders. He thought of his wound. *What's a scar to men at our age, Thomas? What's a little scar?* But everything was *not* in its place. Claudia's pills, they were gone. *That lieutenant would have to pay.* His journals. *They had no right. What gave them the right? That lieutenant . . .* His eyes fell on the empty space in his library where he had kept his journals. He screamed Claudia's name as he took a book and flung it across the room. Then another, then another. The books flew across the room like bats flying out of a cave. Book after book. *They had no right. They had no right.* He leaned over on his desk, exhausted. He swept his hand across the desk, every object falling to the floor. He clenched his jaw, then walked toward the basement, his body grotesque in its awkward movements. When he reached the basement, he searched the room with his eyes. Her things, they were gone. The dresses. They were hers. *Goddamn you, Lieutenant.* His shout was the howl of a hungry animal. His face twisted like a cypress tree that had grown crooked and gnarled fighting the wind. No one had seen that face. No one but Claudia. Gloria.

Secrets

At four o'clock in the afternoon, Gloria stared at the hands of the small machine whose only job was to measure the hours—its repetitive task endless and dull and monotonous. The afternoon sky had turned nearly as black as her eyes. As she looked out her window, a cold rain fell like nails on the ground. It was as if everything was so filthy that the sky had decided to give the city a washing it would never forget. Gloria opened the window, stared at the storming sky. She wanted to feel the heaviness of the rain on her skin. She could still smell Thomas in the room. Like the city, she needed to be washed.

Damn the man who was following her, she thought. Damn him. She'd had enough of staying patiently in rooms. She reached for a coat in her closet, then changed her mind. She would walk in the rain without a coat. She would feel the cold. She was tired of being protected.

As she stepped toward the front door, she heard a noise. Someone at the door. She stepped away, saw the knob turning, did not move. It was Jenny—but Jenny worked late, had never been home before seven. Thomas. He had found her. She stood still—as if she had become inanimate. If it was Thomas, perhaps he would not notice her, would think she was nothing more than one of his pieces of art. Nothing real. He would not find her here. Not here. Not now. *Come, my dear.* She could smell his breath, could almost feel his tongue. She did not notice the dog barking, did not even see the door open.

She found herself staring into his eyes. The man in the coffee shop, the man in the elevator, the man who had asked her if she was afraid. The little girls, they were not here to save her. Bessie's growl turned louder. She did not move, found herself as frozen as a piece of ice. She watched as Bessie leapt at the man. She watched as the man flung her off, the dog attacking him, again led by her instincts to survive, to protect the place that belonged to her. Again, he flung her off. And again Bessie leapt, but this time the man met her with a swift and violent kick. The man—he, too, had instincts. The dog fell to the ground, and he kicked her again and again, until her growl turned into a whimper. Finally, the dog's whimper turned into a deep and heavy breathing, loud as the rain outside. Gloria watched the fight, immobile, a paralyzed spectator. She felt the tightness of her chest, her breathing as labored as the dog that lay still on the floor.

The man looked into her eyes. "Don't be afraid." His deep voice echoed in the room.

He took a step toward her.

Gloria said nothing, her eyes glued to his.

"Don't be afraid."

"Afraid of what?" Gloria shut her eyes at the sound of Charlie's voice.

"Charlie," she whispered. "Thank God." She opened her eyes and saw the man and Charlie glaring into each other's faces, a few inches separating them.

"What have you done to Bessie? You sonofabitch, what have you done to my dog?"

The man looked at Charlie and smiled. "The dog had it coming," he said. Charlie leapt at the man, not unlike Bessie had a few moments earlier. But the man was bigger than Charlie, both of them struggling against each other, the force of their bodies almost graceful in their power. Gloria found herself moving toward the men's frenzied dance. She felt her fists close, the pain in her hand as it hit the man's ribs. Then suddenly the man managed to free himself of them—was gone, out the door. Down the stairs.

"You okay?" Charlie whispered. She fell into his arms. "Charlie, Charlie," she whispered. "Charlie, Charlie, Charlie."

"You're shaking like a leaf," he said. "It's okay." He let go of her and smiled, then turned and saw Bessie lying on the floor. He knelt next to her. The hurt dog did not move, but she was still breathing. "We've got to get her to a vet," he said. He placed his hand on the dog's face. "Good dog," he whispered.

Gloria wiped the sweat from her face. She watched Charlie kneeling over the dog he clearly loved. To love, she thought. To love anything. To look at someone like Charlie was looking at the dog. To look at someone like Jenny looked at the lieutenant. Had she looked at Thomas like that? She wanted to know, *had* to know. And that man, he might have helped her to know. But he had made her afraid, too afraid to ask him about Thomas. He was gone. She was safe. Was she safe? She shook herself awake. She stared at the dog and Charlie. They were the only things in the room that mattered. The only thing in the world. They had met the unexpected with a fight. They had not stood like inanimate objects. She made herself stop shaking. *Enough. You are not a thing.* She placed her hand on Charlie's back. "I'll help you carry Bessie," she said.

◆ ◆ ◆

As Jenny placed the key in the door to her apartment, she wondered if Gloria would be more talkative tonight. She had been silent and wordless the past few days, had not even mentioned her family since the day she was told they were dead. They could not be so dead that the living could not speak of them. The dead could rot the living—she knew about that. When she opened the door, she saw Gloria pacing in the living room.

251

Gloria looked at her, then tried to smile. She opened her mouth, but words did not spill out. "Maybe you should sit down," she said finally.

"What's wrong?"

"Bessie's been hurt."

"What?"

"It's my fault. A man—"

"What man?"

"A man—he broke into the house."

"What?" Jenny was surprised at the calmness of her own voice.

Gloria looked at the floor. "He was just a man."

"Just a man?" Jenny's voice lost its composure. "And he just happened to break into my apartment?"

"Yes."

"How?"

"I don't know. I was just standing there—and I looked up. And he'd opened the door and he told me not to be afraid." She looked at Jenny. "Thomas. I think Thomas sent him."

Jenny nodded. "What makes you say that?"

"I don't know. It's just what I think."

"Have you ever seen him before?"

"Never."

Jenny looked at Gloria. "When you went to see the psychiatrist, did you come straight home?"

"Yes."

"And did you notice if anyone was following you?"

"No."

"You're sure?"

Gloria looked into Jenny's eyes and nodded.

"I don't like this. I don't like this at all. Whoever that man was—" She stopped. "What did he say to you?"

"He just said, 'Don't be afraid.' That was all."

"Nothing else."

"Nothing. It all happened so fast, and Bessie—she jumped at him. And he—he hurt her. And then Charlie walked in the door, and—I'm sorry, Jenny. It's my fault. I know it's all my fault. Bessie was just trying to protect me." She sat down on a chair. "I'm a lot of trouble."

"Is my Bessie—"

"She's going to be fine." Gloria noticed the look of relief on Jenny's face. "Charlie has her." She combed her long hair with her fingers. "If Charlie hadn't come along, I don't know what he'd—he and Bessie—I don't know what to do."

"It's okay," Jenny said softly. She lit a cigarette. "It's not your fault. Those sons of bitches—"

Gloria leaned over the table. Jenny couldn't tell if she was crying or laughing. So much emotion on that face, so much feeling—like the winter sky, volatile, alive, no sign of death—and yet so much of death. Jenny thought she would never stop laughing—or crying—whichever she was doing. So much feeling from someone who exhibited so little of it. Slowly, Gloria calmed herself down. She took a deep breath. "I really must be completely out of my mind." She wiped the tears from her face.

Jenny walked into the kitchen and returned with two glasses of wine in her hands. "Drink," she said.

A new season, my dear. She took the glass from Jenny's hand, then nodded. They sat in silence as Jenny finished her cigarette. "Why don't you and I go down to Charlie's place and have a look in on Bessie?"

◆ ◆ ◆

Jenny stood at the door to Gloria's bedroom. "You okay?"

"Yes, I was just reading."

"Bessie's going to be fine."

"I'm glad, she's a good dog." Gloria put down the book she was holding.

"There's something I think you should know—it's in the journals." Jenny's voice was sober. Serious.

"Why don't you just tell me what's in them?"

"This is one thing you have to do for yourself."

"I have no right to read them."

"That's horseshit, Gloria."

"Maybe so."

"Gloria—"

"Don't, Jenny—I can't."

"Listen to me. This is the man who's behind what happened to Charlie. This is the man who's behind the guy who broke into the house this afternoon. It's damn time you learned what the man had planned—" She stopped herself from saying any more. She sat on the bed. "You're afraid, aren't you?"

"Of what?"

"Of what you might find in there."

"What's that supposed to mean?"

"I think you won't read his journals because you're afraid of losing him. If you read what he wrote, then you'll have to let him go. Because you'll know. You'll know everything. And a part of you needs to keep loving him."

"That's an interesting theory. I thought you were a lawyer."

"Yes, I am. They don't call me counselor for nothing."

Gloria laughed. She leaned her chin on her wrist. "Do you mind very much if we change the subject?"

"Yes, I mind a great deal. This man is hurting people, and you're too delicate to read his journals?" She slammed the door as she walked away.

◆ ◆ ◆

Gloria heard a quiet knock at the door. "That you, Jenny?"

She heard the door open. "You awake? I'm sorry I yelled at you. I didn't mean to hurt you."

"I'll be fine."

"Don't lie to me."

"Okay. I'm not fine."

"Good night, then," Jenny said. "I'm waking you up early. I'm not leaving you alone anymore."

"Why?"

"Because I don't want to come home and find your body on my living room floor—that's why."

"Jenny?"

"What?"

"Why are we whispering in the dark?"

"So the man who broke in won't hear us."

She heard the door shut. Gloria laughed to herself. I like this woman, she thought—so impossible to hate. Her anger was not at all like Thomas Blacker's. Stubborn—but not mean. She did not punish with silence, did not withhold words to get what she wanted. She knew how to forgive—how to accept forgiveness. She wondered where she had learned that. And yet Gloria had not told her the whole truth, had not trusted her. If she liked her so much, why was she lying to her? Not lies, really, just secrets. *What's wrong with me?* She called herself Claudia in the dark.

The Swamp Needs Draining

"So where do you plan on hiding me today?"

"You can stay in my office. You can organize my files. God knows, they could use organizing. I'm going to be in court most of the day, anyway. I've got plenty of work for you to do."

"You sound like Lieutenant Murphy."

"Thank you."

"But I have another session with the psychiatrist."

"Again?"

"It was *your* idea."

Jenny nodded. "Okay. When it's time to go to your appointment, take a cab. Then take a cab back. *And no walking.*"

Gloria stared at her. "I promise."

They both smiled, then laughed.

◆ ◆ ◆

"I want you to put a tail on her, Lieutenant."

"Are you nuts, Jenny? You're overreacting. And don't light that cigarette."

"I hate that. How did you know I was going to light one?"

"I just did. I know you."

"No, you don't. You don't know shit."

He laughed. "Where did you come from?"

"New Orleans. I'm the southern bitch from hell. And I'm telling you he would have hurt her. And poor Bessie has two broken ribs."

"She gonna be okay?"

"Charlie's taking care of her."

"Who's taking care of *him*?"

"One of his friends is staying with him."

"Well, tell him not to travel alone."

"Are you going to help us out or not?"

"I'm off the case, Jenny, haven't you heard? What am I supposed to do?"

"What about George?"

"George and I are up to our asses in crocodiles."

"Well, the swamp needs draining."

"God, you're relentless."

She smiled into the receiver, then lit her cigarette. "Sandy, please."

"It's not fair."

"What's not fair?"

"You called me Sandy."

"Nice, huh?"

"You don't play fair."

"Just put a tail on her." She slammed down the phone. She yelled toward Gloria's room. "You ready, honey? We gotta get moving."

◆ ◆ ◆

When Jenny walked into her office, there was a message on her answering machine: "I got it taken care of. You owe me one. Oh, and I forgot to tell you. The professor's journals are missing. That didn't take long, did it?"

Jenny looked at Gloria.

Gloria shrugged. "Well, we have another copy, don't we?"

Jenny nodded. *Yup, and they're nice and safe.*

In the Basement

Thomas Blacker slept into the early afternoon. He was grateful not to remember what he had been dreaming. His dreams had always made him feel tired and heavy, and he detested waking with a weight that made him want to sink into the earth. But today, as he opened his eyes, he felt light, found himself in Claudia's bed, her smell still lingering on the sheets. He breathed in her scent, then stood up. He looked around the empty room, then walked into the closets. All those lovely dresses, he thought. He had taught her to—"*Would you like to dance, my dear?*"

"*I don't know how to dance, Thomas.*"

"*Here, I'll show you how.*" *He reached for her left hand and placed it in his.* "*Now place your other hand on my shoulder. Yes, just like that. Now, pretend you're listening to a Schubert waltz, and just follow my steps. It's really very simple.*"

"*Schubert,*" *she repeated.* "*I'm trying to remember—*" He thought of the curious look on her face, the way she carried herself, the way all those dresses fell on her body. Some had come from Europe, some from Los Angeles, some from New York—all of them now sitting in a filthy property room. He would get them back. The dresses and the journals. He pictured her changing into a dress.

◆ ◆ ◆

He heard the receptionist's voice, told her it was urgent, that he had to speak to Mr. Burns. He waited impatiently, pacing the floor, his eyes darting restlessly from one object in the room to another as if nothing he saw satisfied or pleased him. When he heard Herald's voice on the telephone, he spoke angrily. "They have my journals, Herald. They have no right to them. I want them back. I want them immediately. Now!"

"Calm down, Thomas. They're not going to use them—I've seen to that. You needn't worry—"

"I want them back! And the dresses, I want them back, too. I want you to have them back to me as soon—"

"I'm afraid that's impossible, Thomas."

"Nothing is impossible, Herald."

"I'll see what I can do."

"That's not good enough."

"It will have to be good enough."

"I said, get them. Do I make myself clear?" Thomas slammed down the phone. He reached for his medication, then stared out the window. His garden was bare. *I'll make it grow again.*

◆ ◆ ◆

The poor bastard. Herald Burns held the phone receiver in his hand, then placed it back in its cradle. I'm trying to save his ass, and he's thinking of dresses and journals. How to save him from himself, he thought. They had to follow their plan. They'd agreed to it. He picked up the phone, pushed the numbers, and waited. When he heard his voice, he just spoke: "Thomas, I'm sorry. I'll get you the journals. I'll get them as soon as I can. Today may be too soon. But I'll get them. You have my word. And you have to trust me. But you may have to let the dress thing drop. I'm sorry about that." He spoke firmly into the phone. He waited for Thomas to answer.

"That will be fine, Herald." His voice was calmer now.

"I think they'll agree to everything at this point. Just leave it to me."

"I want to see her," he said quietly.

"I don't think that's very wise, Thomas."

"But she wants to see me, too."

"What are you talking about?"

"Nothing, Herald. Never mind." It was better not to tell him that she had already come in search of him. Herald was only his lawyer—nothing more than that. "We'll stick to the plan," he said. "I'm sorry to have yelled at you, Herald. You'll pardon me, won't you. I'm not myself."

What Are You Gonna Do—
Call the Cops?

"We should have called the feds in from the beginning."

"We still can."

"All we have is a lot of missing evidence."

"We have Gloria. She can prove our case for us. *And she looks exactly like the little girl in the picture.* There are records in the hospital where she was born, I'm sure. And we have Charlie's testimony. Bet we can match the handwriting on that note. We have enough. We have more than enough. The feds can take it from there. *And without the fucking interference of Chicago's finest.*"

"So let's do it."

"It'll mean going over everybody's head." George made a face as he took a sip of his morning coffee. "You make terrible coffee."

"So don't marry me." Murphy took a drink from the mug he was holding. "It's not so bad. I'm just trying to be a good roommate." He laughed. "Give me a break. I'll be out of here soon enough."

"I don't mind the company, Murph."

He nodded. "We go over everybody's head, George, it'll mean our asses."

"What can they do to us?"

"You want to work in this town again, George?"

"I can always do something else."

"Like what?"

"I know how to mow lawns."

"You're full of shit, George."

George shook his head. "You want to be a cop for the rest of your life?"

Murph waited a long time before he shook his head. "I don't know. Maybe not. You?"

"Look, this is what I know. I've worked my black ass off for this. But not at any cost, Murph."

Murphy bit down on his lip, then winced. He flashed his teeth at George. "What if we go down?"

"Then we go down."

Murph smiled. "We won't go down alone."

"Now you're talkin' the talk."

"You've worked toward sergeant a long time. Captain hates my ass. You can hold on if you want."

"Can't let you do that, Murph."

"You sure, George?"

"Let me tell you something, my man." He dug his finger into Murph's chest. "Fifteen years ago, when I came into this department, no one liked me. Affirmative-action cop. Worked my ass off out in the streets. Took the tests, went to school, got called everything in the book—by both sides. The whole fucking bit. You were the only white guy in that whole fucking place who didn't pretend I wasn't black." He pulled his finger away from his chest. "You go down—*I go down.*"

"And what you worked for, George?"

"My old man told me to be a good cop—so I'm gonna do that, Murph." George took another sip of coffee. He made a face. "This tastes like piss."

Murph nodded. He felt relieved. Whatever happened, he was glad for this. In all his years in the department, he had won a lot of respect. And no friends. Except for George. He smiled. "I talked to Jenny Richard on the phone this morning."

"That who called?"

"Yup."

"Gave her this number?"

"Yup. She wants a tail put on Gloria Santos. Someone's been following her."

"You thinking what I'm thinking?"

"What happened to Charlie could happen to Gloria."

"Or worse."

"Can't let that happen, George."

"Who we gonna get?"

He took out a coin. "Heads or tails?"

Captain, My Captain

The captain was waiting in Lieutenant Murphy's empty office when George and the lieutenant arrived. "Are we late?" George asked as he offered the captain a smile.

"I've got better things to do than keep time cards." The captain seemed more impatient than usual.

"Don't sell yourself short, Captain. You'd be good at it." George's voice was even and friendly.

"I got no battles with you, George."

"It's me he hates," Murph said. There was a hint of a grin on his face. "What's this about, Captain?" He rubbed his palm on his unshaven face.

"Haven't you got a razor?"

"Lost it. I'll get a new one when I get my next raise."

"Then you'll have to wait a while, Lieutenant."

Murph took out a cigarette, tapped it on his wrist. "Is there something I can do for you?"

"Why don't we talk about it in my office?"

Murph pointed at George. "He comes."

"This is about a case—"

"We work on a lot of cases together. He comes."

The captain said nothing, walked out of the room, then turned to make sure they were following him. When they entered his office, he stared at both of them. "Shut the door."

George slammed it shut.

"I'm frankly tired of your lack of cooperation around here."

"I'll make a note of it," George said.

The captain nodded, not at all hiding his disgust.

But he was holding back. He wanted something. Maybe this wouldn't be so bad, George thought. Maybe they'd come out on top.

The captain looked at Murphy. "Lieutenant, I understand you're currently overinvolved with—" He stared at Murphy, cold as the lake. "With Ms. Jenny Richard."

"I'm hardly overinvolved with Ms. Richard. Not that it's any of your business, Captain."

"When it interferes with departmental—"

"Can it, Captain."

"I could throw your ass out of here right now—right fucking now."

"And you would—except you want something."

The captain did his best to ignore his remark. "Your involvement with Jenny Rich—"

"My involvement with Jenny Richard consists of two lunches—one of which ended with her walking out on me over a professional disagreement—and three or four telephone calls. And—"

"And one night."

"You sonofabitch. You been tailing me? Tailing your own men?" He took out a cigarette and lit it.

"No smoking in my office."

"Would you like to put it out for me, Captain?"

The captain sat up in his chair and crossed his arms. "Let me get to the point."

"Do that." George stared stoically into the captain's eyes, then looked at his watch.

"You guys are a helluva tag team." He uncrossed his arms. "Look, whatever our differences, I'm sure we can work them out. I'm new here. I'm sure you could teach me a few things."

"Are you gonna get to it soon, Captain?" Murph took another drag from his cigarette.

"Look, just tell your friend Jenny to back off. Tell her Mr. Blacker's lawyer has a deal for her client. All she's gotta do is make sure she doesn't get too cozy with Ms. Santos. I mean, no one's going to prosecute her for stabbing the professor. You got my word on that."

"Oh, this is a big favor. The sonofabitch kidnaps her, keeps her for twenty-three years—and you're not going to prosecute her for trying to set herself free. You got a heart as big as Texas, don't you, Captain?" Murphy looked as if he were going to spit. "She's going to the feds."

"Not if you tell her not to."

"Now, why would I do that?"

"Because you want to keep your job."

Murph looked over at George, who nodded, smiled, then broke out laughing. Murph combed his hair back with his finger, then joined in the laughter.

"There's one thing you never learned, Captain."

"What's that, George?" His face was red with anger.

"You can't bribe an honest cop."

The captain pointed at Murph. "I could tell you stories about your father that would make you weep, Lieutenant. But he was just one out of a long line of—well, do I need to go into it? The Murphy family never knew an honest cop."

"It knows one now," Murph said, his eyes as steady as his voice. He dropped his cigarette on the floor and crushed it with his foot.

At the Movies

Gloria stepped out of the cab, looked at the building, then moved toward the entrance. She stopped, as if a wall were preventing her from crossing the threshold, then turned away. It was stupid to go through this charade yet another time. She looked down the street, then walked. She felt the eyes. Again. She was certain. She did not want to look around. She felt like bait in a trap. She felt a chill up her spine as if a pair of cold hands were using her body as a piano. She shut her eyes, opened them. She would have to tell Jenny she had not gone to see the therapist. It was the honest thing to do. She could go back to her office right now, tell her. But she liked the feel of the air on her face, liked that she could walk on the streets of the city without a leash or a keeper. But those eyes. She tried to ignore what she felt. She noticed a movie theater, tried to remember the last time she had been in one. Too long. Too long to remember. She had enough money. There was a matinee—had to be one. They still had matinees, didn't they? There was a woman in the glass box selling tickets. She would go in, relax, think of nothing. She would not think of Thomas; she would not think of the man following her. He could not hurt her—not at the movies. She reached in her pocket, pulled out some of the money Jenny had given her for cab fare, and bought a ticket. I'll just stay awhile, she thought. She bought a box of popcorn, tasted it, then laughed. No one could hurt her.

◆ ◆ ◆

She waited for her eyes to adjust to the darkness, found a seat away from most of the scattered few in the theater. The movie had long since started, the woman on the screen was waiting for someone. A man walked into the room. "Where have you been?" she yelled. "I was out," he said as if she were crazy. "Out? That's all you have to say?" Her eyes filled the screen, then the lens showed the distance between them. She wondered about them, if they were married, if they were lovers. They must be lovers, she thought, lovers were always so angry. She tried to let the movie absorb her, wanted it to swallow her up. But the darkness of the theater made her feel uneasy. The woman on the screen was walking on a sidewalk in the city. She seemed lost, tears falling down her face. The man had left her, had made her cry. She did not like this movie— too sad, too serious. She did not notice that a big man had moved into the chair behind her. A few minutes passed before she felt an arm dig into her shoulder. She felt her heart nearly stop. "Don't scream. I won't hurt you." The voice was deep, she could hear it in his whisper.

She turned her head.

"Don't," he whispered. "Just watch the movie."

She could feel her heart thumping, could hardly breathe. She felt his hand pull away, then something dig into her skin. His finger, no, not a finger, something colder. Too cold to be a finger. Something made of—

"You won't get hurt."

She nodded.

"I have some instructions for you, Ms. Santos."

She waited. The coldness of the metal dug deeper into her shoulder— as if he wanted to let her know that this was not a game. A gun, must be that, though she could not be certain. Too blunt to be a knife—it would have cut. She made herself sit perfectly still. "I'm listening," she heard herself say. She kept her eyes on the screen.

"Just sign the papers."

"I don't know what—"

"Just sign them, and nothing will happen to you. Remember Charlie." The gun dug deeper and deeper into her shoulders as if he wanted to push it through her body, but her body pushed back. "Just remember Charlie."

She wanted to scream. He was hurting her. She found it hard to breathe, was suddenly lost, did not know where she was. She felt the room moving around her, felt as if she were no longer in her body. She did not even know she had jerked herself away from his grasp, was not even aware of the fact that she had run out of the movie theater when she found herself leaning against the building. She did not know how long she had stood there, unable to move. Perhaps she had been there a long time. When she felt she could walk, she saw a cab. It seemed to be moving so slowly. The driver stopped for her. She must have had her arm raised. She looked at the cabdriver's face, wondered if he would take her to Thomas or to Jenny. She did not remember giving him an address.

Dresses

The street was crowded. It had been such a long time since he had walked among the masses. He found the odors on the sidewalk distasteful—the cheap colognes on men, the garbage carelessly tossed, the undignified way the women carried themselves. They wore their clothes with such disrespect—not at all like Claudia, these women.

He used a wood cane his wife had given him when he'd twisted his ankle—though he did not think of his wife as he made his way down the street. He spotted the dress shop. He'd bought something there once. He still remembered.

The woman behind the counter smiled at him. He did not want to be noticed, did not want to look out of place. "I'd like something for my niece," he said, then smiled like the kindly uncle he was pretending to be.

"A special occasion?"

"She's attending her first opera."

The woman nodded in a sincere and professional way, wanted to know the size of the dress. He told her he'd know by looking, smiled, told her he had a good eye, laughed at himself. She was charmed or perhaps just wanted to sell a dress. She showed him dresses. No, no, not that one, too severe, no, not red, not black either, oh, and she did not take to pink or lilac, and yes, the deep blue one was lovely, but she had one that was almost identical, but did she have something similar to it in a cream color—something almost white? Yes, that was the one, elegant without being gaudy, yes, of course it would fit. He was sure. And could he have it wrapped? He wanted so much to surprise her. The woman wrapped it herself as he watched. She took such good care of him. She placed the wrapped package in a strong paper bag with handles and handed it to him. Could he manage? Yes, yes, it was not heavy.

The old man walked out of the store smiling.

An Ordinary Courtship

Jenny walked out of the courtroom frowning and shaking her head. She looked up and saw Lieutenant Murphy smiling at her. "Bad day in court, Counselor?"

"You could say that."

"Judge wouldn't go for the plea bargain, huh?"

"You really want to talk about this?" She handed him her briefcase. "Wanna carry my books?"

"Yeah, sure." He laughed, then shook his head.

"How'd you find me?"

"Your new secretary told me you were in court. She's very efficient."

"I didn't want to leave her at home. Not after what happened."

"You know that girl—" He stopped.

"What?"

"This hallway's a little crowded. There's a coffee shop around the corner."

◆ ◆ ◆

"Good coffee," Jenny said as she put down her cup. "Not as good as mine, though."

"You'll have to make some for me sometime." He nodded, then looked at Jenny. "Do me a favor, will you?"

"What's wrong with you?"

He handed her his cellular phone. "You know that psychiatrist Ms. Santos is supposed to be seeing?"

"Yeah?"

"You set it up, right?"

"Of course I did."

"You want to give him a call?"

"It's a her. And why would I want to call her?"

"Just call and ask her if Ms. Santos has been keeping her appointments."

"What—"

"Just do it, okay?"

Jenny shrugged, searched for a card in her purse, then dialed the phone. She looked at the lieutenant. "I feel like an overprotective mother." She grabbed the telephone tightly. "I hate these things." She kept her eyes on the lieutenant as she heard the voice on the other end of the telephone. "Yes, this is Jenny Richard at the public defender's office." She paused, then made a face at the lieutenant. "I set up some appointments with a client under my supervision, and I was wondering if she's been showing up—Yes, yes, I know you don't normally give out that information—Yes, yes, I understand, but if you let me speak to Irene for just a moment, I'm sure she wouldn't mind giving me the information—Yes, I'll hold." She clenched her teeth. "I can't believe I'm doing this, Lieutenant. You know, she's not a—yes, Irene, how are you?" She nodded as she spoke to the therapist. "Look, I'm sorry to bother you, but remember the woman I called you about, the one that had been kidnapped?—Gloria Santos, that's right." Her face grew serious. "Oh, I see—problem—Well, I'm sorry, I see—No, no, I wouldn't worry about it—Yes, thank you. I'll be in touch—I appreciate—Yes, thank you—Me? I've never been better. Thanks for asking—Yes, that would be great. Let's do that." She handed the phone to Lieutenant Murphy and stared at him. "How did you know she hadn't been showing up to her appointments?"

"You hate being the last to know, don't you, Jenny?"

"I sure as hell do."

"I bet you hate surprises."

"Absolutely."

"And me? Am I a—"

"Surprise? No, Lieutenant, you're a cop." She smiled, then laughed. "Why am I laughing? I'm mad as hell."

"Just wait till you hear the rest of it." He rubbed his hands together.

"You're enjoying this, aren't you?"

"Hell, no, I'm not enjoying this. I'm trying to piece it all together." He took another sip of coffee, then bit his lip. "George had her followed—just like you asked. And she didn't go into the building where the cab left her off. She just walked around the city for a while—then went into a movie theater."

"What?"

"It gets better. Someone's following that girl."

"What? Who?"

"George's man got pictures—we'll know soon enough. And he said Ms. Santos and the man had a conversation in the movie theater. Said she just ran out of there like a scared rabbit."

"Did he hear what they said?"

"Nope. Guess we'll have to ask her ourselves." He looked at her and smiled. "You look upset."

"You're damned right I'm upset." She took out a cigarette, put it in her mouth, took it out again, then tossed it on the table. "I've got to get some air."

She grabbed her purse and coat and was halfway out the door of the coffee shop before Murph yelled at her. "Hey, where you going?"

"I'm going to Lincoln Park—where did you think I was going?"

"What?"

"That's where I go, goddamnit." She stood a moment, looked at him, then walked out the door.

Leaves

It was peaceful to be sitting there, on a bench at Lincoln Park.
Such a small and easy thing to do. Chicago was full of parks, full of art, and shows, and plays and blues joints. It was a city full of music and buildings—and even trees—and yet all she did was live in the underbelly of the beast. Even this park—when she came here, it was only to think, never just to see it. She wondered to herself if she could see anything. What was she seeing when she saw Gloria—someone she could save? And Murphy—did she see a man who had finally come to get her? She laughed. There was no longer any joy in her life. There were satisfactions, sometimes, but never any joy. Never that. There had never been anything but the fight. The battle—that was what she had. It wasn't enough. And now Gloria. The utter frustration of taking someone in—then being lied to. "How the fuck am I supposed to help you?" She tossed her hair in the cold breeze and tried to calm herself down. She wondered why everything was upsetting her, why she was so on edge. Change of life—wasn't that another word for death?

She had left Murphy at the coffee shop, had wanted to be alone. *He must think I'm a real piece of work.* She breathed in the cold air, cold like the water in the lake. It might storm, she thought, but there was still some blue in the sky. She reached into her coat pocket and took out a cigarette. She lit it. She liked the cold wind, how it felt on her face, how it made her feel. She picked up a leaf lying at her feet. She stared at it. Her mother had loved leaves, had collected them, kept them in a book, labeled them. She had always wondered why. "Mama, I don't remember anymore." She wondered what had happened—what had really happened. Nothing was clear, nothing of those events in her past. There was only the fact that her mother had shot somebody in her house when she was small. She didn't even remember how old she had been, didn't remember why. Her mother had simply refused to talk about it. It was as if it never happened. Something about her brother. Was it? All her life, she had rewritten that story. Why did it matter? It was done, it was over, it had no hold on her. There were only pieces, fragments—and those fragments were so old that they were too fragile to be touched. They would crumble like the leaf she was holding, becoming utterly inaccessible, impossible to grasp. The history she was so obsessed with—the history that had shaped how she responded to things—it wasn't real. It was just a story. A piece of fiction. "Oh, Mama, I have to leave you now. I can't hate you anymore. I can't even love you." She put the leaf in her pocket.

"Save leaves, do you?"

She looked up at the familiar voice, his long coat unbuttoned. "You've been following me all day," she said softly.

"It's part of my job."

She wanted to tell him she loved him. She wasn't even sure it was true. "Yeah, guess so."

"Penny for your thoughts."

"I was thinking about my mother."

"She okay?"

"She's been dead a long time. Only I was just thinking that I've never really let her die. I think maybe it's time." She smiled at him. "She killed someone. I was always afraid of her after that. But I don't even think I had a reason to be afraid."

"What happened?"

"I don't know. I never knew. I just made things up."

"And you never asked her about it?"

"No." She took a deep breath and let it out. She could see the vapor in front of her. "You know what I like about Chicago winters?"

"What?"

"When you breathe, you can see that you're alive, that you're warm."

"You gonna be okay?"

"Yeah. I have a temper. I'll be fine."

"Is that what you do when you're mad—just go away like a wounded animal?"

"Guess so." She grabbed her hair, pulled it, let it go. "I don't know how to help her. It scares me. I guess lately I'm afraid of a lot of things."

"Like what?" He sat next to her on the bench.

"The winter. This case. You."

"Well, there's nothing we can do about Chicago winters. And this case, well, we're doing the best we can. You just have to talk to her, that's all. I've a funny feeling Herald Burns will be in touch with you soon. Things aren't as bad as they seem." He bit his lip and winced. "And me? There's a lot of things to be afraid of in this city, but I'm not one of them." He put his hand in her coat pocket and squeezed her hand.

"Are you always going to be a cop?"

"I don't know. Maybe, maybe not. Maybe it's time to move on."

"Why?"

"Because I think it might be time. Because of Gloria. You know, she"—he squeezed her hand again—"she made me take a good look. For days, she wouldn't answer one damn question. And I would go home, and I would ask myself, 'Who is she?' And then my wife asked me, 'Who are you?' I thought it was a stupid question. 'What the hell's that—who are you?' That was my answer. And here was this woman. It didn't make any sense, but there she was. And suddenly she was free. It took a knife to make it happen, well, what choice did she have? She wanted a life so desperately that she would have done anything to get it. And now she has it. Something new."

"She didn't exactly leave the old life behind, Sandy. That's the problem."

"No. But there's a world, Jenny, and she's seeing it, trying to make sense of it. It's not invisible to her. We're in it every fucking day, and we don't even see it. And here I am, a cop. And I hate being a cop. And I've always hated it."

"But you've loved it, too. I've seen that."

"Yes, I've loved it, too. But I have to decide which is more real—the love or the hate." He nodded, then smiled at her. "Jenny, you know why I became a cop? Because my great-grandfather was a cop. And my grandfather was a cop. And my father was a cop. And they were all crooked. Every single goddamn one of them. I think I wanted to atone. I was going to be the cop who redeemed the family name. Sometimes I laugh and tell myself I should have been a priest. But a cop? What a waste. Let the dead bury the dead." He let out a laugh. "And then my wife leaves me. I didn't even love her—and yet I would have never left her. What's wrong with me? Gloria didn't have a choice. But when she had a chance, she took it. What's my excuse? Who's kept me?" He looked at Jenny. He wiped the tears from her face. "Don't cry."

"Gloria says you and I always act like we're fighting a war."

"Yes," he said, "but at least we're not fighting each other."

"Who *are* we fighting?"

"*Them.* Thomas Blacker. Herald Burns. The captain. They're rotten and corrupt, and I hate them. I hate them because they don't have hearts. I hate them because they think everyone else is just trash. They run this city—and then blame other people for its violence. But the fucking violence begins with them, goddamnit. I hate them, Jenny. They fuck up the city because they think it belongs to them. And it doesn't, goddamnit. It belongs to us. We're the ones who have to walk on the fucking streets. You hate them, too. You're fighting this dirty little war because you feel the same way."

"And what about Gloria?"

"Isn't she part of the reason?"

"No. We're not doing this for her, Sandy."

"Well, maybe you're right. But I'm not sorry. I'm not a pure being with pure motives. I've always wanted to be that, but I'm not. I'm not sorry, Jenny."

She smiled. "I guess I'm not sorry, either." She leaned against him.

"We're like her, you know. We keep things. And the things we keep, we keep so we can survive."

"But we don't always need the things we keep."

"That why you're trying to quit smoking?"

"Ahh, you noticed." He nodded. "Smoking just may be one of those things I don't need to keep." He smelled her hair. "I'll tell you one thing, though, she's damn lucky she has you."

She pulled away from him. She wanted to look at him, see what his face told her. "Tell me something. Did you hate me?"

"Well, I didn't really. I just thought I hated you."

She laughed, then hit him on the shoulder.

"But even when I *thought* I hated you, I always knew you were good. Have you ever seen yourself when you're defending a client? You're the fiercest damn thing I've ever seen. You're the best lawyer in this whole godforsaken town."

"I thought Herald Burns was the best lawyer in this godforsaken town."

"Nope. He's just another pig. He's just another man who thinks he can own something that can't be owned. He's an old story, Jen." He took his hand out of her coat pocket, then rubbed his palms together. He looked like a miser who had just finished counting his money. "And we have some surprises in store for our friend Mr. Burns. I have a plan."

"Oh, really?" She took out another cigarette and placed it in her mouth. He reached for it, tossed it on the ground, and handed her a stick of gum.

The Things We Keep

Jenny walked into her office, shut the door, waved at Gloria, and took her shoes off. "What a day," she said. "What a nightmare. Not one, but two judges threatened me today. Problem with the system is that all judges are like feudal lords. I hate them. Six out of ten are morons." She fell into the one comfortable chair in her office. She had dragged that chair with her all the way from New Orleans, the soft old leather peeling away like an old coat of paint. "My kingdom for an honest judge with brains." She looked at Gloria, who was looking up at her from behind her desk. "How was your day?"

"Fine."

"How was your visit with our friend?"

"Our friend?"

"Madame shrink."

Gloria shrugged. "Working here was much more interesting. I learned a lot."

Jenny took out a cigarette and lit it.

Gloria smiled at her. "I labeled all your files—just like you asked." She pointed at a neat stack of files. "I don't know where to put these."

"They're all pending. Bottom left-hand drawer will be fine. That's where I put them."

Gloria nodded, opened the drawer. "There's nothing in there."

Jenny laughed. "There is now."

"How can you be so disorganized? I wouldn't be able to stand it. And I wouldn't be able to stand all the phone calls. I took down all the messages. Some of your callers aren't very friendly."

"Welcome to my world."

"It's a little hectic."

"Quiet is a luxury. This is the world, honey—and it's noisy as hell. And it sucks."

"You love the noise, don't you?"

"Damn right. It's what I know."

But was it better than a garden? "Oh, and the lieutenant called. I think he expected to hear your answering machine. He sounded surprised when I answered. Your boss—he was surprised, too."

"I'm sure he was."

"You should have told him."

"Ahh, what's it to him? He doesn't really care, anyway, so long as he doesn't have to pay for you out of his budget. Lesson number one in any racket you get into—budgets. If you're not in the budget, you don't exist."

"The lieutenant wanted to talk to you. It sounded important."

"I spoke to him."

"Good. Is everything okay?"

"Gloria, I need to—" She stared at the phone as it rang.

"Should I answer it?"

"What the hell. It'll give me a chance to observe your telephone manners." She winked.

"It's like acting," Gloria said seriously. She picked up the receiver. "Jenny Richard's office. May I help you?" She was a natural, Jenny thought. A damn quick study. "Just a minute." She pushed the hold button.

"You do that pretty well."

"It's Mr. Herald Burns."

"What does that sonofabitch want?"

She could see nothing on Gloria's face. That's what she did when she heard something she didn't like—she erased all sign of emotion. She wondered if that illegible look would ever go away. She got up from her chair and reached for the phone. She took a deep breath. "Honey, I want you to listen to this." She pushed the intercom button.

"Mr. Burns, to what do I owe this pleasure? Slumming, Counselor?"

"Nothing of the sort. As a matter of fact, I've been wanting to meet you for a long time. You have quite a reputation in this town."

"As do you, Mr. Burns. Only you make more money."

He laughed, though she knew his laugh was forced—nothing natural about it. "Your sense of humor is legendary."

"What can I do for you, Mr. Burns?"

He cleared his throat. Gloria stared into the place on the telephone where his was voice was entering the room. "I understand you represent Gloria Santos."

"Oh, your client gave you her real name, did he?"

"Jenny. May I call you Jenny?"

"You certainly may not."

"Charming," he said. "As charming as everyone said you'd be."

"I'm a busy woman, Mr. Burns."

"Then I'll only take a moment of your time. I'd like to arrange a meeting with your client—that is, before this situation gets out of hand."

"The situation got out of hand a long time ago, Mr. Burns."

"I know your client must be—"

"You know nothing about my client. Nothing at all, Mr. Burns. If you'd like to arrange a meeting with her, then I'll be happy to inform her. If she decides that a meeting with you is in her best interest—and I am not at all sure it is—then rest assured that I will accompany her."

"Of course. You're more than welcome—"

"When would you like to meet?"

"Say tomorrow at—"

"Tomorrow? I'll have to check my calendar." She paused, pretended she was thumbing through her papers. "Tomorrow. I don't know if I can swing it."

"Say four o'clock? My office."

"Let me see what I can do. I'll check with Ms. Santos. I'll call your secretary in the morning." She did not bother to say good-bye, did not bother with professional courtesies. She simply pushed a button and his voice disappeared.

"I'm not exactly the queen of etiquette, am I? *I've been wanting to meet you for a long time.* What horseshit. What does he take me for? He has the charm of scorpion."

Gloria sat in the chair soberly. "I'm not sure I'm up for—"

Jenny placed her hand on her cheek. "Look, I know how you feel. If it were up to me, I'd say fuck 'em. They can eat Bessie's dog food for dinner. But, Gloria—" She stopped, then looked at her as firmly as she could. "You have some explaining to do."

Gloria watched Jenny's eyes as she watched her. She said nothing. When Thomas had looked at her like that, she had always wanted to run. She wondered for an instant if Jenny was going to hit her. She made herself sit perfectly still.

"Who's the man that's been following you?" Jenny's eyes did not move, and her voice was cool, firm—but not too harsh.

"That's the same tone of voice the lieutenant used on me when I was in jail. Am I in jail again?"

"Are you going to answer my question?"

"I don't know." Gloria looked down at the desk.

"One of the lieutenant's colleagues followed you today. And don't look at me that way—I wasn't spying."

Gloria nodded but said nothing.

"I was just worried," Jenny said. "And it turns out I had a right to be."

"Okay," Gloria said softly. "So I didn't go see the psychiatrist. It's not a crime." She looked at Jenny. "I'm sorry. I just couldn't go. I couldn't. I was going to tell you."

"Never mind the goddamned psychiatrist. Who's the man who followed you?"

"A man, Jenny—I don't know who he is."

"How long's he been following you?"

"Since the first day you left me off to see the therapist."

"And you didn't go see her on that day, either, did you?"

"No."

"Where did you go?"

"I just walked around the city."

"And he was following you?"

"Yes."

"Gloria, why didn't you tell me?"

"Because, Jenny, I didn't want to tell you!" She placed her hands over her mouth, then dropped them. "I didn't mean to scream." She placed both her palms on the desk. "I didn't want to tell you."

"Why?"

"I need a reason, Jenny? Why can't I just keep what I want to keep?"

Dresses, Basements, and Wine

When Thomas Blacker arrived back at his house after his shop-ping expedition, he felt a little tired. But not too tired. When he parked his car in the garage, he noticed his old black car was missing. Good. Herald was earning his keep. He walked placidly into his house, decided he'd enjoy a nice wine. He deserved it. He walked down the stairs to the basement, the bag from the dress shop still in his hand. He placed the wrapped box carefully on Gloria's bed, stared at it, then nudged it toward the center. He liked things nice and even. He nodded as he stared at the perfectly wrapped box, then walked out of the room and made his way to where he kept his wines. He turned on the light, examined his bottles, then picked a wine with some spice. He cradled the bottle in his arms and made his way back up the stairs.

He opened the bottle carefully, then let the wine breathe. He noticed the message light blinking on his answering machine. He pressed the button and listened to Herald's baritone voice. "Thomas, it's all arranged. I've spoken to Gloria Santos's lawyer. She's a royal pain, pretended not to be interested. But they'll come. I've made sure of it. Not to worry. I think we'll be home free come tomorrow. I'll call you. . . . " He stopped listening. He hated the fact that Herald referred to Claudia as Gloria Santos. He had never spoken that name. Never! And never would. Herald was so sure of his little scheme. *I should have handled this myself.* He poured himself a glass of wine, took a sip, and held it in his mouth as if it were Claudia. He walked back down the stairs and sat in her room staring at the wrapped box. He pictured her opening the box, admiring the dress he had bought for her. When she came, he would make her stay. He held up his glass to the empty room. "To you, my dear."

What Real People Do

"White or red?"

"Somehow I never pictured you with a wine list in your hands."

"I'm not a complete philistine." Lieutenant Murphy moved his gum from one side of his mouth to the other. "What are you going to have?"

"I think I'll have the lamb."

"Red." He looked at Gloria. "Is red okay?"

"Red is fine." She looked around the restaurant. "This is fun."

He smiled at her. "It's the company."

"I think you've fallen in love with the restaurant."

Gloria nodded. "It's nice. And it's so crowded."

"You think crowded is nice?"

"Look at them. Listen. A hundred conversations. It's like music." Gloria looked around the room again. "Where do they come from?"

"They empty out every evening from all those tall buildings you like so much like water flowing from a dam." Jenny looked around the room, too. "Couldn't we have sat in a smoking section?" She looked at the lieutenant. "That gum is annoying."

"It's a replacement for cigarettes."

"I prefer the cigarettes."

"So do I, but I've decided I don't want to die."

"You should have thought of that before you lit your first cigarette."

"I was young and stupid. Now I'm just old and stupid."

"Is it hard to quit?" Gloria asked.

"Not compared to most things."

"Like what? Compared to what?" Jenny's question hung in the air like smoke.

Alexander Murphy thought a moment, then shrugged. He waved the waiter over and pointed at something on the wine list. "This one," he said. "Quitting smoking isn't as hard as"—he looked up at Gloria—"not as hard as walking into a psychiatrist's office."

Jenny watched as the lieutenant stared at Gloria.

Gloria stared back at the lieutenant. "I think that was supposed to be a joke," she said.

The lieutenant nodded. "But you didn't laugh."

"It's a sore subject. Jenny just yelled at me—"

"I did not yell at you. I only demanded an explanation. He could have killed you, you know?"

"He only wanted to deliver that message."

Lieutenant Murphy cocked his head. "And the message was?"

"Sign the paper."

"Sign the paper—what the hell does that mean?"

"I haven't the slightest idea."

"Well, that's a helluva thing to say." Lieutenant Murphy wore a look of exasperation on his face.

"Well, I'm sure now that he's delivered his message, he'll leave me alone."

"I'm not so sure about that." Lieutenant Murphy's voice was pensive. "I wouldn't rest so easy if I were you." He shook his head as if he were shaking water from his hair.

"Bessie does that." Jenny laughed.

"Yeah, and how is our resident basset hound?"

"Just talked to Charlie this morning—they're both laying low and doing fine."

"Wish I could say the same. Everybody's playing spy. Man follows Charlie—Charlie gets beat up. Man follows Gloria"—he smiled at her—"Gloria gets scared."

"I didn't say I was scared."

"You sound defensive, Ms. Santos. You're losing your poker face." He grinned. "Man follows man who was following Gloria. Oh, and it gets even better." He loosened his tie. "The captain wanted me to get you to back off. He's been keeping an eye on me. Even knows I spent the night at your house. See, even I'm in on the act."

"And did he also know you slept on the couch?"

"That's not the point. He thinks there's something going on between us."

"He has a good imagination." Jenny smiled.

"Don't be mean."

Gloria laughed. These two people amused her. Their affection was so obvious, the way they tossed words at each other, caught them, then threw them back. Nothing like that had ever happened between her and Thomas. There was something much more innocent in the way they treated each other. She felt happy in their presence. Watching them.

Listening to the sounds of the busy restaurant. Smelling the food. *This is what real people do.* But what was she? What was Thomas?

"What did you tell the captain?"

"I told the captain to go to hell. And tomorrow George is going to the feds. I gave him the copy of the report. And he's getting in touch with the people in El Paso. The feds can move in on Thomas Blacker. I don't give a shit if he's dying or not. It's time to turn up the heat."

Neither Jenny nor the lieutenant noticed the look of discomfort on Gloria's face as the lieutenant spoke. The look disappeared immediately, and she listened intently, saying nothing.

"Maybe they've seen this coming."

"They've done everything to try and prevent it. We've got more missing evidence than there are commercials on TV."

"Yeah, well, guess who called me at the office today?"

"Thomas Blacker."

"Close. Herald Burns."

"Oh, so he finally called you. Knew he would."

"He wanted to arrange a meeting."

"What did you tell him?"

"I wanted to tell him to go fuck himself."

Gloria chuckled. "There's that word again."

Jenny pointed at her. "I'm living with the morality police."

"I'm not the morality police. I'm just not used to that word." Gloria looked at her menu as she spoke. She smiled. "So many choices."

Murph touched Jenny's elbow. "So, you going to meet with him or what?"

"I'd rather not," Gloria said. Her voice was soft but emphatic. "Unless you can give me a good reason why we should."

"I can give you several reasons," he said as he leaned into the table.

"Such as?" He liked the challenge in her voice. She had come a long way from the woman who sat in an interview pretending to be a creature with no auditory sense.

"To begin with, we don't know what they want. What we have is what we think. What we think isn't good enough. We can theorize till the cows come home. If you don't go, we won't learn a thing. They've been on Charlie to get you to do something they want. But we don't know what that is. It's probably got something to do with that paper they want you to sign—whatever the hell that is. I say you should go fishing. You never know what you might catch." He nudged Jenny again. "And anyway, she'll protect you. She could make the devil beg for mercy."

"Don't refer to me in the third person. And Herald Burns *is* the devil."

"So now's your chance."

Jenny and Lieutenant Murphy both looked in Gloria's direction.

She shook her head as she looked from one face to the other. "This isn't a fair fight."

"We're all on the same side."

"I have the most to lose," she said quietly.

"And the most to gain."

She thought now that Alexander Murphy had a nice voice. He wasn't the enemy. "What exactly do I have to gain?"

"Your life," Jenny said, her voice almost inaudible in the noisy restaurant.

"I thought I'd already gained that back."

"Have you?" Jenny's eyes were soft and serious.

"No. I guess I haven't." She ran her finger over her menu. "So many choices." She looked at Jenny and the lieutenant. "I'm not used to making them." She looked back down at her menu. She thought of Charlie that night, how he'd been punished—how his face was frightened and swollen. She thought of Bessie, how she had sensed danger and had not even considered running from an intruder who had hurt her. Everyone around her was fighting, was protecting her. She was doing nothing—as if she were some kind of princess. It was time to face the enemy. *Enemy*, she thought—that was Jenny's word. She looked at them. *But don't hurt Thomas. Please don't hurt him.* "Let's meet, then. But don't expect a lot from me—except my presence."

"That's always enough."

"I mean it, Jenny. I'm not going to say one damned word."

"You're very good at saying nothing."

"You're still angry with me, aren't you?"

"I'll get over it." She reached over and touched Gloria's arm. "I just don't want you to get hurt."

I've already been hurt. "Tell Mr. Burns we'll see him." She looked at her menu. "And I don't want the lamb. It's what we never ate the day I—" She clenched her jaw. "The day I stabbed him." She placed the menu on the table. "Halibut. I'll have the halibut."

◆ ◆ ◆

The three of them walked down the street in Old Town, the sidewalks scattered with strollers. The day's rain had ended, and with the clearing sky, the cold was settling into the Chicago night like a child in his mother's arms.

"Would you like some coffee?" Lieutenant Murphy's voice seemed soft and small in the city air, not at all the voice of a seasoned cop. "There's a great coffee shop up the street."

"Will you take a rain check?" Jenny liked that he was tall. He *was* handsome. But not in that disgustingly pretty way so many men were cultivating. She liked that he didn't spend much time on himself—the kind of man who got up, shaved, showered, and went out the door. She wondered what he was like in the morning.

He nodded. Nobody was very eager to talk.

"I'm tired," Gloria confessed. "I'm not used to being out this late. I just want to sleep."

"You like to sleep, don't you?"

"It's one of the few pleasures in my life that I've really been able to indulge in. It's not Thomas's fault. I was always a sleeper. My mother used to drag me out of bed when I started school. I never wanted to get up." She placed her hands in front of her mouth and tried to warm them with her own breath.

When they reached the car, Murphy stopped and looked at Jenny. Gloria felt as if she should disappear. There was nowhere to go. He smiled, kissed Jenny on the cheek, then leaned over and kissed her on the cheek, too. "I hope you had a good time."

Gloria smiled back at him. "I did."

"Me too," he said. "Two beautiful women—what a lucky man." He stuck his arms out as if he wanted to embrace the entire city. "Who cares if I got stuck with the bill—it was worth it."

Jenny laughed as she watched him walk away. "He's not so bad."

"You like looking at him."

"Maybe."

"Not maybe. He likes looking at you, too."

"It's called sexual attraction, honey."

"It suits you."

"It'll come to no good." She laughed. "I'm a disaster with men."

"How many times did you say he'd been married?"

"Twice."

"Well, he's a disaster with women. Maybe you're a match."

"Interesting logic."

"How come he kissed me, too?"

"Some men do. When they see women friends, they kiss them on the cheek—when they say hello or say good-bye. It's not an uncommon practice."

"It's a lovely ritual," Gloria said as she opened the car door. *This is what real people do.* She tried to picture Thomas kissing her on the sidewalk. Maybe it was too real a thing for him to do.

The Case of the Missing Journals

Gloria and Jenny stood in the doorway and silently stared at the torn-up apartment. They looked at each other but did not speak. Except for the couch and the paintings on the walls, nothing was in its place. Books had been tossed on the floor, along with some of Jenny's files.

"Just like in the movies," Jenny said. "Goddamnit, someone's going to pay for this." She stormed into her bedroom, then came out again. "They found them."

"Found what?"

"The professor's journals. I hid them in my closet. Goddamnit, I'm so mad. Oh, I'm so fucking mad." Gloria followed Jenny as she rushed into the kitchen. "It's a good thing Bessie wasn't here. They would have hurt her worse than they did while you were here."

"If I wasn't living here—"

"Stop it. Put your guilt on hold, honey." Jenny thought for a minute. "Oh, I know—" She read a number written on a calendar on the wall. She pushed the seven buttons. She waited for an answer, heard a voice. "Yes, I'd like to speak to Lieutenant Murphy."

"I'm sorry, he's not in."

"Is this Detective Johnson?"

"Yes, it is."

"George, this is Jenny Richard. I'd like the lieutenant to come over here right away. Someone's broken into my apartment."

"You okay?"

"They tore the place up."

"Did they take anything?"

"Thomas Blacker's journals—the copy the lieutenant made for me. Can you just tell him to come over? And if he doesn't get home soon, can you come?"

"You got an address?"

"Yes, it's—"

"Never mind, he just walked in the door."

◆ ◆ ◆

"She sounds upset."

He nodded. "Just drive a little faster, George."

"They're fine. They took what they wanted and left, Murph."

"What? You're afraid of getting a ticket?"

"I'll get us there." He took a left turn onto Lake Shore Drive, then drove north. "So they know about the copies?"

"These bastards know everything."

"We know everything, too."

"What are you talking about?"

George pointed to his briefcase in the backseat. "Grab that."

Murph stretched back and swung it onto his lap. "I was wondering why you brought your briefcase along."

"There's a picture in there—several pictures."

"The man who's been following Gloria Santos."

"Bingo."

"Who is he?"

"Name's Don Parker. Ex-cop. Works as a private dick for—"

"Herald Burns."

"Yup, you guessed it."

◆ ◆ ◆

Gloria held the photograph of the man she had seen in the coffee shop, the same man who had followed her to the top of the John Hancock Building—who had kicked Bessie, had followed her into the movie theater. "It's the same man," she said. "It's him." She kept staring at the picture. "Charlie saw him, too."

The lieutenant nodded. "It's time I had a chat with your friend Charlie."

Jenny looked at Murphy. "Sounds serious, Lieutenant. What about?"

"You'll find out soon enough."

Jenny smiled, puffed on her cigarette, and played with her mug of coffee. "Aren't you guys going to dust the place?"

George laughed.

"What's so funny?"

"You've been watching too many movies. Besides, we won't find anything. They're careful. They took what they wanted. The rest is just for show. They wanted you to know they'd been here."

"Those bastards."

Murphy smiled at the disgust on Jenny's face.

"But we know who they are." George sounded so sure of himself.

"Do we?"

"Herald Burns, for one. But he's got someone on the inside." He smiled. "I have a hunch, though. Got any more of that coffee?"

Gloria poured George another cup.

"What are we going to do now?" Jenny asked.

"Does it matter?" Gloria asked. "Can't we just move on? Can't we just drop it?"

"You want to let that bastard go free?"

"Jenny, does it really matter what I think?"

"Of course it matters."

"I'm not so sure." She looked at Jenny, then at the lieutenant, then at George. "I've said this before to you, Jenny. You're all fighting a war. And I don't even matter."

"No, it's not like that at all." The empathy in Jenny's voice was difficult to argue with.

"Then, Jenny, stop fighting all my battles for me. I don't want to be taken care of as if I'm just some kind of helpless little girl. I'm not seven anymore. I'm not just a fu—I'm not just a fucking victim."

"You're not a fucking anything."

She looked at the lieutenant, then at Jenny. "You and Lieutenant Murphy—you really love all this. Makes you alive. You hate Thomas Blacker more than I do. And you don't even know him. *I know him. I know him better than anybody in the world. He's not evil.*"

"You don't have to believe Thomas Blacker is evil in order to conclude that what he did was wrong."

"But you *do* believe he's evil."

"You're damned right I do. I think it's time you read his journals."

"A man is not what he writes."

There was a long silence in the room, no one speaking. "I'm sorry," Gloria said finally. "I don't know. I just want to have a peaceful life. I just want to be able to walk around the streets of the city and not feel like I'm being watched. I want to get a job, and go to college, and have a career. I don't care if he's punished. What's that to me? And he's dying, damnit. Isn't that what you said, Jenny—that he was dying? Let him die in peace."

"Don't ask me to do something I can't do."

Gloria shook her head. "I have to think," she said. She forced herself to smile.

Jenny noticed the look on Alexander Murphy. "Why are you smiling?"

"It's not the only copy."

"What?" Jenny looked at him. "Why, you sneaky sonofabitch."

"Not sneaky. Just careful. I got to thinking before I turned those journals in. The woman who made those copies for me—she's a friend of mine. Known her a long time. I trusted her to keep her mouth shut. But then I heard something that day. She's the captain's sister-in-law. Just didn't feel right. So I went somewhere else. Had another copy made—at a regular copy place. They're not notarized, but they'll work." He laughed again.

"Where'd you put 'em, Murph?"

"It doesn't matter."

He looked at Gloria. "You still up for that meeting with Mr. Burns?"

Gloria looked at the lieutenant, then at Jenny, then at George, their faces so expectant. They seemed so ready for anything, so eager to fight this necessary little war. Maybe it *was* necessary. For her, too. And she wanted so much to please them, wanted to be a part of them. She remembered how passive she'd been when the man had walked into the apartment. Bessie and Charlie—they had been alive. "Yes," she said. Such a simple word, yes. *Yes.*

Jenny nodded, put her cigarette out.

"Well," George said softly, "I hate to break this up, but I gotta get me some sleep. We're done here. I say we pack it in."

Murphy nodded. "Why don't you go on home without me, George. I think I'll sack out on the couch. Just in case."

"Make sure you stay on the couch." George laughed.

He looked at Jenny. "Do you mind?"

◆ ◆ ◆

As he lay on the couch, he felt a figure standing over him. The night was still and dark, and he was tired. "Is that you, Jenny?"

He felt a warm hand on his face. He kissed it. "Am I dreaming?"

"No," she said. "I just wanted to thank you."

He kissed her hand again. "I love your hands," he whispered.

"Just my hands?"

She bent over and kissed him. "Good night, Sandy."

"You smell good." He felt her move away. Must be a dream. But it felt so real.

Jenny Richard, Jenny Richard

A good man in the next room. No court hearings, no trials. And perhaps a showdown with the infamous Herald Burns. For some inexplicable reason, she was looking forward to meeting him. It would be better than going to court. The threat did not seem large, and she knew herself well enough to know she loved a good fight. And she would be with Gloria. Gloria who had already faced the devil, had survived to bring her news of life. *I don't want to die.* That's what Sandy had said. "I don't want to die, either, damnit. Not yet. Jenny Richard, Live."

She walked into the living room. Maybe he was still asleep. She would watch him sleep. But when she stared at the couch, it was empty. No Alexander Murphy. He was gone. She was disappointed. She saw the note on the coffee table. At least he's consistent, she thought.

Dear Jenny Richard—

> *At least this time I was sober. No sign of our friend Parker. I'm not at all convinced he wouldn't have hurt Gloria. If she disappeared, their problems would be solved. I'm certain the captain is involved. I think George thinks so, too. It will be hard to prove—but we got something on one of his stooges (and it has something to do with our friend Charlie). I'll tell you more about it later. Just set up that meeting with Burns. George is gonna nail Parker. This could turn out to be a great day. We sure as hell could use one.*

Oh, and tell Gloria I'd be happy to drop off the copies of the journals if she changes her mind. After today nobody's going to be stealing anything from your apartment.

SANDY

P.S. My wife has filed for divorce. I'll be back in my own house soon. When's the basset hound coming back? I miss her.

"He quits smoking and he goes crazy." She put the note in the pocket of her robe, walked into the kitchen, and put on the coffee. *Maybe it's not love. Maybe it's just my rapidly evolving hormones.* She laughed. So what if she was in her midforties? So was he. She thought of their conversation at lunch, how he had seemed unhappy about being a cop, almost as if he wouldn't mind leaving. But he had always seemed to her to be a cop's cop. She had not liked him because he had seemed to be such a true believer. Like a marine. He had seemed so hard and egotistical. But he wasn't that way at all. Maybe he behaved that way because it had helped him to survive. Maybe she had misread him—or maybe he had changed. Or maybe she had changed.

One thing was certain: He was an honest cop. *I'm falling in love with an honest cop.*

You Have the Right to . . .

"You need me for something, Lieutenant?"

Murph looked up at Tim Cain and smiled. "Yeah, just for a second. Come on in. Shut the door."

"Sure thing. If it's only for a sec. The captain wants—" He stopped as he saw Charlie sitting in Lieutenant Murphy's office.

Lieutenant Murphy smiled. "Something wrong?"

Tim Cain tried unsuccessfully to hide his nervousness. "No." He gestured toward Charlie. "Guy startled me. Didn't know you had someone in your office. Listen, if you don't mind, I got a few things—"

"It can wait."

"The captain—"

"*Can wait.*"

"Now, Murph, don't start in on the captain."

"Okay. How 'bout I start in on you?"

Tim Cain gestured toward Charlie again. "He goes."

"Nope. He stays." The lieutenant stared at Tim Cain's left hand. "Tell me again how you got those scars."

"In a fire. It was a long time ago—I've told you this story. What the hell's all this about?"

"Know any good lawyers?"

The sergeant looked at him. "What would I need a good lawyer for?"

"To help you out of the shit you're in."

"I'm not in any shit."

"Save it, Sergeant. You're as dirty as the shorts you wear."

"Oh, yeah? Well, at least I don't chum around with faggots."

Murphy looked at Charlie, then back at Sergeant Cain. "And how would you happen to know Mr. Robertson's sexual persuasion? Looks like a country boy to me."

"I happen to know for a fact that the guy sitting in that chair is a god-damned—" Tim Cain suddenly caught himself. He bit his lip.

Lieutenant Murphy smiled. "You've just never known when to keep your mouth shut, have you, Sergeant?" He looked over at Charlie. "This the guy?"

Charlie nodded. "That's him."

"I don't know what you're talking about."

"Well, you'll have some time to think about it." Lieutenant Murphy kept a smiled pasted to his face. "I'll take your badge, Sergeant. I wouldn't take it with me, if I were you—not where you're going." He put a stick of gum in his mouth. "I'm going to read something to you that I'm absolutely certain you've heard before: You have the right to remain silent. You have the right to . . ." As Lieutenant Alexander Murphy spoke, he did not know what made him happier, the look on Tim Cain's face or the look on Charlie's. It would give him one more thing to think about on nights when sleep would not come.

I'm Fine

George walked into Jenny's office and smiled at Gloria sitting behind the desk, a pile of files in front of her. "You look good behind a desk," he said.

"Hi," she said. She placed both her hands in front of her and rubbed the wood. "Jenny's not here. She should be here any sec—"

"She got held up in court. Won't be out until just before your meeting with Mr. Burns. Murph asked me to take you. That okay with you?"

Gloria nodded. "That's fine." She looked at her watch, thought of Thomas for an instant, then looked back at George.

"Tell me something, Ms. Gloria—you afraid of me?"

She looked at him, his dark eyes not so different from hers, his skin darker than the wood of the desk. "No."

"You look at me different than you do Lieutenant Murphy."

She was quiet, wanted to tell the truth, wanted to use the right words. "You were the first black man I ever saw."

"You've seen more now, haven't you?"

"Yes." She smiled at him.

"Do black people scare you?"

"Should they?"

"We scare a lot of white people."

"You mean people like Thomas."

"Didn't he teach you to be afraid of me—I mean people like me?"

"He wanted me to be afraid of everything. Of everyone. I don't think he succeeded." She stared at her hands. "You don't look like Lieutenant Murphy, and I don't look like Jenny. Am I white?"

George shrugged.

"They blame you, don't they?"

He looked at her. "What do you mean?"

"Nothing," she whispered. "Never mind." She paused. "That's what Thomas did—he blamed me. He kidnapped me—and then everything that went wrong was my fault." She smiled at him. "I'm not afraid of you, George. I'm a little cautious. But I'm no more cautious of you than I am of the lieutenant. He's easier to read than you are, you know? He wears everything on his face. You don't. You smile a lot—it seems a natural thing for you to do. It puts people at ease, but I think it hides a lot." She was surprised by her own honesty. She was conversing with a man she didn't know, but it seemed like the right thing to do. And he wasn't a stranger—not like the man in the coffee shop who had tried to talk to her. Not like the man who had followed her.

George nodded. "You're a pretty smart lady," he said. He wanted to tell her she was right. He looked at his watch. They would have to finish this conversation at a later date. "I think we should get going. You all right?"

"I'm fine." She felt the knots in her stomach. *I will never be fine again.*

Nice View

When Jenny arrived at Herald Burns's office, George and Gloria were waiting for her. She hugged Gloria casually. "Don't be scared," she whispered in her ear. "You look great." She smiled at George, kissed him on the cheek. He slipped a note into her hand.

"What was that for?" George asked.

"For luck."

"I'm not the one that's walking into the lions' den."

"That kiss will bring me luck."

"Hope so." He grinned. "I sure as hell hope so." He looked at his watch. "It's almost time for your appointment. And it's almost time for my disappearing act." He stared at Jenny's briefcase. "You remember to bring everything?"

"This is better than going to trial."

"Just win this one." He looked at Gloria. "We could use a win." He walked toward the glass doors, turned around, smiled, then disappeared from their view.

Jenny read the note George had handed to her. She nodded. "You know what's in it?"

Gloria shook her head.

"Lieutenant Murphy's arrested the man who—" She looked around the room. "I'll tell you later. This place is too big for my taste," she whispered. "And too modern."

"Cold," Gloria said, "like the weather."

They turned toward the sound of the buzz on the receptionist's phone. The woman picked it up and nodded. She looked toward the two women. "Are you Ms. Richard and Ms. Santos?"

"Yes." Jenny felt her heart pound. Adrenaline is good, she thought.

"Mr. Burns will see you now. Just follow me."

"Be a rock," Jenny whispered to Gloria. "Still and solid as a rock." She squeezed her hand. They walked down a long hall, pictures and plaques hanging all over the clean white walls. The woman opened a set of double doors. When they entered the room, Herald Burns stood behind a desk made of oak. The skyline of Chicago was behind him as if he had ordered it to appear there for his own enjoyment.

"Nice view," Jenny said.

He stood and offered his hand. "I'm glad you like it."

He had a firm handshake, but Jenny thought his grasp was too eager. "How much you pay for the view?"

He smiled but did not answer.

He offered to shake Gloria's hand, but she made no effort to reciprocate.

"You must be Ms. Santos."

She did not acknowledge his presence.

He offered them a seat. He looked at Gloria. "You're as lovely as Thomas said you were. I can certainly see why—"

"—he'd want to kidnap her." Jenny sat down on an overstuffed leather chair. "Nice chairs," she said. She looked around the room, then stared at the painting he had on the wall. Saint Michael had always been one of her favorite saints. "Nice painting. Looks like it belongs in a church." She kept her voice flat and steady, then smiled. "Which one of the two are you?"

"I know which one you think you are," he said, his tone as flat as hers.

"Do you?"

"There's no need to be so antagonistic, Ms. Richard," he replied, his voice softening.

"There's no need to be so friendly, either. I'm not Emily Post, and this isn't a social visit."

Gloria sat on an identical chair next to Jenny. She sat down as if it were a box seat at the opera.

Jenny kept herself from smiling. "What is it that you wanted?"

He placed a document on his desk. "I simply wanted you to read this."

"You've gone to a lot of trouble over that little piece of paper."

"I'm sure I don't know what you mean."

"I have a friend named Charlie who could explain it you."

"I don't know anything about your friends." He looked at the document and slid it toward Jenny. "Wouldn't you like to read it?"

"Not particularly. I read documents for a living. I don't care to read another."

"Perhaps Ms. Santos would like to read it?"

"I don't think she would," Gloria said. Her voice was distant and dispassionate. She was surprised at herself, surprised she'd spoken.

"Maybe you'd like to tell us what's in it." Jenny took out a pack of cigarettes from her purse. "Do you mind if I smoke?"

"I don't have any ashtrays."

Jenny lit her cigarette. "I'll use the carpet."

He opened his drawer and took out an ashtray, then placed it on his desk.

Jenny reached for it and placed it on the table next to her chair. "Amazing how things appear and disappear, isn't it? Take, for instance, journals."

"You talk in riddles. I don't like riddles."

"If you have a sense of humor, they can be fun."

He looked at the document on his desk. "I have in my possession Thomas Blacker's will."

"What is that to us?"

"It might interest you to know that Ms. Santos is Mr. Blacker's sole beneficiary. As you probably already know, my client is quite ill."

"He's been sick most of his life."

Herald Burns ignored her comment. He looked at Gloria. She sat as still as if she were sitting for a portrait. "It's a considerable fortune. Several million—not including the value of the house."

"She's more than earned it."

"There's only one small—"

"I thought there was a catch."

"All Ms. Santos has to do is sign this document." He held up a piece of paper.

"What's in it?"

"I'm sure you can both read."

"I'm sure you can tell us what's in it." She glared at him.

"If Ms. Santos agrees never to speak of the events that have occurred over the past twenty-three years, either publicly or privately for as long as she lives—then everything is all hers. If she ever violates the agreement, then his estate will be transferred to another party."

"In other words, it's a bribe."

"It's a legal agreement. It's a common enough clause—"

"In lawsuit settlements. I'm a lawyer, Mr. Burns, and as far as I'm concerned, legal agreements and bribes are not mutually exclusive terms." She inhaled her cigarette and blew the smoke toward Mr. Burns. "I don't think we're interested."

"You'll never get him."

"What makes you so sure?"

"You haven't got any evidence."

"You've seen to that, haven't you?"

"It's a moot point, really. He'll die long before you ever get to trial."

"Oh, you'll see to that, too. No one can slow down the wheels of justice better than you, Mr. Burns. You've built a career on it."

"I do my job. I've never done anything to be ashamed of."

"*Shame* isn't in your vocabulary."

"That will be enough, Ms. Richard. I didn't come here to be insulted."

"You didn't come here at all. You sent for us—like a pope allowing an audience with a couple of peasants."

"I'm sure it comes as no surprise that I don't give a damn what you think of me. As you've said, Ms. Richard, this is not a social visit. As Thomas Blacker's attorney, my only interest is to represent his wishes." He looked at the document, then pointed at it. "It's a very generous offer."

"By generous, do you mean he didn't deduct what it cost to raise and feed her for twenty-three years?"

Herald Burns stared at Jenny for a moment, then decided not to engage her. He looked at Gloria as if he had decided to shift strategies. "You'll have everything you've ever wanted. This is your chance. Why blow it for a wiseass attorney who has a chip on her shoulder about rich people? What have you got now? As your attorney has pointed out, you've more than earned it. Why walk away with nothing?"

There was no fear, no disbelief, no surprise, nothing written on Gloria's face that he could read. "Think about it, Ms. Santos. And there might even be a fee for your attorney."

"Her attorney would rather suck the heads of rotting crawfish than take a penny from Mr. Blacker's fortune." She smiled at Mr. Burns, then took another puff from her cigarette. "Tomorrow the feds are going to be all over your ass. And the day after, the press is going to be all over your ass. Your ass is going to be a busy place."

"The feds won't pay any attention to you. They're busy people. And the press is even busier."

"Oh, I wouldn't be so sure." She opened her briefcase. She shoved a photograph on his desk. "That man works for you. His name is Parker. He recently threatened Ms. Santos in a movie theater. He broke into my apartment—twice. Once he threatened Ms. Santos and hurt my dog, and my dog has decided to press charges." She smiled. "The second time he broke into my apartment, he stole copies of Thomas Blacker's journals. He and Tim Cain just got arrested. You know Tim Cain?"

"Never heard of him."

"Well, they're in the slammer together."

"On what grounds?"

"You want me to list all the charges? What matters most is that we have them in jail—even as we speak."

"The charges will never stick."

"Maybe." She winked at him. "Problem is that your Mr. Parker thought I had the only copy of Mr. Blacker's journals." She stared right into his face. "Lieutenant Murphy owns *another* copy. You didn't know about that one, did you?"

"Well, that's of no—"

"I'm not finished yet, Mr. Burns. There's a certain Mr. Rusty Rayborn. He used to do favors for the professor. He was able to get him shackles, he was able to get him birth control pills—oh, and other things. We found him—and it just so happens that he hates Thomas Blacker. He had plenty to say. A little immunity can go a long way for a small-time peddler. He's even agreed to talk to the feds. And your man, Mr. Parker, well he's nothing but a patsy ex-cop who does your dirty work—I think he'll talk plenty. In any case, he's a small fish. But you—you're a rather large fish. And so is Thomas Blacker. And you're caught. And day after tomorrow, I'm gonna be in the newspaper holding two big fish."

"You can't touch me."

"Yes I can."

He laughed. "And all this time I thought you were in the business of defending criminals. Since when did you switch sides? You would have made a splendid prosecutor. Still, you're strictly an amateur. Your little theories aren't gonna get you anywhere but on the dole. I'll have your ass for these little insinuations."

"The only way you'll ever have my ass is in your dreams." She leaned over the desk. "In a few days, I'll have your balls on a platter." She shoved the photo toward him. "And keep the picture. Put it on your wall—next to your painting."

"I'll have you brought up on ethics charges."

"Really? I was about to say the same thing."

"Oh, you're so self-righteous, aren't you? Who the hell do you think you are? All you've ever done is make a living defending criminals."

"As have you, Mr. Burns. The difference between us is that your guilty clients get off. Mine go to prison. You get rich. I don't."

He placed his palms on the table. "I've worked for everything I have." He spread his hands as is he were sweeping the entire city with his arms. "And I don't owe you—*I don't owe anybody*—any explanations for anything."

"Answer me this, Mr. Burns. If your client is so free of guilt, then why the generous offer?"

"My client is one of the finest human beings I've ever met."

"Your client, Mr. Burns, kidnapped *my* client when she was seven years old. What do you make of that?"

"You don't know anything about Thomas Blacker—"

"I do," Gloria said. Her voice was soft, and yet her words made Herald Burns stop in midsentence. Nothing that Jenny had said had rattled him—but now he seemed almost startled. "May I see that piece of paper?" she asked quietly.

Jenny looked at her. *What could she be thinking?*

Herald Burns slid it toward her.

"Would you be good enough to hand it to me?"

He walked around the desk slowly, then placed it in Gloria's hand. "The agreement is clear enough," he said.

She looked at the page, read it to herself.

Herald Burns returned to his chair, then kept his eyes on her.

When Gloria finished with the document, she stared at him—then ripped the paper in half.

"I don't think we have anything more to discuss," Gloria said. His eyes were the most frightening things she had ever seen. More frightening than Thomas Blacker's had been. But at least Thomas had been capable of kindness. She doubted this man had any kindness in him at all. Every day, she learned something new. About the world. About herself.

"I'm no one," Gloria said. "I'm not anyone at all. And Thomas wants to give me money? Is that all he wants to give?"

Jenny stood up, looked out the glass wall behind the figure at the desk, then walked around the room. She wanted to slap him, slap him for what he'd done to Charlie, slap him for arranging for all the evidence to disappear. And all to make sure Gloria signed a piece of paper—all this to save a man who was not worth saving. She hated him for the things he worshipped. Such empty gods. She stared at the picture of Saint Michael. She faced Herald Burns and burned her hatred into him with her glare. She pointed at the painting. "Yes, Mr. Burns, I do know which one of those two I am. Do you?" She looked at Gloria, then both of them walked toward the door. Jenny turned around and faced Herald Burns one more time. He was surprised, she thought. He had been so certain she'd sign. She wanted to laugh but managed only to smile. "Whatever you paid for your view, Mr. Burns, it was too much."

Fallen Angels

How he had held on to that small particle of hope on Thomas's face when he told them they had to fight. How he had crossed a line because he wanted to help. How he was so certain they would win, because losing seemed a vague and distant idea—an idea he had abandoned long ago, an idea that could not touch him. How his arrogance had led him to miscalculate the whole situation, how unfamiliar this feeling was as he sat in his office in a chair that no longer felt so comfortable. How those women had left him dazed. How he hated them, how he hated that lawyer, how she refused to obey the rules of professional diplomacy. How she looked at him, as if he were a rat carrying an infectious disease. How she had fooled herself into believing she was above the dirt the city was made of. How she had smiled at his painting as if, by looking at it, she knew what he was made of. How her client had sat, superior, unfazed by her surroundings, as if she had created the world. How he would have to go back to Thomas. How he had to tell him. How, this time, he had overplayed his hand.

He walked over to his closet and looked at Thomas's journals. He had promised Thomas he would get them back to him. He would take them to him, he thought, give him the journals, and tell him their plan had not worked, tell him they were in trouble. Or perhaps, he thought, he would return the journals to the captain, tell him they had better put them back where they belonged. It would go better for all of them if the journals had simply been misfiled. Yes, that would be better. For him. He would tell Thomas it was over, that he had tried. It was time for him to think of himself, to think of a way out. He had not planned on this. He was so certain he'd frightened them, so certain of everything. There was a way, he thought, there must be a way. *And fuck Thomas Blacker.* He found himself moving away from his thoughts, found himself reading Thomas's journals.

Almost Home

Jenny took out a cigarette, placed it in her mouth, but did not light it. She bit down on the unlit filter in her mouth as she drove. Neither she nor Gloria had said a word after they'd left Herald Burns's office.

"It's okay if you light it," Gloria said.

"I can wait."

"You've earned it."

Jenny reached into her purse fumbling for her lighter.

"Here," Gloria said, "I'll find it." She found a lighter at the bottom of Jenny's purse, then handed it to her. "One of these days you're going to kill yourself on the road as you search for a light."

Jenny lit her cigarette and let the smoke out of her lungs slowly. "I'm sorry I told you to be a rock. I just meant that—"

"I didn't have that much to say." She ran her finger across her lip. "Something about that man." She looked out the window of the car and stared at the people on the sidewalk. "What you did in his office—you were amazing."

"I'll have to put you on a jury someday." She laughed. "I *was* good, wasn't I?"

"You enjoyed it."

"I guess I did."

"I didn't like him. He scared me."

"You didn't look scared—but then you never do."

"I'm trying not to be so stoic."

"Sometimes it's a virtue. When you ripped up his cheesy little contract. Oh, I loved the look on the bastard's face when you did that. I was afraid—"

"You were afraid I was going to sign it. You were the one who told me I should take him for all he was worth."

"Yeah, well, I was wrong about that."

"But you thought I might reconsider."

"Yes. I could be wrong, but a big part of you still wants to protect him."

"You think I was ripping Thomas—but I wasn't. It's not his money I want. What I want is—" She stopped. "I don't know what I want. Yes, I do. I just want all this to end. Oh, God, Jenny—" She clenched her fists tight and wiped her tears with them. "When we get home, can you call the lieutenant and ask him to bring his copy of the journals? It's time I read them."

"I think I can arrange that," she said. "Don't fight the tears, honey."

"I don't want to cry," she yelled. "I just want to hit someone."

"I can pull the car over and we can pick any guy wearing a suit."

"You're impossible." She reached for a tissue in Jenny's purse.

"Well, you haven't lost your sense of humor."

"I never knew I had one till I met you."

Jenny took a drag of her cigarette as she reached a stoplight. She looked at Gloria. "We still have a few things left to do."

"Like?"

"I've talked to some reporters—they're interested in the story. They won't do it if you don't want to." She watched for a sign on Gloria's face. The car behind her honked at her. "Yeah, yeah," she said as she continued making her way through the evening traffic.

"What will we gain?"

"We got him, you know? We have Thomas Blacker right where we want. Only one thing, Gloria—he's dying. And Herald Burns isn't bluffing when he says he'll keep us out of court. Thomas Blacker will be long dead before he ever gets what's coming to him."

"So you want a public trial—is that it?"

"Something like that."

"What's in it for you, Jenny?"

"Why are you so angry with me because I want that bastard to get what's coming to him?"

"I'm not angry."

"The hell you aren't. I'm not this vulture waiting to land on the carcass's flesh."

"I didn't imply that, Jenny."

"Yes, you did. What's in it for me, Gloria? I'll tell you what's in it for me. I get to help expose someone who committed a crime—a crime against someone I happen to like. Tell me why he should get away with it. I want a good reason."

"Because he's dying."

"That's not good enough."

"Why don't we take our little victory in Herald Burns's office and walk away? They arrested that man, didn't they? And you told Herald

Burns the lieutenant arrested the man who'd beat up Charlie. We're fine, now, aren't we? Can't we just leave Thomas alone?"

"We're not finished." When Gloria read the journals, she would know that nothing was finished.

They were silent for a long time. Jenny turned onto Lake Shore Drive and made her way north. Gloria noticed how easily she maneuvered through traffic. "You want me to tell them—what?" Gloria said finally.

"The press? Don't do this to please me." She lit another cigarette. "If you do this, do it because you believe it's the right thing to do."

"Thomas used to say the press was stupid and crass. He said newspaper reporters couldn't write, couldn't think, either."

"In a way, he was right," Jenny said, trying to let go of her frustration. "The press is like the Chicago Police Department—you can't live with 'em, you can't live without 'em."

"I can't think right now."

"Is it because you think you'll be put on display?"

There was a distinct bitterness in Gloria's laugh. "I've been on display for over twenty years—what's a newspaper? I just need to think."

"Well, there's time."

"So you'll tell the lieutenant to bring the journals?"

"Yes."

"*Right away?*"

"Yes."

"Do you love him?"

"I didn't know we were discussing my personal life."

"Is that a yes?"

"You're an impossible woman, you know that?"

"And you're so easy."

Jenny laughed. "We'll survive. We both will."

"And the lieutenant?" Gloria smiled.

"He's sweet, don't you think?"

Gloria noticed the look on her face. She loves. She wondered if that's what she felt for Thomas.

Jenny turned onto her street and smiled. "We're almost home."

The Sides We Take

She liked the feel of her bare feet on the wood floor—it made her feel younger. She thought of Herald Burns, the way he'd looked at them—like some superior being. And yet, she knew she and Gloria had gotten the best of that bastard. What was in it for him, she wondered? Motivation—that was an important word in her vocabulary. Gloria had asked the same question of her. Did motivation apply to lawyers, too? She laughed. She could not help but wonder about Burns. Had he done all this for friendship? Did he love? Was he loyal? Did he feel the same things she felt? Was he as human? Or had he done all these things because the world he lived in dictated what he should do? Perhaps he felt untouchable, and so it had been his arrogance that was his ruin—was that it? Was it as simple as that? Maybe the sides people took was not a simple matter. She had told Gloria that Blacker and Burns were evil. She had believed it when she'd said it, and a part of her believed it even now. But what was it exactly that made them evil? Were some born to do good, and others born to do evil? She had always thought of herself as being on the right side. Was she as good as she thought? Alexander Murphy had told her it was a sin to believe you were good. She had not known how to respond—so she had laughed and dismissed his Catholic answer. But as she felt the cold wood against her bare feet, she thought she understood what he had meant.

She listened to the water running in the shower. Gloria liked long showers, probably never missed cleaning any part of her body. I've never been that thorough, she thought to herself. She rubbed her feet on the floor. Now that they were so close to the end, how could she let all of this go so easily? It made no sense. *What's in it for you?* Maybe Gloria was right. Hadn't she got what she wanted? They had beaten Herald Burns. He would leave them all alone—Charlie, Gloria—all of them. No one would follow them on the streets. Gloria would have her life back to make of it what she would. That was what mattered. The public revenge—humiliating them? What would that accomplish? She wondered what the difference was between justice and revenge. And wondered, too, which she preferred in this instance. So what if Thomas Blacker never went to trial? He would be dead. There was a kind of justice in that. She shook her head. No—that was not enough. If Thomas Blacker had been poor, had had no influence, had not been famous, had not had friends—if he had just been another anonymous man, what might have happened to him? Her clients, *her clients*, most of them were as guilty as Thomas Blacker. And many of them were guilty of lesser crimes. And none of them would walk—all of them hounded by cops and prosecutors who pretended to have insatiable appetites for justice— no Glorias to show them mercy or compassion. It was simple. They had to pay. Let them rot.

She walked to the refrigerator, poured herself a glass of wine. The cold wood floors felt hard on her feet. She wasn't a girl anymore. Alexander Murphy would arrive with copies of the journals. Gloria would read them. She would decide whether to try the sonofabitch in public—or not. Let *him* rot. She wished to Alexander Murphy's Catholic God that it was up to her.

Herself on a Map

5 MAY 1987

This last speaking tour lasted too long. I tire of travel. Sometimes the audience asks such inane questions. Don't they read my books? I have spent a lifetime writing them. Am I just another celebrity? What about the books I've written—what about that? I wonder, sometimes, if it matters. I feel myself losing my patience. I will accept fewer and fewer invitations to speak. I must spend more time on my writing. The life of the mind—this is what matters. I once enjoyed my fame. It grows larger with each book. I only grow more weary.

Claudia and I had a lovely weekend. She cooked dinner every evening. She made love to me, comforted me, rubbed my back. I brought her four new dresses from New York. She adored them all, looked radiant in all of them. She hasn't any idea how lovely she is. That's part of her beauty, I suppose. We are very happy, she and I, though she does not tell me many things. She continues to keep things from me. I will never know her as well as she knows me. This bothers me. It is, I think, a flaw in her personality. But she is virtuous in other ways, and I have learned to be patient with her. . . .

16 SEPTEMBER 1991

It's been twenty years now. I hardly remember my life before her. She seemed unhappy yesterday. I asked her why she seemed sad. "It's the weather," she said. "It rained all day." She would say nothing else. After twenty years, she still does not trust me. I have done everything for her. I sent her to her room early tonight, though she did not wish to go. I gave her a good book to keep her entertained, and I let her take a glass of wine down with her. A glass of wine now and again relaxes her—though I much prefer she drink with me. I sometimes wish we could go out together. She has never seen the symphony, has never been to the park, seen the lake, gone to the Art Institute. Would she run? I wonder. I will always wonder. Twenty years. If I let her go, could she return to where she came from? She would be like a trained animal unable to return to her former habitat. She would not survive. It's too late. It's too late for both of us.

Tomorrow I will cook for her, place some flowers from the garden on the table. We'll drink a bottle of wine, discuss the book I gave her. And then we will go to my room. She needs some time away from the basement. She's spent altogether too much time down there. . . .

Gloria tossed each page on the floor as she finished it. The entries sounded so much like him, and nothing in them was new or revealing. She knew everything that was in them—except the passages that mentioned incidents at the university that he had not told her about. He seemed egotistical about certain things. About other things he was almost humble. And that man—that man who got things for him. She found it out of character that he would mention him. There were so many things he did *not* mention. He had struck her many times in the beginning when she displeased him—yet most of those occasions were missing from the journals. And yet he mentioned this man who would get him birth control pills, who bought her sanitary napkins. Thomas made him sound despicable. But he was doing it for money—doing it for someone else. Doing it for Thomas. What a strange thing his memory was. More arrogant than intelligent, she thought. And she had been so intimidated by his mind.

Reading his words made her feel numb, almost as if she were back in his house. As humiliating as it had been to live with Thomas, to live with his moods, she realized living with him had also been a dull and boring existence. She remembered how she'd torn that *contract* in half in Mr. Burns's office. She had the same feeling now—felt like tearing each page of the journal. But they were only copies. They were not the real journals. Not real in any way. But if she ripped them up, what good would it do? She stared at his handwriting. It was neat, firm, confident, bordering on ornate. Even in these copies, she could see the kind of man he was. He was like these pieces of paper—nothing original in them. She wondered why she was so afraid of hurting him. All this time, she thought it was *he* who had protected *her*.

◆ ◆ ◆

"She's been reading for hours." Jenny looked at her watch.

"It's only seven o'clock."

"Yes, but she's been reading since four."

"Relax, Genevieve. Eat. Or don't you like my cooking? I never cooked for my wives—not ever."

She looked at the half-eaten steak on her plate and sat back down.

She was sure he was exaggerating. "You must have cooked for them," she said. "Of course, it's pretty hard to screw up a steak, Lieutenant."

"So, it's back to Lieutenant, is it?"

"I meant it as a term of endearment." She played with her baked potato.

"It's not going to bite you."

"I'm sorry—I'm not very hungry."

"Tell me again, what do we have?"

"Evidence."

"Yes, *evidence*."

"Don't yell."

"I'm not yelling. Mind if I smoke?"

"After dinner."

"God, we haven't even had sex yet, and already we're fighting."

"We're not fighting. We're eating dinner." He laughed. He pushed his hair back with his fingers. "So when *are* we going to have sex?"

"I don't sleep with married men."

"My wife filed. Nolo contendere." He smiled, proud of himself.

"Nolo contendere only applies to criminal cases."

"My marriage was criminal. And really I'm not married anymore."

"Technically, you are."

"Oh, God, this is going to be the longest foreplay in history."

She leaned over and kissed him on the cheek. "You didn't tell me what we had."

"We have, for the millionth time: the hundred dresses—someone in New York has to recognize this guy, they're expensive as hell. We have birth control pills, which no one will believe he was taking—and they were in *his* bathroom. We have Mr. Rusty Rayborn, who's willing to testify to getting him the pills, the shackles, and Gloria's monthly supply of sanitary napkins—and other little items he got for the professor as needed."

"But we don't have the shackles themselves."

"We know that."

"How could they be missing?"

"The car's missing."

"But the car was never picked up as evidence. So, as far as anyone is concerned, it was just a car theft."

"Yeah, and they left the newer, better car behind? Fat chance."

"Okay, and we have, we have what else?"

"We have the copies of the journals. George's testimony that he found the journals in the professor's library, my testimony that I made copies. And a corroborating witness."

"And when the feds ask you why you just didn't send down the people from the property room to fetch the evidence, what are you going to tell them?"

"The truth—that we didn't trust anyone. And most important, we have Tim Cain and Don Parker in custody. They'll talk. Cain can't keep his mouth shut, and Parker's not gonna take the rap by himself. We're not just gonna nail Blacker, we're gonna nail his goddamned lawyer." He smiled. "You should have seen the look on Cain's face. Made Charlie's day. Made mine, too. Sometimes this career has its moments."

"So what happens now?"

"If we were going to court, they'd be begging at the doorstep trying to plea-bargain their way out of the shithole they've dug themselves into."

"But there isn't going to be a trial—not for Blacker, anyway."

"You're right about that. Feds are moving in just the same. George and I had a long talk with our government friends. But he'll be pushing up daisies long before anything comes of it. Anyway, we're the big winners. I mean, *we have* Thomas Blacker." He pushed his plate away, drew a square, then brought his fist down on it. "And we have the captain, too. Cain will talk. Captain's out of there." He drew another square, and again his fist came down on the table. "And Herald Burns, if we don't out-and-out get him, we'll have managed to scare the holy shit out of the sonofabitch. He'll never be the same again." He drew another square, but before he could bring his fist down on it, Jenny beat him to it. "That one's mine."

"Well, that one you can have. By the sounds of things, you had your day in court with him already. And you won."

"Gloria won." She pushed her plate away and lit a cigarette. "Want some coffee?"

"Yeah, sure." He stared at her cigarette. "Anyway, all this is a moot point. Tomorrow afternoon, you're gonna have a couple of reporters over here, and it's gonna hit the papers, and it'll all be over."

"If Gloria agrees."

"And if she doesn't?"

"I don't know." She played with her cigarette. "Why'd they go after Charlie? Why Charlie?"

"Makes sense if you think about it. I figure it like this: Herald Burns steps in, wants to help an old friend. And why not—he's helped out worse—"

"They don't come worse than Thomas Blacker."

"Wanna bet?"

She made a face at him.

"Anyway, probably Burns thinks, best thing to do is keep Gloria in jail. Guy finds out what the deal is on us—me and you. Well, finds out I can't be bought. Gets me off the case. Too late, though—I'd let her out."

"Yeah, only because I was all over your ass."

He nodded. "Yes, yes."

"Just yes, yes?"

"You're not the only good Catholic in the room, you know? I was on her side, too." He kissed her. "Ummm, cigarette. You want me to go on?"

She nodded.

"And then he wants to get *you* off the case. But he can't do that, see? So he wants to scare you into keeping your mouth shut. Wants to keep everything nice and quiet. So he wants to get to you. He asks around about you, knows you fight like hell, won't scare. Ahh, but he knows your weakness. You got a friend, see? You love that friend. That's how he gets to you. Just wants you to know he's there—to know he can hurt you. Makes sense to me."

Jenny nodded. "You think they would have hurt Gloria?"

"Killed her, you mean? Hard to say. I don't take Burns for a killer. All they wanted was for her to sign that piece of paper. Scare you, scare her—life gets very complicated and all the evidence is missing. Kidnapped her? That's crazy. Prove it. Can't prove it, huh? Not enough evidence. Reasonable doubt—all that money looks like a pretty good settlement. It's a lot of money. All she has to do is shut up, forget about it, live her life."

"Herald Burns and the captain went to a lot of trouble."

"Yup. Captain's easy to figure out. Money. It's that simple. He was bought and paid for a long time ago."

"And Burns? And Blacker?"

"Burns—well, it's his job to defend his clients. So his methods were a little unorthodox. So were yours. So were mine." He shrugged. "I could spend a lot of nights trying to figure those guys out. Some kidnappings make more sense than others. Perverts, that's one thing. Use a kid for sex—then kill 'em. Sick. Really sick. But we understand it—somehow the why is answered. And estranged parents—happens all the time. They take the kid for a weekend and make a run for it. Sad, but there's a logic there. Kidnapping for money—well, there's a logic there, too. This case—well, you read the journals same as me. All I can say is he needed a virgin for his garden. I don't understand that kind of logic—if that's what it is."

Jenny put out her cigarette, nodded. She was glad he didn't understand Thomas Blacker's logic.

"You're going to hand over copies of the journals to the press, aren't you?"

"Damn right I am. I'm defending my client the best way I know how. Same as Burns. This is the closest we'll ever get to nailing him. Besides, it was your idea that I go to the press in the first place."

He nodded. "Good memory."

22 OCTOBER 1994

She stared at the date of the last entry. He had written it that morning— that Sunday morning. It was not a long entry, and his handwriting was more hurried. He had written it as if in a rush. She stared at the words:

It won't be difficult. I'll give her the pills. She's used to taking pills. Rusty will get them for me. In this regard, he is reliable. She'll take them. And if she refuses, I'll put them in her food. Just the right drug—just the right amount. It will be over quickly. She'll never even know. She won't suffer. I'll hold her. I'll tell her how lovely she is.

She'd be lost in the world. This city would eat her up alive. I thought we'd have more time—just us. I should have retired from the world instead of trying to convince it to mend its ways. Such a waste. I'm sorry now. She would be completely lost.

I'll bury her in my garden. In the spring, she'll make things grow. No one will ever know she was here. I can die in peace. Without worrying about her. And soon enough we'll be together. My Claudia and I.

She reread his words. "Didn't want me to suffer!" she yelled. "Be together! Thomas, be together!" She didn't hear herself yelling, didn't realize she was talking through her sobs. "You loved me—you said you loved me. Goddamn you, Thomas." She yelled his name over and over. She did not feel herself as she walked out of the room, away from the words he had written.

◆ ◆ ◆

Jenny and Lieutenant Murphy ran toward the sound of her sobs. By then Gloria was standing in the living room, her fists pounding on the wall. Jenny moved toward her, but Gloria shoved her away. She moved toward the front door. "He loved me," she sobbed. "I believed him." There was disgust and weariness in her voice. Jenny tried to get close to her, and again Gloria pushed her away. "I believed him. I hate myself. *I hate myself.*"

"It's okay, honey," Jenny said as she tried to calm her with her voice.

"Stop saying that. You always say that. What's going to be okay, Jenny? Tell me." She kept her fists clenched. "I have to go. I can't breathe. I have to get some air." She stared at Jenny. "And don't come near. Just don't."

Jenny nodded.

"I have to get out of here. I'm suffocating."

"Gloria—"

Jenny stopped Lieutenant Murphy from speaking by putting out her hand. She shook her head at him. She tossed Gloria a coat that was lying on a chair.

"Take this," she said. "It's cold."

Gloria took the coat reluctantly, hugged it, then ran out the door.

Jenny followed her with her eyes until she disappeared into the night.

◆ ◆ ◆

"You're going to let her go?" Lieutenant Murphy moved toward the door.

"I can't be her guardian angel forever. And neither can you."

"She shouldn't be out on the streets. She doesn't even know her way around. What if something happens to her?"

"Something's already happened to her."

"So what are we going to do?"

"I think I'll have a drink. Want one?"

"Yeah, sure. And then what?"

"We'll wait."

"Guess I have to—you gave her my coat."

◆ ◆ ◆

It was as if she had been sleepwalking. And when she woke, she found herself walking down a busy street. She was awake now, and there had to be a way—a way to save herself. And it was she who had to do it. What Jenny and Lieutenant Murphy were doing—that belonged to *them*. The city belonged to Thomas Blacker, though he hated it. The city belonged to Herald Burns, who wanted to own it and looked down on it from his office. The city belonged to Jenny Richard and Alexander Murphy because they knew it, worked in it, understood its evils and its illogical beauty. The city belonged to the people who walked these streets and understood it better than they understood themselves—above all, it belonged to them. *But it does not belong to me.* And it would never be hers, not ever—not if she did not take a piece of it by force.

She took a deep breath. "Jenny," she whispered. But Jenny could not tell her what to do. Jenny did not know about her and Thomas. She pushed her hair back. It felt so heavy. *Pull it out—pull it all out.* Thomas.

He was always there, would always be there. Unless, unless she made peace with him. A knife in his chest was not making peace. She had to. She looked around for a phone booth, saw one down the street. She walked up to the phone, read the instructions. She needed a quarter. But she had no money. She felt something in the pocket of the coat she was wearing. She took out the crisp piece of paper—not paper—a five-dollar bill. She walked into a nearby store, bought a pack of gum, made sure they gave her a quarter.

She walked back to the phone booth and picked up the receiver. She heard the strange buzz, pictured the phone number that was caught in her mind like a trapped animal. She tried to place the quarter in the slot, her hands trembling, the quarter falling on the sidewalk, rolling away as if it had a mind of its own, voicing its resistance. She dropped the receiver, her entire body shaking, and for a moment she was as lost as she had ever been. She thought of the last time she had seen Thomas, the look on his face, thought of what he'd written, could not keep out the words he had spoken to her again and again: *I love you. I love you.* But did she, did she love him? Even after all this? What would she say to him? She stood, the noises of the city in the background, and yet all she could hear was his voice, all she could see was the last time she'd seen him—the look on his face as he lay on the floor calling her an ingrate, and asking why. *Thomas, you kept me in shackles. You slapped me until I behaved. You had sex with me because you could—because you willed me to. You took me from my parents—from my people. My people, Thomas. And you still asked why?* That look on his face, as if she had devastated him. It was as if *she* were the one. She, who had punished him, she who had been cruel, she who had made him suffer under her moods, under the power of a look that threatened as surely as a raised hand.

How do you tell a man you owe him nothing? How do you tell a man who has decided that you are lame that you have reclaimed your legs? The last time she had seen him—was that an ending? Was that any way to end? She wanted to tell him, talk to him, ask him. *Because you wanted power, Thomas, is that why? Because you saw me once walking down a street and loved me as you had loved nothing else? Because your garden needed just one more flower to make it perfect?* She remembered that Jenny had said he was evil. Perhaps he was—but that was not the answer. He was no more evil than she had been when she'd held the knife and stuck it in his chest. Evil did not answer the question. *Evil* was an even bigger word than *freedom*.

She could see his pleading eyes as he bled on the floor of his cold house. It would be wrong not to see him one last time. She could not deny him, could not deny herself this one last chance. There were so many things she wanted to say to him. She would go to him and tell him, and he would, at last, understand. She wanted him to know. *Do you want to know about my life, Thomas? I will tell you what it was like. I have lived in a place far from the voices of my people. I have sat and listened to the silence of the stillest nights as the leaves fell quiet on the ground. I have listened to my heart break in half as if it were nothing more than a stiff and useless bone. I have knelt down and wailed like a wolf forced to chew off her own leg in order to free herself from the trap. I have had enough of hunger. I have had enough of sorrow, have had enough of the dark. Do you understand, Thomas?* She pictured herself in a forest full of trees, a forest nobody owned. She saw herself as she gathered the leaves in her arms. *Thomas, do you remember how once, in a time called spring, the leaves were new and tender and green? Come the summer, Thomas, come the summer, I will be a tree.* That is what she would tell him. She smiled to herself. Her thoughts were so perfect and lucid and articulate. He *would* understand. Finally, he would know what he had done, and know, too, the greatness of her hope. And she would forgive him. Then they would both be at peace.

For an instant she was unable to move, then finally her eyes fell on the quarter that was lying on the sidewalk. She wanted to walk away from the coin, but it was there, had stopped running, was waiting for her to pick it up. She found herself reaching for it. She took the receiver in her hand, listened to the void. She wanted to hear a voice. Again, she placed the quarter in the slot. She found she had stopped trembling. She dialed the number and somehow felt free of it as she pushed the square buttons. She held her breath as it rang. Perhaps, she thought, he had returned home. It rang again. And again it rang. On the fourth ring, the machine would answer. She did not want to talk into a machine. She wanted to hear his voice, speak to him. And then she heard his voice, his familiar voice that sounded so much like home. Hello, he kept repeating. Hello. Hello. And then she heard herself speak. "It's me," she said.

He was silent for a moment. "I've been waiting," he said. "Where are you?"

"I'm on a street corner in a phone booth. I can take a cab."

"You know the address?"

"Of course."

"Of course," he said, that familiar tone in his voice.

"I don't have the money to pay the cab."

"I'll leave the gates open. Just drive in. I'll pay the fare at the door." He paused a moment. "It will be lovely to see you again."

"Are you angry with me, Thomas?"

"Anger is such a waste of time, my dear. I've been waiting for so long."

He sounded peaceful, happy. They would have a nice visit. This was the only way, she thought, the only way to find herself on a map. After this, she would never be lost again. She walked toward the edge of the sidewalk and watched for a cab to take her to Thomas.

A Woman

Herald Burns nodded as he finished reading Thomas Blacker's journals. He'd had no one's permission to read them, but he needed none. He refrained from smiling. He was certain now he had misplaced his faith in Thomas. If Thomas only knew the trouble he had gone to— the trouble Thomas had demanded in his own manipulative way. "Beautiful," he laughed. "Just beautiful." At least he knew how to pick 'em. When she had walked into his office, she had almost taken his breath away. Thomas had at least had a good imagination: When he'd seen her as a child, he had imagined what she would look like as a woman. Not many men could have done that. When Thomas had told him what he'd done, he had not understood. So out of character, he'd thought—Thomas, the quintessential cautious man, had committed a spontaneous act. Thomas had not planned to kidnap her. But he had seen her, wanted to possess her. Perfection. He remembered Thomas had once told him he was working on his masterpiece. He had assumed he was referring to a new book. But now he knew that he had been referring to *her*. Why not? He had turned his yard into a perfect garden. He had turned blank pages into brilliant books. What was left to challenge him? Why not take a woman? His own Frankenstein—his own creation. He laughed. Wasn't that what he'd done? It wasn't inconsistent. Not inconsistent in the least. Maybe he had not had such a good imagination after all. He was just like every other man in the world—every other little man. He had been wrong about Thomas. Thomas had never had a moral compass—he had only been driven by the idea of perfection. And she *was* perfect—sat and spoke and looked like an angel. *Not my type, Thomas, but then again, I've never been interested in angels.*

He was completely disgusted—more with himself than with Thomas. He had always looked at everything with such clarity—except Thomas. He had very nearly worshipped him. He pushed the intercom button. He heard his secretary's voice on the speaker. "I don't want to be disturbed," he said. He did not wait for her to answer before he walked to the place where he kept his liquor. He poured himself half a glass of scotch and stared at it. He remembered how Thomas had helped him get into law school, the checks he'd written to pay for his books, the conversations they'd had. Thomas had believed in him—the great Thomas Blacker. The father he'd never had. He saw clearly now that he, too, had been seduced. He had behaved like a starry-eyed boy, the overzealous, obedient son, repaid his debt. *Whatever you paid for the view—it was too much.* He took a drink. Repaid him for what? "She's nothing, Thomas. What have I done? All for you, Thomas. For what? All for a woman." He looked out into the city, the lights like halos in the twilight. It could have all been his. The sonofabitch would have killed her. Killed her just to keep her. "Fuck you, Thomas. Fuck you all the way to hell."

He poured himself another drink, then paced around the room. He needed to think. It would have been better for everyone if he had died in the hospital. He stared at the picture of Saint Michael and wondered what Thomas had seen in it.

Return

The cab ride seemed to take an eternity. She felt as if she would be traveling forever, traveling and traveling, never reaching the place where she really wanted to be, the place where she belonged. She felt she had been journeying somewhere all of her life. It had all begun on a sunny September day in El Paso. Nothing had been the same since that day. In her mind, she had always wanted to be somewhere else. She had yearned for so long to be away from Thomas, from his cruelty, from his voice, from his awful anger. But once away from it, she found she could not live without him—as if he were the only air she could breathe. Maybe she belonged to him now. It did not matter that he'd taken her. The fact of that taking was irrevocable. When a cow was branded, it belonged to the man who branded it. When the slaves were freed, they took the master's name. The taking. No one could change what had happened. Jenny could rail against it with an indignation that only showed how innocent she was. The lieutenant and Jenny, no matter how hard they were, could never see her for what she was. She was a product of the taking. It had happened. If she was going back to him, it was because she wanted to know where she belonged. Maybe, going there, she would discover she no longer needed him. Maybe she would discover that she was more than a cow, more than a slave, more than a leaf on a tree in his garden. But she could not live in the land of not knowing. Didn't Jenny love? She could see it when she looked at the lieutenant. And the lieutenant, didn't he love, too? Who was to say that she and Thomas did not love?

She tried to picture his face. But his face was out of focus, and as the cab got closer to Thomas's house, she was forgetting the speech she had uttered to herself before she called him. What was it that she had wanted to say? She found herself trembling, did not bother to make herself stop. Perhaps when she saw him, she would remember. She heard the cab-driver ask, "This the place?" She heard herself answer, heard herself tell him that he should drive up to the house. When the cab stopped in the driveway near the front door, she stepped out, rang the doorbell. Such an odd thing, to stand outside his house.

He was dressed in a plain white shirt, lightly starched. He smiled at her, gave her money, told her to tell the driver to keep the change. She returned to the car, gave the man the money, and thanked him. She watched as the cab drove away. She saw Thomas standing at the door. She walked toward him, entered his house. It was better this way—to walk into his house of her own volition. That was a kind of freedom, she thought. He held the door open for her. "I knew you would come," he said. She wanted to kiss him on the cheek, embrace him. Instead, she smiled, her eyes searching the room. Nothing had changed. She did not even notice that he had stuck his key in the dead bolt and locked the door.

Waiting

Lieutenant Murphy looked at his watch and got up from the couch. He started to pace. "She's been gone a long time, don't you think?"

Jenny placed her drink on the coffee table and took a deep breath out of exasperation. "Does that look mean I told you so?" She took out a cigarette and lit it. "Shit."

"That's your fifth cigarette in an hour, Jenny."

"But who's counting." She looked up at him. "It's only been a couple of hours. She'll walk in the door any minute."

"You don't sound very convinced."

"Well, what the hell was I supposed to do? We should've chained her to her room? That's been done, Alexander Murphy."

"Don't yell."

"Tell me what to do."

"We'll wait awhile. If she doesn't come soon, I'll have some squad cars comb the neighborhood. She won't be hard to find."

Jenny nodded, leaned her head back, then took a deep drag from her cigarette. She blew the smoke out through her nose. "I don't get a good feeling, Sandy. You ever get those feelings? You don't think anything's happened to her, do you?"

"Nah, she'll be fine."

Jenny nodded. "You're right." She put out her cigarette. "Can I ask you a question?"

"Sure."

"Do you think she loves him—Blacker, I mean—do you think she loves him?"

"I don't know. It's not an uncommon thing, you know—to love a captor."

"I know—it even has a name. God, I hope she's all right."

He looked at her. "Jenny, I like that you care so much."

An Ordinary Courtship

She felt confused and wordless. She could tell he was waiting for her to speak. She looked at him, wondered if he sensed she was different. Perhaps she was. They looked at each other for a long time. "You're looking well," she said finally, then felt stupid for saying it.

He nodded. "I don't look well at all."

"Of course you do."

He smiled at her. "Did you come here to argue with me?"

She shook her head. "No, Thomas, I haven't." She could feel herself trembling. "I just wanted—wanted to talk to you. I wanted to tell you—" She stopped. "We're civilized people, aren't we, Thomas?"

He nodded.

She smiled at him. "Won't you offer me a seat?"

"I'm sorry. I think I've misplaced my manners. Seeing you again— it's—would you like some wine?" It was so difficult to read his mood. He stood a moment, looked at her.

Gloria looked back at him, thought of the way Lieutenant Murphy had looked at Jenny when he kissed her on the cheek as they stood on the sidewalk outside the restaurant. His eyes were paler than the lieutenant's.

He looked at the way she was dressed—a man's overcoat, a pair of jeans and a sweater. "But wouldn't you like to change into something more—" He shrugged, his palms up, his face happy. "—something more suitable?"

"You always did like me in dresses, didn't you, Thomas?" He seemed so happy, so calm. Maybe he'd changed, maybe she'd done the right thing by coming to see him. The good thing. That's what she wanted, to do the good thing. To feel that she was good. She wanted him to see she was not an ingrate.

"And I have just the thing. It's waiting for you in your room."

"Were you so sure I'd come?"

He nodded.

"You know me that well?"

"Part of loving someone is knowing them well."

"And do you?"

"Do I what, my dear?"

"Love me. Do you love me, Thomas?"

"How many times did you hear me say it? Did you never hear me? Such a stubborn girl." He laughed. "It's so lovely to see you again. Can't you see that?"

She nodded. She had felt so strong coming here, so sure of what she'd do, of what she'd say. But something in his voice made her afraid, made her feel like an addict returning to a bad habit. "Would you like me to change?" She heard her own helpless answer.

He smiled. "I'll walk you to your room."

She wondered why she was smiling back at him.

◆ ◆ ◆

The steps were so familiar, the smell, the creaks in the wood, Thomas beside her, the feel of his hand. They had walked down these steps together a thousand times. "Did you know I used to count these steps?" she said.

"And how many are there?"

"Sixteen."

"I've never counted them, myself. All these years, and I never counted them." He smiled at her. When they reached her room, she hesitated before the open door. She saw the wrapped gift box in the center of the bed. She entered the room. She moved toward the bed, then sat down. She looked up at Thomas, who was standing in the doorway.

"I'll leave you to change," he said. He closed the door.

She heard the click of the lock, and his footsteps as he went up the stairs. She remembered the first time she had felt trapped in this room. *Why have I come back?* She opened the box slowly, then stared at the dress. It was almost exactly the same dress she'd worn on their last evening together. *Oh God, no. No.*

A Door Opens

Herald Burns sat in his dimly lit office, the lights of the city sparkling in the background. He placed his hand on the telephone, paused, then pressed the familiar digits. What would he tell him, he thought, this man he had wasted an entire lifetime admiring? He heard the old man's familiar voice. He had no stomach for the sound of it now. "Thomas," he said quietly, "sorry to call you so late. I know I promised to call you after the meeting, but—" He paused. "Something came up. Couldn't be helped." He stared at the journals he'd finished reading, turned one of them over in his hand. He made a face. "Thomas—" He paused again. "She wouldn't sign."

His announcement was greeted with silence. He expected an explosion; this was just the calm before the storm hit. Instead, when Thomas spoke, he seemed almost giddy. "You did what you could, Herald, but it no longer matters." He laughed. "It's all worked out for the best."

"What? Thomas, you don't understand. I think we may be in a good deal of trouble—"

"Trouble, Herald. It's all taken care of." He sounded odd, like a boy.

"Are you drunk, Thomas?"

"Drunk? No, no, Herald, don't you see? She's here."

"What are you talking about?"

"She's come back. Really, it's all I wanted."

"Thomas, have you gone stark raving mad? You haven't gone and—"

"I've done nothing, Herald. It was she who came to me. You needn't worry about anything anymore. Everything's going to be fine."

He thought of the journals, what Thomas had written. "Thomas, she's not worth it. You must send her back to Ms. Richard."

"Back to her? Never. It's all been decided. Can't you see?"

"I don't think this is very wise."

"I've had enough of wisdom, Herald. We're together—that's all that matters. Be happy for me."

"Thomas—" He held the dead phone in his hand. He's gone fucking mad, he thought. They both have. He shook his head, tossed away the journal, watched it slide across his desk, then fall to the floor. Doesn't she know? Doesn't that fool woman know? He got up from his desk, paced the room. He looked up at the painting of Saint Michael. He smiled. It was Thomas who had always had his foot on him. Thomas had been the angel, and he had been the devil under his foot. He could see that now. But now it was time to reverse the roles. He could change sides, yes, it was still possible. There was still hope—not for Thomas. Thomas was lost. But there was still a chance—for him.

Waiting

The lieutenant reached for Jenny's pack of cigarettes sitting on the coffee table and lit one. He took a puff, then shook his head. "This is the last one," he said. He stared at Jenny's face, nothing but worry and regret written on it. "We've waited long enough, don't you think?"

Jenny nodded. "I should never have let her go."

"And I thought *I* was full of mea culpas." He took another drag from his cigarette, reached for his cellular phone, then dialed a number. "George." His voice was professional, serious, calm. "Ms. Santos left the house four or five hours ago. I think something—listen, we've a bad feeling over here. Get some cars on the street. Find her. Now, George— Yeah, yeah, we're here. You can reach me on my phone." He pressed a button and flipped the phone in the air as if it were a ball. He caught it. "Goddamnit!"

She looked at him. "Murphy, are we just going to sit here and do nothing?"

"You have any better suggestions?"

"We could go look for her, couldn't we? It beats the hell out of sitting here."

He nodded. "Get your coat."

Dinner for Two

She looked at her watch. She had been in her room for more than two hours. Where had he gone? Why was he keeping her again? It wasn't supposed to be like this—not this time. This time it was supposed to be different. She was supposed to tell him everything she'd ever felt. He was supposed to listen. She had come here just to tell him—just to—it wasn't true, she knew that. Somehow, she knew she had wanted to hear him say he was sorry, hear him beg her for forgiveness, hear him say *I love you. I have always*—it was not supposed to be like a prison again. It was supposed to be like love. She had wanted him to understand. Understanding—that's what love was. She stared at the new dress. Nothing had changed. She had expected to find a new man just as she felt herself to be a new woman. But he was the same. And she, she was the same, too—the same woman who put on dresses Thomas bought for her. She took off the clothes Jenny had given her, left them in a pile on the floor. She stepped into her new dress, such a familiar sensation. She walked into the bathroom and looked at herself in the mirror. She looked at the images of herself. How many of her were there? She shivered and hugged herself. She could feel herself trembling.

She could think of nothing now except her fear. He had pretended to be kind and happy, then locked her in this room again. She had missed the smell and the familiarity of this room—its comfort. But now it did not feel like it was hers anymore. Something *had* changed. She had lived in a room with windows, and she preferred the windows. I have to get away, she thought. Telling him what she felt did not matter now. He would not listen. He would not ask for forgiveness. He would not tell her he loved her. He would only keep her. Coming here had been a mistake, but now—*He will not keep*—she heard the door open. She walked back out into the room. *Not this time, Thomas.* She saw him standing at the door, a black coat, a black tie. She would not show him anything, would not ask him why he had locked her in. "You look very handsome," she said.

He smiled. "Dinner is served, my dear. I've set the table myself."

"I could have helped you," she said.

"No, no, I wanted everything to be a surprise."

She smiled, did not tremble as she took his arm.

They did not speak as they climbed the stairs. When she walked into the dining room, she stared at the elegantly set table: the white tablecloth, the white napkins, the white and red flowers, the crystal, the sparkling china, the spinach salad, the opened bottle of wine, the silver tray of steaming lamb. She noticed his cuff links. She felt a chill. She fought the urge to hug herself.

"My dear, you look a little pale." He smiled. He pulled out her chair and offered her a seat. "I thought this time we could finish our meal."

She looked at him, then took the seat he offered. But she did not smile. It was the same as it had been. She had not come here for this. "Thomas, I don't want to play games anymore."

"Isn't that why you came—because you liked our games so much?"

"No, that's not why I came. I came because I wanted to tell you I was sorry."

"Sorry? You're sorry?"

"And I wanted you to know that I've forgiven you."

"Forgiven me?" He laughed. "You've always had such a good sense of humor." He poured them both some wine. He lifted his glass. "To your sense of humor, my dear." He laughed again.

"I actually thought I could come here and we could talk. There are so many things I've wanted to—"

"Oh, let's not rush into conversations we might regret. Let's enjoy our meal, shall we?"

"I'm not hungry, Thomas."

"I've gone to a great deal of trouble."

"You shouldn't have."

"It's not your place to say, my dear."

"You can't tell me what to do anymore, Thomas. That's not what love is."

"What do you know of love, my dear? Would you like me to show you my scar—the one you left on my chest? Is that what love is?"

She had almost forgotten his anger, the deliberate and threatening way he spoke to her when he was displeased. "I shouldn't have come. I want to go home."

"Home, Claudia? My dear, you *are* home. Even you know that."

"My name isn't Claudia."

"In *my* house that is what you are called."

The Sides We Take

Jenny strained her eyes as she looked for Gloria on the street.
The lieutenant drove slowly, his eyes half on the road, half on the sidewalk.

"If anything happens to her, I'll never forgive myself. This is all my
fault."

"All your fault, huh? Isn't it just like a lawyer to take all the credit?"

She laughed. "Don't try and make me feel better. I want to feel lousy."
She saw a woman walking down the street, it looked like—"There she
is!" The lieutenant brought the car to a stop. "No, it's not her. Damn!"
She stared at Lieutenant Murphy's phone as it rang. She reached for it.

He took it from her and listened to the voice on the other end.
"What? Now? Urgent, huh—what the hell could he want? Can't it
wait? . . . Yeah, George, give me the number." He nodded, pushed a button, then mumbled the numbers to himself. "Burns," he said.

"What are you mumbling about?"

"Herald Burns. He's trying to reach me, says it's urgent." He
shrugged, heard the telephone ring, heard a voice on the other end.
"Yes, this is Lieutenant Murphy. I understand—"

"Lieutenant. That Santos girl—she missing?"

"How'd you—"

"Never mind, Lieutenant. If I were you, I'd get my ass over to Thomas
Blacker's house."

"How do I know you're not sending me on a—"

"Listen, Lieutenant, Blacker told me himself. She's there!"

He nodded. "I don't get it, Burns. How come you're being so help-
ful?"

"Let's just say I've switched sides."

"What's in it for you?"

"I can read the handwriting on the wall."

The lieutenant nodded and tossed the phone onto the seat. He
looked at Jenny. "She went to him."

"What?"

"She's there."

They looked at each other. "Sandy, you don't think—"

The Last Dance

"I thought this time it would be different."

"What would be different?"

"Us."

He took another sip of wine. "Dinner's getting cold," he said. He looked at the lamb. "Damn," he said, then smiled. "I've forgotten something." He smiled at her. "So many familiar things about this dinner. You *will* wait for me, won't you?"

Gloria sat expressionless in her chair. Jenny had been so right about so many things. She watched him walk into the kitchen, placed her hand on her glass of wine, and tasted it. It's bitter, she thought, gone bad. Couldn't Thomas taste that it was nothing but vinegar?

"There we are," he said as he placed a knife on the table.

◆ ◆ ◆

"Won't this heap go any faster?"

"I'm driving as fast as I can, damnit! And anyway, I'm sure a squad car's arrived by now." He winced. "Stay calm. Have another cigarette." He smiled. "He won't hurt her."

"Yeah, sure." She lit a cigarette and cracked the window. *Thomas Blacker, if anything happens to her, I'll kill you myself.*

◆ ◆ ◆

Gloria stared at the knife.

"It's not the same one, my dear, but it will have to do."

She looked up at him, then looked back at the knife.

329

"This time, I'll beat you to it."

She looked into his burning eyes. But his smile was so calm. So this is what made him happy. Jenny had said he was evil. Jenny had been right. But it was too late. He laughed, reached for the knife, then picked it up.

"No." Her whisper filled the room. "Thomas, you—"

"What? Are you trying to tell me I can't? Why can't I? You did. You ruined everything we had. You cut me down as if I were nothing more than an animal. And you come here telling me you've forgiven me. *You forgive me!* It is mine to forgive—and yours to ask forgiveness. And I choose not"—his voice shook, the knife in his grasp moving closer and closer—"not to forgive."

She heard his voice, but she was no longer sure of what was happening. She remembered the man who had broken into the apartment, remembered how she had tried to remain as still as the air of the desert. *But she was not air.* She remembered Bessie and Charlie, how they had fought. Their instincts had been to survive. All she could see was Bessie jumping at the man. She was moving, could see her arm reaching for the hand that held the knife, felt the blade slice her skin, the thin red line on her arm like ink on a piece of paper. And then the blood. But the hurt did not matter. She bled. She was alive. He stared at her arm, laughed, but her chance lay in his laughter, in that pause. She felt her whole body leap, watched him fall on the floor. But he was up again, screaming, the sounds coming out of him barely human. She turned to run, but where? His house, he would find her, would not rest until he did what he'd written in his journal. But she did not want to lie in the earth, not in his garden. It was true, he would have killed her. He was a killer—she had not thought of him like that, but it was true, and now she knew it, knew why Jenny had said those things. But she had not listened. He snarled at her, pointed the knife at her. She did not know if she was more afraid of his eyes or the blade he was holding, but she could see his body, could see he was weak, could not even stand straight. She could face him now. The first time she had been a coward, had taken him by surprise. But now she could be brave. When he thrust the knife toward her, she was ready, she had good reflexes. She grabbed his hand, both of them struggling for the knife. Whoever had the knife held the power. She would get—he was stronger than she thought, would not let go, his breath on her, the vinegar of the wine, sour—face-to-face, she could see what he was, the monster, and then they were on the floor, almost like making love, she on top, the knife slipping away from him. She reached for it, and suddenly it was in her hands. But he was fast, would not give up, and now it was he who was on top, but she would not be passive in his arms, not tonight, not ever again. She held on to the knife, felt as if it had become a part of her hand. He could not take it away, not this—he was tiring, too old and sick. And she, she would never be tired again. She pushed her weight, and rolled—on top again, and he was yelling through his labored breath, still yelling, his voice relentless, *you'll have to kill me, kill me. Me or you, my dear. You, you, dead, because that's the way love is, my dear* . . . He kept saying that and other things, and she wondered for an instant if they were both dead, dead and damned to struggle in this hell for an eternity. But her blood was real, and his breath—that, too, was real. And the knife, warm from their touch, wet from their sweat. Real, the knife, she could feel it—and with one last pull, the knife was hers, and there was no thinking anymore. There was only the knife and she did not even feel it as it went into his chest. She felt him go limp the same way he'd melt after sex. She stared at his final look of disbelief. There were no more words in him. She did not pull the knife out of his lifeless body. She would leave it there where it belonged. His blood did not scare her. She was not afraid of anything, not afraid of him or herself, not afraid of what she had done. She had wanted to live. That is why she had come. She looked at him. Still. His face was twisted, his eyes open. But he could not see her.

She could leave now. She walked toward the door, pulled on the knob. But the door was locked. Again. She almost wanted to laugh. She walked back to Thomas, stood over him, then knelt down next to him. She searched for the keys in his pants pockets, felt them. She was not afraid to touch him. She pulled them out, held them in her hand. Now it was she who held the keys. She walked to the front entrance, stuck the key in the lock, and flung open the door. She stared at her arm. It was cut and bleeding. She felt no pain, felt only that she was alive. She looked out into the night. The sky was clear, the air was cold. She took a breath. She felt she could stand and breathe in this night for an eternity.

331

epilogue

The Sonofabitch Never Looked Better

Jenny and Lieutenant Murphy sped into Thomas Blacker's driveway minutes after the first squad car arrived. When they walked in the door, Gloria stood in the living room, a young officer about to handcuff her. She looked up, her eyes meeting Jenny's.

Lieutenant Murphy nodded. He flashed his badge. "We won't be needing the handcuffs," he said. "I'll take it from here, Officer." The young patrolman nodded, then disappeared into the other room. He moved toward Gloria and smiled at her. "You okay?"

She nodded.

"We better get this arm taken care of. Hurt much?"

"Not much."

"Looks pretty nasty to me." He took out a handkerchief and tied it around her arm. "This'll help. Let's get you to a doctor."

She nodded, tried to smile. He was kind. "I'm going to have to go back to jail," she whispered. "I know that."

"Oh, I wouldn't worry too much about that. You have a damn good lawyer."

Gloria nodded, slowly walked toward Jenny. She looked into Jenny's face—it was so kind, sincere. She fell into Jenny's arms, felt her body searching for a home.

"Soon as George gets here I'll—" Lieutenant Murphy looked up. "Speak of the devil."

George waved. "Fancy meeting you here."

Lieutenant Murphy winced, then looked at Jenny, Gloria sobbing in her arms. "Get her out of here."

George and Lieutenant Murphy moved toward the dining room, the two officers staring at the body, a knife in its chest.

Lieutenant Murphy shook his head. "The sonofabitch never looked better."

The Trial

Having been presented with the entire sordid story, the district attorney's office did not look forward to prosecuting Gloria Erlinda Santos for the murder of Thomas Blacker. In the end, Gloria had insisted on having her day in court. Jenny had agreed to go ahead with a jury trial only because she was certain no sane jury would convict her. Jenny held press conferences, answered questions, made sure the trial stayed in the headlines. The more publicity, the better. Who would side with Thomas Blacker? And besides, as she told Alexander Murphy, "Camera sure likes her." The camera liked Jenny, too—though Murphy complained that it didn't do a damn thing for him, only made him look like a middle-aged man who used to smoke too much.

Not that Jenny Richard took anything for granted. Good Catholic girl that she was, she kept believing the whole incident was caused by her lack of attentiveness. If she had paid closer attention to what Gloria had been going through, she would never have gone back to Thomas Blacker—that's what she told herself. She was determined to atone for her sins of omission by presenting as thorough a defense as was humanly possible. Even the judge (who, in the past, had found Ms. Richard altogether too shrill and strident for his taste) was impressed by her presentation. She left nothing to chance, prepared night and day, chain-smoked, did not sleep. She only ate because Lieutenant Murphy forced her to eat all the meals Gloria cooked for her.

Jenny's parade of witnesses included not one, not two, but three experts on Stockholm syndrome (one of them flew in from London at his own expense after hearing about the case); Sergeant Tim Cain (who agreed to testify against the captain in exchange for a lesser charge against his own person); Lieutenant Alexander Murphy (who was completely embarrassed by the publicity); Mr. Rusty Rayborn (who was more than happy to testify—especially since Thomas Blacker was dead and could no longer be counted on to bring more business his way); and Mr. Charlie Robertson (who became a fifteen-second celebrity in the local gay rag). Jenny's biggest coup came with the testimony of Herald

Christian Burns, who almost succeeded in making himself out to be a hero. Almost. Later, Jenny admitted that his testimony had proven to be invaluable, but she insisted she would have won the case without him. "And besides, he only joined our side because the sonofabitch needed a good PR campaign."

The missing evidence turned up like a bad penny. The journals, the shackles—even the car Thomas Blacker used to kidnap Gloria Santos.

On the last day of the trial, Gloria took the stand. Jenny was unable to talk her out of it. "You don't have to do this to yourself."

"Yes, I do," Gloria said. She even went so far as to refuse to rehearse her answers. "I'm not in a play," she said. Under oath, she answered all of Jenny's questions calmly and with poise—not a trace of self-pity. In his cross-examination, the prosecutor asked her why she had gone to visit Thomas Blacker. Gloria deferred to the expert witnesses who had previously testified. When the prosecutor asked: "Did you have to kill him? Was it necessary?" Gloria simply answered, "It was only necessary to kill him if I wanted to live." When Gloria stepped down, Jenny knew they had won. It took the jury half an hour to come back with an acquittal.

Lieutenant Murphy faithfully watched all of the proceedings from the back of the courtroom. When the verdict was announced, he felt as if the spring had come, though the ground was still covered with snow. He did not crowd around Jenny and Gloria, did not insinuate himself on them as if it were *his* victory. It was all theirs.

Aftermath

At midnight of the first Saturday in March, the clouds let loose the snow. When Gloria awoke, she looked out the window, the snow falling like confetti in a parade. It seemed as if the city had been covered with a new coat of paint, the streets glowing as if they were made of light. She walked into the quiet kitchen, signs of Jenny everywhere in the room. She shook her head and wondered if Lieutenant Murphy would ever get her to quit smoking.

She walked into the bathroom, brushed her teeth, poured cold water over her face. She brushed her hair, so much shorter now, so much lighter. She looked at herself in the mirror. He was dead, but she was not.

She walked into the bedroom, changed into a pair of jeans, and threw on a sweater she'd bought with her first paycheck from working in Jenny's office. When she reached for her coat in her closet, she noticed the dress—so strange and out of place hanging there. Thomas's dress, she thought. She had other clothes now. She took it from the hanger, wadded it up as if it were made of useless paper, and stuffed it in her coat. She opened the door to the apartment, then shut it. Opened the door, then shut it. Then did it again. Such a simple thing. A door. She walked out into the streets of the city, her nostrils freezing as she breathed in the cold. She headed toward the lake, wanted to see the snow falling on the water.

She looked down at the white ground as she walked. She remembered a dream she'd had a long time ago: There had been a battle for her arms as she walked through a desert of snow—and her body had lost that battle. It was just a dream. She smiled to herself as she felt the cold wind on her face. The cold was bitter, but it was also fleeting. It was almost spring.

When she reached the lake, she looked out at the cold, gray waters. She looked back at the city. It was unclear and unfocused through the snow, and she could not see the city for what it was. But it was there. She could not help but think of El Paso as she walked. She was sorry she had been taken from her home and from the people who were hers. It was too late to go back. There was nothing there but the graves of her family. She did not want to think of El Paso as the place where they were buried. She wanted to think of El Paso as the city of her birth, as the city where, once, all of them had lived—the place where all of them had loved. Now she belonged to a new place—a place that was large and unfathomable, a place she would never understand. She remembered her mother telling her that it was a small thing to be patient with the world. Her mother had been wrong—it was a very big thing. As she looked out at the city, she could not help but think of it as home. Today it was dressed in white.

She took the dress out from under her coat. She placed it on the ground and made a mound of it. She took out a book of matches, lit the dress on fire, and watched it as it burned. The flames warmed her for an instant. The fire burned so brightly, then was gone. She wished her memories would burn so easily. She pulled up the sleeve of her coat, looked at the scar. The slash of a knife. She would never forget. Memory was a blessing. Memory was a curse. Memory was an old god. An old god never dies.

She walked away from the ashes.

Acknowledgments

I could not have written this book without the help of expert legal advice, which I received from El Paso's district attorney, Jaime Esparza, who took time out from his busy schedule to answer questions and allow members of his staff to speak to me. I thank him for his generosity.

When I was lost in my own sentences, struggling to find my way through, Richard Green's voice became a compass. His good sense, his vision, his unwavering enthusiasm, and his support were indispensable to me. Every author should have a Richard Green.

Jennie McDonald patiently read and reread countless drafts of this book and never failed in her encouragement. Always gracious in her criticism, she was there at the beginning, there during the tiresome middle, and there at the end. Without her fine critical acumen, and her infectious sense of humor, this book would have been impossible to complete. I owe her a debt that can never be repaid.

Fiona Hallowell at HarperCollins, with her great editorial eye and her professionalism, made this book become a reality. She is a credit to her profession and living proof that the editorial process doesn't have to hurt.

Lastly, I thank the woman who shares my life, Patricia Macias. Her fine legal mind, generous spirit, and moral presence gave my writing a center. She has dedicated herself to the advancement of children's rights in the city in which we live, and her relentlessly compassionate vision is everywhere to be found in this book.